Pride and Passion

Also by Nora Roberts

Series

Irish Born Trilogy
BORN IN FIRE
BORN IN ICE
BORN IN SHAME

Dream Trilogy
DARING TO DREAM
HOLDING THE DREAM
FINDING THE DREAM

Chesapeake Bay Saga
SEA SWEPT
RISING TIDES
INNER HARBOR
CHESAPEAKE BLUE

Gallaghers of Ardmore Trilogy
JEWELS OF THE SUN
TEARS OF THE MOON
HEART OF THE SEA

Three Sisters Island Trilogy
DANCE UPON THE AIR
HEAVEN AND EARTH
FACE THE FIRE

Key Trilogy
KEY OF LIGHT
KEY OF KNOWLEDGE
KEY OF VALOR

In the Garden Trilogy
BLUE DAHLIA
BLACK ROSE
RED LILY

Circle Trilogy
MORRIGAN'S CROSS
DANCE OF THE GODS
VALLEY OF SILENCE

Sign of Seven Trilogy
BLOOD BROTHERS
THE HOLLOW
THE PAGAN STONE

Bride Quartet
VISION IN WHITE
BED OF ROSES
SAVOR THE MOMENT
HAPPY EVER AFTER

The Inn BoonsBoro Trilogy
THE NEXT ALWAYS
THE LAST BOYFRIEND
THE PERFECT HOPE

The Cousins O'Dwyer Trilogy
DARK WITCH
SHADOW SPELL
BLOOD MAGICK

The Guardians Trilogy
STARS OF FORTUNE
BAY OF SIGHS
ISLAND OF GLASS

Chronicles of The One
YEAR ONE

Nora Roberts and J. D. Robb

REMEMBER WHEN

J. D. Robb

Anthologies

FROM THE HEART

A LITTLE MAGIC

A LITTLE FATE

MOON SHADOWS
(with Jill Gregory, Ruth Ryan Langan, and Marianne Willman)

The Once Upon Series
(with Jill Gregory, Ruth Ryan Langan, and Marianne Willman)

ONCE UPON A CASTLE

ONCE UPON A STAR

ONCE UPON A DREAM

ONCE UPON A ROSE

ONCE UPON A KISS

ONCE UPON A MIDNIGHT

SILENT NIGHT
(with Susan Plunkett, Dee Holmes, and Claire Cross)

OUT OF THIS WORLD
(with Laurell K. Hamilton, Susan Krinard, and Maggie Shayne)

BUMP IN THE NIGHT
(with Mary Blayney, Ruth Ryan Langan, and Mary Kay McComas)

DEAD OF NIGHT
(with Mary Blayney, Ruth Ryan Langan, and Mary Kay McComas)

THREE IN DEATH

SUITE 606
(with Mary Blayney, Ruth Ryan Langan, and Mary Kay McComas)

IN DEATH

THE LOST
(with Patricia Gaffney, Mary Blayney, and Ruth Ryan Langan)

THE OTHER SIDE
(with Mary Blayney, Patricia Gaffney, Ruth Ryan Langan, and Mary Kay McComas)

TIME OF DEATH

THE UNQUIET
(with Mary Blayney, Patricia Gaffney, Ruth Ryan Langan, and Mary Kay McComas)

MIRROR, MIRROR
(with Mary Blayney, Elaine Fox, Mary Kay McComas, and R. C. Ryan)

DOWN THE RABBIT HOLE
(with Mary Blayney, Elaine Fox, Mary Kay McComas, and R. C. Ryan)

Also Available . . .

THE OFFICIAL NORA ROBERTS COMPANION
(edited by Denise Little and Laura Hayden)

Pride and Passion

Search for Love AND *Irish Thoroughbred*

NORA ROBERTS

ST. MARTIN'S GRIFFIN ❧ NEW YORK

PRIDE AND PASSION. Copyright © 2018 by Nora Roberts. All rights reserved. Printed in the United States of America. For information, address St. Martin's Press, 175 Fifth Avenue, New York, N.Y. 10010.

www.stmartins.com

The Library of Congress Cataloging-in-Publication Data is available upon request.

ISBN 978-1-250-18487-0 (trade paperback)

Our books may be purchased in bulk for promotional, educational, or business use. Please contact your local bookseller or the Macmillan Corporate and Premium Sales Department at 1-800-221-7945, extension 5442, or by email at MacmillanSpecialMarkets@macmillan.com.

Search for Love was first published in 1991 by Silhouette Books.

Irish Thoroughbred was first published in 1981 by Silhouette Books.

First St. Martin's Griffin Paperback Edition: November 2018

10 9 8 7 6 5 4 3 2 1

CONTENTS

Pride and Passion

SEARCH FOR LOVE

CHAPTER ONE

The train ride seemed endless, and Serenity was tired. The argument the night before with Tony had not helped her disposition, plus the long flight from Washington to Paris, and now the arduous hours in the stuffy train had her gritting her teeth to hold back the groan. All in all, she decided miserably, she was a poor traveler.

The trip had been the excuse for the last, terminal battle between Serenity and Tony, their relationship having been strained and uneven for weeks. Her continued refusal to be pressured into marriage had provoked several minor tiffs, but Tony had wanted her, and his patience seemed inexhaustible. Not until her announcement of the intended trip had his forbearance cracked, and the war had begun.

"You can't go rushing off this way to France to see some

supposed grandmother you never knew existed until a couple of weeks ago." Tony had paced, his agitation obvious by the way he allowed his hand to disturb his well-styled fair hair.

"Brittany," Serenity had elaborated. "And it doesn't matter when I found out she existed; I know now."

"This old lady writes you a letter, tells you she's your grandmother and wants to see you, and off you go, just like that." He had been totally exasperated. She knew his logical mind was unable to comprehend her impulse, and she had hung on to the threads of her own temper and had attempted to speak calmly.

"She's my mother's mother, Tony, the only family I have left, and I intend to see her. You know I've been making plans to go since her letter arrived."

"The old girl lets twenty-four years go by without a word, and now suddenly, this big summons." He had continued to pace the large, high-ceilinged room before whirling back to her. "Why in heaven's name did your parents never speak of her? Why did she wait until they were dead to contact you?"

Serenity had known he had not meant to be cruel; it was not in Tony's nature to be cruel, merely logical, his lawyer's mind dealing constantly in facts and figures. Even he could not know the slow, deadly ache that remained, lingering after two months, the time since her parents' sudden, unexpected deaths. Knowing that his words had not been intended to hurt did not prevent her from lashing out, and the argument had grown in proportion until Tony had stomped out and left her alone, seething and resentful.

Now, as the train chugged its way across Brittany, Serenity was forced to admit that she, too, had doubts. Why had her grandmother, this unknown Comtesse Françoise de Kergallen, remained silent for nearly a quarter of a century? Why had her mother, her lovely, fragile, fascinatingly different mother, never mentioned a relative in far-off Brittany? Not even her father, as volatile, outspoken, and direct as he had been, had ever spoken of ties across the Atlantic.

They had been so close, Serenity mused with a sigh of memory. The three of them had done so much together. Even when she had been a child, her parents had included her when they visited senators, congressmen, and ambassadors.

Jonathan Smith had been a much-sought-after artist; a portrait created by his talented hand, a prized possession. Those in Washington society had clamored for his commissions for more than twenty years. He had been well liked and respected as a man as well as an artist, and the gentle charm and grace of Gaelle, his wife, had made the couple a highly esteemed addition to the capital set.

When Serenity had grown older, and her natural artistic abilities became apparent, her father's pride had known no bounds. They had sketched and painted together, first as tutor and pupil, then as man and woman, and they drew even closer with the shared joy of art.

The small family had shared an idyllic existence in the elegant row house in Georgetown, a life full of love and laughter, until Serenity's world had crashed in around her, along with the plane which had been carrying her parents to California. It had been impossible to believe they were dead, and she still lived on. The high-ceilinged rooms would no longer echo with her father's booming voice or her mother's gentle laughter. The house was empty but for memories that lay like shadows in each corner.

For the first two weeks, Serenity could not bear the sight of a canvas or brush, or the thought of entering the third-floor studio where she and her father had spent so many hours, where her mother would enter and remind them that even artists had to eat.

When she had finally gathered up the courage to climb the stairs and enter the sun-filled room, she found, rather than unbearable grief, a strange, healing peace. The skylight showered the room with the sun's warmth, and the walls retained the love and laughter which had once existed there. She had begun to live again, paint again, and Tony had been kind and gentle, helping to fill the hollowness left by loss. Then, the letter had come.

Now she had left Georgetown and Tony behind in a quest for the part of her that belonged to Brittany and an unknown grandmother. The strange, formal letter which had brought her from the familiarity of Washington's crowded streets to the unaccustomed Breton countryside lay safely tucked in the smooth leather bag at her side. There had been no affection in the missive, merely facts and an invitation, more like a royal command, Serenity mused, half-annoyed, half-amused. But if her pride would have scoffed at the command, her curiosity, her desire to know more of her mother's family, had accepted. With her innate impulsiveness and organization, she had arranged her trip, closed up the beloved house in Georgetown, and burned her bridges with Tony.

The train groaned and screeched in protest as it dragged into the station at Lannion. Tingling excitement warred with jet lag as Serenity gathered her hand luggage and stepped onto the platform, taking her first attentive look at her mother's native country. She stared around her with an artist's eyes, lost for a moment in the simple beauty and soft, melding colors that were Brittany.

The man watched her concentration, the small smile playing on her parted lips, and his dark brow rose slightly in surprise. He took his time surveying her, a tall, willow-slim figure in a powder-blue traveling suit, the soft skirt floating around long, shapely legs. The soft breeze ran easy fingers through her sunlit hair, feathering it back to frame the delicate-boned, oval face. The eyes, he noted, were large and wide, the color of brandy, surrounded by thick lashes shades darker than her pale hair. Her skin looked incredibly soft, smooth like alabaster, and the combination lent an ethereal appearance: a delicate, fragile orchid. He would all too soon discover that appearances are often deceptive.

He approached her slowly, almost reluctantly. "You are Mademoiselle Serenity Smith?" he inquired in lightly accented English.

Serenity started at the sound of his voice, so absorbed in the countryside she had not noted his nearness. Brushing back a lock of hair, she turned her head and found herself looking up, much higher than was her habit, into dark, heavy-lidded brown eyes.

"Yes," she answered, wondering why those eyes made her feel so strange. "Are you from the Château Kergallen?"

The slow lifting of one dark brow was the only change in his expression. "*Oui,* I am Christophe de Kergallen. I have come to take you to the countess."

"De Kergallen?" she repeated with some surprise. "Not another mysterious relative?"

The brow remained lifted, and full, sensuous lips curved so slightly as to be imperceptible. "One could say, Mademoiselle, that we are, in an obscure manner, cousins."

"Cousins," she murmured as they studied each other, rather like two prizefighters sizing each other up before a bout.

Rich black hair fell thick and straight to his collar, and the dark eyes which continued to remain steady seemed nearly as black against his deep bronze skin. His features were sharp, hawklike, somewhat piratical, and he exuded a basic masculine aura which both attracted and repelled her. She immediately wished for her sketch pad, wondering if she could possibly capture his aristocratic virility with pencil and paper.

Her lengthy scrutiny left him unperturbed, and he held her gaze, his eyes cool and aloof. "Your trunks will be delivered to the château." He bent down, picking up the bags she had set on the platform. "If you will come with me, the countess is anxious to see you."

He led her to a gleaming black sedan, assisted her into the passenger's side, and stowed her bags in the back, his manner so cold and impersonal that Serenity felt both annoyed and curious. He began to drive in silence, and she turned in her seat and examined him with open boldness.

"And how," she demanded, "are we cousins?" *What do I call him?* she wondered. *Monsieur? Christophe? Hey, you?*

"The countess's husband, your mother's father, died when your mother was a child." He began his explanation in polite, faintly bored tones, and she was tempted to tell him not to strain himself. "Several years later, the countess married my grandfather, the Comte de Kergallen, whose wife had died and left him with a son, my father." He turned his head and spared her a brief glance. "Your mother and my father were raised as brother and sister in the château. My grandfather died, my father married, lived long enough to see me born, and then promptly killed himself in a hunting accident. My mother pined for him for three years, then joined him in the family crypt."

The story had been recited in remote, unemotional tones, and the sympathy Serenity would have normally felt for the child left orphaned never materialized. She watched his hawklike profile for another moment.

"So, that makes you the present Comte de Kergallen and my cousin through marriage."

Again, a brief, negligent glance. *"Oui."*

"I can't tell you how both facts thrill me," she stated, a definite edge of sarcasm in her tone. His brow rose once more as he turned to her, and she thought for an instant that she had detected laughter lighting the cool, dark eyes. She decided against it, positive that the man sitting next to her never laughed. "Did you know my mother?" she inquired when the silence grew.

"Oui. I was eight when she left the château."

"Why did she leave?" Serenity demanded, turning to him with direct amber eyes. He twisted his head and met them with equal directness, and she was assaulted by their power before he turned his attention back to the road.

"The countess will tell you what she wishes you to know."

"What she wishes?" Serenity sputtered, angered by the deliberate rebuff. "Let's understand each other, Cousin. I fully intend to find out exactly why my mother left

Brittany, and why I've spent my life ignorant of my grandmother."

With slow, casual movements, Christophe lit a cheroot, expelling smoke lazily. "There is nothing I can tell you."

"You mean," she corrected, narrowing her eyes, "there is nothing you *will* tell me."

His broad shoulders moved in a purely Gallic shrug, and Serenity turned to stare out the front window, copying his movement with the American version, missing the slight smile which played on his mouth at her gesture.

They continued to drive in sporadic silence, with Serenity occasionally inquiring about the scenery, Christophe answering in polite monosyllables, making no effort to expand the conversation. Golden sun and pure sky might have been sufficient to soothe the disposition ruffled by the journey, but his continued coolness outbalanced nature's gift.

"For a count from Brittany," she observed with deceptive sweetness after being spared another two syllables, "you speak remarkably fine English."

Sarcasm rolled off him like a summer's breeze, and his response was lightly patronizing. "The countess also speaks English quite well, Mademoiselle. The servants, however, speak only French or Breton. If you find yourself in difficulty, you have only to ask the countess or myself for assistance."

Serenity tilted her chin and turned her rich golden eyes

on him with haughty disdain. *"Ce n'est pas nécessaire, Monsieur le Comte. Je parle bien le français."*

One dark brow lifted in harmony with his lips. *"Bon,"* he replied in the same language. "That will make your visit less complicated."

"Is it much farther to the château?" she inquired, continuing to speak in French. She felt hot, crumpled, and tired. Due to the long trip and the time change, it seemed as if she had been in some kind of vehicle for days, and she longed for a stationary tub filled with hot, soapy water.

"We have been on Kergallen land for some time, Mademoiselle," he replied, his eyes remaining on the winding road. "The château is not much farther."

The car had been climbing slowly to a higher elevation. Serenity closed her eyes on the headache which had begun to throb in her left temple, and wished fervently that her mysterious grandmother lived in a less complicated place, like Idaho or New Jersey. When she opened her eyes again, all aches, fatigue, and complaints vanished like a mist in the hot sun.

"Stop!" she cried, reverting to English, unconsciously laying a hand on Christophe's arm.

The château stood high, proud, and solitary: an immense stone edifice from another century with drum towers and crenellated walls and a tiled conical roof glowing warm and gray against a cerulean-blue sky. The windows were many, high and narrow, reflecting the diminishing sunlight with a myriad of colors. It was ancient, arrogant, confident, and Serenity fell immediately in love.

Christophe watched the surprise and pleasure register on her unguarded face, her hand still warm and light on his arm. A stray curl had fallen loose onto her forehead, and he reached out to brush it back, catching himself before he reached her and staring at his own hand in annoyance.

Serenity was too absorbed with the château to notice his movement, already planning what angles she would use for sketches, imagining the moat that might have encircled the château at one time in the past.

"It's fabulous," she said at last, turning to her companion. Hastily, she removed her hand from his arm, wondering how it could have gotten there. "It's like something out of a fairy tale. I can almost hear the sound of trumpets, see the knights in armor, and ladies in full, floating dresses and high, pointed hats. Is there a neighborhood dragon?" She smiled at him, her face illuminated and incredibly lovely.

"Not unless one counts Marie, the cook," he answered, lowering the cool, polite wall for a moment and allowing her a quick glimpse of the wide, disarming smile which made him seem younger and approachable.

So, he's human, after all, she concluded. But as her pulse leaped in response to the sudden smile, she realized that when human, he was infinitely more dangerous. As their eyes met and held, she had the strange sensation of being totally alone with him, the rest of the world only a backdrop as they sat alone in private, enchanted solitude, and Georgetown seemed a lifetime away.

The stiffly polite stranger soon replaced the charming escort, and Christophe resumed the drive in silence, all the more thick and cold after the brief friendly interlude.

Watch it, Serenity, she cautioned herself. *Your imagination's running rampant again. This man is most definitely not for you. For some unknown reason, he doesn't even like you, and one quick smile doesn't change him from a cold, condescending aristocrat.*

Christophe pulled the car to a halt in a large, circular drive bordered by a flagstone courtyard, its low stone walls spilling over with phlox. He alighted from the car with swift, agile grace, and Serenity copied him before he had rounded the hood to assist her, so enchanted by the storybook atmosphere that she failed to note the frown which creased his brow at her action.

Taking her arm, he led her up stone steps to a massive oaken door, and, pulling a gleaming brass handle, inclined his head in a slight bow and motioned her to enter.

The entrance hall was huge. The floors were buffed to a mirrorlike shine and scattered with exquisite hand-hooked rugs. The walls were paneled, hung with tapestries, wide and colorful and incredibly old. A large hall rack and hunt table, both oak and glowing with the patina of age, oaken chairs with hand-worked seats, and the scent of fresh flowers graced the room, which seemed oddly familiar to her. It was as if she had known what to expect when she had crossed the threshold into the château, and the room seemed to recognize her, and welcome her.

"Something is wrong?" Christophe asked, noting her expression of confusion.

She shook her head with a slight shiver. *"Déjà vu,"* she murmured, and turned to him. "It's very strange; I feel as though I've stood right here before." She caught herself with a jolt of shock before she added, "with you." Letting out a deep breath, she made a restless movement with her shoulders. "It's very odd."

"So, you have brought her, Christophe."

Serenity turned away from suddenly intense brown eyes to watch her grandmother approach.

La Comtesse de Kergallen was tall and nearly as slender as Serenity. Her hair was a pure, brilliant white, lying like clouds around a sharp, angular face that defied the network of wrinkles age had bestowed on it. The eyes were clear, a piercing blue under well-arched brows, and she carried herself regally, as one who knew that more than six decades had not dimmed her beauty.

No Mother Hubbard, this, Serenity thought quickly. *This lady is a countess right down to her fingertips.*

The eyes surveyed Serenity slowly, completely, and she observed a flicker of emotion cross the angular face before it once again became impassive and guarded. The countess extended a well-shaped, ringed hand.

"Welcome to the Château Kergallen, Serenity Smith. I am Madame la Comtesse Françoise de Kergallen."

Serenity accepted the offered hand in her own, wondering whimsically if she should kiss it and curtsy. The clasp was brief and formal—no affectionate embrace, no smile of welcome. She swallowed disappointment and spoke with equal formality.

"Thank you, Madame. I am pleased to be here."

"You must be tired after your journey," the countess stated. "I will show you to your room myself. You will wish to rest before you change for dinner."

She moved to a large, curving staircase, and Serenity followed. Pausing on the landing, she glanced back to find Christophe watching her, his face creased in a brooding frown. He made no effort to smooth it away or remove his eyes from hers, and Serenity found herself turning swiftly and hurrying after the countess's retreating back.

They walked down a long, narrow corridor with brass lights set at intervals into the walls, replacing, she imagined, what would have once been torches. When the countess stopped at a door, she turned once more to Serenity, and after giving her another quick study, she opened the door and motioned her to enter.

The room was large and open, yet somehow retained an air of delicate grace. The furniture was glossy cherry, and a large four-poster canopied bed dominated the room, its silk coverlet embroidered with time-consuming stitches. A stone fireplace was set in the wall opposite the foot of the bed, its mantel carved and ornate, a collection of Dresden figures reflecting in the large framed mirror over it. One end of the room was curved and glassed, an upholstered windowseat inviting one to sit and ponder the breathtaking view.

Serenity felt the uncontrollable pull of the room, an aura of love and happiness, the gentle elegance well remembered. "This was my mother's room."

Again, the quick play of emotion flickered, like a candle caught in a draft. "*Oui*. Gaelle decorated it herself when she was sixteen."

"Thank you for giving it to me, Madame." Even the cool reply could not dispel the warmth the room brought her, and she smiled. "I shall feel very close to her during my stay."

The countess merely nodded and pressed a small button next to the bed. "Bridget will draw your bath. Your trunks will arrive shortly, and she will see to your unpacking. We dine at eight, unless you would care for some refreshment now."

"No, thank you, Countess," Serenity replied, beginning to feel like a boarder in a very well-run hotel. "Eight will be fine."

The countess moved to the doorway. "Bridget will show you to the drawing room after you have rested. We have cocktails at seven-thirty. If there is anything you require, you have only to ring."

The door closed behind her, and Serenity took a deep breath and sat heavily on the bed.

Why did I come? she asked herself, closing her eyes on a sudden surge of loneliness. *I should have stayed in Georgetown, stayed with Tony, stayed with what I could understand. What am I searching for here?* Taking a long breath, she fought the encompassing depression and surveyed her room again. *My mother's room,* she reminded herself and felt the soothing hands of comfort. *This is something I can understand.*

Moving to the window, Serenity watched day soften into twilight, the sun flashing with final, brilliant fire before surrendering to slumber. A breeze stirred the air, and the few scattered clouds moved with it, rolling lazily across the darkening sky.

A château on a hill in Brittany. Shaking her head at the thought, she knelt on the windowseat and watched evening's nativity. *Where does Serenity Smith fit into this?* Somewhere. She frowned at the knowledge which sprang from her heart. *Somehow I belong here, or a part of me does. I felt it the moment I saw those incredible stone walls, and again when I walked into the hall.* Pushing the feeling to the depths of her brain, she concentrated on her grandmother.

She certainly wasn't overwhelmed by the reunion, Serenity decided with a rueful smile. Or perhaps it was just the European formality that made her seem so cold and distant. *It hardly seems reasonable that she would ask me to* come if she hadn't wanted to see me. I suppose I expected more because I wanted more. Lifting her shoulders, she allowed them to fall slowly. Patience has never been one of my virtues, but I suppose I'd better develop it. Perhaps if my greeting at the station had been a bit more welcoming . . . Her frown appeared again as she replayed Christophe's attitude.

I could swear he would have liked to bundle me back on the train the minute he set eyes on me. Then, that infuriating conversation in the car. Frown deepened into scowl, and she ceased to focus on the quiet dimness of dusk. That is a very frustrating man, and she added, her scowl softening into thoughtfulness, the very epitome of a Breton count. Perhaps that's why he affected me so strongly. Resting her chin on her palm, she recalled the awareness which had shimmered between them as they had sat alone in the lengthening shadow of the château. He's unlike any man I've ever known: elegant and vital at the same time. There's a potency there, a virility wrapped inside the sophistication. Power. The word flashed into her brain, drawing her brows close. Yes, she admitted with a reluctance she could not quite understand, there's power there, and an essence of self-assurance.

From an artist's standpoint, he's a remarkable study. He attracts me as an artist, she told herself, certainly not as a woman. A woman would have to be mad to get tangled up with a man like that. Absolutely mad, she repeated to herself firmly.

CHAPTER TWO

The oval, free-standing gilt-framed mirror reflected a slim, fair-haired woman. The flowing, high-necked gown in a muted "ashes of roses" shade lent a glow to the creamy skin, leaving arms and shoulders bare. Serenity met the reflection's amber eyes, held them, and sighed. It was nearly time to go down and again meet her grandmother—the regal, reserved countess—and her cousin, the formal, oddly hostile count.

Her trunks had arrived while she was enjoying the bath drawn by the small, dark Breton maid. Bridget had unpacked and put away her clothes, shyly at first, then chattering and exclaiming over the articles as she hung them in the large wardrobe or folded them in the antique bureau. The simple friendliness had been a marked contrast to the attitude of those who were her family.

Serenity's attempts to rest between the cool linen sheets of the great canopied bed had been futile, all her emotions in turmoil. The strange awareness she had experienced upon entering the château, the stiff, formal welcome of her grandmother, and the strong, physical response to the remote count had all banded together to make her unaccustomedly nervous and unsure of herself. She found herself wishing again she had allowed Tony to sway her, and had remained among the things and people she knew and understood.

Letting out a deep breath, she straightened her shoulders and lifted her chin. She was not a naïve schoolgirl to be awed by castles and overdone formality, she reminded herself. She was Serenity Smith, Jonathan and Gaelle Smith's daughter, and she would hold her head up and deal with counts and countesses.

Bridget knocked softly at her door, and Serenity followed her down the narrow corridor and began her descent down the curved staircase, cloaked in confidence.

"*Bonsoir,* Mademoiselle Smith." Christophe greeted her with his usual formality as she reached the bottom landing, and Bridget made a quick, unobtrusive exit.

"*Bonsoir,* Monsieur le Comte," Serenity returned, equally ritualistic, as they once more surveyed each other closely.

The black dinner suit lent a certain Satanic appearance to his aquiline features, the dark eyes glistening to near jet-black, the skin against the black and stark white of his shirt gleaming dusky-bronze. If there were pirates in his lineage, Serenity decided, they were elegant ones—and, she concluded further, as his eyes lingered on her, probably highly successful in all aspects of piratical pursuits.

"The countess awaits us in the drawing room," he announced when he had looked his fill, and with unexpected charm, he offered her his arm.

The countess watched as they entered the room, the tall, haughty man and the slim, golden-haired woman, a perfect foil at his side. A remarkably handsome couple, she reflected, one that would cause heads to turn wherever they went. "*Bonsoir,* Serenity, Christophe," she greeted them, regally resplendent in a gown of sapphire-blue, diamonds shooting fire from her throat. "*Mon apéritif,* Christophe, *s'il te plaît.* And for you, Serenity?"

"Vermouth, thank you, Madame," she replied, the practiced social smile on her lips.

"You rested well, I hope," the older woman inquired as Christophe handed her the small crystal glass.

"Yes, very well, Madame." She turned to accept the offered wine. "I . . ." The inane words she was about to utter stuck in her throat as the portrait caught her eye, and she turned around fully and faced it.

A cream-skinned, pale-haired woman looked back at her, the face the mirror image of her own. But for the length of the light gold mist of hair, falling to the shoulders, and the eyes that shone deep blue rather than amber, the portrait was Serenity: the oval face, delicate, with interesting hollows, the full, shapely mouth, the fragile, elusive beauty of her mother, reproduced in oil a quarter of a century earlier.

Her father's work—Serenity knew this immediately and unmistakably. The brush strokes, the use of color, the individual technique that shouted Jonathan Smith as surely as if she had read the small signature in the bottom corner. Her eyes filled, and she blinked back the threatening mist. Seeing the portrait had brought her parents close for a moment, and she was saturated with a deep sense of warmth and belonging that she had just been learning to live without.

She continued to study the painting, allowing herself to take in the details of her father's work, the folds of the oyster-white gown which seemed to float on a hidden breeze, the rubies at her mother's ears, a sharp contrast of color, the stone repeated in the ring on her finger. During the survey, something nagged at the back of her mind, some small detail out of place which refused to bring itself out of her consciousness, and she let it fade and merely experienced.

"Your mother was a very beautiful woman," the countess remarked after a time, and Serenity answered absently, still absorbed by the glowing look of love and happiness in her mother's eyes.

"Yes, she was. It's amazing how little she changed since my father painted this. How old was she?"

"Barely twenty," the countess replied, cultured tones

edging with curtness. "You recognized your father's work quickly."

"Of course," Serenity agreed, not noticing the tones, and turning, she smiled with honest warmth. "As his daughter and a fellow artist, I recognize his work as quickly as his handwriting." Facing the portrait again, she gestured with a slim, long-fingered hand. "That was painted twenty-five years ago, and it still breathes with life, almost as if they were both right here in this room."

"Your resemblance to her is very strong," Christophe observed as he sipped his wine from his place by the mantel, capturing her attention as completely as if he had put his hands on her. "I was quite struck by it when you stepped from the train."

"But for the eyes," the countess pronounced before Serenity could form a suitable comment. "The eyes are his."

There was no mistaking the bitterness which vibrated in her voice, and narrowing the eyes under discussion, Serenity spun around, the skirt of her gown following lazily. "Yes, Madame, I have my father's eyes. Does that displease you?"

Elegant shoulders moved in dismissal, and the countess lifted her glass and sipped.

"Did my parents meet here, in the château?" Serenity demanded, patience straining. "Why did they leave and never come back? Why did they never speak to me of you?" Glancing from her grandmother to Christophe, she met two cool, expressionless faces. The countess had lifted a shield, and Serenity knew Christophe would help her maintain it. He would tell her nothing; any answers must come from the woman. She opened her mouth to speak again when she was cut off with a wave of a ringed hand.

"We will speak of it soon enough." The words were spoken like a royal decree as the countess rose from her chair. "Now, we will go in to dinner."

The dining room was massive, but Serenity had decided everything was massive in the château. High-beamed ceilings towered like those in a cathedral, and the dark wainscotted walls were broken by high windows framed with rich velvet drapes the color of blood. A fireplace large enough to stand in commanded an entire wall, and she thought, when lit, it must be an awesome sight. A heavy chandelier gave the room its lights, its crystals trembling in a glistening rainbow of colors on the suite of dark majestic oak.

The meal began with an onion soup, thick, rich, and very French, and the trio maintained a polite conversation throughout the course. Serenity glanced at Christophe, intrigued against her will by his darkly handsome looks and haughty bearing.

He certainly doesn't like me, she concluded with a puzzled frown. *He didn't like me the moment he set eyes on me. I wonder why.* With a mental shrug, she began to eat her creamed salmon. *Perhaps he doesn't like women in general.* Looking over, his eyes met hers with a force that rivaled an electric storm, and her heart leaped suddenly, as if seeking to escape from behind her ribs. *No,* she amended quickly, tearing her eyes from his and studying the clear white wine in her glass, *he's no woman hater; those eyes are full of knowledge and experience. Tony never made me react like this.* Lifting her glass, she sipped with determination. *No one ever made me react like this.*

"Stevan," the countess commanded, "*du vin pour* Mademoiselle."

The countess's order to the hovering servant brought Serenity back from her contemplations. *"Mais non, merci. C'est bien."*

"You speak French very well for an American, Serenity," the dowager observed. "I am grateful your education was complete, even in that barbarous country."

The disdain in the last few words was so blatant that Serenity was unsure whether to be insulted or amused by the slight on her nationality. "That 'barbarous' country, Madame," she said dryly, "is called America, and it's nearly civilized these days. Why, we go virtually weeks between Indian attacks."

The proud head lifted imperiously. "There is no need for impudence, young woman."

"Really?" Serenity asked with a guileless smile. "Strange, I was sure there was." Lifting her wineglass, she saw, to her surprise, Christophe's teeth flash white against his dark skin in a wide, quick grin.

"You may have your mother's gentle looks," the countess observed, "but you have your father's tongue."

"Thank you." She met the clear blue eyes with an acknowledging nod. "On both counts."

The meal concluded, the conversation was allowed to drift back into generalities. And if the interlude took on the aspect of a truce, Serenity was still floundering as to the reason for the war. They adjourned once more to the main drawing room, Christophe lounging idly in an overstuffed chair swirling his after-dinner brandy while the countess and Serenity sipped coffee from fragile china cups.

"Jean-Paul le Goff, Gaelle's fiancé, met Jonathan Smith in Paris." The countess began to speak without preamble, and Serenity's cup halted on its journey to her lips, her eyes flying to the angular face. "He was quite taken with your father's talent and commissioned him to paint Gaelle's portrait as a wedding gift."

"My mother was engaged to another man before she married my father?" Serenity asked, setting down her cup with a great deal of care.

"*Oui.* The betrothal had been understood between the families for years; Gaelle was content with the arrangement. Jean-Paul was a good man, of good background."

"It was to be an arranged marriage, then?"

The countess waved away Serenity's sense of distaste with a gesture of her hand. "It is an old custom, and as I said, Gaelle was content. Jonathan Smith's arrival at the château changed everything. Had I been more alert, I would have recognized the danger, the looks which passed between them, the blushes which rose to Gaelle's cheeks when his name was spoken."

Françoise de Kergallen sighed deeply and gazed up at the portrait of her daughter. "Never did I imagine Gaelle would break her word, disgrace the family honor. Always she was a sweet, obedient child, but your father blinded her to her duty." The blue eyes shifted from the portrait to the living image. "I had no knowledge of what had passed between them. She did not, as she had always done before, confide in me, seek my advice. The day the portrait was completed, Gaelle fainted in the garden. When I insisted on summoning a doctor, she told me there was no need—she was not ill, but with child."

The countess stopped speaking, and the silence spread like a heavy cloak through the room. "Madame," Serenity said, breaking the silence in clear, even tones, "if you are attempting to shock my sensibilities by telling me I was conceived before my parents were married, I must disappoint you. I find it irrelevant. The days of stone-throwing and branding have passed, in my country at least. My parents loved each other; whether they expressed that love before or after they exchanged vows does not concern me."

The countess sat back in her chair, laced her fingers, and studied Serenity intently. "You are very outspoken, n'est-ce pas?"

"Yes, I am." She gave the woman a level look. "However, I try to prevent my honesty from causing injury."

"Touché," Christophe murmured, and the arched white brows rose fractionally before the countess gave her attention back to Serenity.

"Your mother had been married a month before you were conceived." The statement was given without a change of expression. "They were married in secret in a small chapel in another village, intending to keep the knowledge to themselves until your father was able to take Gaelle to America with him."

"I see." Serenity sat back with a slight smile. "My existence brought matters into the open a bit sooner than expected. And what did you do, Madame, when you discovered your daughter married and carrying the child of an obscure artist?"

"I disowned her, told them both to leave my home. From that day, I had no daughter." The words were spoken quickly, as if to throw off a burden no longer tolerable.

A small sound of anguish escaped Serenity, and her eyes flew to Christophe only to meet a blank, brooding wall. She rose slowly, a deep ache assailing her, and turning her back on her grandmother, she faced the gentle smile in her mother's portrait.

"I'm not surprised they put you out of their lives and kept you out of mine." Whirling back, she confronted the countess, whose face remained impassive, the pallor of her cheeks the only evidence of emotion. "I'm sorry for you, Madame. You robbed yourself of great happiness. It is you who have been isolated and alone. My parents shared a deep, encompassing love, and you cloistered yourself with pride and bruised honor. She would have forgiven you; if you knew her at all, then you know that. My father would have forgiven you for her sake, for he could deny her nothing."

"Forgive me?" High color replaced the pallor, and rage shook the cultured voice. "What need I with the forgiveness of a common thief and a daughter who betrayed her heritage?"

Amber eyes grew hot, like golden flames against flushed cheeks, and Serenity shrouded her fury in frigidity. "Thief? Madame, do you say my father stole from you?"

"*Oui,* he stole from me." The answering voice was hard and steady, matching the eyes. "He was not content to steal my child, a daughter I loved more than life. He added to his loot the Raphael Madonna which had belonged to my family for generations. Both priceless, both irreplaceable, both lost to a man I foolishly welcomed into my home and trusted."

"A Raphael?" Serenity repeated, lifting a hand to her temple in confusion. "You're implying my father stole a Raphael? You must be mad."

"I imply nothing," the countess corrected, lifting her head like a queen about to pronounce sentence. "I am stating that Jonathan Smith took both Gaelle and the Madonna. He was very clever. He knew it was my intention to donate the painting to the Louvre and he offered to clean it. I trusted him." The angular face was once more a grim mask of composure. "He exploited my trust, blinded my daughter to her duty, and left the château with both my treasures."

"It's a lie!" Serenity raged, anger welling up inside her with a force of a tidal wave. "My father would never steal—never! If you lost your daughter, it was because of your own pride, your own blindness."

"And the Raphael?" The question was spoken softly, but it rang in the room and echoed from the walls.

"I have no idea what became of your Raphael." She looked from the rigid woman to the impassive man and felt very much alone. "My father didn't take it; he was not a thief. He never did one dishonest thing in his life." She began to pace the room, battling the urge to shout and shatter their wall of composure. "If you were so sure he had your precious painting, why didn't you have him arrested? Why didn't you prove it?"

"As I said, your father was very clever," the countess rejoined. "He knew I would not involve Gaelle in such a scandal, no matter how she had betrayed me. With or without my consent, he was her husband, the father of the child she carried. He was secure."

Stopping her furious pacing, Serenity turned, her face incredulous. "Do you think he married her for security? You have no conception of what they had. He loved her more than his life, more than a hundred Raphaels."

"When I found the Raphael missing," the dowager continued, as if Serenity had not spoken, "I went to your father and demanded an explanation. They were already preparing to leave. When I accused him of taking the Raphael, I saw the look which passed between them—this man I had trusted, and my own daughter. I saw that he had taken the painting, and Gaelle knew him to be a thief but would stand with him against me. She betrayed herself, her family, and her country." The speech ended on a weary whisper, a brief spasm of pain appearing on the tightly controlled face.

"You have talked of it enough tonight," Christophe stated and rose to pour a brandy from a decanter, bringing the countess the glass with a murmur in Breton.

"They did not take it." Serenity took a step closer to the countess, only to be intercepted by Christophe's hand on her arm.

"We will speak of it no more at this time."

Jerking her arm away from his hold, she emptied her fury on him. "You won't tell me when I will speak! I will not tolerate my father being branded a thief! Tell me, Monsieur le Comte, if he had taken it, where is it? What did he do with it?"

Christophe's brow lifted, and his eyes held hers, the meaning in his look all too clear. Serenity's color ebbed, then flowed back in a rush, her mouth opening helplessly, before she swallowed and spoke in calm, distinct tones.

"If I were a man, you would pay for insulting both my parents and me."

"*Alors,* Mademoiselle," he returned with a small nod, "it is my good fortune you are not."

Serenity turned from the mockery in his tone and addressed the countess, who sat watching their exchange in silence. "Madame, if you sent for me because you believed I might know the whereabouts of your Raphael, you will be disappointed. I know nothing. In turn, I have my own disappointment, because I came to you thinking to find a family tie, another bond with my mother. We must both learn to live with our disappointments."

Turning, she left the room without so much as a backward glance.

Giving the door to her bedroom a satisfactory slam, Serenity dragged her cases from the wardrobe and dropped them onto the bed. Mind whirling in near-incoherent fury, she began pulling neatly hung clothing from its sanctuary and tossing it into the mouth of the open suitcases in a colorful jumble of confusion.

"Go away!" she called out with distinct rudeness as a knock sounded on her door, then turned and spared Christophe a lethal glare as he ignored the command.

He gave her packing technique a raised-brow study before closing the door quietly behind him. "So, Mademoiselle, you are leaving."

"Perfect deduction." She tossed a pale pink blouse atop the vivid mountain on her bed and proceeded to ignore him.

"A wise decision," he stated as she pointedly kept her back to him. "It would have been better if you had not come."

"Better?" she repeated, turning to face him as the slow, simmering rage began to boil. "Better for whom?"

"For the countess."

She advanced on him slowly, eyes narrowing as one prepared for battle, giving one brief mental oath on his advantage of height. "The countess invited me to come. Summoned," she corrected, allowing her tone to edge. "Summoned is more accurate. How dare you stand there and speak to me as if I had trampled on sacred ground! I never even knew the woman existed until her letter came, and I was blissfully happy in my ignorance."

"It would have been more prudent if the countess had left you to your bliss."

"That, Monsieur le Comte, is a brilliant example of understatement. I'm glad you understand I could have struggled through life without ever knowing any of my Breton connections." Turning in dismissal, Serenity vented her anger on innocent clothing.

"Perhaps you will find the struggle remains simple since the acquaintance will be brief."

"You want me out, don't you?" Spinning, she felt the last thread of dignity snap. "The quicker the better. Let me tell you something, Monsieur le Comte de Kergallen. I'd rather camp on the side of the road than accept your gracious hospitality. Here." She tossed a flowing flowered skirt in his general direction. "Why don't you help me pack?"

Stooping, he retrieved the skirt and laid it on a graceful upholstered chair, his cool, composed manner infuriating Serenity all the more. "I will send Bridget to you." The astringent politeness of his tone caused Serenity to glance quickly for something more solid to hurl at him. "You do seem to require assistance."

"Don't you dare send anyone!" she shouted as he turned for the door, and he faced her again, inclining his head at the order.

"As you wish, Mademoiselle. The state of your attire is your own concern."

Detesting his unblemished formality, Serenity found herself forced to provoke him. "I'll see to my own packing, Cousin, when I decide to leave." Deliberately, she turned and lifted a garment from the heap. "Perhaps I'll change my mind and stay for a day or two, after all. I've heard the Breton countryside has much charm."

"It is your privilege to remain, Mademoiselle." Catching the faint tint of annoyance in his tone, Serenity found it imperative to smile in victory. "I would, however, not recommend it under the circumstances."

"Wouldn't you?" Her shoulders moved in a small, elegant shrug, and she tilted her face to his in provocation. "That is yet another inducement for remaining." She saw both her words and actions had touched a chord of response as his eyes darkened with anger. His expression, however, remained calm and composed, and she wondered what form his temper would take when and if he unleashed it.

"You must do as you wish, Mademoiselle." He surprised her by closing the distance between them and capturing the back of her neck with strong fingers. At the touch, she realized his temper was not as far below the surface as she had imagined. "You may, however, find your visit not as comfortable as you might like."

"I'm well able to deal with discomfort." Attempting to pull away, she found the hand held her stationary with little effort.

"Perhaps, but discomfort is not something sought by a person of intelligence." The politeness of Christophe's smile was more arrogant than a sneer, and Serenity stiffened and endeavored to draw away again. "I would have said you possessed intelligence, Mademoiselle, if not wisdom."

Determined not to surrender to slowly growing fear, Serenity kept both eyes and voice level. "My decision to go or stay is not something I need to discuss with you. I will sleep on it and make the suitable arrangements in the morning. Of course, you can always chain me to a wall in the dungeon."

"An interesting alternative." His smile became both mocking and amused, his fingers squeezing lightly before they finally released her. "I will sleep on it." He moved to the door, giving her a brief bow as he turned the knob. "And make the suitable arrangements in the morning."

Frustrated by being outmaneuvered, Serenity hurled a shoe at the panel which closed behind him.

CHAPTER THREE

The quiet awoke Serenity. Opening her eyes, she stared without comprehension at the sun-filled room before she remembered where she was. She sat up in bed and listened. Silence, the deep, rich quality of silence, broken only by the occasional music of a bird. A quiet lacking the bustling, throbbing city noises she had known all of her life, and she decided she liked it.

The small, ornate clock on the cherry writing desk told her it was barely six, so she lay back for a moment in the luxury of elegant pillows and sheets and wallowed in laziness. Though her mind had been crowded with the facts and accusations her grandmother had disclosed, the fatigue from the long journey had taken precedence, and she had slept instantly and deeply, oddly at peace in the bed which had once been her mother's. Now, she stared up at the ceiling and ran through the previous evening again in her mind.

The countess was bitter. All the layers of practiced composure could not disguise the bitterness, or, Serenity admitted, the pain. Even through her own anger she had glimpsed the pain. Though she had banished the daughter, she had kept the portrait, and perhaps, Serenity concluded, the contradiction meant the heart was not as hard as the pride.

Christophe's attitude, however, still left her simmering. It seemed he had stood towering over her like a biased judge, ready to condemn without trial. *Well,* she determined, *I have my own share of pride, and I won't cower and shrink while my father's name is muddied, and my head put on the block. I can play the game of cold politeness, as well. I'm not running home like a wounded puppy; I'm going to stay right here.*

Gazing at the streaming sunlight, she gave a deep sigh. "*C'est un nouveau jour,* Maman," she said aloud. And, slipping from the bed, she walked over to the window. The garden spread out below her like a precious gift. "I'll go for a walk in your garden, Maman, and later I'll sketch your home." Sighing, she reached for her robe. "Then perhaps the countess and I can come to terms."

She washed and dressed quickly, choosing a pastel-printed sundress which left her arms and shoulders bare. The château remained in tranquil silence as she made her way to the main floor and stepped out into the warmth of the summer morning.

Strange, she mused, turning in a large circle. How strange not to see another building or cars or even another human being. The air was fresh and mildly scented, and she took a deep breath, consuming it before she began to circle the château on her way to the garden.

It was even more astonishing at close range than it had been from her window. Lush blooms exploded in an incredible profusion of colors, scents mixing and mingling into one exotic fragrance, at once tangy and sweet. There were a variety of paths cutting through the well-tended arrangements, smooth flagstones catching the morning sun and holding it glistening on their surface. Choosing one path at random, she strolled in idle contentment, enjoying the solitude, the artist in her reveling in the riot of hues and shapes.

"*Bonjour,* Mademoiselle." A deep voice broke the quiet, and Serenity whirled around, startled at the intrusion on her solitary contemplations. Christophe approached her slowly, tall and lean, his movements reminding her of an arrogant Russian dancer she had met at a Washington party. Graceful, confident, and very male.

"*Bonjour,* Monsieur le Comte." She did not waste a smile, but greeted him with careful cordiality. He was casually dressed in a buff-colored shirt and sleek-fitting brown jeans, and if she had felt the breeze of the buccaneer before, she was now caught in the storm.

He reached her and stared down with his habitual thorough survey. "You are an early riser. I trust you slept well."

"Very well, thank you," she returned, angry at having to battle not only animosity, but also attraction. "Your gardens are beautiful and very appealing."

"I have a fondness for what is beautiful and appealing." His eyes were direct, the dark brown smothering the amber, until she felt unable to breathe, dropping her eyes from the power of his.

"Oh, well, hello." They had been speaking in French, but at the sight of the dog at Christophe's heels, Serenity reverted back to English. "What's his name?" She crouched down to ruffle the thick, soft fur.

"Korrigan," he told her, looking down at her bent head as the sun streamed down, making a halo of pale curls.

"Korrigan," she repeated, enchanted by the dog and forgetting her annoyance with his master. "What breed is he?"

"Brittany spaniel."

Korrigan began to reciprocate her affection with tender licks on smooth cheeks. Before Christophe could command the dog to stop, Serenity laughed and buried her face against the animal's soft neck.

"I should have known. I had a dog once; it followed me home." Glancing up, she grinned as Korrigan continued to love her with a moist tongue. "Actually, I gave him a great deal of encouragement. I named him Leonardo, but my father called him Horrible, and that's the name that stuck. No amount of washing or brushing ever improved his inherent scruffiness."

As she went to rise, Christophe extended his hand to assist her to her feet, his grasp firm and disturbing. Checking the urge to jerk away from him, she disengaged herself casually and continued her walk. Both master and dog fell into step beside her.

"Your temper has cooled, I see. I found it surprising that such a dangerous temper exists inside such a fragile shell."

"I'm afraid you're mistaken." She twisted her head, giving him a brief but level glance. "Not about the temper, but the fragility. I'm really quite sturdy and not easily dented."

"Perhaps you have not yet been dropped," he countered, and she gave her attention to a bush pregnant with roses. "You have decided to stay for a time?"

"Yes, I have," she admitted and turned to face him directly, "although I get the distinct impression you'd rather I didn't."

His shoulders moved in an eloquent shrug. "*Mais non,* Mademoiselle. You are welcome to remain as long as it pleases you to do so."

"Your enthusiasm overwhelms me," muttered Serenity. *"Pardon?"*

"Nothing." Letting out a quick breath, she tilted her head and gave him a bold stare. "Tell me, Monsieur, do you dislike me because you think my father was a thief, or is it just me personally?"

The cool, set expression did not alter as he met her stare. "I regret to have given you such an impression. Mademoiselle, my manners must be at fault. I will attempt to be more polite."

"You're so infernally polite at times it borders on rudeness," she snapped, losing control and stomping her foot in exasperation.

"Perhaps you would find rudeness more to your taste?" His brow lifted as he regarded her temper with total nonchalance.

"Oh!" Turning away, she reached out angrily to pluck a rose. "You infuriate me! Darn!" she swore as a thorn pricked her thumb. "Now look what you made me do." Lifting her thumb to her mouth, she glared.

"My apologies," Christophe returned, a mocking light in his eyes. "That was most unkind of me."

"You are arrogant, patronizing, and stuffy," Serenity accused, tossing her curls.

"And you are bad-tempered, spoiled, and stubborn," he rejoined, narrowing his gaze and folding his arms across his chest. They stared at each other for a moment, his polite veneer slipping, allowing her a glimpse of the ruthless and exciting man beneath the coolly detached covering.

"Well, we seem to hold high opinions of each other after so short an acquaintance," she observed, smoothing back displaced curls. "If we know each other much longer, we'll be madly in love."

"An interesting conclusion, Mademoiselle." With a slight bow, he turned and headed back toward the château. Serenity felt an unexpected but tangible loss.

"Christophe," she called on impulse, wanting inexplicably to clear the air between them. He turned back, brow lifted in question, and she took a step toward him. "Can't we just be friends?"

He held her eyes for a long moment, so deep and intense a look that she felt he stripped her to the soul. "No, Serenity, I am afraid we will never just be friends."

She watched his tall, lithe figure stride away, the spaniel once more at his heels.

An hour later, Serenity joined her grandmother and Christophe at breakfast, with the countess making the usual inquiries as to how she had spent her night. The conversation was correct, if uninspired, and Serenity felt the older woman was making an effort to ease the tension brought on by the previous evening's confrontation. Perhaps, Serenity decided, it was not considered proper to squabble over croissants. *How amazingly civilized we are!* Suppressing an ironical smile, she mirrored the attitude of her companions.

"You will wish to explore the château, Serenity, *n'est-ce pas?*" Lifting her eyes as she set down the creamer, the countess stirred her coffee with a perfectly manicured hand.

"Yes, Madame, I would enjoy that," Serenity agreed with the expected smile. "I should like to make some sketches from the outside later, but I would love to see the inside first."

"*Mais oui*. Christophe," she said, addressing the dark man who was idly sipping his coffee, "we must escort Serenity through the château this morning."

"Nothing would give me greater pleasure, Grandmère," he agreed, placing his cup back in its china saucer. "But I regret I shall be occupied this morning. The new bull we imported is due to arrive, and I must supervise its transport."

"Ah, the cattle," the countess sighed and moved her shoulders. "You think too much about the cattle."

It was the first spontaneous statement Serenity had noted, and she picked it up automatically. "Do you raise cattle, then?"

"Yes," Christophe confirmed, meeting her inquiring gaze. "The raising of cattle is the château's business."

"Really?" she countered with exaggerated surprise. "I didn't think the de Kergallens bothered with such mundane matters. I imagined they just sat back and counted their serfs."

His lips curved slightly and he gave a small nod. "Only once a month. Serfs do tend to be highly prolific."

She found herself laughing into his eyes. Then as his quick, answering grin pounded a warning in her brain, she gave her attention to her own coffee.

In the end, the countess herself escorted Serenity on her tour of the rambling château, explaining some of its history as they moved from one astonishing room to another.

The château had been built in the late seventeenth century, and being in existence for just slightly less than three hundred years, it was not considered old by Breton standards. The château itself and the estates which belonged to it had been handed down from generation to generation to the oldest son, and although some modernizations had been made, it remained basically the same as it had been when the first Comte de Kergallen brought his bride over the drawbridge. To Serenity it was the essence of a lost and timeless charm, and the immediate affection and enchantment she had felt at first sight only grew with the explorations.

In the portrait gallery, she saw Christophe's dark fascination reproduced over the centuries. Though varied from generation to generation, the inveterate pride remained, the aristocratic bearing, the elusive air of mystery. She paused in front of one eighteenth-century ancestor whose resemblance was so striking that she took a step nearer to make a closer study.

"You find Jean-Claud interesting, Serenity?" the countess questioned, following her gaze. "Christophe is much like him in looks, *n'est-ce pas?*"

"Yes, it's remarkable." The eyes, she decided, were much too assured, and much too alive, and unless she were very much mistaken, the mouth had known a great many women.

"He is reputed to have been a bit, uh, *sauvage*," she continued with a hint of admiration. "It is said smuggling was his pastime; he was a man of the sea. The story is told that once when in England, he fell enamored of a woman of that country, and not having the patience for a long, formal, old-fashioned courtship, he kidnapped her and brought her to the château. He married her, of course; she is there." She pointed to a portrait of a rose-and-cream-fleshed English girl of about twenty. "She does not look unhappy."

With this comment, she strolled down the corridor, leaving Serenity staring up at the smiling face of a kidnapped bride.

The ballroom was huge, the far wall being opened with lead-paned windows adding to the space. Another wall was entirely mirrored, reflecting the brilliant prisms of the trio of chandeliers which would throw their sparkling light like silent stars from the high-beamed ceiling. Stiff-backed Regency chairs with elegant tapestry seats were strategically arranged for those who merely wished to look on as couples whirled across the highly polished floor. She wondered if Jean-Claud had given a wedding ball for his Sabine wife, and decided he undoubtedly had.

The countess led Serenity down another narrow corridor to a set of steep stone steps, winding spiral-like to the topmost tower. Although the room they entered was bare, Serenity immediately gave a cry of pleasure, moving to its center and gazing about as though it had been filled with treasures. It was large and airy and completely circular, and the high windows which encompassed it allowed the streaming sunlight to kiss every inch of space. Without effort, she pictured herself painting here for hours in blissful solitude.

"Your father used this room as his studio," the countess informed her, the stiffness returning to her voice, and Serenity broke off her fantasies and turned to confront her grandmother.

"Madame, if it is your wish that I remain here for a time, we must come to an understanding. If we cannot, I will have no choice but to leave." She kept her voice firm and controlled and astringently polite, but the eyes betrayed the struggle with temper. "I loved my father very much, as I did my mother. I will not tolerate the tone you use when you speak of him."

"Is it customary in your country for a young woman to address her elders in such a manner?" The regal head was held high, temper equally apparent.

"I can speak only for myself, Madame," she returned, standing straight and tall in the glow of sunlight. "And I am not of the opinion that age always equates with wisdom. Nor am I hypocrite enough to pay you lip service while you insult a man I loved and respected above all others."

"Perhaps it would be wiser if we refrained from discussing your father while you are with us." The request was an unmistakable command, and Serenity bristled with anger.

"I intend to mention him, Madame. I intend to discover precisely what became of the Raphael Madonna and clear the black mark you have put on his name."

"And how do you intend to accomplish this?"

"I don't know," she tossed back, "but I will." Pacing the room, she spread her hands unconsciously in a completely French gesture. "Maybe it's hidden in the château; maybe someone else took it." She whirled on the other woman with sudden fury. "Maybe you sold it and placed the blame on my father."

"You are insulting!" the countess returned, blue eyes leaping with fire.

"You brand my father a thief, and you say that *I* am insulting?" Serenity retorted, meeting her fire for fire. "I knew Jonathan Smith, Countess, and he was no thief, but I do not know you."

The countess regarded the furious young woman silently for several moments, blue flames dying, replaced by consideration. "That is true," she acknowledged with a nod. "You do not know me, and I do not know you. And if we are strangers, I cannot place the blame on your head. Nor can I blame you for what happened before you were born."

Moving to a window, she stared out silently. "I have not

changed my opinion of your father," she said at length, and turning, she held up a hand to silence Serenity's automatic retort. "But I have not been just where his daughter is concerned. You come to my home, a stranger, at my request, and I have greeted you badly. For this much, I apologize." Her lips curved in a small smile. "If you are agreeable, we will not speak of the past until we know each other."

"Very well, Madame," Serenity agreed, sensing both request and apology were an olive branch of sorts.

"You have a soft heart to go with a strong spirit," the dowager observed, a faint hint of approval in her tone. "It is a good match. But you also have a swift temper, *n'est-ce pas?*"

"*Évidemment,*" Serenity acknowledged.

"Christophe is also given to quick outbursts of temper and black moods," the countess informed her in a sudden change of topic. "He is strong and stubborn and requires a wife of equal strength, but with a heart that is soft."

Serenity stared in confusion at her grandmother's ambiguous statement. "She has my sympathy," she began, then narrowed her eyes as a small seed of doubt began to sprout. "Madame, what have Christophe's needs to do with me?"

"He has reached the age when a man requires a wife," the countess stated simply. "And you are past the age when most Breton women are well married and raising a family."

"I am only half-Breton," she asserted, distracted for a moment. Her eyes widened in amazement. "Surely you don't . . . you aren't thinking that Christophe and I . . . ? Oh, how beautifully ridiculous!" She laughed outright, a full, rich sound that echoed in the empty room. "Madame, I am sorry to disappoint you, but the count does not care for me. He didn't like me the moment he set eyes on me, and I'm forced to admit that I'm not overly fond of him, either."

"What has liking to do with it?" the countess demanded, her hands waving the words away.

Serenity's laughter stilled, and she shook her head in disbelief even as realization seeped through. "You've spoken to him of this already?"

"Oui, d'accord," the countess agreed easily.

Serenity shut her eyes, nearly swamped with humiliation and fury. "No wonder he resented me on sight— between this and thinking what he does of my father!" She turned away from her grandmother, then back again full of righteous indignation. "You overreach your bounds, Comtesse. The time of arranged marriages has long since passed."

"Poof!" It was a dismissive exclamation. "Christophe is too much his own man to agree to anything arranged by another, and I see you are too headstrong to do so. But"—a slow smile creased the angular face as Serenity looked on with wide, incredulous eyes—"you are very lovely, and Christophe is an attractive and virile man. Perhaps nature will—what is it? Take its course."

Serenity could only gape openmouthed into the calm, inscrutable face.

"Come." The countess moved easily toward the door. "There is more for you to see."

CHAPTER FOUR

The afternoon was warm, and Serenity was simmering. Indignation had spread from her grandmother to encompass Christophe, and the more she simmered, the more it became directed at him.

Insufferable, conceited aristocrat! she fumed. Her pencil ran violently across her pad as she sketched the drum towers of the château. *I'd rather marry Attila the Hun than be bound to that stiff-necked boor!* She broke the midday hush with a short burst of laughter. *Madame is probably picturing dozens of miniature counts and countesses playing formal little games in the courtyard and growing up to carry on the imperial line in the best Breton style!*

What a lovely place to raise children, she thought, pencil pausing, and eyes softening. *It's so clean and quiet and beautiful.* A deep sigh filled the air, and she started. Then realizing that it had emitted from her own lips, she frowned furiously. *La Comtesse Serenity de Kergallen,* she said silently and frowned with more feeling. *That'll be the day!*

A movement caught her attention, and she twisted her head, squinting against the sun to watch Christophe approach. His strides were long and sure, and he crossed the lawn with an effortless rhythm of limbs and muscles. *He walks as if he owns the world,* she observed, part in admiration, part in resentment. By the time he reached her, resentment had emerged victorious.

"You!" she spat without preamble, rising from the soft tuft of grass and standing like a slender avenging angel, gold and glowing.

His gaze narrowed at her tone, but his voice remained cool and controlled. "Something disturbs you, Mademoiselle?"

The ice in his voice only fanned the fire of anger, and dignity was abandoned. "Yes, I'm disturbed! You know very well I'm disturbed! Why in heaven's name didn't you tell me about this ludicrous idea of the countess's?"

"Ah." Brows rose, and lips curved in a sardonic smile. "*Alors,* Grandmère has informed you of the plans for our marital bliss. And when, my beloved, shall we have the banns announced?"

"You conceited . . ." she sputtered, unable to dream up an appropriately insulting term. "You know what you can do with your banns! I wouldn't have you on a bet!"

"Bon," he replied with a nod. "Then we are at last in full agreement. I have no desire to tie myself to a wasp-tongued brat. Whoever christened you Serenity had very little foresight."

"You're the most detestable man I have ever met!" she raged, her temper a direct contrast to his cool composure. "I can't abide the sight of you."

"Then you have decided to cut your visit short and return to America?"

She tilted her chin and shook her head slowly. "Oh, no, Monsieur le Comte, I shall remain right here. I have inducements for staying which outweigh my feelings for you."

The dark eyes narrowed into slits as he studied her face. "It would appear the countess has added a few francs to make you more agreeable."

Serenity stared at him in puzzlement until his meaning slowly seeped through, draining her color and darkening her eyes. Her hand swung out and struck him with full force in a loud, stinging slap, and then she spun on her heel and began to run toward the château. Hard hands dug into her shoulders and whirled her around, crushing her against the firm length of his body as his lips descended on hers in a brutal, punishing kiss.

The shock was electric, like a brilliant light flashed on, then extinguished. For a moment, she was limp against him, unable to surface from a darkness teeming with heat and demand. Her breath was no longer her own; she re-

alized suddenly he was stealing even that, and she began
to push at his chest, then pound with helpless, impotent
fists, terrified she would be captured forever in the swirling, simmering darkness.

His arms banded around her, molding her soft slender-
ness to the hard, unyielding lines of his body, merging
them into one passionate form. His hand slid up to cup
the back of her neck with firm fingers, forcing her head to
remain still, his other arm encircling her waist, maintaining absolute possession.

Her struggles slipped off him as though they were not
taking place, emphasizing his superior strength and the
violence which bubbled just beneath the surface. Her lips
were forced apart as his mouth continued its assault, exploring hers with an intimacy without mercy or compassion. The musky scent of his maleness was assailing her
senses, numbing both brain and will, and dimly she heard
her grandmother describing the long-dead count with
Christophe's face. *Sauvage,* she had said. *Sauvage.*

He gave her mouth its freedom, his grip returning to
her shoulders as he looked down into clouded, confused
eyes. For a moment, the silence hung like a shimmering
wall of heat.

"Who gave you permission to do that?" she demanded
unevenly, a hand reaching to her head to halt its spinning.

"It was either that or return your slap, Mademoiselle,"
he informed her, and from his tone and expression, she
could see he had not yet completed the transformation

from pirate to aristocrat. "Unfortunately, I have a reluctance to strike a woman, no matter how richly she may deserve it."

Serenity jerked away from his restraint, feeling the treacherous tears stinging, demanding release. "Next time, slap me. I'd prefer it."

"If you ever raise your hand to me again, my dear cousin, rest assured I will bruise more than your pride," he promised.

"You had it coming," she tossed back, but the temerity of her words was spoiled by wide eyes shimmering like golden pools of light. "How dare you accuse me of accepting money to stay here? Did it ever occur to you that I might *want* to know the grandmother I was denied all my life? Did you ever think that I might *want* to know the place where my parents met and fell in love? That I need to stay and prove my father's innocence?" Tears escaped and rolled down smooth cheeks, and Serenity despised each separate drop of weakness. "I only wish I could have hit you harder. What would you have done if someone had accused *you* of being bought like a side of beef?"

He watched the journey of a tear as it spilled from her eye and clung to satin skin, and a small smile tilted one corner of his mouth. "I would have beat them soundly, but I believe your tears are a more effective punishment than fists."

"I don't use tears as a weapon." She wiped at them with

the back of her hand, wishing she could have stemmed the flow.

"No; they are therefore all the more potent." A long bronzed finger brushed a drop from ivory skin, the contrast of colors lending her a delicate, vulnerable appearance, and he removed his hand quickly, addressing her in a casual tone. "My words were unjust, and I apologize. We have both received our punishment, so now we are—how do you say?—quits."

He gave her his rare, charming smile, and she stared at him, drawn by its power and enchanted by the positive change it lent to his appearance. Her own smile answered, the sudden shining of the sun through a veil of rain. He made a small, impatient sound, as though he regretted the momentary lapse, and nodding, he turned on his heel and strode away, leaving Serenity staring after him.

During the evening meal, the conversation was once more strictly conventional, as if the astonishing conversation in the tower room and the tempestuous encounter on the château grounds had not taken place. Serenity marveled at the composure of her companions as they carried on a light umbrella of table talk over *langoustes à la crème.* If it had not been for the fact that her lips still felt the imprint, she would have sworn she had imagined the stormy, breathtaking kiss Christophe had planted there. It had been a kiss which had stirred some deep inner feeling of response and had jolted her cool detachment more than she cared to admit.

It meant nothing, she insisted silently and applied herself to the succulent lobster on her plate. She'd been kissed before and she would be kissed again. She would not allow any moody tyrant to give her one more moment's concern. Deciding to resume her role in the game of casual formality, she sipped from her glass and made a comment on the character of the wine.

"You find it agreeable?" Christophe picked up the trend of conversation in an equally light tone. "It is the château's own Muscadet. We produce a small quantity each year for our own enjoyment and for the immediate vicinity."

"I find it very agreeable," Serenity commented. "How exciting to enjoy wine made from your own vineyards. I've never tasted anything quite like it."

"The Muscadet is the only wine produced in Brittany," the countess informed Serenity with a smile. "We are primarily a province of the sea and lace."

Serenity ran a finger over the snowy-white cloth that adorned the oak table. "Brittany lace, it's exquisite. It looks so fragile, yet years only increase the beauty."

"Like a woman," Christophe murmured, and Serenity lifted her eyes to meet his dark regard.

"But then, there are also the cattle." She grabbed at the topic to cover momentary confusion.

"Ah, the cattle." His lips curved, and Serenity had the

uncomfortable impression that he was well aware of his effect on her.

"Having lived in the city all my life, I'm totally ignorant when it comes to cattle." She floundered on, more and more disconcerted by the directness of his eyes. "I'm sure they make quite a picture grazing in the fields."

"We must introduce you to the Breton countryside," the countess declared, drawing Serenity's attention. "Perhaps you would care to ride out tomorrow and view the estate?"

"I would enjoy that, Madame. I'm sure it will be a pleasant change from sidewalks and government buildings."

"I would be pleased to escort you, Serenity," Christophe offered, surprising her. Turning back to him, her expression mirrored her thoughts. He smiled and inclined his head. "Do you have the suitable attire?"

"Suitable attire?" she repeated, surprise melting into confusion.

"But yes." He appeared to be enjoying her changing expressions, and his smile spread. "Your taste in clothing is impeccable, but you would find it difficult to ride a horse in a gown like that."

Her gaze lowered to the gently flowing lines of her willow-green dress before rising to his amused glance. "Horse?" she said, frowning.

"You cannot tour the estate in an automobile, *ma petite*. The horse is more adaptable."

At his laughing eyes, she straightened and drew out her dignity. "I'm afraid I don't ride."

"*C'est impossible!*" the countess exclaimed in disbelief. "Gaelle was a marvelous horsewoman."

"Perhaps equestrian abilities are not genetic, Madame," Serenity suggested, amused by her grandmother's incredulous expression. "I am no horsewoman at all. I can't control a merry-go-round pony."

"I will teach you." Christophe's words were a statement rather than a request, and she turned to him, amusement fading into hauteur.

"How kind of you to offer, Monsieur, but I have no desire to learn. Do not trouble yourself."

"Nevertheless," he stated and lifted his wineglass, "you shall. You will be ready at nine o'clock, *n'est-ce pas?* You will have your first lesson."

She glared at him, astonished by his arbitrary dismissal of her refusal. "I just told you . . ."

"Try to be punctual, *chérie,*" he warned with deceptive laziness as he rose from the table. "You will find it more comfortable to walk to the stables than to be dragged by your golden hair." He smiled as if the latter prospect held great appeal for him. "*Bonne nuit,* Grandmère," he added with affection before he disappeared from the room, leaving Serenity fuming, and his grandmother unashamedly pleased.

"Of all the insufferable nerve!" she sputtered when she

located her voice. Turning angry eyes on the other woman, she added defiantly, "If he thinks I'm going to meekly obey and . . ."

"You would be wise to obey, meekly or otherwise," the dowager interrupted. "Once Christophe has set his mind . . ." With a small, meaningful shrug, she left the rest of the sentence to Serenity's imagination. "You have slacks, I presume. Bridget will bring you a pair of your mother's riding boots in the morning."

"Madame," Serenity began slowly, as if attempting to make each word understood, "I have no intention of getting on a horse in the morning."

"Do not be foolish, child." A slender, ringed hand reached negligently for a wineglass. "He is more than capable of carrying out his threat. Christophe is a very stubborn man." She smiled, and for the first time Serenity felt genuine warmth. "Perhaps even more stubborn than you."

Muttering strong oaths, Serenity pulled on the sturdy boots that had been her mother's. They had been cleaned and polished to a glossy black shine and fit her small feet as if custom-made for them.

It seems even you are conspiring against me, Maman, she silently chided her mother in despair. Then she called out a casual *"Entrez"* as a knock sounded on her door. It was not the little maid, Bridget, who opened the door, however, but Christophe, dressed with insouciant elegance in fawn riding breeches and a white linen shirt.

"What do you want?" she asked with a scowl, pulling on the second boot with a firm tug.

"Merely to see if you are indeed punctual, Serenity," he returned with an easy smile, his eyes roaming over her mutinous face and the slim, supple body clad in a silkscreen-printed T-shirt and French tailored jeans.

Wishing he would not always look at her as if memorizing each feature, she rose in defense. "I'm ready, Captain Bligh, but I'm afraid you won't find me a very apt pupil."

"That remains to be seen, *ma chérie*." His eyes swept over her again, as if considering. "You seem to be quite capable of following a few simple instructions."

Her eyes narrowed into jeweled slits, and she struggled with the temper he had a habit of provoking. "I am reasonably intelligent, thank you, but I don't like being bull-dozed."

"Pardon?" His blank expression brought out a smug smile.

"I shall have to recall a great many colloquialisms, Cousin. Perhaps I can slowly drive you mad."

Serenity accompanied Christophe to the stables in haughty silence, determinedly lengthening her strides to match his gait and preventing the necessity of trailing after him like an obedient puppy. When they reached the outbuilding, a groom emerged leading two horses, bridled and saddled in anticipation. One was full black and gleaming, the other a creamy buckskin, and to Serenity's apprehensive eyes, both were impossibly large.

She halted suddenly and eyed the pair with a dubious frown. *He wouldn't really drag me by the hair,* she thought carefully. "If I just turned around and walked away, what would you do about it?" Serenity inquired aloud.

"I would only bring you back, *ma petite.*" The dark brow rose at her deepening frown, revealing he had already anticipated her question.

"The black is obviously yours, Comte," she concluded in a light voice, struggling to control a mounting panic. "I can already picture you galloping over the countryside in the light of a full moon, the gleam of a saber at your hip."

"You are very astute, Mademoiselle." He nodded, and taking the buckskin's reins from the groom, he walked the mount toward her. She took an involuntary step back and swallowed.

"I suppose you want me to get on him."

"Her," he corrected, mouth curving.

She flashed at him, angry and nervous and disgusted with her own apprehension. "I'm not really concerned about its sex." Looking over the quiet horse, she swallowed again. "She's . . . she's very large." Her voice was fathoms weaker than she had hoped.

"Babette is as gentle as Korrigan," Christophe assured

her in unexpectedly patient tones. "You like dogs, *n'est-ce pas?*"

"Yes, but . . ."

"She is soft, no?" He took her hand and lifted it to Babette's smooth cheek. "She has a good heart and wishes only to please."

Her hand was captured between the smooth flesh of the horse and the hard insistence of Christophe's palm, and she found the combination oddly enjoyable. Relaxing, she allowed him to guide her hand over the mare and twisted her head, smiling over her shoulder.

"She feels nice," she began, but as the mare blew from wide nostrils, she jumped nervously and stumbled back against Christophe's chest.

"Relax, *chérie.*" He chuckled softly, his arms encircling her waist to steady her. "She is only telling you that she likes you."

"It just startled me," Serenity returned in defense, disgusted with herself, and decided it was now or never. She turned to tell him she was ready to begin, but found herself staring wordlessly into dark, enigmatic eyes as his arms remained around her.

She felt her heart stop its steady rhythm, remaining motionless for a stifling moment, then race sporadically at a wild pace. For an instant, she believed he would kiss her again, and to her own astonishment and confusion, she realized she wanted to feel his lips on hers above all else. A frown creased his brow suddenly, and he released her in a sharp gesture.

"We will begin." Cool and controlled, he stepped effortlessly into the role of instructor.

Pride took over, and Serenity became determined to be a star pupil. Swallowing her anxiety, she allowed Christophe to assist her in mounting. With some surprise, she noted that the ground was not as far away as she had anticipated, and she gave her full attention to Christophe's instructions. She did as he bade, concentrating on following his directions precisely, determined not to make a fool of herself again.

Serenity watched Christophe mount his stallion with a fluid grace and economy of movement she envied. The spirited black suited the dark, haughty man to perfection, and she reflected, with some distress, that not even Tony at his most ardent had ever affected her the way this strange, remote man did with his enveloping stares.

She couldn't be attracted to him, she argued fiercely. He was much too unpredictable, and she realized, with a flash of insight, that he could hurt her as no man had been able to hurt her before. *Besides,* she thought, frowning at the buckskin's mane, *I don't like his superior, dominating attitude.*

"Have you decided to take a short nap, Serenity?" Christophe's mocking voice brought her back with a snap, and meeting his laughing eyes, she felt herself flush to her undying consternation. *"Allons-y, chérie."* Her deepening color was noted with a curve of his lips, as he directed his horse away from the stables and proceeded at a slow walk.

They moved side by side, and after several moments Serenity found herself relaxing in the saddle. She passed Christophe's instructions on to the mare, which responded with smooth obedience. Confidence grew, and she allowed herself to view the scenery, enjoying the caress of the sun on her face and the gentle rhythm of the horse under her.

"Maintenant, we trot," Christophe commanded suddenly, and Serenity twisted her head to regard him seriously.

"Perhaps my French is not as good as I supposed. Did you say trot?"

"Your French is fine, Serenity."

"I'm quite content to amble along," she returned with a careless shrug. "I'm in no hurry at all."

"You must move with the jogging of the horse," he instructed, ignoring her statement. "Rise with every other jog. Press gently with your heels."

"Now, listen . . ."

"Afraid?" he taunted, his brow lifting high in mockery. Before common sense could overtake pride, Serenity tossed her head and pressed her heels against the horse's side.

This must be what it feels like to operate one of those dam-

nable jackhammers they're forever tearing up the streets with, she thought breathlessly, bouncing without grace on the trotting mare.

"Rise with every other jog," Christophe reminded her, and she was too preoccupied with her own predicament to observe the wide grin which accompanied his words. After a few more awkward moments, she caught on to the timing.

"Comment ça va?" he inquired as they moved side by side along the dirt path.

"Well, now that my bones have stopped rattling, it's not so bad. Actually"—she turned and smiled at him—"it's fun."

"Bon. Now we canter," he said simply, and she sent him a withering glance.

"Really, Christophe, if you want to murder me, why not try something simpler like poison, or a nice clean stab in the back?"

He threw back his head and laughed, a full, rich sound that filled the quiet morning, echoing on the breeze. When he turned his head and smiled at her, Serenity felt the world tilt, and her heart, ignoring the warnings of her brain, was lost.

"Allons, ma brave." His voice was light, carefree, and contagious. "Press in your heels, and I will teach you to fly."

Her feet obeyed automatically, and the mare responded, quickening her gait to a smooth, easy canter. The wind played with Serenity's hair and brushed her cheeks with cool fingers. She felt as though she were riding on a cloud, unsure whether the lightness was a result of the rush of wind or the dizziness of love. Enthralled with the novelty of both, she did not care.

At Christophe's command, she drew back on the reins, slowing the mare from a canter to a trot to a walk before finally coming to a halt. Lifting her face to the sky, she gave a deep sigh of pleasure before turning to her companion. The wind and excitement had whipped a rose blush onto her cheeks, her eyes were wide, golden, and bright, and her hair was tousled, an unruly halo around her happiness.

"You enjoyed yourself, Mademoiselle?"

She flashed him a brilliant smile, still intoxicated with love's potent wine. "Go ahead; say 'I told you so.' It's perfectly all right."

"*Mais non, chérie,* it is merely a pleasure to see one's pupil progress with such speed and ability." He returned her smile, the invisible barrier between them vanishing. "You move naturally in the saddle; perhaps the talent is genetic, after all."

"Oh, Monsieur." She fluttered her lashes over a gleam of mischief. "I must give the credit to my teacher."

"Your French blood is showing, Serenity, but your technique needs practice."

"Not so good, huh?" Pushing back disheveled hair, she

gave a deep sigh. "I suppose I'll never get it right. Too much American Puritan from my father's ancestors."

"Puritan?" Christophe's full laugh once more disturbed the quiet morning. "*Chérie,* no Puritan was ever so full of fire."

"I shall take that as a compliment, though I sincerely doubt it was intended as one." Turning her head, she looked down from the hilltop to the spreading valley below. "Oh, how beautiful."

A scene from a postcard slumbered in the distance, gentle hills dotted with grazing cattle against a backdrop of neat cottages. Farther in the distance, she observed a tiny village, a small toy town set down by a giant hand, dominated by a white church, its spire reaching heaven-ward.

"It's perfect," she decided. "Like slipping back in time." Her eyes roamed back to the grazing cattle. "Those are yours?" she asked, gesturing with her hand.

"*Oui,*" he asserted.

"This is all your property, then?" she asked again, feeling a sudden sinking sensation.

"This is part of the estates." He answered with a careless movement of his shoulders.

We've been riding for so long, she thought with a frown, *and we're still on his land. Lord knows how far it spreads in other directions. Why can't he be an ordinary man?* Turning her head, she studied his hawklike profile. *But he is not an ordinary man,* she reminded herself. *He is the Comte de Kergallen, master of all he surveys, and I must remember that.* Her gaze moved back to the valley, her frown deepening. *I don't want to be in love with him.* Swallowing the sudden dryness of her throat, she used her words as a defense against her heart.

"How wonderful to possess so much beauty."

He turned to her, brow raising at her tone. "One cannot possess beauty, Serenity, merely care for and cherish it."

She fought against the warmth his soft words aroused, keeping her eyes glued to the valley. "Really? I was under the impression that young aristocrats took such things for granted." She made a wide, sweeping gesture. "After all, this is only your due."

"You have no liking for aristocracy, Serenity, but you have aristocratic blood, as well." Her blank look brought a slow smile to his chiseled features, and his tone was cool. "Yes, your mother's father was a count, though his estates were ravaged during the war. The Raphael was one of the few treasures your grandmother salvaged when she escaped."

The damnable Raphael again! Serenity thought dismally. He was angry; she determined this from the hard light in his eyes, and she found herself oddly pleased. It would be easier to control her feelings for him if they remained at odds with each other.

"So, that makes me half-peasant, half-aristocrat," she retorted, moving her slim shoulders in dismissal. "Well, *mon cher cousin,* I much prefer the peasant half myself. I'll leave the blue blood in the family to you."

"You would do well to remember there is no blood between us, Mademoiselle." Christophe's voice was low, and meeting his narrowed eyes, Serenity felt a trickle of fear. "The de Kergallens are notorious for taking what they want, and I am no exception. Take care how you use your brandy eyes."

"The warning is unnecessary, Monsieur. I can take care of myself."

He smiled, a slow, confident smile, more unnerving than a furious retort, and turned his mount back toward the château.

The return ride was accomplished in silence, broken only by Christophe's occasional instructions. They had crossed swords again, and Serenity was forced to admit he had parried her thrust easily.

When they reached the stables, Christophe dismounted with his usual grace, handing the reins to a groom and moving to assist her before she could copy his action.

Defiantly, she ignored the stiffness in her limbs as she eased herself from the mare's back and Christophe's hands encircled her waist. They remained around her for a moment, and he brooded down at her before releasing the hold that seemed to burn through the light material of her shirt.

"Go have a hot bath," he ordered. "It will ease the stiffness you are undoubtedly feeling."

"You have an amazing capacity for issuing orders, Monsieur."

His eyes narrowed before his arm went around her with incredible speed, pulling her close and crushing her lips in a hard, thorough kiss that left no time for struggle or protest, but drew a response as easily as a hand turning a water tap.

For an eternity he kept her the prisoner of his will, plunging her deeper and deeper into the kiss. Its bruising intensity released a new and primitive need in her, and abandoning pride for love, she surrendered to demands she could not conquer. The world evaporated, the soft Breton landscape melting like a watercolor left out in the rain, leaving nothing but warm flesh and lips which sought her surrender. His hand ran over the slim curve of her hip, then up her spine with sure authority, crushing her against him with a force which would have cracked her bones had they not already dissolved in the heat.

Love. Her mind whirled with the word. Love was walks in soft rain, a quiet evening beside a crackling fire. How could it be a throbbing, turbulent storm which left you weak and breathless and vulnerable? How could it be that one would crave the weakness as much as life itself? Was this how it had been for Maman? Was this what put the dreamy mists of knowledge in her eyes? *Will he never set me free?* she wondered desperately, and her arms encircled his neck, body contradicting will.

"Mademoiselle," he murmured with soft mockery,

keeping his mouth a breath from hers, his fingers teasing the nape of her neck, "you have an amazing capacity for provoking punishment. I find the need to discipline you imperative."

Releasing her, he turned and strode carelessly away, stopping to acknowledge the greeting of Korrigan, who trotted faithfully at his heels.

CHAPTER FIVE

Serenity and the countess shared their lunch on the terrace, surrounded by sweet-smelling blossoms. Refusing the offered wine, Serenity requested coffee instead, enduring the raised white brow with tranquil indifference.

I suppose this makes me an undoubted Philistine, she concluded, suppressing a smile as she enjoyed the strong black liquid along with the elegant shrimp bisque.

"I trust you found your ride enjoyable," the countess stated after they had exchanged comments on the food and weather.

"To my utter amazement, Madame," Serenity admitted, "I did. I only wished I had learned long ago. Your Breton scenery is magnificent."

"Christophe is justifiably proud of his land," the countess asserted, studying the pale wine in her glass. "He loves it as a man loves a woman, an intense sort of passion. And though the land is eternal, a man needs a wife. The earth is a cold lover."

Serenity's brows rose at her grandmother's frankness, the sudden abandonment of formality. Her shoulders moved in a faintly Gallic gesture. "I'm sure Christophe has little trouble finding warm ones." *He probably merely snaps his fingers and dozens tumble into his arms,* she added silently, almost wincing at the fierce stab of jealousy.

"Naturellement," the countess agreed, a glimmer of amusement lighting up her eyes. "How could it be otherwise?" Serenity digested this with a scowl, and the dowager lifted her wineglass. "But men like Christophe require constancy rather than variety after a time. Ah, but he is so like his grandfather." Looking over quickly, Serenity saw the soft expression transform the angular face. "They are wild, these Kergallen men, dominant and arrogantly masculine. The women who are given their love are blessed with both heaven and hell." Blue eyes focused on amber once more and smiled. "Their women must be strong or be trampled beneath them, and they must be wise enough to know when to be weak."

Serenity had been listening to her grandmother's words as if under a spell. Shaking herself, she pushed back the plate of shrimp for which her appetite had fled. "Madame," she began, determined to make her position clear, "I have no intention of entering into the competition for the present count. As I see it, we are incredibly ill matched." She recalled suddenly the feel of his lips against hers, the demanding pressure of his hard body, and she trembled. Raising her eyes to her grandmother's, she shook her head in fierce denial. "No." She did not stop to reason if she was speaking to her heart or the woman across from her, but stood and hurried back into the château.

The full moon had risen high in the star-studded sky, its silver light streaming through the high windows as Serenity awoke, miserable, sore, and disgusted. Though she had retired early, latching on to the inspiration of a fictitious headache to separate herself from the man who clouded her thoughts, sleep had not come easily. Now, just a few short hours since she had captured it, it had escaped. Turning in the oversized bed, she moaned aloud at her body's revolt.

I'm paying the price for this morning's little adventure. She winced and sat up with a deep sigh. *Perhaps I need another hot bath,* she decided with dim hope. *Lord knows it couldn't make me any stiffer.* She eased herself from the mattress, legs and shoulders protesting violently. Ignoring the robe at the foot of the bed, she made her way across the dimly lit room toward the adjoining bath, banging her shin smartly against an elegant Louis XVI chair.

She swore, torn between anger and pain. Still muttering, she nursed her leg, pulling the chair back into position and leaning on it. "What?" she called out rudely as a knock sounded on her door.

It swung open, and Christophe, dressed casually in a robe of royal-blue silk, stood observing her. "Have you injured yourself, Serenity?" It was not necessary to see his expression to be aware of his mockery.

"Just a broken leg," she snapped. "Pray, don't trouble yourself."

"May one inquire as to why you are groping about in the dark?" He leaned against the doorframe, cool, calm, and in total command, his arrogance all the catalyst Serenity's mercurial temper required.

"I'll tell you why I'm groping about in the dark, you smug, self-assured beast!" she began, her voice a furious whisper. "I was going to drown myself in the tub to put myself out of the misery you inflicted on me today!"

"I?" he said innocently, his eyes roaming over her, slim and golden in the shimmering moonlight, her long, shapely legs and pure alabaster-toned skin exposed by the briefness of her flimsy nightdress. She was too angry to be aware of her dishabille or his appreciation, oblivious to the moonlight which seeped through the sheerness of her gown and left her curves delectably shadowed.

"Yes, you!" she shot back at him. "It was you who got me up on that horse this morning, wasn't it? And now each individual muscle in my body despises me." Groaning, she rubbed her palm against the small of her back. "I may never walk properly again."

"Ah."

"Oh, what a wealth of meaning in a single syllable." She glared at him, doing her best to stand with some dignity. "Could you do it again?"

"Ma pauvre petite," he murmured in exaggerated sympathy. *"Je suis désolé."* He straightened and began to move toward her. Then, suddenly recalling her state of dress, her eyes grew wide.

"Christophe, I . . ." she began as his hands descended on her bare shoulders, but the words ended in a sigh as his fingers massaged the strain.

"You have discovered new muscles, yes? And they are not being agreeable. It will not be so difficult the next time." He led her to the bed and pressed her shoulders so that she sat, unresisting, savoring the firm movements on her neck and shoulders. Easing down behind her, his long fingers continued down her back, kneading away the ache as if by magic.

She sighed again, unconsciously moving against him. "You have wonderful hands," she murmured, a blessed lethargy seeping into her as the soreness disappeared and a warm contentment took its place. "Marvelous strong fingers; I'll be purring any minute."

She was not aware when the transition occurred, when the gentle relaxation became a slow kindling in her stomach, his objective massage an insistent caress, but she felt her head suddenly spinning with the heat.

"That's better, much better," she faltered and made to move away, but his hands went quickly to her waist, holding her immobile as his lips sought the soft vulnerability of her neck in a gentle feather of a kiss. She trembled, then started like a frightened doe, but before she could escape, he had twisted her to face him, his lips descending in possession on hers, stilling all protests.

Struggle died before it became a reality, the kindling erupting into a burst of flame, and her arms encircled his neck as she was pressed against the mattress. His mouth seemed to devour hers, hard and assured, and his hands followed the curves of her body as if he had made love to her countless times. Impatiently, he pushed aside the thin strap on her shoulder, seeking and finding the satin smoothness of her breast, his touch inciting a tempest of desire, and she began to move under him. His demands became more urgent, his hands more insistent as they moved down the whisper of silk, his lips leaving hers to assault her neck with an insatiable hunger.

"Christophe," she moaned, knowing she was incapable of combating both him and her own weakness. "Christophe, please, I can't fight you here. I could never win."

"Do not fight me, *ma belle*," he whispered into her neck. "And we shall both win."

His mouth took hers again, soft and lingering, causing desire to swell, then soar. Slowly, his lips explored her face, brushing along the hollows of her cheeks, teasing the vulnerability of parted lips before moving on to other conquests. A hand cupped her breast in lazy possession, fingers tracing its curve, tarrying over the nipple until a dull, throbbing ache spread through her. The sweet, weakening pain brought a moan, and her hands began to seek the rippling muscles of his back, as if to accentuate his power over her.

His lazy explorations altered to urgency once more, as if her submission had fanned the fires of his own passions. Hands bruised soft flesh, and her mouth was savaged by his, the teeth which had nibbled along her bottom lip replaced by a mouth which ravaged her senses, and demanded more than surrender, but equal passion.

The hand left her breast to run down her side, pausing over her hip before he continued on, claiming the smooth, fresh skin of her thigh, and her breath came only in shuddering sighs as his lips moved lower along her throat to taste the warm hollow between her breasts.

With one final flash of lucidity, she knew she stood on the edge of a precipice, and one more step would plunge her into an everlasting void.

"Christophe, please." She began to tremble, though nearly suffocating with the heat. "Please, you frighten me, I frighten me. I've never . . . I've never been with a man before."

His movements stopped, and the silence became thick as he lifted his face and stared down at her. Slivers of moonlight slept on her pale hair, tousled on the snowy pillow, her eyes smoky with awakened passion and fear.

With a short, harsh sound, he lifted his weight from her. "Your timing, Serenity, is incredible."

"I'm sorry," she began, sitting up.

"For what do you apologize?" he demanded, anger just below the surface of icy calm. "For your innocence, or for allowing me to come very close to claiming it?"

"That's a rotten thing to say!" she snapped, fighting to steady her breathing. "This happened so quickly, I couldn't think. If I had been prepared, you would never have come so close."

"You think not?" He dragged her up until she was kneeling on the surface of the bed, once more molded against him. "You are prepared now. Do you think I could not take you this minute with you more than willing to allow it?"

He glared down at her, the air around him tingling with assurance and fury, and she could say nothing, knowing she was helpless against his authority and her own surging need. Her eyes were huge in her pale face, fear and innocence shining like beacons, and he swore and pushed her away.

"*Nom de Dieu!* You look at me with the eyes of a child. Your body disguises your innocence well; it is a dangerous masquerade." Moving to the door, he turned back to survey the lightly clad form made small by the vastness of the bed. "Sleep well, *mignonne*," he said with a touch of mockery. "The next time you choose to run into the furniture, it would be wise if you lock your door; I will not walk away again."

Serenity's cool greeting to Christophe over breakfast was returned in kind, his eyes meeting hers briefly, showing no trace of the passion or anger they had held the previous night. Perversely, she was annoyed at his lack of reaction as he chatted with the countess, addressing Serenity only when necessary, and then with a strict politeness which could be detected only by the most sensitive ear.

"You have not forgotten Geneviève and Yves are dining with us this evening?" the countess asked Christophe.

"*Mais non,* Grandmère," he assured her, replacing his cup in its saucer. "It is always a pleasure to see them."

"I believe you will find them pleasant company, Serenity." The countess turned her clear blue eyes on her granddaughter. "Geneviève is very close to your age, perhaps a year younger, a very sweet, well-mannered young woman. Her brother, Yves, is very charming and quite attractive." A smile was born on her lips. "You will find his company, uh, *diverting.* Do you not agree, Christophe?"

"I am sure Serenity will find Yves highly entertaining."

Serenity glanced over quickly at Christophe. Was there a touch of briskness to his tone? He was sipping his coffee calmly, and she decided she had been mistaken.

"The Dejots are old family friends," the countess went

on, drawing Serenity's attention back to her. "I am sure you will find it pleasant to have company near your own age, *n'est-ce pas?* Geneviève is often a visitor to the château. As a child she trotted after Christophe like a faithful puppy. *Bien sûr,* she is not a child any longer." She threw a meaningful glance at the man at the head of the long oak table, and Serenity used great willpower not to wrinkle her nose in disdain.

"Geneviève grew from an awkward pigtailed child into an elegant, lovely woman," Christophe replied, and the affection in his voice was unmistakable.

Good for her, Serenity thought, struggling to keep an interested smile in place.

"She will make a marvelous wife," the countess predicted. "She has a quiet beauty and natural grace. We must persuade her to play for you, Serenity. She is a highly skilled pianist."

Chalk up one more for the paragon of virtue, Serenity brooded to herself silently, miserably jealous of the absent Geneviève's relationship with Christophe. Aloud, she said, "I shall look forward to meeting your friends, Madame." Silently, she assured herself that she would dislike the perfect Geneviève on sight.

The golden morning passed quietly, a lazy mid-morning hush falling over the garden as Serenity sketched. She had exchanged a few words with the gardener before they had both settled down to their respective tasks. Finding him an interesting study, she sketched him as he bent over the bushes, trimming the overblown blossoms and chattering, scolding, and praising his colorful, scented friends.

His face was timeless, weathered and lined with character, unexpectedly bright blue eyes shining against a ruddy complexion. The hat covering his shock of steel-gray hair was black, a wide, flat-brimmed cap with velvet ribbons streaming down the back. He wore a sleeveless vest and aged knickers, and she marveled at his agility in the wooden *sabots*.

So deep was her concentration on capturing his Old World aura with her pencil that she failed to hear the footsteps on the flagstones behind her. Christophe watched her for some moments as she bent over her work, the graceful curve of her neck calling to his mind an image of a proud white swan floating on a cool, clear lake. Only when she tucked her pencil behind her ear and brushed an absent hand through her hair did he make his presence known.

"You have captured Jacques admirably, Serenity." His brow rose in amusement at the startled jump she made and the hand that flew to her heart.

"I didn't know you were there," she said, cursing the breathlessness of her voice and the pounding of her pulse.

"You were deep in your work," he explained, casually sitting next to her on the white marble bench. "I did not wish to disturb you."

Ho, she amended silently, *you'd disturb me if you were a thousand miles away.* Aloud, she spoke politely: "*Merci.*

You are most considerate." In defense, she turned her attention to the spaniel at their feet. "Ah, Korrigan, *comment ça va?*" She scratched behind his ear, and he licked her hand with loving kisses.

"Korrigan is quite taken with you," Christophe remarked, watching the long, tapering fingers being bathed. "He is normally much more reserved, but it appears you have captured his heart." Korrigan collapsed in an adoring heap over her feet.

"A very sloppy lover," she remarked, holding out her hand.

"A small price to pay, *ma belle,* for such devotion."

He drew a handkerchief from his pocket, captured her hand, and began to dry it. The effect on Serenity was violent. Sharp currents vibrated from the tips of her fingers and up her arm, spreading a tingling heat through her body.

"That's not necessary. I have a rag right here." She indicated her case of chalks and pencils and attempted to pull her hand away from his.

His eyes narrowed, his grip increasing, and she found herself outmatched in the short, silent struggle. With a sigh of angry exasperation, she allowed her hand to lay limp in his.

"Do you always get your own way?" she demanded, eyes darkening with suppressed fury.

"Bien sûr," he replied with irritating confidence, releasing her now-dry hand and giving her a long, measuring

look. "I feel you are also used to having your own way, Serenity Smith. Will it not be interesting to see who, how do you say, 'comes out on top' during your visit?"

"Perhaps we should put up a scoreboard," she suggested, retreating behind the armor of frigidity. "Then there would be no doubt as to who comes out on top."

He gave her a slow, lazy smile. "There will be no doubt, *cousine*."

Her retort was cut off by the appearance of the countess, and Serenity automatically smoothed her features into relaxed lines to avoid the other woman's speculation.

"Good morning, my children." The countess greeted them with a maternal smile that surprised her granddaughter. "You are enjoying the beauty of the garden. I find it at its most peaceful at this time of day."

"It's lovely, Madame," Serenity concurred. "One feels there is no other world beyond the colors and scents of this one solitary spot."

"I have often felt that way." The angular lines softened. "The hours I have spent here over the years are uncountable." She seated herself on a bench across from the dark man and fair-skinned woman and sighed. "What have you drawn?" Serenity offered her pad, and the countess studied the drawing before raising her eyes to study the woman in turn. "You have your father's talent." At the grudging admission, Serenity's eyes sharpened, and her mouth opened to retort. "Your father was a very talented artist," the countess continued. "And I begin to see he had some quality of goodness to have earned Gaelle's love and your loyalty."

"Yes, Madame," Serenity replied, realizing she had been awarded a difficult concession. "He was a very good man, both a constant loving father and husband."

She resisted the urge to bring up the Raphael, unwilling to break the tenuous threads of understanding being woven. The countess nodded. Then, turning to Christophe, she made a comment about the evening's dinner party.

Picking up drawing paper and chalks, Serenity began idly to draw her grandmother. The voices hummed around her, soothing, peaceful sounds suited to the garden's atmosphere. She did not attempt to follow the conversation, merely allowing the murmuring voices to wash over her as she began to concentrate on her work with more intensity.

In duplicating the fine-boned face and the surprisingly vulnerable mouth, she saw more clearly the countess's resemblance to her mother, and so, in fact, to herself. The countess's expression was relaxed, an ageless beauty that instinctively held itself proud. But somehow now, Serenity saw a glimpse of her mother's softness and fragility, the face of a woman who would love deeply—and therefore be hurt deeply. For the first time since she had received the formal letter from her unknown grandmother, Serenity felt a stirring of kinship, the first trickle of love for the woman who had borne her mother, and so had been responsible for her own existence.

Serenity was unaware of the variety of expressions flitting across her face, or of the man who sat beside her, observing the metamorphosis while he carried on his conversation. When she had finished, she lay down her chalks and wiped her hands absently, starting when she turned her head and encountered Christophe's direct stare. His eyes dropped to the portrait in her lap before coming back to her bemused eyes.

"You have a rare gift, *ma chérie,*" he murmured. And she frowned in puzzlement, unsure from his tone whether he was speaking of her work or something entirely different.

"What have you drawn?" the countess inquired. Serenity tore her eyes from his compelling regard and handed her grandmother the portrait.

The countess studied it for several moments, the first expression of surprise fading into something Serenity could not comprehend. When the eyes rose and rested on her, the face altered with a smile.

"I am honored and flattered. If you would permit me, I would like to purchase this." The smile increased. "Partly for my vanity, but also because I would like a sample of your work."

Serenity watched her for a moment, hovering on the line between pride and love. "I'm sorry, Madame." She shook her head and took the drawing. "I cannot sell it." She glanced down at the paper in her hand before handing it back and meeting the blue eyes. "It is a gift for you,

Grandmère." She watched the play of emotion move both mouth and eyes before speaking again. "Do you accept?"

"*Oui.*" The word came on a sigh. "I shall treasure your gift, and this"—she looked down once more at the chalk portrait—"shall be my reminder that one should never allow pride to stand in the way of love." She rose and touched her lips to Serenity's cheeks before she moved down the flagstone path toward the château.

Standing, Serenity moved away from the bench. "You have a natural ability to invite love," Christophe observed, and she rounded on him, her emotions highly tuned.

"She's my grandmother, too."

He noted the veil of tears shimmering in her eyes and rose to his feet in an easy movement. "My statement was a compliment."

"Really? I thought it a condemnation." Despising the mist in her eyes, she wanted both to be alone and to lean against his broad shoulder.

"You are always on the defensive with me, are you not, Serenity?" His eyes narrowed as they did when he was angry, but she was too involved with battling her own emotions to care.

"You've given me plenty of cause," she tossed back. "From the moment I stepped off the train, you made your feelings clear. You'd condemned both my father and me. You're cold and autocratic and without a bit of compassion or understanding. I wish you'd go away and leave me alone. Go flog some peasants or something; it suits you."

He moved so quickly that she had no chance to back away, his arms nearly splitting her in two as they banded around her. "Are you afraid?" he demanded, and his lips crushed hers before she could answer, and all reason was blotted out.

She moaned against the pain and pleasure his mouth inflicted, going limp as his hold increased, conquering even her breath.

How is it possible to hate and love at the same time? her heart demanded of her numbed brain, but the answer was lost in a flood of turbulent, triumphant passion. Fingers tangled ruthlessly in her hair, pulling her head back to expose the creamy length of her neck, and he claimed the vulnerable skin with a mouth hot and hungry. The thinness of her blouse was no defense against the sultry heat of his body, but he disposed of the brief barrier, his hand sliding under, then up along her flesh to claim the swell of her breast with a consummate and absolute possession.

His mouth returned to ravage hers, bruising softness with a demand she could not deny. No longer did she question the complexity of her love, but yielded like a willow in a storm to the entreatment of her own needs.

He lifted his face, and his eyes were dark, the fires of anger and passion burning them to black. He wanted her, and her eyes grew wide and terrified at the knowledge. No one had ever wanted her this intensely, and no one had ever possessed the power to take her this effortlessly.

For even without his love, she knew she would submit, and even without her submission, he would take.

He read the fear in her eyes, and his voice was low and dangerous. "*Oui, petite cousine,* you have cause to be afraid, for you know what will be. You are safe for the moment, but take care how and where you provoke me again."

Releasing her, he walked easily up the path his grandmother had chosen, and Korrigan bounded up, sent Serenity an apologetic glance, and then followed close on his master's heels.

CHAPTER SIX

Serenity dressed with great care for dinner that evening, using the time to put her feelings in order and decide on a plan of action. No amount of arguments or reasoning could alter the fact that she had plunged headlong into love with a man she had known only a few days, a man who was as terrifying as he was exciting.

An arrogant, domineering, audaciously stubborn man, she added, pulling up the zipper at the back of her dress. And one who had condemned her father as a thief. *How could I let this happen?* she berated herself. *How could I have prevented it?* she reflected with a sigh. *My heart may have deserted me, but my head is still on my shoulders, and I'm going to have to use it. I refuse to allow Christophe to see that I've fallen in love with him and subject myself to his mockery.*

Seated at the cherrywood vanity, she ran a brush through soft curls and touched up her light application of makeup. War paint, she decided, and grinned at the reflection. *It fits; I'd rather be at war with him than in love. Besides*—the grin turned into a frown—*there is also Mademoiselle Dejot to contend with tonight.*

Standing, she surveyed her full reflection in the free-standing mirror. The amber silk echoed the color of her eyes and added a warm glow to her creamy skin. Thin straps revealed smooth shoulders, and the low, rounded bodice teased the subtle curve of breast. The knife-pleated skirt floated gently to her ankles, the filminess and muted color adding to her fragile, ethereal beauty.

She frowned at the effect, seeing fragility when she had desired poise and sophistication. The clock informed her that there was no time to alter gowns, so slipping on shoes and spraying a cloud of scent around her, she hurried from the room.

The murmur of voices emitting from the main drawing room made Serenity realize, to her irritation, that the dinner guests had already arrived. Her artist's eye immediately sketched the tableau which greeted her as she entered the room: the gleaming floor and warm polished paneling, the high, lead-paned windows, the immense stone fireplace with the carved mantel—all set the perfect backdrop for the elegant inhabitants of the château's drawing room, with the countess the undisputed queen in regal red silk.

The severe black of Christophe's dinner suit threw the snow-white of his shirt into relief and accented the tawny color of his skin. Yves Dejot was also in black, his skin more gold than bronze, his hair an unexpected chestnut. But it was the woman between the two dark men who caught both Serenity's eye and reluctant admiration. If her grandmother was the queen, here was the crown princess. Jet-black hair framed a small, elfin face of poignant beauty. Almond-shaped eyes of pansy-brown dominated the engaging face, and the gown of forest-green glowed against the rich golden skin.

Both men rose as she entered the room, and Serenity gave her attention to the stranger, all too aware of Christophe's habitual all-encompassing survey. As introductions were made, she found herself looking into chestnut eyes, the same shade as his hair, which held undeniable masculine approval and an unmistakable light of mischief.

"You did not tell me, *mon ami,* that your cousin was a golden goddess." He bent over Serenity's fingers, brushing them with his lips. "I shall have to visit the château more often, Mademoiselle, during your stay."

She smiled with honest enjoyment, summing up Yves Dejot as both charming and harmless. "I am sure my stay will be all the more enjoyable with that prospect in mind, Monsieur," she responded, matching his tone, and she was rewarded with a flashing smile.

Christophe continued his introductions, and Serenity's

hand was clasped in a small, hesitant grip. "I am so happy to meet you at last, Mademoiselle Smith." Geneviève greeted her with a warm smile. "You are so like your mother's portrait, it is like seeing the painting come to life."

The voice was sincere, and Serenity concluded that no matter how hard she tried, it would be impossible to dislike the pixielike woman who gazed at her with the liquid eyes of a cocker spaniel.

The conversation continued light and pleasant throughout *apéritifs* and dinner, delectable oysters in champagne setting the mood for an elegantly prepared and served meal. The Dejots were curious about America and Serenity's life in its capital, and she attempted to describe the city of contrasts as the small group enjoyed *le ris de veau au Chablis*.

She began to draw a picture with words of stately old government buildings, the graceful lines and columns of the White House. "Unfortunately, there has been a great deal of modernization, with huge steel and glass monstrosities replacing some of the old buildings. Neat, vast, and charmless. But there are dozens of theatres, from Ford's, where Lincoln was assassinated, to the Kennedy Center."

Continuing, she took them from the stunning elegance of Embassy Row to the slums and tenements outside the federal enclave, through museums and galleries and the bustle of Capitol Hill.

"But we lived in Georgetown, and this is a world apart from the rest of Washington. Most of the homes are row houses or semi-detached, two or three stories, with small bricked-in yards edged with azaleas and flowerbeds. Some of the side streets are still cobblestoned, and it still retains a rather old-fashioned charm."

"Such an exciting city," Geneviève commented. "You must find our life here very quiet. Do you miss the animation, the activity of your home?"

Serenity frowned into her wineglass, then shook her head. "No," she answered, somewhat surprised by her own admission. "That's strange, I suppose." She met the brown eyes across from her. "I spent my entire life there, and I was very happy, but I don't miss it at all. I had the strangest feeling of affinity when I first walked into the château, a feeling of recognition. I've been very content here."

Glancing over, she found Christophe's eyes on her, brooding and penetrating, and she felt a quick surge of panic. "Of course, it's a relief not to enter into the daily contest for a parking space," she added with a smile, attempting to shake off the mood of seriousness. "Parking spaces are more precious than gold in Washington, and behind the wheel even the most mild-mannered person would commit murder and mayhem to obtain one."

"Have you resorted to such tactics, *ma chérie?*" Christophe asked. Raising his wineglass, he kept his eyes on her.

"I shudder to think of my crimes," she answered, relieved by the light turn of topic. "I dare not confess what lengths I've gone to in order to secure a few feet of empty space. I can be terribly aggressive."

"It is not possible to believe that aggression is a quality of such a delicate willow," Yves declared, blanketing her in his charming smile.

"You would be surprised, *mon ami*," Christophe commented with an inclination of his head. "The willow has many unexpected qualities."

Serenity continued to frown at him as the countess skillfully changed the subject.

The drawing room was gently lit, lending an air of intimacy to the vast room. As the group enjoyed after-dinner coffee and brandy, Yves seated himself next to Serenity and began dispensing his abundant supply of Gallic charm. She noted, with a great deal of discomfort around her heart, which she was forced to recognize as pure, honest jealousy, that Christophe devoted himself to entertaining Geneviève. They spoke of her parents, who were touring the Greek islands, of mutual acquaintances and old friends. He listened attentively as Geneviève related an anecdote, flattered, laughed, teased, his attitude being one of overall gentleness, a softness Serenity had not seen in him before. Their relationship was so obviously special, so close and long standing, that Serenity felt a swift pang of despair.

He treats her as though she were made of fine, delicate

crystal, small and precious, and he treats me as though I were made of stone, sturdy, strong, and dull.

It would have been infinitely easier if Serenity could have disliked the other woman, but natural friendliness overcame jealousy, and as time went by, she found herself liking both Dejots more and more.

Geneviève consented, after some gentle prompting by the countess, to play a few selections on the piano. The music floated through the room as sweet and fragile as its mistress.

I suppose she's perfect for him, Serenity concluded dismally. *They have so much in common, and she brings out a tenderness in him that will keep him from hurting her.* She glanced over to where Christophe sat, relaxed against the cushions of the sofa, his dark, fascinating eyes fixed on the woman at the piano. A swift variety of emotions ran through her—longing, despair, resentment, settling into a hopeless fog of depression as she realized no matter how perfect Geneviève might be for him, she could never happily watch Christophe court another woman.

"As an artist, Mademoiselle," Yves began as the music ended and conversation resumed, "you require inspiration, *n'est-ce pas?*"

"Of one kind or another," she agreed and smiled at him.

"The gardens of the château are immensely inspirational in the moonlight," he pointed out with an answering smile.

"I am in the mood for inspiration," she decided on quick impulse. "Perhaps I could impose on you to escort me."

"Mademoiselle," he answered happily, "I would be honored."

Yves informed the rest of the party of their intention, and Serenity accepted his proffered arm without seeing the dark look thrown at her by the remaining male member.

The garden was indeed an inspiration, the brilliance of colors muted in the silver shimmer of moonlight. The scents intertwined into a heady perfume, mellowing the warm summer evening into a night for lovers. She sighed as her thoughts strayed back to the man in the château's drawing room.

"You sigh from pleasure, Mademoiselle?" Yves questioned as they strolled down a winding path.

"Bien sûr," she answered lightly, shaking off her somber mood and granting her escort one of her best smiles. "I'm overcome by the overwhelming beauty."

"Ah, Mademoiselle." He lifted her hand to his lips and kissed it with much feeling. "The beauty of each blossom pales before yours. What rose could compare with such lips, or gardenia with such skin?"

"How do French men learn to make love with words?"

"It is taught from the cradle, Mademoiselle," he informed her with suspicious sobriety.

"How difficult for a woman to resist such a setting."

Serenity took a deep, consuming breath. "A moonlit garden outside a Breton château, the air filled with perfume, a handsome man with poetry on his lips."

"*Hélas!*" Yves gave a heavy sigh. "I fear you will find the strength to do so."

She shook her head with mock sorrow. "I am unfortunately extremely strong, and you," she added with a grin, "are a charming Breton wolf."

His laughter broke the night's stillness. "Ah, already you know me too well. If it were not for the feeling I had when we met that we were destined to be friends and not lovers, I would pursue my campaign with more feeling. But we Bretons are great believers in destiny."

"And it is so difficult to be both friends and lovers."

"*Mais oui.*"

"Then friends it shall be," Serenity stated, extending her hand. "I shall call you Yves, and you shall call me Serenity."

He accepted her hand and held it a moment. "*C'est extraordinaire* that I should be content with friendship with one like you. You possess an elusive beauty that locks into a man's mind and keeps him constantly aware of you." His shoulders moved in a Gallic shrug which said more than a three-hour speech. "Well, such is life," he remarked fatalistically. Serenity was still laughing when they re-entered the château.

The following morning, Serenity accompanied her grandmother and Christophe to Mass in the village she had viewed from the hilltop. A light, insistent rain had begun during the pre-dawn hours, its soft hissing against her window awakening her until its steady rhythm had lulled her back to sleep.

The rain continued as they drove to the village, drenching leaves and causing flowers in the cottage's neat garden to droop heavy-headed, lending them an air of a colorful congregation at prayer. She had noticed, with some puzzlement, that Christophe had maintained a strange silence since the previous evening. The Dejots had departed soon after Serenity and Yves had rejoined the group in the drawing room, and though Christophe's farewells to his guests were faultlessly charming, he had avoided addressing Serenity directly. The only communication between them had been a brief—and, she had imagined, forbidding—glance, quickly veiled.

Now, he spoke almost exclusively to the countess, with occasional comments or replies made directly to Serenity, polite, with a barely discernible hostility which she decided to ignore.

The focal point of the small village was the chapel, a tiny white structure with its neatly trimmed grounds an almost humorous contrast to its slightly apologetic, crumbling state. The roof had had more than one recent repair, and the single oak door at the entrance was weathered and battered from age and constant use.

"Christophe has offered to have a new chapel built," the countess commented. "But the villagers will not have it. This is where their fathers and grandfathers have worshipped for centuries, and they will continue to worship here until it crumbles about their ears."

"It's charming," Serenity decided, for somehow the tiny chapel's faintly dilapidated air gave it a certain steadfast dignity, a sense of pride at having witnessed generations of christenings, weddings, and funerals.

The door groaned in apology as Christophe opened it, allowing the two women to precede him. The interior was dark and quiet, the high-beamed ceiling adding an illusion of space. The countess glided to the front pew, taking her place in the seats which had been reserved for the Château Kergallen for nearly three centuries. Spying Yves and Geneviève across the narrow aisle, Serenity threw them both a full smile and was rewarded with an answering one from Geneviève and a barely discernible wink from Yves.

"This is hardly the proper setting for your flirtations, Serenity," Christophe whispered in her ear as he assisted her out of her damp trenchcoat.

Her color rose, making her feel like a child caught giggling in the sacristy, and she turned her head to retort as the priest, who seemed as old as the chapel, approached the altar, and the service began.

A feeling of peace drifted over her like a soft, down-filled quilt. The rain insulated the congregation from the outside, its soft whispering on the roof adding to the quiet rather than detracting from it. The low drone of Breton from the ancient priest, and the light rumble of response, an occasional whimper from an infant, a muffled cough, the dark stained glass with rivulets of rain running down its surface—all combined into a quiet timelessness. Sitting in the well-worn pew, Serenity felt the chapel's magic and understood the villagers' refusal to give up the crumbling building for a more substantial structure, for here was peace, and the serenity for which she had been named. A continuity with the past, and a link with the future.

As the service ended, so did the rain, and a vague beam of sunlight filtered through the stained glass, introducing a subtle, elusive glow. When they emerged outside, the air was fresh, sparkling from the clean scent of rain. Drops still clung to the newly washed leaves, glistening like tears against the bright green surfaces.

Yves greeted Serenity with a courtly bow and a lingering kiss on the fingers. "You have brought out the sun, Serenity."

"Mais oui," she agreed, smiling into his eyes. "I have ordered all my days in Brittany to be bright and sunny."

Removing her hand, she smiled at Geneviève, who resembled a dainty primrose in a cool yellow dress and narrow-brimmed hat. Greetings were exchanged, and Yves leaned down toward Serenity like a conspirator.

"Perhaps you would care to take advantage of the sunshine, *chérie,* and come for a drive with me. The countryside is exquisite after a rain."

"I'm afraid Serenity will be occupied today," Christophe answered before she could accept or decline, and she glared at him. "Your second lesson," he said smoothly, ignoring the battle lights in her amber eyes.

"Lesson?" Yves repeated with a crooked smile. "What are you teaching your lovely cousin, Christophe?"

"Horsemanship," he responded with a like smile, "at the moment."

"Ah, you could not find a finer instructor," Geneviève observed with a light touch on Christophe's arm. "Christophe taught me to ride when Yves and my father had given me up as hopelessly inadequate. You are so patient." Her cocker spaniel eyes gazed up at the lean man, and Serenity stifled an incredulous laugh.

Patient was the last word she would use to describe Christophe. Arrogant, demanding, autocratic, overconfident—she began silently listing qualities she attributed to the man at her side. Cynical and overbearing, also. Her attention wandered from the conversation, her gaze lighting on a small girl sitting on a patch of grass with a frisky black puppy. The dog was alternately bathing the child's face with enthusiastic kisses and running in frantic circles around her as the child's high, sweet laughter floated on the air. It was such a relaxing, innocent picture that it took Serenity a few extra seconds to react to what happened next.

The dog suddenly darted across the grass toward the road, and the child scrambled up, dashing after it, calling the dog's name in stern disapproval. Serenity watched without reaction as a car approached. Then a cold draft of fear overtook her as she observed the child's continuing flight toward the road.

Without thought, she streaked in pursuit, frantically calling in Breton for the child to stop, but the girl's attention was riveted on her pet, and she rushed over the grass, stepping out in the path of the oncoming car.

Serenity heard the squeal of brakes as her arms wrapped around the child, and she felt the rush of wind and slight bump of the fender against her side as she hurled both herself and the girl across the road, landing in a tangled heap on its surface. There was absolute silence for a split-second, and then pandemonium broke loose as the puppy, which Serenity was now sitting on rather heavily, yelped in rude objection, and the child's loud wails for her mother joined the animal's indignation.

Suddenly, excited voices in a mixture of languages joined the wailing and yelping, adding to Serenity's dazed, befuddled state. She could find no strength to remove her weight from the errant puppy, and the girl struggled from her now-limp grasp and ran into the arms of her pale, tearful mother.

Strong, hard arms lifted Serenity to her feet, holding her shoulders and tilting back her head so that she met Christophe's dark, stormy eyes. "Are you hurt?" When she shook her head, he continued in a tight, angry voice: "*Nom de Dieu!* You must be mad!" He shook her slightly, increasing the dizziness. "You could have been killed! How you missed being struck is a miracle."

"They were playing so sweetly," she recalled in a vague voice. "Then that silly dog goes tearing off into the street. Oh, I wonder if I hurt it; I sat right on it. I don't think the poor animal liked it."

"Serenity." Christophe's furious voice and the vigorous shaking brought her attention back to him. "*Mon Dieu!* I begin to believe you really are mad!"

"Sorry," she murmured, feeling empty and light-headed. "Silly to think of the dog first and the child later. Is she all right?"

He let out a soft stream of curses on a long breath. "*Oui,* she is with her mother. You moved like a cheetah; otherwise, both of you would not be standing up babbling now."

"Adrenaline," she muttered and swayed. "It's gone now."

His grip increased on her shoulders as he surveyed her face. "You are going to faint?" The question was accompanied by a deep frown.

"Certainly not," she replied, attempting to sound firm and dignified, but succeeding in a rather wavering denial.

"Serenity." Geneviève reached her, taking her hand and abandoning formality. "That was so brave." Tears swam in the brown eyes, and she kissed both of Serenity's pale cheeks.

"Are you hurt?" Yves echoed Christophe's question, his eyes concerned rather than angry.

"No, no, I'm fine," she assured him, unconsciously leaning on Christophe for support. "The puppy got the worst of it when I landed on it." *I just want to sit down,* she thought wearily, *until the world stops spinning.*

Suddenly, she found herself being addressed in rapid, tearful Breton by the child's mother. The words were slurred with emotion, and the dialect was so thick she had difficulty following the stream of conversation. The woman continually wiped brimming eyes with a wrinkled ball of handkerchief, and Serenity made what she hoped were the correct responses, feeling incredibly tired and faintly embarrassed as the mother grabbed and kissed Serenity with fervent gratitude. At a low order from Christophe, they were relinquished, and she retreated, gathering up her child and melting away into the crowd.

"Come." He slipped an arm around Serenity's waist, and the mass of people parted like the waves of the Red Sea as he led her back toward the chapel. "I think both you and the mongrel should be put on a short leash."

"How kind of you to lump us together," she muttered, then caught sight of her grandmother sitting on a small stone bench, looking pale and suddenly old.

"I thought you would be killed," the countess stated in a thick voice, and Serenity knelt in front of her.

"I'm quite indestructible, Grandmère," she claimed with a confident smile. "I inherited it from both sides of my family."

The thin, bony hand gripped Serenity's tightly. "You are very impudent and stubborn," the countess declared in a firmer voice. "And I love you very much."

"I love you, too," Serenity said simply.

CHAPTER SEVEN

Serenity insisted on receiving her riding lesson after the midday meal, vetoing both the suggested prescription of a long rest and the prospect of summoning a doctor.

"I don't need a doctor, Grandmère, and I don't need a rest. I'm perfectly all right." She shrugged aside the morning's incident. "A few bumps and bruises; I told you I'm indestructible."

"You are stubborn," the countess corrected, and Serenity merely smiled and shrugged again.

"You have had a frightening experience," Christophe inserted, studying her with critical eyes. "A less strenuous activity would be more suitable."

"For heaven's sake, not you, too!" She pushed away her coffee impatiently. "I'm not some mid-Victorian weakling who subsides into fits of vapors and needs to be coddled.

If you don't want to take me riding, I'll call Yves and accept his invitation for the drive which you refused for me." Her fine-boned face was set, and her chin lifted. "I am not going to go to bed in the middle of the day like a child."

"Very well." Christophe's eyes darkened. "You will have your ride, though perhaps your lesson will not be as stimulating as what Yves intended."

She stared at him for a moment in bewilderment before color seeped into her cheeks. "Oh, really, what a ridiculous thing to say."

"I will meet you at the stables in half an hour." He interrupted her protestations, rose from the table, and strode from the room before she could formulate a suitable rebuttal.

Turning to her grandmother, her face was a picture of indignation. "Why is he so insufferably rude to me?"

The countess's slim shoulders moved expressively, and she looked wise. "Men are complicated creatures, *chérie*."

"One day," Serenity predicted with an ominous frown, "one day he's not going to walk away until I've had my say."

Serenity met Christophe at the appointed time, determined to focus every ounce of energy into developing the proper riding technique. She mounted the mare with concentrated confidence, then followed her silent instructor as he pointed his horse in the opposite direction from that which they had taken on their last outing. When he broke into a light canter, she copied his action, and she experienced the same intoxicating freedom as she had before. There was, however, no sudden, exciting flash of smile on his features, no laughter or teasing words, and she told herself she was better off without them. He called out an occasional instruction, and she obeyed immediately, needing to prove both to him and herself that she was capable. So, she contented herself with the task of riding and an infrequent glance at his dark, hawklike profile.

Lord help me, she sighed in defeat, taking her eyes from him and staring straight ahead. *He's going to haunt me for the rest of my life. I'll end up a crotchety old maid, comparing every man I see to the one I couldn't have. I wish to God I'd never laid eyes on him.*

"Pardon?" Christophe's voice broke into her silent meditations, and she started, realizing she must have muttered something aloud.

"Nothing," she stammered, "it was nothing." Taking a deep breath, she frowned. "I could swear I smell the sea." He slowed his mount to a walk, and she reined in beside him as a faint rumble broke the silence. "Is that thunder?" She gazed up into a clear blue sky, but the rumble continued. "It *is* the sea!" she exclaimed, all animosity forgotten. "Are we near it? Will I be able to see it?" He merely halted his horse and dismounted. "Christophe, for heaven's sake!" She watched in exasperation as he tied his mount's reins to a tree. "Christophe!" she repeated, struggling from the saddle with more speed than grace. He took her arm as she landed awkwardly and tied her mount beside his before leading her farther down the path. "Choose whatever language you like," she invited magnanimously, "but talk to me before I go crazy!"

He stopped, turned, and drew her close, covering her mouth with a brief, distracting kiss. "You talk too much," he stated simply and continued on his way.

"Really," she began, but subsided when he turned and looked down at her again. Satisfied with her silence, he led her on, the distant rumbling growing nearer and more insistent. When he stopped again, Serenity caught her breath at the scene below.

The sea stretched as far as she could see, the sun's rays dancing on its deep green surface. The surf rolled in to caress the rocks, its foam resembling frothy lace on a deep velvet gown. Teasingly, it flowed back from the shore, only to roll back like a coquettish lover.

"It's marvelous," she sighed, reveling in the sharp salt-sprayed air and the breeze which ruffled her hair. "I suppose you must be used to this by now; I doubt I ever could be."

"I always enjoy looking at the sea," he answered, his eyes focused on the distant horizon, where the clear blue sky kissed the deep green. "It has many moods; perhaps that is why the fishermen call it a woman. Today she is calm and gentle, but when she is angry, her temper is a magnificent thing to see."

His hand slid down her arm to clasp her in a simple, intimate gesture she had not expected from him, and her heart did a series of somersaults. "When I was a boy, I thought to run away to the sea, live my life on the water, and sail with her moods." His thumb rubbed against the tender skin of her palm, and she swallowed before she could speak.

"Why didn't you?"

His shoulders moved, and she wondered for a moment if he remembered she was there. "I discovered that the land has its own magic—vivid-colored grass, rich soil, purple grapes, and grazing cattle. Riding a horse over the long stretches of land is as exciting as sailing over the waves of the sea. The land is my duty, my pleasure, and my destiny."

He looked down into the amber eyes, fixed wide and open on his face, and something passed between them, shimmering and expanding until Serenity felt submerged by its power. Then, she was crushed against him, the wind swirling around them like ribbons to bind them closer as his mouth demanded an absolute surrender. She clung to him as the roar of the sea swelled to a deafening pitch, and suddenly she was straining against him and demanding more.

If the mood of the sea was calm and gentle, his did not mirror it. Helpless against her own need, she reveled in the savage possession of his mouth, the urgent insistence of the hands which claimed her, as if by right. Trembling, not with fear, but with the longing to give, she pressed yet closer, willing him to take what she offered.

His mouth lifted once, briefly, and she shook her head against the liberation, pulling his face back to hers, lips begging for the merging. Her fingers dug into the flesh of his shoulders at the force of the new embrace, his mouth seeking hers with a new hunger, as if he would taste her or starve. His hand slipped under the silk of her blouse to claim the breast which ached for his touch, the warmth of his fingers searing like glowing embers against her skin, and though her mouth was conquered, his tongue demanding the intimacy of velvet moisture, her mind murmured his name over and over until there was nothing else.

Arms banded around her again, hands abandoning their explorations, and breath flew away and was forgotten in the new, crushing power. Soft breasts pressed against the hard leanness of his chest, thigh straining against thigh, heart pounding against heart, and Serenity knew she had taken the step from the precipice and would never return to the solidity of earth.

He released her so abruptly, she would have stumbled had his hand not gripped her arm to steady her. "We must go back," he stated as if the moment had never been. "It grows late."

Her hands reached up to push the tumbled curls from

her face, her eyes lifting to his, wide and full of confused pleading. "Christophe." She said his name on a whisper, unable to form any other sound, and he stared down at her, the brooding look familiar and, as always, unfathomable.

"It grows late, Serenity," he repeated, and the underlying anger in his tone brought only more bewilderment.

Suddenly cold, her arms wrapped around her body to ward off the chill. "Christophe, why are you angry with me? I haven't done anything wrong."

"Haven't you?" His eyes narrowed and darkened with familiar temper, and through the ache of rejection, her own rose to meet it.

"No. What could I do to you? You're so infuriatingly superior, up there on your little golden throne. A partial aristocrat like myself could hardly climb up to your level to cause any damage."

"Your tongue will cause you endless trouble, Serenity, unless you learn to control it." His voice was precise and much too controlled, but Serenity found discretion buried under a growing mountain of fury.

"Well, until I choose to do so, perhaps I'll use it to tell you precisely what I think about your arrogant, autocratic, domineering, and infuriating attitude toward life in general, and myself in particular."

"A woman," he began, in a voice she noted was entirely too soft and too silky, "with your temperament, *ma petite cousine,* must be continually shown there is only one master." He took her arm in a firm hold and turned away from the sea. "I said we will go."

"*You*, Monsieur," she returned, holding her ground and sending him a look of smoldering amber, "can go whenever you want."

Her exit of furious dignity took her three feet before her shoulders were captured in a viselike grip, then whirled around to face a fury which made her own temper seem tranquil. "You cause me to think again about the wisdom of beating a woman." His mouth took hers swiftly, hard and more punishing than a fist, and Serenity felt a quick surge of pain, tasting only anger on his lips, and no desire. Fingers dug into her shoulders, but she allowed herself neither struggle nor response, remaining passive in his arms as courage fled into hopelessness.

Set free, she stared up at him, detesting the veil of moistness which clouded her eyes. "You have the advantage, Christophe, and will always win a physical battle." Her voice was calm and carefully toned, and she watched his brows draw close, as if her reaction puzzled him. His hand lifted to brush at a drop which had escaped to flow down her cheek, and she jerked away, wiping it away herself and blinking the rest back.

"I've had my quota of humiliations for one day, and I will not dissolve into a pool of tears for your benefit." Her voice became firmer as she gained control, and her shoulders straightened as Christophe watched the transformation in silence. "As you said, it's getting late." Turning, she walked back up the path to where the horses waited.

The days passed quietly, soft summer days filled with the sun and the sweet perfume of flowers. Serenity devoted most of the daylight hours to painting, reproducing the proud, indomitable lines of the château on canvas. She had noted, at first with despair and then with increasing anger, Christophe's calculated avoidance of her. Since the afternoon when they had stood on the cliff above the sea, he had barely spoken to her, and then only with astringent politeness. Pride soon covered her hurt like a bandage over an open wound, and painting became a refuge against longing.

The countess never mentioned the Raphael, and Serenity was content for the time to drift, wanting to strengthen the bond between them before delving further into its disappearance and the accusation against her father.

She was immersed in her work, clad in faded jeans and a paint-splattered smock, her hair disheveled by her own hand, when she spotted Geneviève approaching across the smooth carpet of lawn. A beautiful Breton fairy, Serenity imagined, small and lovely in a buff-colored riding jacket and dark brown breeches.

"*Bonjour,* Serenity," she called out when Serenity raised a slim hand in greeting. "I hope I am not disturbing you."

"Of course not. It's good to see you." The words came easily because she meant them, and she smiled and put down her brush.

"Oh, but I have made you stop," Geneviève began in apology.

"You've given me a marvelous excuse to stop," she corrected.

"May I see?" Geneviève requested. "Or do you not like your work viewed before it is finished?"

"Of course you may see. Tell me what you think."

She moved around to stand beside Serenity. The background was completed: the azure sky, lamb's-wool clouds, vivid green grass, and stately trees. The château itself was taking shape gradually: the gray walls glowing pearly in the sunlight, high glistening windows, the drum towers. There was much left to complete, but even in its infancy, the painting captured the fairy-tale aura Serenity had envisioned.

"I have always loved the château," Geneviève stated, her eyes still on the canvas. "Now I see you do, as well." Pansy eyes lifted from the half-completed painting and sought Serenity's. "You have captured its warmth, as well as its arrogance. I am glad to know you see it as I do."

"I fell in love with it the first moment I saw it," Serenity admitted. "The longer I stay, the more hopelessly I'm lost." She sighed, knowing her words described the man, as well as his home.

"You are lucky to have such a gift. I hope you will not think less of me if I confess something."

"No, of course not," Serenity assured her, both surprised and intrigued.

"I am terribly envious of you," she blurted out quickly, as if courage might fail her.

Serenity stared down at the lovely face incredulously. "You, envious of me?"

"*Oui.*" Geneviève hesitated for a moment, and then began to speak in a rush. "Not only of your talent as an artist, but of your confidence, your independence." Serenity continued to gape, her mouth wide open in astonishment. "There is something about you which draws people to you—an openness, a warmth in your eyes that makes one want to confide, feeling somehow you will understand."

"How extraordinary," Serenity murmured, astonished. "But, Geneviève," she began in a lighter tone, "you're so lovely and warm, how could you envy anyone, least of all me? You make me feel like a veritable Amazon."

"Men treat you as a woman," she explained, her voice faintly desperate. "They admire you not only for the way you look, but for what you are." She turned away, then back again quickly, a hand brushing at her hair. "What would you do if you loved a man, had loved him all of your life, loved with a woman's heart, but he saw you only as an amusing child?"

Serenity felt a cloud of despair envelop her heart. *Christophe,* she concluded. *Dear Lord, she wants my advice about Christophe.* She stifled the urge to give a shout of hysterical laughter. *I'm supposed to give her pointers on the man I love. Would she seek me out if she knew what he thinks of me . . . of my father?* Her eyes met Geneviève's dark ones, filled with hope and trust. She sighed.

"If I were in love with such a man, I would take great pains to let him know I was a woman, and that was how I wanted him to see me."

"But how?" Geneviève's hand spread in a helpless gesture. "I am such a coward. Perhaps I would lose even his friendship."

"If you really love him, you'll have to risk it or face the rest of your life as only his friend. You must tell . . . your man, the next time he treats you as a child, that you are a woman. You must tell him so that there is no doubt in his mind what you mean. Then, the move is his."

Geneviève took a deep breath and squared her shoulders. "I will think about what you have said." She turned her warm eyes on Serenity's amber ones once more. "Thank you for listening, for being a friend."

Serenity watched the small, graceful figure retreat across the grass. *You're a real martyr, Serenity,* she told herself. *I thought self-sacrifice was supposed to make one glow with inner warmth; I just feel cold and miserable.* She began packing up her paints, no longer finding pleasure in the sunshine. *I think I'll give up martyrdom and take up foreclosing on widows and orphans; it couldn't make me feel any worse.*

Depressed, Serenity wandered up to her room to store her canvas and paints. With what she considered a herculean effort, she managed to produce a smile for the maid, who was busily folding freshly laundered lingerie into the bureau drawer.

"*Bonjour,* Mademoiselle." Bridget greeted Serenity with a dazzling smile of her own, and amber eyes blinked at the power.

"*Bonjour,* Bridget. You seem in remarkably good spirits." Glancing at the shafts of sunlight which flowed triumphantly through the windows, Serenity sighed and shrugged. "I suppose it is a beautiful day."

"*Oui,* Mademoiselle. *Quel jour!*" She gestured toward the sky with a hand filled with filmy silk. "I think I have never seen the sun smile more sweetly."

Unable to cling to depression under the attack of blatant good humor, Serenity plopped into a chair and grinned at the small maid's glowing face. "Unless I read the signs incorrectly, I would say it's love which is smiling sweetly."

Heightened color only added more appeal to the young face as Bridget paused in her duties to beam yet another smile over Serenity. "*Oui,* Mademoiselle, I am very much in love."

"And I gather from the look of you"—Serenity continued battling a sweet surge of envy of the youthful confidence—"that you are very much loved."

"*Oui*, Mademoiselle." Sunlight and happiness formed an aura around her. "On Saturday, Jean-Paul and I will be married."

"Married?" Serenity repeated, faintly astonished as she studied the tiny form facing her. "How old are you, Bridget?"

"Seventeen," she stated with a sage nod for her vast collection of years.

Seventeen, Serenity mused with an unconscious sigh. "Suddenly, I feel ninety-two."

"We will be married in the village," Bridget continued, warming to Serenity's interest. "Then everyone will come back to the château, and there will be singing and dancing in the garden. The count is very kind and very generous. He says we will have champagne." Serenity watched as joy turned to awe.

"Kind," she murmured, turning the adjective over in her mind. *Kindness is not a quality I would have attributed to Christophe.* Letting out a long breath, she recalled his gentle attitude toward Geneviève. *Obviously, I simply don't bring it out in him.*

"Mademoiselle has so many lovely things." Glancing up, Serenity saw Bridget fondling a flowing white negligee, her eyes soft and dreamy.

"Do you like it?" Rising, she fingered the hem, remembering the silky texture against her skin, then let it drift like a pure fall of snow to the floor.

"It's yours," Serenity declared impulsively, and the maid turned back, soft eyes now as wide as dark saucers.

"*Pardon,* Mademoiselle?"

"It's yours," she repeated, smiling into astonishment. "A wedding present."

"Oh, *mais non,* I could not . . . it is too lovely." Her voice faltered to a whisper as she gazed at the gown with wistful desire, then turned back to Serenity. "Mademoiselle could not bear to part with it."

"Of course I can," Serenity corrected. "It's a gift, and it would please me to know you were enjoying it." Studying the simple white silk which Bridget clutched to her breast, she sighed with a mixture of envy and hopelessness. "It was made for a bride, and you will look beautiful in it for your Jean-Paul."

"Oh, Mademoiselle!" Bridget breathed, blinking back tears of gratitude. "I will treasure it always." She followed this declaration with a joyful stream of Breton thanks, the simple words lifting Serenity's spirits. She left the future bride gazing into the mirror, negligee spread over apron as she dreamed of her wedding night.

The sun again smiled sweetly on Bridget's wedding day, the sky a cerulean-blue touched with a few friendly white wisps of clouds.

As the days had passed, Serenity's depression had altered to a frigid resentment. Christophe's aloof demeanor fanned the fires of temper, but determinedly, she had buried them under equally haughty ice. As a result, their conversations had been limited to a few stony, formally polite sentences.

She stood, flanked by him and the countess, on the tiny lawn of the village church awaiting the bridal procession. The raw-silk suit she had chosen deliberately for its cool, untouchable appearance had been categorically dismissed by a wave of her grandmother's regal hand. Instead, she had been presented with an outfit of her mother's, the scent of lavender still clinging, as fresh as yesterday. Instead of appearing sophisticated and distant, she now appeared like a young girl awaiting a party.

The full gathered skirt just brushed bare calves, its brilliant vertical stripes of red and white topped with a short white apron. The peasant scoop-necked blouse was tucked into the tiny waist, its short puffed sleeves leaving arms bare to the sun. A black sleeveless vest fitted trimly over the subtle curve of breast, her pale halo of curls topped with a beribboned straw hat.

Christophe had made no comment on her appearance, merely inclining his head when she had descended the stairs, and now Serenity continued the silent war by addressing all her conversation exclusively to her grandmother.

"They will come from the house of the bride," the

countess informed her, and though Serenity was uncomfortably aware of the dark man who stood behind her, she gave the appearance of polite attentiveness. "All of her family will walk with her on her last journey as a maiden. Then, she will meet the groom and enter the chapel to become a wife."

"She's so young," Serenity murmured in a sigh, "hardly more than a child."

"*Alors,* she is old enough to be a woman, my aged one." With a light laugh, the countess patted Serenity's hand. "I was little more when I married your grandfather. Age has little to do with love. Do you not agree, Christophe?"

Serenity felt, rather than saw, his shrug. "So it would seem, Grandmère. Before she is twenty, our Bridget will have a little one tugging on her apron and another under it."

"*Hélas!*" the countess sighed with suspicious wistfulness, and Serenity turned to regard her with careful curiosity. "It appears neither of my grandchildren see fit to provide me with little ones to spoil." She gave Serenity a sad, guileless smile. "It is difficult to be patient when one grows old."

"But it becomes simpler to be shrewd," Christophe commented in a dry voice, and Serenity could not prevent herself from glancing up at him. He gave her a brief, raised-brow look, and she met it steadily, determined not to falter under its spell.

"To be wise, Christophe," the countess corrected,

unperturbed and faintly smug. "This is a truer statement. *Voilà!*" she announced before any comment could be made. "They come!"

Soft new flower petals floated and danced to earth as small children tossed them from wicker baskets. They laid a carpet of love for the bride's feet. Innocent petals, wild from the meadow and forest, and the children danced in circles as they offered them to the air. Surrounded by her family, the bride walked like a small, exquisite doll. Her dress was traditional, and obviously old, and Serenity knew she had never seen a bride more radiant or a dress more perfect.

Aged white, the full, pleated skirt flowed from the waist to dance an inch from the petal-strewn road. The neck was high and trimmed with lace, and the bodice was fitted and snug, touched with delicate embroidery. She wore no veil, but instead had on a round white cap topped with a stiff lace headdress which lent the tiny dark form an exotic and ageless beauty.

The groom joined her, and Serenity noted, with a near-maternal relief, that Jean-Paul looked both kind and nearly as innocent as Bridget herself. He, too, was attired traditionally: white knickers tucked into soft boots, and a deep blue double-breasted jacket over an embroidered white shirt. The narrow-brimmed Breton cap with its velvet ribbons accentuated his youth, and Serenity surmised he was little older than his bride.

Shining young love glowed around them, pure and

sweet as the morning sky, and the sudden, unexpected pang of longing caused Serenity to draw in her breath, then clutch her hands together tightly to combat a convulsive shudder. *Just once,* she thought, and swallowed against the dryness of her throat, *just once I would have Christophe look at me that way, and I could live on it for the rest of my life.*

Starting as a hand touched her arm, she looked up to find his eyes on her, faintly mocking and altogether cool. Tilting her chin, she allowed him to lead her inside the chapel.

The château's garden was a perfect world in which to celebrate a new marriage, vivid and fresh and alive with scents and hues. The terrace was laden with white-clothed tables brimming over with food and drink. The château had laid on its finest for the village wedding, silver and crystal gleaming with the pride of age in the glory of sunlight. And the village, Serenity observed, accepted it as their due. As they belonged to the château, so it belonged to them. Music rose over the mixture of voices and laughter: the sweet, lilting strain of violins and the softly nasal call of bagpipes.

Serenity watched from the terrace as bride and groom performed their first dance as man and wife, a folk dance, full of charm and saucy movements, and Bridget flirted with her husband with tossing head and teasing eyes, much to the approval of the audience. Dancing continued, growing livelier, and Serenity found herself being pulled into the crowd by a charmingly determined Yves.

"But I don't know how," she protested, unable to prevent the laugh his persistence provoked.

"I will teach you," he returned simply, taking both her hands in his. "Christophe is not the only one with the ability to instruct." He inclined his head in acknowledgment of her frown. "Ah-ha! I thought as much." Her frown deepened at the ambiguity, but he merely smiled, lifted one hand to his lips briefly, and continued. "*Maintenant,* first we step to the right."

Caught up first in her lesson, then in the pleasure of the simple music and movements, Serenity found the tensions of the past days drifting away. Yves was attentive and charming, taking her through the steps of the dances and bringing her glasses of champagne. Once seeing Christophe dancing with a small, graceful Geneviève, a cloud of despair threatened her sun, and she turned away quickly, unwilling to fall back into the well of depression.

"You see, *chérie,* you take to the dance naturally." Yves smiled down at her as the music paused.

"Assuredly, my Breton genes have come to the fore to sustain me."

"So," he said in mock censure, "will you not give credit to your instructor?"

"*Mais oui.*" She gave him a teasing smile and a small curtsy. "My instructor is both charming and brilliant."

"True," he agreed, chestnut eyes twinkling against the gravity of his tone. "And my student is both beautiful and enchanting."

"True," she agreed in turn, and laughing, she linked her arm through his.

"Ah, Christophe." Her laughter froze as she saw Yves's gaze travel above her head. "I have usurped your role as tutor."

"It appears you are both enjoying the transition." Hearing the icy politeness in his voice, Serenity turned to him warily. He looked entirely too much like the seafaring count in the portrait gallery for her comfort. The white silk shirt opened carelessly to reveal the strong, dark column of throat, the sleeveless black vest a startling contrast. The matching black pants were mated to soft leather boots, and Serenity decided he looked more dangerous than elegant.

"A delightful student, *mon ami,* as I am sure you agree." Yves's hand rested lightly on Serenity's shoulder as he smiled into the set, impassive face. "Perhaps you would care to test the quality of my instructions for yourself."

"Bien sûr." Christophe acknowledged the offer with a slight inclination of his head. Then, with a graceful, rather old-fashioned gesture, he held out his hand, palm up, for Serenity's acquiescence.

She hesitated, both fearing and longing for the contact of flesh. Then seeing the challenge in his dark eyes, she placed her palm in his with aristocratic grace.

Serenity moved with the music, the steps of the old, flirting dance coming easily. Swaying, circling, joining briefly, the dance began as a confrontation, a formalized contest between man and woman. Their eyes held, his bold and confident, hers defiant, and they moved in alternating circles, palms touching. As his arm slipped lightly around her waist, she tossed her head back to keep the gaze unbroken, ignoring the sudden thrill as their hips brushed.

Steps quickened with the music, the melody growing more demanding, the ancient choreography growing more enticing, the contact of bodies lengthening. She kept her chin tilted insolently, her eyes challenging, but she felt the heat begin its insistent rise as his arm became more possessive of her waist, drawing her closer with each turn. What had begun as a duel was now a seduction, and she felt his silent power taking command of her will as surely as if his lips had claimed hers. Drawing on one last shred of control, she stepped back, seeking the safety of distance. His arm pulled her against him, and helplessly, her eyes sought the mouth which hovered dangerously over hers. Her lips parted, half in protest, half in invitation, and his lowered until she could taste his breath on her tongue.

The silence when the music ended was like a thunderclap, and she watched wide-eyed as he drew the promise of his mouth away with a smile of pure triumph.

"Your teacher is to be commended, Mademoiselle." His hands dropped from her waist, and with a small bow, he turned and left her.

The more remote and taciturn Christophe became, the more open and expansive became the countess, as though sensing his mood and seeking to provoke him.

"You seem preoccupied, Christophe," the countess stated artlessly as they dined at the large oak table. "Are your cattle giving you trouble, or perhaps an *affaire de coeur?*"

Determinedly, Serenity kept her eyes on the wine she swirled in her glass, patently fascinated by the gently moving color.

"I am merely enjoying the excellent meal, Grandmère," Christophe returned, not rising to the bait. "Neither cattle nor women disturb me at the moment."

"Ah." The countess breathed life into the syllable. "Perhaps you group both together."

Broad shoulders moved in a typical gesture. "They both demand attention and a strong hand, *n'est-ce pas?*"

Serenity swallowed a bit of *canard à l'orange* before it choked her.

"Have you left many broken hearts behind in America, Serenity?" The countess spoke before Serenity could voice the murderous thoughts forming in her brain.

"Dozens," she returned, aiming a deadly glance at Christophe. "I have found that some men lack the intelligence of cattle, more often having the arms, if not the brains, of an octopus."

"Perhaps you have been dealing with the wrong men," Christophe suggested, his voice cool.

This time it was Serenity's shoulders which moved. "Men are men," she said in dismissal, seeking to annoy him with her own generalization. "They either want a warm body for groping in corners, or a piece of Dresden to sit on a shelf."

"And how, in your opinion, does a woman wish to be treated?" he demanded as the countess sat back and enjoyed the fruits of her instigation.

"As a human being with intellect, emotions, rights, needs." Her hands moved expressively. "Not as a happy convenience for a man's pleasure to be tucked away until the mood strikes him, or a child to be petted and amused."

"You seem to have a low opinion of men, *ma chérie*," Christophe intimated, neither of them aware they were speaking more in this conversation than they had in days.

"Only of antiquated ideas and prejudice," she contradicted. "My father always treated my mother as a partner; they shared everything."

"Do you look for your father in the men you meet, Serenity?" he asked suddenly, and her eyes widened, surprised and disconcerted.

"Why, no, at least I don't think so," she faltered, trying to see into her own heart. "Perhaps I look for his strength and his kindness, but not a replica. I think I look for a man who could love me as completely as he loved my mother—someone who could take me with all my faults and imperfections and love me for what I am, not what he might want me to be."

"And when you find such a man," Christophe asked, giving her an unfathomable stare, "what will you do?"

"Be content," she murmured, and made an effort to give her attention to the food on her plate.

Serenity continued her painting the following day. She had slept poorly, disturbed by the admission she had made to Christophe's unexpected question. She had spoken spontaneously, the words the fruit of a feeling she had not been aware of possessing. Now with the warmth of the sun at her back and brush and palette in hand, she endeavored to lose her discomfort in the love of painting.

She found it difficult to concentrate, Christophe's lean features invading her mind and blurring the sharp lines of the château. Rubbing her forehead, she finally threw down her brush in disgust and began to pack her equipment, mentally cursing the man who insisted on interfering with both her work and her life. The sound of a car cut into her eloquent swearing, and she turned, her hand shading her eyes from the sun, to watch the approaching vehicle wind down the long drive.

It halted a few yards from where she stood, and her mouth dropped open in amazement as a tall, fair man got out and began walking toward her.

"Tony!" she cried in surprise and pleasure, rushing across the grass to meet him.

His arms gripped her waist, and his lips covered hers in a brief but thorough kiss.

"What are you doing here?"

"I could say I was just in the neighborhood." He grinned down at her. "But I don't think you'd buy that." He paused and studied her face. "You look terrific," he decided, and bent to kiss her again, but she eluded him.

"Tony, you haven't answered me."

"The firm had some business to conduct in Paris," he explained. "So I flew over, and when I set things straight, I drove out here to see you."

"Two birds with one stone," she concluded wryly, feeling a vague disappointment. *It would have been nice,* she reflected, *if he had dropped his business and charged across the Atlantic because he couldn't bear to be parted from me.* But not Tony! She studied his good-looking, clear-cut features. *Tony's much too methodical for impulses, and that's been part of the problem.*

He brushed her brow with a casual kiss. "I missed you."

"Did you?"

He looked slightly taken aback. "Well, of course I did,

Serenity." His arm slipped around her shoulders as he began walking toward her painting apparatus. "I'm hoping you'll come back with me."

"I'm not ready to go yet, Tony. I have commitments here. There are things I have to clear up before I can even think about going back."

"What things?" he asked with a frown.

"I can't explain, Tony," she evaded, unwilling to take him into her confidence. "But I've barely had time to know my grandmother; there are so many lost years to make up for."

"You can't expect to stay here for twenty-five years and make up for lost time." His voice was filled with exasperation. "You have friends back in Washington, a home, a career." He stopped and took her by the shoulders. "You know I want to marry you, Serenity. You've been putting me off for months."

"Tony, I never made any promises to you."

"Don't I know it." Releasing her, he stared around in abstraction. With a pang of guilt, she tried harder to make him understand.

"I've found part of myself here. My mother grew up here; her mother still lives here." She turned and faced the château, making a wide, sweeping gesture. "Just look at it, Tony. Have you ever seen anything to compare with it?"

He followed her gaze and studied the large stone structure with another frown. "Very impressive," he stated without enthusiasm. "It's also huge, rambling, and, more than likely, drafty. Give me a brick house on P Street any day."

She sighed, deflated, then turning to her companion, smiled with affection. "Yes, you're right, you don't belong here."

"And you do?" The frown deepened.

"I don't know," she murmured, her eyes roaming over the conical roof and down to the courtyard. "I just don't know."

He studied her profile a moment, then strategically changed the subject. "Old Barkley had some papers for you." He referred to the attorney who had handled her parents' affairs and for whom he worked as a junior partner. "So instead of trusting them to the mail, I'm delivering them in person."

"Papers?"

"Yes, very confidential." He grinned in his familiar way. "Wouldn't give me a clue as to what they were about; just said it was important that you get them as soon as possible."

"I'll look at them later," she said in dismissal, having had enough of papers and technical forms since her parents' death. "You must come inside and meet my grandmother."

If Tony had been unimpressed with the château, he was overwhelmed by the countess. Serenity hid her smile as she introduced Tony to her grandmother, noting the widening of his eyes as he accepted the offered hand. She was, Serenity thought with silent satisfaction, magnificent. Leading Tony into the main drawing room, the countess ordered refreshments and proceeded to pump Tony in the most charming way for every ounce of information about himself. Serenity sat back and observed the maneuver, proud of her straight face.

He doesn't stand a chance, she decided as she poured tea from the elegant silver pot. Handing the dainty china cup to her grandmother, their eyes met. The unexpected mischief in the blue eyes almost caused a burst of laughter to escape, so she busied herself with the pouring of more tea with intense concentration.

The old schemer! she thought, surprised that she was not offended. *She's determining if Tony's a worthy candidate for her granddaughter's hand, and poor Tony is so awed by her magnificence, he doesn't see what's going on.*

At the end of an hour's conversation, the countess had learned Tony's life history: his family background, education, hobbies, career, politics, many details of which Serenity had been ignorant herself. The inquisition had been skillful, so subtly accomplished that Serenity suppressed the urge to stand and applaud when it was completed.

"When do you have to get back?" she asked, feeling she should save Tony from disclosing his bank balance.

"I have to leave first thing in the morning," he told her,

relaxed and totally oblivious to the gentle third degree to which he had been subjected. "I wish I could stay longer, but . . ." He shrugged.

"*Bien sûr,* your work comes first," the countess finished for him, looking understanding. "You must dine with us tonight, Monsieur Rollins, and stay with us until morning."

"I couldn't impose on your hospitality, Madame," he objected, perhaps halfheartedly.

"Impose? Nonsense!" His objection was dismissed with a regal wave of the hand. "A friend of Serenity's from so far away—I would be deeply offended if you would refuse to stay with us."

"You are very kind. I'm grateful."

"It is my pleasure," the countess stated as she rose. "You must show your friend around the grounds, and I will see that a room is prepared for him." Turning to Tony, she extended her hand once more. "We have cocktails at seven-thirty, Monsieur Rollins. I will look forward to seeing you then."

CHAPTER EIGHT

Serenity stood in front of the full-length mirror without seeing the reflection. The tall, slender woman in the amethyst gown, soft waves of crepe flowing like a jeweled breeze, might not have stared back from the highly polished glass. Serenity's mind was playing back the afternoon's events, her emotions running from pleasure, irritation, and disappointment to amusement.

After the countess had left them alone, Serenity had conducted Tony on a brief tour of the grounds. He had been vaguely complimentary about the garden, taking in its surface beauty, his logical, matter-of-fact mind unable to see beyond the roses and geraniums to the romance of hues and textures and scents. He was lightly amused by the appearance of the ancient gardener and slightly uncomfortable with the overwhelming spaciousness of the view from the terrace. He preferred, in his words, a few houses or at least a traffic light. Serenity had shaken her head at this in indulgent affection, but had realized how little she had in common with the man with whom she had spent so many months.

He was, however, completely overawed by the château's *châtelaine*. Anyone less like a grandmother, he had stated with great respect, he had never encountered. She was incredible, he had said, to which Serenity silently agreed, though perhaps for different reasons. She looked as if she belonged on a throne, indulgently granting audiences, and she had been so gracious, so interested in everything he had said. *Oh, yes,* Serenity had concurred silently, trying and failing to be indignant. *Oh, yes, dear, gullible Tony, she had been vastly interested.* But what was the purpose of the game she was playing?

When Tony was settled in his room, strategically placed, Serenity noted, at the farthest end of the hall from herself, she had sought out her grandmother with the excuse of thanking her for inviting Tony to stay.

Seated in her room at an elegant Regency writing desk penning correspondence on heavy-crested stationery, the countess had greeted Serenity with an innocent smile, which somehow resembled the cat who swallowed the canary.

"Alors." She had put down her pen and gestured to a

low brocade divan. "I hope your friend has found his room agreeable."

"*Oui,* Grandmère, I am very grateful to you for inviting Tony to stay for the night."

"*Pas de quoi, ma chérie.*" The slender hand had gestured vaguely. "You must think of the château as your home, as well as mine."

"*Merci,* Grandmère," Serenity had said demurely, leaving the next move to the older woman.

"A very polite young man."

"*Oui,* Madame."

"Quite attractive . . ."—a slight pause—". . . in an ordinary sort of way."

"*Oui,* Madame," Serenity had agreed conversationally, tossing the ball into her grandmother's court. The ball was received and returned.

"I have always preferred more unusual looks in a man, more strength and vitality. Perhaps"—a slight teasing curve of the lips—"more of the buccaneer, if you know what I mean."

"Ah, *oui,* Grandmère." Serenity had nodded, keeping a guileless open gaze on the countess. "I understand very well."

"*Bien.*" The slim shoulders had moved. "Some prefer a tamer male."

"So it would seem."

"Monsieur Rollins is a very intelligent, well-mannered man, very logical and earnest."

And dull. Serenity had added the unspoken remark before speaking aloud in annoyance. "He helps little old ladies across the street twice a day."

"Ah, a credit to his parents, I am sure," the countess had decided, either unaware or unperturbed by Serenity's mockery. "I am sure Christophe will be most pleased to meet him."

A faint glimmer of uneasiness had been born in Serenity's brain. "I'm sure he will."

"Mais oui." The countess smiled. "Christophe will be very interested to meet such a close friend of yours." The emphasis on "close" had been unmistakable, and Serenity's senses had sharpened as her uneasiness had grown.

"I fail to see why Christophe should be overly interested in Tony, Grandmère."

"Ah, *ma chérie,* I am sure Christophe will be fascinated by your Monsieur Rollins."

"Tony is not *my* Monsieur Rollins," Serenity had corrected, rising from the divan and advancing on her grandmother. "And I really don't see anything they have in common."

"No?" the countess asked with such irritating innocence that Serenity fought with amusement.

"You are a devious minx, Grandmère. What are you up to?"

Blue eyes met amber with the innocence of sweet childhood. "Serenity, *ma chérie,* I have no idea what you are talking about." As Serenity had opened her mouth to retort, the countess once more cloaked herself in her royalty. "I must finish my correspondence. I will see you this evening."

The command had been crystal clear, and Serenity had been forced to leave the room unsatisfied. The closing of the door with undue force had been her only concession to her rising temper.

Serenity's thoughts returned to the present. Slowly, her slim form, draped in amethyst, came into focus in the mirror. She smoothed her blond curls absently and erased the frown from her face. *We're going to play this very cool,* she informed herself as she fastened on pearl earrings. *Unless I am very much mistaken, my aristocratic grandmother would like to stir up some fireworks this evening, but she won't set off any sparks in this corner.*

She knocked on the door of Tony's room. "It's Serenity, Tony. If you're ready, I'll walk down with you." Tony's call bade her to enter, and she opened the door to see the tall, fair man struggling with a cufflink. "Having trouble?" she inquired with a wide grin.

"Very funny." He looked up from his task with a scowl. "I can't do anything left-handed."

"Neither could my father," she stated with a quick, warm feeling of remembrance. "But he used to curse beautifully. It's amazing how many adjectives he used to describe a small pair of cufflinks." She moved to him and took his wrist in her hand. "Here, let me do it." She began to work the small object through his cuff. "Though what you would have done if I hadn't come along, I don't know." She shook her head and bent over his hand.

"I would have spent the evening with one hand thrust in my pocket," he answered smoothly. "Sort of a suave and continental stance."

"Oh, Tony." She looked up with a bright smile and shining eyes. "Sometimes you're positively cute."

A sound outside the door caught her attention, and she turned her head as Christophe walked by, paused for a moment to take in the intimate picture of the laughing woman fastening the man's cufflink, two fair heads close together. One dark brow raised fractionally, and with a small bow, Christophe continued on his way, leaving Serenity flushed and disconcerted.

"Who was that?" Tony asked with blatant curiosity, and she bent her head over his wrist to hide her burning cheeks.

"Le Comte de Kergallen," she answered with studied nonchalance.

"Not your grandmother's husband?" His voice was incredulous, and the question elicited a bright peal of laughter from Serenity, doing much to erase her tension.

"Oh, Tony, you are cute." She patted his wrist, the errant cufflink at last secured, and she looked up at him with sparkling eyes. "Christophe is the present count, and he's her grandson."

"Oh." Tony's brow creased in thought. "He's your cousin, then."

"Well . . ." She drew the word out slowly. "Not precisely." She explained the rather complicated family history and the resulting relationship between herself and the Breton count. "So, you see," she concluded, taking Tony's arm and walking from the room, "in a roundabout sort of way, we could be considered cousins."

"Kissing cousins," Tony observed with a definite frown.

"Don't be silly," she protested too quickly, unnerved by the memories of hard, demanding lips on hers.

If Tony noted the rushed denial and flushed cheeks, he made no comment.

They entered the drawing room arm in arm, and Serenity felt her flush deepen at Christophe's brief but encompassing appraisal. His face was smooth and unreadable, and she wished with sudden fervor that she could see the thoughts that lived behind his cool exterior.

Serenity watched his gaze shift to the man at her side, but his gaze remained impassive and correct.

"Ah, Serenity, Monsieur Rollins." The countess sat in the high-backed, richly brocaded chair framed by the massive stone fireplace, the image of a monarch receiving her subjects. Serenity wondered whether this placement had been deliberate or accidental. "Christophe, allow me to present Monsieur Anthony Rollins from America, Serenity's guest." The countess, Serenity noted with irony, had neatly categorized Tony as her personal property.

"Monsieur Rollins," she continued without breaking her rhythm, "allow me to present your host, Monsieur le Comte de Kergallen."

The title was emphasized delicately, and Christophe's position as master of the château was established. Serenity shot her grandmother a knowing glance.

The two men exchanged formalities, and Serenity was observant enough to note the age-old routine of sizing up, like two male dogs gauging the adversary before entering into combat.

Christophe served his grandmother an *apéritif*, then inquired as to Serenity's pleasure before continuing with his duties with Tony. He echoed Serenity's request for vermouth, and she stifled a smile, knowing Tony's taste ran strictly to dry vodka martinis or an occasional brandy.

The conversation flowed smoothly, the countess inserting several of the facts pertaining to Tony's background he had so conveniently provided her with that afternoon.

"It is so comforting to know that Serenity is in such capable hands in America," she stated with a gracious smile, and continued, ignoring the scowl Serenity threw at her. "You have been friends for some time, *non?*" The faint hesitation, barely perceptible, on the words "friends" caused Serenity's scowl to deepen.

"Yes," Tony agreed, patting Serenity's hand with affection. "We met about a year ago at a dinner party. Remember, darling?" He turned to smile at her, and she erased her scowl quickly.

"Of course. The Carsons' party."

"Now you have traveled so far just for a short visit." The countess smiled with fond indulgence. "Was that not considerate, Christophe?"

"Most considerate." With a nod, he lifted his glass.

Why, you artful minx, Serenity thought irreverently. *You know very well Tony came on business. What are you up to?*

"Such a pity you cannot remain longer, Monsieur Rollins. It is pleasant for Serenity to have company from America. Do you ride?"

"Ride?" he repeated, baffled for a moment. "No, I'm afraid not."

"*C'est dommage.* Christophe has been teaching Serenity. How is your pupil progressing, Christophe?"

"*Très bien,* Grandmère," he answered easily, his gaze moving from his grandmother to Serenity. "She has a natural ability, and now that the initial stiffness has passed"—a fleeting smile appeared, and her color rose in memory—"we are progressing nicely, eh, *mignonne?*"

"Yes," she agreed, thrown off balance by the casual endearment after days of cool politeness. "I'm glad you persuaded me to learn."

"It has been my pleasure." His enigmatic smile only served to increase her confusion.

"Perhaps you in turn will teach Monsieur Rollins,

Serenity, when you have the opportunity." The count-ess drew her attention, and amber eyes narrowed at the innocence of the tone.

The meddler! she fumed inwardly. *She's playing the two against each other, dangling me in the middle like a meaty bone.* Irritation transformed into reluctant amusement as the clear eyes met hers, a devil of mischief dancing in their depths.

"Perhaps, Grandmère, though I doubt I shall be able to make the jump from student to instructor for some time. Two brief lessons hardly make me an expert."

"But you shall have others, *n'est-ce pas?*" She tossed off Serenity's counterploy and rose with fluid grace. "Mon-sieur Rollins, would you be so kind as to escort me to dinner?"

Tony smiled, greatly flattered, and took the countess's arm, though who was leading whom from the room was painfully obvious to the woman left behind.

"Alors, chérie." Christophe advanced on Serenity and held out his hand to assist her to her feet. "It seems you must make do with me."

"I guess I can just about bear it," she retorted, ignoring the furious thumping of her heart as his hand closed over hers.

"Your American must be very slow," he began conver-sationally, retaining her hand and towering over her in a distracting manner. "He has known you for nearly a year, and still he is not your lover."

Her face flamed, and she glared up at him, grasping at her dignity. "Really, Christophe, you surprise me. What an incredibly rude observation."

"But a true one," he returned, unperturbed.

"Not all men think exclusively of sex. Tony is a very warm and considerate person, not overbearing like some others I could name."

He only smiled with maddening confidence. "Does your Tony make your pulse race as it does now?" His thumb caressed her wrist. "Or your heart beat like this?" His hand covered the heart that galloped like a mad horse, and his lips brushed hers in a gentle, lingering kiss so unlike any of the others he had given her that she could only stand swaying with dazed sensations.

Lips feathered over her face, teasing the corners of her mouth, withholding the promise with the experience of seduction. Teeth nibbled at the lobe of her ear, and she sighed as the small spark of pain shot inestimable currents of pleasure along her skin, drugging her with delight and slow, smoldering desire. Lightly, his fingers traced the length of her spine, then moved with devastating laziness along the bare flesh of her back until she was pliant and yielding in his arms, her mouth seeking his for fulfillment. He gave her only a brief taste of his lips before they roamed to the hollow of her throat, and his hands moved slowly from curve to curve, fingers teasing but not taking the fullness of breast before they began a circling, gentle massage at her hips.

Murmuring his name, she went limp against him, unable to demand what she craved, starving for the mouth he denied her. Wanting only to be possessed, needing what only he could give, her arms pulled him closer in silent supplication.

"Tell me," Christophe murmured, and through mists of languor, she heard the light mockery of his tone. "Has Tony heard you sigh his name, or felt your bones melt against him as he held you so?"

Stunned, she jerked back convulsively from his embrace, anger and humiliation warring with desire. "You are overconfident, Monsieur," she choked. "It's none of your business how Tony makes me feel."

"You think not?" he asked in a politely inquiring tone. "We must discuss that later, *ma belle cousine.* Now I think we had best join Grandmère and our guest." He gave her an engaging and exasperating grin. "They may well wonder what has become of us."

They need not have concerned themselves, Serenity noted as she entered the dining room on Christophe's arm. The countess was entertaining Tony beautifully, currently discussing the collection of antique Fabergé boxes displayed on a large mirrored buffet.

The meal commenced with vichyssoise, cold and refreshing, the conversation continuing in English for Tony's benefit. Talk was general and impersonal, and Serenity felt herself relaxing, commanding her muscles to uncoil as the soup course was cleared and the *homard grillé* was served. The lobster was nothing less than perfection, and she mused idly that, if the cook was indeed a dragon, as Christophe had joked on that first day, she was indeed a very skilled one.

"I imagine your mother made the transition from the château to your house in Georgetown very easily, Serenity," Tony stated suddenly, and she regarded him with a puzzled frown.

"I'm not sure I understand what you mean."

"There are so many basic similarities," he observed, and as she continued to look blank, he elaborated. "Of course, everything's on a much larger scale here, but there are the high ceilings, the fireplaces in every room, the style of furniture. Why, even the banisters on the stairs are similar. Surely you noticed?"

"Why, yes, I suppose I did," she answered slowly, "though I didn't realize it until now." Perhaps, she reasoned, her father had chosen the Georgetown house because he, too, had noted the similarities, and her mother had selected the furnishings from the memories of her childhood. The thought was somehow comforting. "Yes, even the banisters," she continued aloud with a smile. "I used to slide down them constantly, down from the third-floor studio, smack into the newel post, then slide to the ground floor and smack into the next one." The smile turned into a laugh. "Maman used to say that another part of my anatomy must be as hard as my head to take such punishment."

"She used to say the same to me," Christophe stated suddenly, and Serenity's eyes flew to him in surprise. *"Mais oui, petite."* He answered her look of surprise with one of his rare, full smiles. "What is the sense of walking if one can slide?"

A picture of a small, dark boy flying down the smooth rail, and her mother, young and lovely, watching and laughing, filled her mind. Her startled look faded slowly into a smile which mirrored Christophe's.

She helped herself to the raisin soufflé, light as a cloud, accompanied by a dry and sparkling champagne. She felt herself drifting through dinner in a warm, contented glow, happy to let the easy conversation flow around her.

When they moved to the drawing room after dinner, she decided to refuse the offer of a liqueur or brandy. The glow persisted, and she suspected that at least part of it (she was determined not to think about the other part and the quick, tantalizing embrace before dinner) was due to the wine served with each course. No one appeared to notice her bemused state, her flushed cheeks, and her almost mechanical answers. She found her senses almost unbearably sharpened as she listened to the music of the voices, the deep hum of the men's mingling with the lighter tones of her grandmother. She inhaled with sensuous pleasure the tangy smoke of Christophe's cheroot drifting toward her, and she breathed deeply of the women's mingled subtle perfumes overpowered by the sweet scent of the roses spilling from every porcelain vase. A pleasing balance, she decided, the artist in her responding to and enjoying the harmony, the fluid continuity of the scene. The soft lights, the night breeze gently lifting the curtains, the quiet clink of glasses being set on the table—all merged into an impressionistic canvas to be registered and stored in her mind's eye.

The dowager countess, magnificent on her brocade throne, presided, sipping crème de menthe from an exquisite gold-rimmed glass. Tony and Christophe were seated across from each other, like day and night, angel and devil. The last comparison brought Serenity up short. *Angel and devil?* she repeated silently, surveying the two men.

Tony—sweet, reliable, predictable Tony, who applied the gentlest pressure. Tony of the infinite patience and carefully thought-out plans. What did she feel for him? Affection, loyalty, gratitude for being there when she needed him. A mild, comfortable love.

Her eyes moved to Christophe. Arrogant, dominating, exasperating, exciting. Demanding what he wanted, and taking it, bestowing his sudden, unexpected smile and stealing her heart like a thief in the night. He was moody, whereas Tony was constant; imperious, whereas Tony was persuasive. But if Tony's kisses had been pleasant and stirring, Christophe's had been wildly intoxicating, turning her blood to fire and lifting her into an unknown world of sensation and desire. And the love she felt for him was neither mild nor comfortable, but tempestuous and inescapable.

"Such a pity you do not play the piano, Serenity." The countess's voice brought her back with a guilty jerk.

"Oh, Serenity plays, Madame," Tony informed her with a wide grin. "Dreadfully, but she plays."

"Traitor!" Serenity gave him a cheerful grin.

"You do not play well?" the countess was clearly incredulous.

"I'm sorry to bring disgrace to the family once again, Grandmère," Serenity apologized. "But not only do I not play well, I play quite miserably. I even offend Tony, who is absolutely tone deaf."

"You'd offend a corpse with your playing, darling." He brushed a lock of hair from her face in a gesture of casual intimacy.

"Quite true." She smiled at him before glancing at her grandmother. "Poor Grandmère, don't look so stricken." Her smile faded somewhat as she met Christophe's frigid stare.

"But Gaelle played so beautifully," her grandmother countered with a gesture of her hand.

Serenity brought her attention back, attempting to shake off the chill of Christophe's eyes. "She could never understand the way I slaughtered music, either, but even with her abundant patience, she finally gave in and left me to my paints and easel."

"Extraordinaire!" The countess shook her head, and Serenity shrugged and sipped her coffee. "Since you cannot play for us, *ma petite,*" she began in a change of mood, "perhaps Monsieur Rollins would enjoy a tour of the garden." She smiled wickedly. "Serenity enjoys the garden in the moonlight, *n'est-ce pas?*"

"That sounds tempting," Tony agreed before Serenity could respond. Sending her grandmother a telling look, Serenity allowed herself to be led outside.

CHAPTER NINE

For the second time Serenity strolled in the moonlit garden with a tall, handsome man, and for the second time she wished dismally that it was Christophe by her side. They walked in companionable silence, enjoying the fresh night air and the pleasure of familiar linked hands.

"You're in love with him, aren't you?"

Tony's question broke the stillness like a rock being hurled through glass, and Serenity stopped and stared up at him with wide eyes.

"Serenity." He sighed and brushed a finger down her cheek. "I can read you like a book. You're doing your best to hide it, but you're crazy about him."

"Tony, I . . ." she stammered, feeling guilty and miserable. "I never meant to. I don't even like him, really."

"Lord." He gave a soft laugh and a grimace. "I wish you

didn't like me that way. But then," he added, cupping her chin, "you never have."

"Oh, Tony."

"You were never anything but honest, darling," he assured her. "You've nothing to feel guilty about. I thought that with constant, persistent diligence I would wear you down." He slipped an arm around her shoulders as they continued deeper into the garden. "You know, Serenity, your looks are deceptive. You look like a delicate flower, so fragile a man's almost afraid to touch you for fear you'll break, but you're really amazingly strong." He gave her a brief squeeze. "You never stumble, darling. I've been waiting for a year to catch you, but you never stumble."

"My moods and temper would have driven you over the edge, Tony." Sighing, she leaned against his shoulder. "I could never be what you needed, and if I tried to mold myself into something else, it wouldn't have worked. We'd have ended up hating each other."

"I know. I've known for a long time, but I didn't want to admit it." He let out a long breath. "When you left for Brittany, I knew it was over. That's why I came to see you; I had to see you one more time." His words sounded so final that she looked up in surprise.

"But we'll see each other again, Tony; we're still friends. I'll be coming back soon."

He stopped again and met her eyes, the silence growing long between them. "Will you, Serenity?" Turning, he led her back toward the lights of the château.

The sun was warm on her bare shoulders as Serenity said her goodbyes to Tony the next morning. He had already made his farewells to the countess and Christophe, and Serenity had walked with him from the coolness of the main hall to the warmth of the flagstone courtyard. The little red Renault waited for him, his luggage already secured in the boot, and he glanced at it briefly before turning to her, taking both of her hands in his.

"Be happy, Serenity." His grip tightened, then relaxed on her hands. "Think of me sometimes."

"Of course I'll think of you, Tony. I'll write and let you know when I'll be back."

He smiled down at her, his eyes roaming over her face, as if imprinting every detail in his memory. "I'll think of you just as you are today, in a yellow dress with the sun in your hair and a castle at your back—the everlasting beauty of Serenity Smith of the golden eyes."

He lowered his mouth to hers, and she was swamped by a sudden surge of emotion, a strong premonition that she would never see him again. She threw her arms around his neck and clung to him and to the past. His lips brushed her hair before he drew her away.

"Goodbye, darling." He smiled and patted her cheek.

"Goodbye, Tony. Take care." She returned his smile, determinedly battling back the tears which burned her eyes.

She watched as he walked to the car and got in, and with a wave headed down the long, winding drive. The car became a small red dot in the distance and then gradually faded from sight, and she continued to stand, allowing the silent tears to have their freedom. An arm slipped around her waist, and she turned to see her grandmother standing beside her, sympathy and understanding in the angular face.

"You are sad to see him go, *ma petite?*" The arm was comforting, and Serenity leaned her head against the slim shoulder.

"*Oui,* Grandmère, very sad."

"But you are not in love with him." It was a statement rather than a question, and Serenity sighed.

"He was very special to me." Pushing a tear from her cheek, she gave a childish sniffle. "I shall miss him very much. Now, I shall go to my room and have a good cry."

"*Oui,* that is wise." The countess patted her shoulder. "Few things clear the brain and cleanse the heart like a good cry." Turning, Serenity enveloped her in a hug. "*Va, vite, mon enfant.*" The countess held her close for a moment before disengaging herself. "Go shed your tears."

Serenity ran up the stone steps and entered through the heavy oak doors into the coolness of the château. Rushing toward the main staircase, she collided with a hard object. Hands gripped her shoulders.

"You must watch where you are going, *ma chérie,*" Christophe's voice mocked. "You will be running into walls and damaging your beautiful nose." She attempted to pull away, but one hand held her in place without effort as another came under her chin to tilt back her head. At the sight of brimming eyes, the mockery faded, replaced by surprise, then concern, and lastly an unfamiliar helplessness. "Serenity?" Her name was a question, the tone gentle as she had not heard it before, and the tenderness in the dark eyes broke what little composure she could still lay claim to.

"Oh, please," she choked on a desperate sob, "let me go." She struggled from his grasp, striving not to crumble completely, yet wanting to be held close by this suddenly gentle man.

"Is there something I can do?" He detained her by placing a hand on her arm.

Yes, you idiot! her brain screamed. *Love me!* "No," she said aloud, running up the stairs. "No, no, no!"

She streaked up the stairs, like a golden doe pursued by hunters, and finding her bedroom door, she opened it, then slammed it behind her, and threw herself on her bed.

The tears had worked their magic. Finally, Serenity was able to rinse them away and face the world and whatever the future had in store. She glanced at the manila envelope which she had tossed negligently on her bureau.

"Well, I suppose it's time to see what old Barkley sent

me." Serenity got up reluctantly and went over to the bureau to pick up the envelope. She threw herself down on the bed again to break the seal, dumping its contents on the spread.

There was merely a page with the firm's impressive letterhead, which brought thoughts of Tony flooding back to her mind, and another sealed envelope. She picked up the neatly typewritten page listlessly, wondering what new form the family retainer had discovered for her to fill out. As she read the letter's contents, and the totally unexpected message it contained, she sat bolt upright.

Dear Miss Smith,

Enclosed you will find an envelope addressed to you containing a letter from your father. This letter was left in my care to be given to you only if you made contact with your mother's family in Brittany. It has come to my attention through Anthony Rollins that you are now residing at the Château Kergallen in the company of your maternal grandmother, so I am entrusting same to Anthony to be delivered to you at the earliest possible date.

Had you informed me of your plans, I would have carried out your father's wishes at an earlier date. I, of course, have no knowledge of its contents, but I am sure your father's message will bring you comfort.

M. Barkley

Serenity read no farther, but put the lawyer's letter aside and picked up the message her father had left in his care. She stared at the envelope which had fallen face down on the bed, and, turning it over, her eyes misted at seeing the familiar handwriting. She broke the seal.

The letter was written in her father's bold, clear hand:

My own Serenity,
When you read this your mother and I will no longer be with you, and I pray you do not grieve too deeply, for the love we feel for you remains true and strong as life itself.

As I write this, you are ten years old, already the image of your mother, so incredibly lovely that I am already fretting about the boys I will have to fight off one day. I watched you this morning as you sat sedately (a most unusual occupation for you, as I am more used to seeing you skating down the sidewalks at a horrifying speed or sliding without thought to bruised skin down the banisters). You sat in the garden, with my sketch book and a pencil, drawing with fierce concentration the azaleas that bloomed there. I saw in that moment, to both my pride and despair, that you were growing up, and would not always be my little girl, safe in the security your mother and I had provided for you. I knew then it was necessary to write down events you might one day have the need to understand.

I will give old Barkley (a small smile appeared on

Serenity's face as she noted that the attorney had been known by that name even so many years ago) *instructions to hold this letter for you until such time as your grandmother, or some member of your mother's family, makes contact with you. If this does not occur, there will be no need to reveal the secret your mother and I have already kept for more than a decade.*

I was painting on the sidewalks of Paris in the full glory of spring, in love with the city and needing no mistress but my art. I was very young, and, I am afraid, very intense. I met a man, Jean-Paul le Goff, who was impressed by my, as he put it, raw young talent. He commissioned me to paint a portrait of his fiancée as a wedding present to her, and arranged for me to travel to Brittany and reside in the Château Kergallen. My life began the moment I entered that enormous hall and had my first glimpse of your mother.

It was not my intention to act upon the love I felt from the first moment I saw her, a delicate angel with hair like sunlight. I tried with all my being to put my art first. I was to paint her; she belonged to my patron; she belonged to the château. She was an angel, an aristocrat with a family lineage longer than time. All these things I told myself a hundred times. Jonathan Smith, itinerant artist, had no right to possess her in dreams, let alone reality. At times, when I made my preliminary sketches, I believed I would die for love of her. I told myself to go, to make some excuse and leave, but I could not find the courage. I thank God now that I could not.

One night, as I walked in the garden, I came upon her. I thought to turn away before I disturbed her, but she heard me, and when she turned, I saw in her eyes what I had not dared dream. She loved me. I could have shouted with the joy of it, but there were so many obstacles. She was betrothed, honor-bound to marry another man. We had no right to our love. Does one need a right to love, Serenity? Some would condemn us. I pray you do not. After much talk and tears, we defied what some would call right and honor, and we married. Gaelle begged me to keep the marriage a secret until she could find the right way to tell Jean-Paul and her mother. I wanted the world to know, but I agreed. She had given up so much for me, I could deny her nothing.

During this time of waiting, a more disturbing problem came to light. The countess, your grandmother, had in her possession a Raphael Madonna, displayed in prominence in the main drawing room. It was a painting, the countess informed me, which had been in her family for generations. Next to Gaelle, she treasured this painting above all things. It seemed to symbolize to her the continuity of her family, a shining beacon remaining constant after the hell of war and loss. I had studied this painting closely and suspected it was a forgery. I said nothing, at first thinking perhaps the countess herself had had a copy made for her own needs. The Germans had taken so much from her—husband, home—that perhaps they had taken the original Raphael, as well. When she made the announcement that she had decided to donate the painting to the Louvre in order to share its greatness, I nearly froze with fear. I had grown fond of this woman, her pride and determination, her grace and dignity. I had no desire to see her hurt, and I realized that she believed the painting to be authentic. I knew Gaelle would be tormented by the scandal if the painting was dismissed as a fraud, and the countess would be destroyed. I could not let this happen. I offered to clean the painting in order to examine it more critically, and I felt like a traitor.

I took the painting to my studio in the tower, and under close study, I had no doubt that it was a very well-executed copy. Even then, I do not know what I would have done, if it had not been for the letter I found hidden behind the frame. The letter was a confession from the countess's first husband, a cry of despair for the treachery he had committed. He confessed he had lost nearly all of his possessions, and those of his wife. He was deep in debt, and having decided the Germans would defeat the Allies, he arranged to sell the Raphael to them. He had a copy made and replaced the original without the countess's knowledge, feeling the money would see him through the hardship of war, and the deal with the Germans would keep his estates secure.

Too late, he despaired of his action, and hiding his confession in the frame of the copy, he went to face the men he had dealt with in the hopes of returning the money. The note ended with his telling of his intention, and pleading for forgiveness if he proved unsuccessful.

As I finished reading the letter, Gaelle came into the studio; I had not the foresight to bolt the door. It was impossible to hide my reaction, or the letter, which I still held in my hand, and so I was forced to share the burden with the one person I most wanted to spare. I found in those moments, in that secluded tower room, that the woman I loved was endowed with more strength than most men. She would keep the knowledge from her mother at all costs. She felt it imperative that the countess be shielded from humiliation and the knowledge that the painting she so prized was but a forgery. We devised a plan to conceal the painting, to make it appear as if it had been stolen. Perhaps we were wrong. To this day I do not know if we did the right thing; but for your mother there was no other way. And so, the deed was done.

Gaelle's plans to tell her mother of our marriage were soon forced into reality. She found, to our unending joy, that she carried our child, you, the fruit of our love that would grow to be the most important treasure of our lives. When she told her mother of our marriage and her pregnancy, the countess flew into a rage. It was her right to do, Serenity, and the animosity she felt for me was well deserved in her eyes. I had taken her daughter from her without her knowledge, and in doing so, I had placed a mark on her family's honor. In her anger, she disowned Gaelle, demanded that we leave the château and never enter again. I believe she would have rescinded her decision in time; she loved Gaelle above all things. But that same day she found the Raphael missing. Putting two and two together, she accused me of stealing both her daughter and her family treasure. How could I deny it? One crime was no worse than the other, and the message in your mother's eyes begged me to keep silent. So I took your mother away from the château, her country, her family, her heritage, and brought her to America.

We did not speak of her mother, for it brought only pain, and we built our life fresh with you to strengthen our bond. And now you have the story, and with it, forgive me, the responsibility. Perhaps by the time you read this, it will be possible to tell the entire truth. If not, let it remain hidden, as the forgery was hidden, away from the world with something infinitely more precious to conceal it. Do what your heart tells you.

Your loving father.

Tears had fallen on the letter since its beginning, and now as Serenity finished reading, she wiped them away and took a long breath. Standing, she moved over to the window and stared down at the garden where her parents had first revealed their love.

"What do I do?" she murmured aloud, still gripping the letter in her hand. *If I had read this a month ago, I would have gone straight to the countess with it, but now I don't know,* she told herself silently.

To clear her father's name, she would have to reveal a secret kept hidden for twenty-five years. Would the telling accomplish anything, or would it undo whatever good the sacrifices made by both her parents had done? Her father had instructed her to listen to her heart, but it was so filled with the love and anguish of his letter that she could hear nothing, and her mind was clouded with indecision. There was a swift, fleeting impulse to go to Christophe, but she quickly pushed it aside. To confide in him would only make her more vulnerable, and the separation she must soon deal with more agonizing.

She had to think, she decided, taking several deep breaths. She had to clear away the fog and think clearly and carefully, and when she found an answer, she had to be sure it was the right one.

Pacing the room, she halted suddenly and began changing her clothes in a frantic rush. She remembered the freedom and openness that had come to her when she rode through the woods, and it was this sensation, she determined, slipping on jeans and shirt, that she required to ease her heart and clear her brain.

CHAPTER TEN

The groom greeted her request to saddle Babette doubtfully. He argued, albeit respectfully, that he had no orders from the count to go riding, and for once Serenity used her aristocratic heritage and haughtily informed him that as the countess's granddaughter, she was not to be questioned. The groom submitted, with a faint muttering of Breton, and she was soon mounted on the how-familiar mare and setting off on the path Christophe had taken on her first lesson.

The woods were quiet and comforting, and she emptied her mind in the hopes that the answer would then find room to make an appearance. She walked the mare easily for a time, finding it simple now to retain command of the animal while still feeling a part of it. She found herself no closer to resolving her problem, however, and urged Babette into a canter.

They moved swiftly, the wind blowing her hair back from her face and engulfing her once more with the sense of freedom which she sought. Her father's letter was tucked into her back pocket, and she decided to ride to the hill overlooking the village and read it once more, hoping by then to find the wisdom to make the right decision.

A shout rang out behind her, and she turned in the saddle to see Christophe coming after her astride the black stallion. As she turned, her foot connected sharply with the mare's side, and Babette took this as a command and streaked forward in a swift gallop. Serenity was nearly unseated in surprise, and she struggled to right herself as the horse raced down the path with unaccustomed speed. At first all of her attention was given to the problem of remaining astride, not even contemplating the mechanics of halting the mare's headlong rush. Before her brain had the opportunity to communicate with her hands and give them the idea to rein in, Christophe came alongside her. Then, reaching over, he pulled back on her reins, uttering a stream of oaths in a variety of languages.

Babette came to a docile halt, and Serenity's eyes closed in relief. The next thing she knew, she was gripped around the waist and dragged from the saddle without ceremony, with Christophe's dark eyes burning into hers.

"What do you hope to accomplish by running away from me?" he demanded, shaking her like a rag doll.

"I was doing no such thing," she protested through teeth that chattered at the movement. "I must have startled the horse when I turned around." Her own anger began to replace relief. "It wouldn't have happened if you hadn't come chasing after me." She began to struggle away, but his grip increased with painful emphasis. "You're hurting me!" she stormed at him. "Why must you always hurt me?"

"You would find a broken neck more painful, *ma petite folle*," he stated, dragging her farther down the path and away from the horses. "That is what could have happened to you. What do you mean by riding off unescorted?"

"Unescorted?" she repeated with a laugh, jerking away from him. "How quaint. Aren't women allowed to ride unescorted in Brittany?"

"Not women who have no brains," he returned with dark fury, "and who have been on a horse only twice before in their lives."

"I was going very well before you came." She tossed her head at his logic. "Now just go away and leave me alone." She watched as his eyes narrowed, and he took a step toward her. "Go away!" she shouted, backing up. "I want my privacy. I have things to think about."

"I will give you something else to think about."

He moved swiftly, gripping her behind the neck and

stealing her breath with his lips. She pushed against him without success, fighting both him and the whirling dizziness which flew to her brain. Gripping her shoulders, he drew her away, his fingers digging into her flesh.

"Enough! *C'est entendu!*" He shook her again, and she saw by his face that the aristocrat had fled and there was only the man. "I want you. I want what no man has had before—and, by God, I *will* have you."

He swept her up into his arms, and she struggled with a wild, primitive fear, beating against his chest like a trapped bird beating against the bars of its cage, but his stride remained steady and sure, as though he carried a complaisant child rather than a terrified woman.

Then she was on the ground, with his body crushing down on hers, his mouth savaging hers like a man possessed, her protests making no more of a ripple than a pebble tossed into the ocean. With a swift, violent motion, her blouse was opened, and he claimed her naked skin with bruising fingers, his lovemaking filled with a desperate urgency which conquered all thought of resistance, all will to struggle.

Struggle became demand, and her mouth became mobile and seeking under his; the hands which had previously pushed him away were now pulling him closer. Drowned in the deluge of passion, she reveled in the intimacy of his masculine hardness, her body moving with the ageless rhythm of instinct beneath him. Urgent and without restraint, his hands traced trails of heat along her naked flesh, his mouth following the blaze, returning again and again to drink from hers. Each time, his thirst grew, his demands taking her into a new and timeless world, the border between heaven and hell, where only one man and one woman can exist.

Deeper and deeper he led her, until pleasure and pain merged into one spiraling sensation, one all-consuming need. Helpless under the barrage of shimmering passion, the trembling began slowly, growing more intense as the journey took her further from the known and closer to the unexperienced. With a moan mixed with fear and desire, her fingers clutched at his shoulders, as if to keep from plummeting into an eternal void.

His mouth left hers suddenly, and with his breath uneven, his cheek rested against her brow for a moment before he lifted his head and looked down at her.

"I am hurting you again, *ma petite*." He sighed and rolled off her to lie on his back. "I tossed you on the ground and nearly ravished you like a barbarian. I seem to find it difficult to control my baser instincts with you."

She sat up quickly, fumbling with the buttons of her blouse with unsteady fingers. "It's all right." She attempted but failed to produce a careless-sounding voice. "No harm done. I've often been told how strong I am. You must learn to temper your technique a bit, though," she babbled on to hide the extent of her pain. "Geneviève is more fragile than I."

"Geneviève?" he repeated, lifting himself on his elbow

to look at her directly. "What has Geneviève to do with this?"

"With this?" she answered. "Oh, nothing. I have no intention of saying anything to her of this. I'm quite fond of her."

"Perhaps we should speak in French, Serenity. I am having difficulty understanding you."

"She's in love with you, you big idiot!" she blurted out, ignoring his request for French. "She told me; she came asking for my advice." She controlled the short burst of hysterical laughter which escaped her. "She asked for my advice," she elaborated, "on how to make you see her as a woman instead of a child. I didn't tell her what your opinion was of me; she wouldn't have understood."

"She told you she was in love with me?" he demanded, his eyes narrowing.

"Not by name," she said shortly, wishing the conversation had never begun. "She said she had been in love with a man all of her life, and he regarded her as a child. I simply told her to set him straight, tell him that she was a woman, and . . . What are you laughing at?"

"You thought she spoke of me?" He was once more flat on his back and laughing more freely than she had ever seen. "Little Geneviève in love with me!"

"How dare you laugh at her! How can you be so callous as to make fun of someone who loves you?" He caught her fists before they made contact with his chest.

"Geneviève did not seek you out for advice about me,

chérie." He continued to hold her off without effort. "She was speaking of Iann. But you have not met Iann, have you, *mon amour?*" He ignored her furious struggles and continued to speak with a wide grin. "We grew up together—Iann, Yves, and I—with Geneviève trailing along like a little puppy. Yves and I remained her 'brothers' after she grew into a woman, but it was Iann she truly loved. He has been in Paris on business for the last month, only returning home yesterday." A small jerk of his wrists brought her down on his chest. "Geneviève called this morning to tell me of their engagement. She also told me to thank you for her, and now I know why." His grin increased as amber eyes grew wide.

"She's engaged? It wasn't you?"

"Yes, she is; and no, it was not," he answered helpfully. "Tell me, *ma belle cousine,* were you jealous when you thought Geneviève to be in love with me?"

"Don't be ridiculous," she lied, attempting to remove her mouth from its proximity to his. "I would be no more jealous of Geneviève than you would be of Yves."

"Ah." In one swift movement he had reversed their positions and lay looking down at her. "Is that so? And should I tell you that I was nearly consumed with jealousy of my friend Yves, and that I very nearly murdered your American Tony? You would give them smiles that should be mine. From the moment I saw you step off the train, I was lost, bewitched, and I fought it as a man fights that which threatens to enslave him. Perhaps this slavery is freedom." His hand moved through the silk of her hair. "Ah, Serenity, *je t'aime*."

She swallowed in the search for her voice. "Would you say that again?"

He smiled, and his mouth teased hers for a moment. "In English? I love you. I loved you from the moment I saw you, I love you infinitely more now, and I will love you for the rest of my life." His lips descended on hers, moving them with a tenderness he had never shown, lifting only when he felt the moistness of her tears. "Why do you weep?" he questioned, his brow creasing in exasperation. "What have I done?"

She shook her head. "It's only that I love you so much, and I thought . . ." She hesitated and let out a long breath. "Christophe, do you believe my father was innocent, or do you think me to be the daughter of a thief?"

His brow creased again with a frown, and he studied her silently. "I will tell you what I know, Serenity, and I will tell you what I believe. I know that I love you, not just the angel who stepped off the train at Lannion, but the woman I have come to know. It would make no difference if your father was a thief, a cheat, or a murderer. I have heard you speak of your father, and I have seen how you look when you tell of him. I cannot believe that a man who earned this love and devotion could have committed such a crime. This is what I believe, but it does not matter; nothing he did or did not do could change my love for you."

"Oh, Christophe," she whispered, pulling his cheek

down to hers, "I've waited all my life for someone like you. There is something I must show you." She pushed him away gently, taking the letter from her pocket and handing it to him. "My father told me to listen to my heart, and now it belongs to you."

Serenity sat across from him, watching his face as he read, and she felt a deep peace, a contentment she had not known since her parents had been taken from her. Love for him filled her, along with a strong sense of security that he would help her to make the right decision. The woods were silent, tranquil, disturbed only by the whisper of wind through the leaves, and the birds that answered it. For a moment, it was a place out of time, inhabited only by man and woman.

When he had finished reading the letter, Christophe lifted his eyes from the paper and met hers. "Your father loved your mother very much."

"Yes."

He folded the letter, replacing it in its envelope, his eyes never leaving hers. "I wish I had known him. I was only a child when he came to the château, and he did not stay long."

Her eyes clung to his. "What should we do?"

He moved nearer, taking her face in his hands. "We must take the letter and show it to Grandmère."

"But they're dead, and she's alive. I love her; I don't want to hurt her."

He bent down and kissed shimmering lashes. "I love

you, Serenity, for so many reasons, and you have just given me one more." He tilted her head so their eyes met again. "Listen to me now, *mon amour,* and trust me. Grandmère needs to see this letter, for her own peace of mind. She believes her daughter betrayed her, stole from her. She has lived with this for twenty-five years. This letter will set her free. She will read in your father's words the love Gaelle had for her, and, equally important, she will see the love your father had for her daughter. He was an honorable man, but he lived with the fact that his wife's mother thought him to be a thief. The time has come to set them all free."

"All right," she agreed. "If you say this is what we must do, this is what we will do."

He smiled, and taking both her hands in his, he lifted them to his lips before helping her to her feet. "Tell me, *cousine*"—the familiar mocking smile was in place—"will you always do as I say?"

"No," she answered with a vigorous shake of her head. "Absolutely not."

"Ah, I thought not." He led her to the horses. "Life will not be dull." He took the reins of the buckskin in his hand, and she mounted without assistance. He frowned as he handed her the reins. "You are disturbingly independent, stubborn, and impulsive, but I love you."

"And you," she commented, as he moved to mount the stallion, "are arrogant, overbearing, and irritatingly confident, but I love you, as well."

They reached the stables. After relinquishing the horses to a groom, they set off toward the château with linked hands. As they approached the garden entrance, Christophe stopped and turned to her.

"You must give this to Grandmère yourself, Serenity." He took the envelope from his pocket and handed it to her.

"Yes, I know." She looked down at it as he placed it in her hand. "But you will stay with me?"

"Oui, ma petite." He drew her into his arms. "I will stay with you." His mouth met hers, and she threw her arms around his neck until the kiss deepened, and they were only aware of each other.

"Alors, mes enfants." The countess's words broke the spell, and they both turned to see her watching them from the edge of the garden. "You have decided to stop fighting the inevitable."

"You are very clever, Grandmère," Christophe commented with a lift of his brow. "But I believe we would have managed even without your invaluable assistance."

Elegant shoulders moved expressively. "But you might have wasted too much time, and time is a precious commodity."

"Come inside, Grandmère. Serenity has something to show you."

They entered the drawing room, and the countess seated herself in her regular thronelike chair. "What is it you have to show me, *ma petite?*"

"Grandmère," Serenity said as she began moving in front of the countess, "Tony brought me some papers from my attorney. I didn't even bother to open them until he left, but I found when I did that they were much more important than I had anticipated." She held out the letter. "Before you read this, I want you to know I love you." The countess opened her mouth to speak, but Serenity hurried on. "I love Christophe, and before he read what I'm giving you, he told me he loved me, as well. I can't tell you how wonderful it was to know that before he saw this letter. We decided to share this with you because we love you." She handed the letter to her grandmother and then seated herself on the sofa. Christophe joined her, and he took her hand in his as they waited.

Serenity's eyes were drawn to her mother's portrait, the eyes that met hers full of joy and happiness, the expression of a woman in love. *I have found it, too, Maman,* she spoke silently, *the overwhelming joy of love, and I hold it here in my hand.*

She dropped her eyes to the joined hands, the strong bronzed fingers intertwined with the alabaster ones, the ruby ring which had been her mother's glowing against the contrasting colors. She stared at the ring on her own hand, then raised her eyes to the replica on her mother's, and she understood. The countess's movement as she rose from her chair interrupted Serenity's thoughts.

"For twenty-five years I have wronged this man, and the daughter whom I loved." The words were soft as she turned to gaze out the window. "My pride blinded me and hardened my heart."

"You were not to know, Grandmère," Serenity replied, watching the straight back. "They wanted only to protect you."

"To protect me from the knowledge that my husband had been a thief, and from the humiliation of public scandal, your father allowed himself to be branded, and my daughter gave up her heritage." Moving back to the chair, she sank down wearily. "I sense from your father's words a great feeling of love. Tell me, Serenity, was my daughter happy?"

"You see the eyes as my father painted them." She gestured to the portrait. "She looked always as she looked then."

"How can I forgive myself for what I did?"

"Oh, no, Grandmère." Serenity rose and knelt in front of her, taking the fragile hands in her own. "I didn't give you the letter to add to your grief, but to take it from you. You read the letter; you see that they blamed you for nothing; they purposely allowed you to believe that they betrayed you. Maybe they were wrong, but it's done, and there can be no going back." She gripped the narrow hands tighter. "I tell you now that I blame you for nothing, and I beg you, for my sake, to let the guilt die."

"Ah, Serenity, *ma chère enfant*." The countess's voice was as tender as her eyes. *"C'est bien,"* she said briskly, drawing her shoulders up straight once more. "We will remember only the happy times. You will tell me more of Gaelle's life with your father in this Georgetown, and you will bring them both close to me again, *n'est-ce pas?*"

"*Oui,* Grandmère."

"Perhaps one day you will take me to the house where you grew up."

"To America?" Serenity asked, deeply shocked. "Wouldn't you be afraid to travel to so uncivilized a country?"

"You are being impudent again," the countess stated regally as she rose from her chair. "I begin to believe I will come to know your father very well through you, *mignonne.*" She shook her head. "When I think of what I allowed that painting to cost me! I am well pleased to be rid of it."

"You still have the copy, Grandmère," Serenity corrected. "I know where it is."

"How do you know this?" Christophe asked, speaking for the first time since they had entered the room.

She turned to him and smiled. "It was right there in the letter, but I didn't realize it at first. It was when we were sitting together just now, and you held my hand, that it came to me. Do you see this?" She held out her hand where the ruby gleamed. "It was my mother's, the same she wears in the portrait."

"I had noticed the ring in the painting," the countess said slowly, "but Gaelle had no such ring. I thought your father merely painted it to match the earrings she wore."

"She had the ring, Grandmère; it was her engagement

ring. She wore it always with her wedding band on her left hand."

"But what has this to do with the copy of the Raphael?" Christophe questioned with a frown.

"In the painting she wears the ring on her right hand. My father would never have made such a mistake in detail unless he did it intentionally."

"It is possible," the countess murmured.

"I know it's there; it says so in the letter. He says he concealed it, covered by something infinitely more precious. Nothing was more precious to him than Maman."

"*Oui,*" the countess agreed, studying the painting of her daughter. "There could be no safer hiding place."

"I have some solution," Serenity began. "I could uncover a corner; then you could be sure."

"*Non.*" She shook her head. "*Non,* there is no need. I would not have you mar one inch of your father's work if the true Raphael were under it." She turned to Serenity and lifted a hand to her cheek. "This painting, Christophe, and you, *mon enfant,* are my treasures now. Let it rest. It is where it belongs." She turned back to her grandchildren with a smile. "I will leave you now. Lovers should have their privacy."

She left the room with the air of a queen, and Serenity watched her in admiration. "She's magnificent, isn't she?"

"*Oui,*" Christophe agreed easily, taking Serenity into his arms. "And very wise. I have not kissed you for more than an hour."

After he had remedied the discrepancy to their mutual satisfaction, he looked down at her with his habitual air of confidence. "After we are married, *mon amour,* I will have your portrait painted, and we will add still another treasure to the château."

"Married?" Serenity repeated with a frown. "I never agreed to marry you." She pushed away as though reluctant. "You can't just order me to do so; a woman likes to be asked." He pulled her against him and kissed her thoroughly, his lips hard and insistent.

"You were saying, *cousine?*" he asked when he freed her.

She regarded him seriously, but allowed her arms to twine around his neck. "I shall never be an aristocrat."

"Heaven forbid," he agreed with sincerity.

"We shall fight often, and I will constantly infuriate you."

"I shall look forward to it."

"Very well," she said, managing to keep a smile from her lips. "I will marry you—on one condition."

"And that is?" His brow raised in question.

"That you walk in the garden with me tonight." She drew her arms around him tighter. "I'm so tired of walking in the moonlight with other men and wishing they were you."

IRISH THOROUGHBRED

CHAPTER ONE

Adelia Cunnane stared out the window without seeing the magic layer of clouds. Some formed into mountains, others glaciers, flattening and thinning into an ice-encrusted lake; but, for one experiencing her first air journey, she found the view uninspiring. Her mind was crowded with doubts and uncertainties that merged with a strong pang of homesickness for a small farm in Ireland. But both farm and Ireland were now very far away, and every minute that crawled by brought her closer to America and strangers. She knew, with a sigh of frustration, that nothing in her life had ever prepared her properly to cope with either.

Her parents had been killed in a lorry accident, leaving her an orphan at the tender age of ten. In the weeks that followed her parents' death, Adelia had drifted through a fog of shock, turning inward to ward off the agony of separation, the strange and terrifying feeling of desertion. Slowly, a wall had been constructed around the pain, and she had thrown herself into the work of the farm with an adult's dedication.

Her father's sister, Lettie Cunnane, had taken over both child and farm, running both with a firm hand. Although never unkind, neither had she been affectionate: She had possessed little patience or understanding for the unpredictable, often tempestuous child.

The farm had been the only common ground between them, and woman and child had built their relationship with the dark, fertile soil and the hours of labor it required. They had lived and worked together for nearly thirteen years; then Lettie had suffered a paralyzing stroke, and Adelia had been forced to divide her time between the duties of the farm and caring for an invalid's needs. Days and nights had merged together as she waged the determined battle to shoulder the increasing responsibility.

Her enemies had been the lack of time and the lack of money. When, after six long months, she was again left alone, Adelia was near the point of exhausted desperation. Her aunt was gone, and though she had worked unceasingly, the farm had had to be sold for taxes.

She had written to her only remaining relative, her father's elder brother, Padrick, who had emigrated to America twenty years previously, informing him of his sister's death. His answer had been immediate, the letter warm and loving, asking her to join him. The last sentence of the missive was a simple, gentle command: "Come to America; your home is with me now."

So she had packed her few belongings, sold or given away what could not be taken with her, and said good-bye to Skibbereen and the only home she had ever known. . . .

A sudden movement of the plane jolted Adelia back from memory. She sat back against the cushions of her seat, fingering the small gold cross she always wore around her neck. There was nothing left for her in Ireland, she told herself, fighting against the flutters of her stomach. Everything she had loved there was dead, and Padrick Cunnane was the only family she had left, the only link with what she had once had. She pushed back a surge of sudden, unaccustomed fear. America, Ireland—what difference did it make? Her shoulders moved restlessly. She would manage. Hadn't she always managed? She was determined not to be a burden to her uncle, the vague, shadowy man she knew only from letters, whom she had last seen when she'd been barely three. There would be work for her, she reasoned, perhaps on the horse farm her uncle had written of so often over the years. Her ability to work with animals was innate, and she had absorbed a varied knowledge of medicine through her experiences, her skill being such that she had often been called on to aid in a difficult calving or stitch up a rent hide. She was strong, despite her diminutive stature—and, she reminded herself with an unconscious squaring of shoulders, she was a Cunnane.

Surely, she told herself with more confidence, there would be a place for her at Royal Meadows, where her uncle worked as trainer for the Thoroughbred racing stock. There'd be no fields needing plowing, no cows needing milking, but she'd earn her bread and butter if she had to work as a scullery maid. She wondered suddenly, with a small frown, if they had scullery maids in America.

The plane touched down, and Adelia disembarked and entered the Dulles terminal in Virginia, where she found herself gaping in confusion, fascinated by the scene, confused by the babble of foreign tongues, the odd mixture of people. Her eyes lingered over an East Indian family in full native dress. She turned to observe two teenagers in faded denims strolling by hand in hand, followed by a scurrying middle-aged businessman clutching a leather briefcase.

Later, standing in the lobby, she looked around hoping to see a familiar face. Everyone rushing and hurrying, she thought. A body could be trampled and never seen again. . . .

"Dee, little Dee!" A man hurried toward her, a stockily built, compact man with a full thatch of curling gray hair, and she caught a glimpse of eyes as bright and blue as her father's before she was enveloped in a warm, crushing hug. The thought occurred to her that it had been a lifetime since anyone had held her so close.

"Little Dee, I would have known you anywhere." He pulled back and studied her face, eyes misty, smile tender. "It's like looking into Kate's face again—it's the image of your mother you are."

He continued to stare at her while she searched for her voice, his gaze taking in the deep, rich auburn hair falling in gleaming waves to her shoulders, the large, deep green of thickly lashed eyes, the tip-tilted nose and full mouth which Aunt Lettie had described as impudent, the face now of a startled pixie.

"What a beautiful sight you are," he said at last on a sigh of pure pleasure.

"Uncle Padrick?" she asked, finding a multitude of questions and emotions racing through her.

"And who else would you be thinking I might be?" He looked down at her with those well-remembered eyes, filled with love and laughter, and doubts, fears, and questions vanished in a wave of joy.

"Uncle Paddy," she whispered as she flung her arms around his neck.

As they drove along the highway from the airport, Adelia stared about her in fresh amazement. Never had she seen so many cars, and all flying by at an outrageous speed. Everything moved so fast, and the noise, she marveled silently, the noise was enough to wake the dead. Shaking her head, she began to bombard her uncle with questions.

How far was it they were going? Did everyone drive so fast in America? How many horses were at Royal Meadows? When could she see them? Questions buzzed in her mind and through her lips, and Paddy answered them tolerantly, finding the soft lilt of her voice as sweet as a summer breeze.

"Where is it I'll be working?"

He removed his eyes from the road a moment and glanced at her. "There's no need for you to be working, Dee."

"Oh, but Uncle Paddy, I must," she disagreed, turning to face him. "I could work with the horses; I've a way with animals."

Thick gray brows drew together in a doubtful frown. "I didn't bring you all this way to be putting you to work." Before she could protest, he went on. "And I don't know what Travis would be thinking about me hiring my own niece."

"Oh, but I'd do anything." She brushed back masses of chestnut hair. "Groom the horses, muck out the stalls, cart hay—it doesn't matter." Unknowingly, she used her eyes in an outrageous manner. "Please, Uncle Paddy, it's crazy I'd be in a week, not having some sort of work to do."

Her eyes won the small battle, and Paddy squeezed her hand. "We'll see."

So engrossed had she been in their conversation and the fascinating stream of traffic that she had lost all track of time. When Paddy pulled into a drive and halted the car, Adelia gazed about her with new wonder.

"Royal Meadows, Dee," he announced with a sweeping gesture of his hand. "Your new home."

The entrance to the long, winding drive was flanked by two tall stone pillars, and bushes studded with the promise of flowering buds continued along its path as far as she could see. The grass was brilliantly green over softly rolling hills, and horses grazed lazily in the distance.

"The finest horse farm in all of Maryland, sure as faith," Paddy added with possessive pride as he proceeded along the curving drive. "And—in Padrick Cunnane's opinion—the finest in the whole of America."

The car rounded a bend in the drive, and Adelia caught her breath as the main house came into view. An immense structure, or so it seemed to her, with three magnificent stories of old and muted stone. Dozens of windows winked in the gleaming sun like large, clear eyes. Wide and boldly glistening, they were a sharp contrast to the stone's mellowness. Skirting the top two stories were balconies, the design of wrought iron as intricate and delicate as the finest lace. The house stood on a gently sloping lawn of close-cropped green, graced with bushes and stately trees just awakening from their winter sleep.

"Beautiful, isn't it, Dee?"

"Aye," she agreed, awed by its size and elegance. "The grandest house I've ever seen."

"Well, our house isn't so grand as this." He turned the car left as the drive forked past the stone building. "But it's a fine place, and I hope you'll be happy there."

Adelia turned her attention to her uncle with a smile that transformed her face into a work of art. "I'll be happy, Uncle Paddy, as long as you're with me." Letting impulse guide her movements, she leaned over and kissed his cheek.

"Ah, Dee, I'm glad you're here." He took her hand in a firm grip. "You've brought the spring with you."

The car came to a halt, and Adelia turned to look out the front window, her mouth falling open at what greeted her eyes. An oval track commanded her view, and across from it stood a large white building, which Paddy identified as the stables. Fences and paddocks checker-boarded the area, and the scent of hay and horses drifted through the air.

In solemn amazement she gazed about, and the thought sped through her brain that she had not moved from one farm to another but from one world to another. At home, the farm had meant the earth, with its blessings and curses, a small barn in constant need of repair, a strip of pasture. Here, the space alone made her eyes widen, so much space to belong to one man. But as well as space, she recognized the efficiency and the order in fresh white buildings and split-rail fences. In the distance, where the hills began their soft roll, she saw mares grazing while their foals frolicked with the joy of spring and youth.

Travis Grant, she mused, recalling the name of the owner from Paddy's letters. *Travis Grant* knows how to care for what he owns. . . .

"There's my house." Now Paddy pointed out the opposite window. "Our house now."

Following his direction, she let out a cry of pleasure. The first story of the building was a large white garage, which she learned later serviced the trailers and trucks used for transporting the Thoroughbreds. Atop this was a stone structure, nearly twice as large as the farmhouse in which she had spent her life. It was a miniature replica of the main house, with the same native stonework and glistening windows graced with balconies.

"Come inside, Dee. Get a look at your new home."

He led her down a narrow, crushed stone path and up the stairs to the front door, opening it wide and nudging her ahead of him.

A bright, cozy room welcomed her, with pale green walls and a shining oak floor. A brightly checked sofa and matching chair invited her to sit in front of the raised hearth when the weather was cool, or contemplate rambling hills through wide, sheer-draped windows.

"Oh, Uncle Paddy!" She sighed, making an inadequate but expressive movement of her hands.

"Come, Dee, I'll show you the rest."

He led her through the house, her wide eyes growing larger with each new discovery, from the kitchen, with its sunny yellow fixtures and spotless counters, to the bath, where creamy ivory tiles made her dream of languishing for hours in hot, soapy water.

"This is your room, darlin'."

He opened the door across from the bath, and Adelia stepped inside. It was not an overly large room, but to her inexperienced eyes it was huge indeed. The walls were painted a robin's-egg blue, and sheer white curtains billowed and swayed at two open windows. The soft blue and white was repeated in the flower print of the bedspread, and a fluffy white rug lay on the wooden floor. The mirror over the maple dresser reflected the expression of stunned pleasure on her face. The knowledge that the room was to be hers brought unaccustomed tears to her eyes. Blinking them away, she turned and threw her arms around her uncle's neck.

Later, they strolled across the lawn toward the stables. Adelia had changed from the dress she had worn for the trip and was now clad in her more customary attire of jeans and cotton shirt, with her auburn curls pulled up and covered by a faded blue hat. She had convinced her uncle that rest was not what she needed, and that seeing the horses was what she wanted above all else. With her face glowing and eyes pleading, Paddy would have found it impossible to deny her anything.

Approaching the stables, they spotted a small group gathered around a chestnut Thoroughbred. The raised voices reached uncle and niece before their presence was noted.

"And what might be the problem here?" Paddy demanded.

"Paddy, glad you're back," a tall, husky man greeted him with obvious relief. "Majesty just had one of his spells. Gave Tom a bad kick."

Paddy transferred his attention to a small, spare young man seated on the ground, nursing his thigh and muttering.

"How bad is it, lad? Did you break anything?"

"Naw, nothing broke." Disgust was more evident than pain in both voice and face. "But I don't guess I'll be riding for a couple of days." Looking over at the dark chestnut, he shook his head with a mixture of resentment and reluctant amusement. "That horse may be the fastest thing on four legs, but he's meaner than a stomped-on cat."

"His eyes aren't mean," Adelia commented, and several pairs of eyes focused on her for the first time.

"This is Adelia, my niece. Dee, this is Hank Manners, assistant trainer. Tom Buckly, on the ground there, is an exercise boy, and George Johnson and Stan Beall, grooms." After introductions had been completed, Adelia quickly turned her attention back to the horse.

"They don't understand you, do they? Ah, but you're a fine fellow."

"Miss," Hank cautioned as she lifted a hand to stroke his muzzle, "I wouldn't do that. He's not in the best of moods to begin with, and he doesn't take to strangers."

"Ooch, but it's not strangers we'll be for long." Smiling, she stroked the length of his strong muzzle, and Majesty blew from wide nostrils.

"Paddy," Hank began in cautious warning, but the other man lifted a hand to silence him.

"A fine, beautiful horse you are. I've never seen another to compare with you, and that's the truth of it." She continued to speak as she ran her hands over his smooth neck and side. "You're built for running—strong, long legs and a fine, wide chest." Her hands moved over him freely as the horse remained still, ears at attention. She fondled his nose before resting her cheek against his neck. "I bet you're lonely for someone to talk to."

"I'll be switched." Hank observed Adelia's confident handling of the frisky colt and shook his head. "He's never let anyone do that before, not even you, Paddy."

"Animals have feelings as well, Mr. Manners." She brought her face from the Thoroughbred's neck and turned around. "He wants some pampering."

"Well, little lady, you certainly seem to have a way with him." He gave her a grin expressive of both amusement and admiration before turning his attention to Paddy. "He still needs to be exercised. I'll give Steve a call."

"Uncle Paddy." Adelia grabbed his arm on impulse, eyes shining with excitement. "I can do it. Let me take him out."

"I don't think a little lady like you could handle a big fire-breather like Majesty," Hank put in before Paddy could speak, and Adelia drew herself up to the full of her five feet two inches and tilted her chin.

"There's nothing on four legs I can't ride."

"Is Travis back yet?" Paddy concealed his smile and addressed Hank.

"No." He eyed Paddy through narrowed lids. "You're not thinking of letting her take him out?"

"I'd say she's about the right size—couldn't weigh over a hundred pounds." He gave his niece a thorough survey, one hand rubbing his chin.

"Paddy." Hank's hand descended on his shoulder, only to be ignored.

"You're a Cunnane, aren't you, lass? If you say you can handle him, then by the saints you can." Adelia beamed at her uncle and told him firmly she was indeed a Cunnane.

"God knows what the boss is going to say when he finds out," Hank muttered, finding himself against a solid wall of family alliance.

"Just leave Travis to me," Paddy answered with calm authority.

With a shrug of his shoulders and another incoherent mutter, Hank resigned himself to Paddy's loss of common sense.

"Once around the track, Dee," her uncle instructed. "Pace him to what you can handle; I can see from the look of him he wants his head."

Pulling her cap lower, she nodded, watching the

well-trimmed hooves paw the ground in impatience. With an easy vault she was in the saddle, and as Hank opened the wide gate she took Majesty onto the dirt track. Leaning forward, she whispered in his ear as he sidestepped and strained to be off.

"Ready, Dee?" Paddy called. As an afterthought he pulled out his stopwatch.

"Aye, we're ready." Straightening, she took a deep breath.

"Go!" he shouted, and horse and rider lunged down the track.

Crouching low over the Thoroughbred's neck, she urged him on to the speed for which he thirsted. The wind beat against her face, stinging her eyes, as they tore over the dirt at a pace she had never experienced, never imagined, but somehow had craved. It was a wild, exhilarating adventure; both horse and rider reveled in the unbridled sensation as they sped as one around the oval track, sun, wind, and speed their companions. She laughed and shouted to her partner, a new sense of freedom liberating her from the concerns and worries that had been a part of her life for so long. For a few short moments she was riding the clouds, away from pressure, away from responsibility, in a glorious haven that returned her to carefree childhood. When they came to the end of the run, she slowed the horse gradually to a halt and flung her arms around his gleaming neck.

"I'll be a son of a gun!" Hank said in simple astonishment.

"What were you expecting?" Paddy questioned, feeling as proud as a peacock with two tails. "She's a Cunnane." He held out the stopwatch for Hank to see. "Not a bad time either." With a final smile, he strutted over as Adelia slipped to the ground.

"Oh, Uncle Paddy!" Her eyes gleamed like emeralds against her flushed face, and she pulled off her cap, flourishing it in excitement. "He's the grandest horse in the world. It was like riding Pegasus himself!"

"That was nice riding, little lady." Hank extended his hand, shaking his head in admiration both for her ability and for the gleaming hair that now spilled over her shoulders.

"Thank you, Mr. Manners." She accepted his hand with a smile.

"Hank."

She grinned. "Hank."

"Well, Adelia Cunnane." Paddy slipped his arm around her shoulders. "Royal Meadows just hired another exercise boy. You've got yourself a job."

Lying in her bed that night, Adelia stared wide-eyed at the ceiling. So many things had happened, in so short a time, that her mind refused to relax and allow her body to rest.

After her ride on the Thoroughbred, she had been taken through the stables, introduced to more hands and more horses, shown into a tackroom that contained more leather than she had ever seen in one place at one time, and exposed to more people and more things than she believed she had ever been exposed to in her life. And all in the course of one day.

Paddy had prepared their dinner, firmly refusing assistance, and she had merely watched as he bustled around the kitchen. The stove, she decided, had more to do with magic than technology. And a machine that washed and dried the dishes at a touch of a button—marvels! Hearing about such things and reading about them was one matter, but seeing them with your own eyes . . . it was easier to believe in the Pooka and the little people. When, with a sigh, she said as much to her uncle, he threw back his head and laughed until tears flowed down his cheeks, then enveloped her in a hug as crushing as the one he had greeted her with at the airport.

They had eaten at the small dinette set in the kitchen window, and she had answered all his questions about Skibbereen. The meal was full of talking and laughing, and Paddy's eyes twinkled continually at her colorful descriptions and outrageous stories. She elaborated here and there, her hands working with her words, brows raising over guileless eyes as she stretched truth into an obvious exaggeration. Her uncle had noticed the faint shadows under them, however, and urged her to retire early, overcoming her protests with the deft suggestion that she had needed to be fresh in the morning.

So Adelia had obeyed, drawing a steaming tub and wallowing in unfamiliar luxury for what she knew Aunt Lettie would have considered a sinful amount of time. When at last she lay between the cool, fresh sheets, she found it impossible to relax. Her mind was full, crowded with new sensations, new images; and her body, so used to complete exhaustion before sleep, was unable to cope with the lack of physical exertion. Easing out of bed, she exchanged her nightdress for jeans and shirt and, piling her hair once more under the absurd cap, slipped noise- lessly from the sleeping house.

The night was clear, cool, and quiet, a vague breeze sweetening the air, only the bright, insistent call of a whippoorwill breaking the stillness. The light of the half moon guided her toward the stables as she strolled with- out thought of destination over the smooth new grass. The stillness, the familiar scent of animals, reminded her of home, and suddenly she felt a contentment and peace she had not even known she had lived without.

Hesitating outside the door of the large white stables, she debated whether she dare enter and spend the last of her evening with the horses. Having decided there was no harm in it, she was reaching out for the handle when an iron grip closed around her arm and whirled her around, and she was lifted off her feet for a moment like a rag doll.

"Just what do you think you're doing? And how did you get in here?"

She stared wordlessly at the owner of the harsh, angry voice, a vague shadow silhouetted in the dim moonlight, looming over her like an avenging giant. She searched for her own voice, but the combination of shock and pain had stolen it. Her words slipped down her throat as she felt herself being dragged into the building.

"Here, let's have a look at you," the voice growled as its owner switched on the lights. He spun her around, dislodging her cap, and the glory of her hair escaped its confinement to form a fiery cascade down her back.

"What the . . . you're a girl!" He released his firm hold and Adelia stepped back and began to give him both sides of her Irish tongue.

"Sure and it's observant you are to be noticing that—" She rubbed her arm vigorously while her green eyes glared up at her astonished assailant. "And who are you coming around grabbing innocent people and crushing their bones? A great, hulking bully you are, sneaking up on a body and dragging and pulling them about! A horse-whipping is what you're deserving for scaring the life from me and nearly breaking my arm in the process—"

"You may be pint-sized, but you're packed with dynamite," the man observed, obviously amused. He wondered as he looked over her softly rounded shape how he could have mistaken her for a boy. "From your accent I could make a guess that you're little Dee, Paddy's niece."

"I'm Adelia Cunnane, but it's not your little Dee I am." She regarded him with unconcealed resentment. "And it's not me who's having the accent. It's you!"

He threw back his head and roared with laughter, increasing Adelia's fury. "Oh, I am glad to have made you so happy." Folding her arms across her chest, she tossed her head, rich dark curls swinging wildly. "And who in the world are you, I'd like to know?"

"I'm Travis," he answered, still grinning. "Travis Grant."

CHAPTER TWO

It was Adelia's turn to gape at her companion. As the mists of fury cleared from her eyes, she saw him clearly for the first time. He was tall and powerfully built, and the sleeves of his shirt were carelessly rolled above his elbows, revealing deeply tanned muscular arms. He had chiseled features, clear and sharp, and his eyes were so blue against the brown of his skin that they startled the casual onlooker. His hair was rich and full, thick black curls in a disarming disarray to his collar, and the mouth that continued to grin at her was well formed, showing strong white teeth.

This was the man she was to work for, this was the man she needed to impress, Adelia's brain registered numbly, and she had just raked him clean with her furious tongue.

"Jakers," she whispered, shutting her eyes a moment and wishing she could disappear in a puff of smoke.

"I'm sorry we met under such, uh . . ."—he hesitated, his mouth twitching again—"confusing circumstances, Adelia. Paddy's been on top of the world since he made arrangements to bring you over from Ireland."

"I didn't expect to be meeting you till tomorrow, Mr. Grant." She clung desperately to pride and kept her voice even. "Uncle Paddy said you wouldn't be back."

"I didn't expect to find a half-pint fairy invading my stables," Travis returned, grinning once again.

Adelia straightened her spine and threw him a haughty look. "I couldn't sleep, so I came for a walk. I was thinking I might look in on Majesty."

"Majesty's a very high-strung animal," Travis admonished, his gaze roaming over her from top to bottom. "You'd best keep a respectable distance."

"And how will I be doing that?" she demanded imperiously, disconcerted by his masculine appraisal. "I'm to be exercising him regularly."

"The devil you are!" His eyes rose to hers and narrowed. "If you think I'd let a slip of a thing like you on my prize colt, you've lost your senses."

"I've already been on your prize colt." Anger returned, and her head tossed with it. "I rode around your track on him in fine time."

"I don't believe it." He took a step toward her, and her

head was forced to tilt still further. "Paddy wouldn't let you up on Majesty."

"I'm not in the habit of lying, Mr. Grant," Adelia retorted with great dignity. "The boy, Tom, got a kick for his trouble, so I rode Majesty instead."

"You rode Majesty?" Travis repeated in slow, even tones.

"That I did," she agreed, then, noting the anger hardening the blue eyes, sped on. "He's a beauty, rides like the wind, but he's not bad-tempered. He wouldn't have been kicking Tom if the boy had understood him better." She was speaking rapidly, not giving Travis an opportunity to comment. "The poor thing just needed someone to talk to him, someone to show him he was loved and appreciated."

"And you can talk to horses?" Travis's lips curved on the question.

"Aye," she agreed, unaware of the mocking gleam that lit his eyes. "Anyone can if they've a mind to. I know animals, Mr. Grant. I worked with the vet back in Skibbereen, and I know a bit about healing as well. I would never do anything to bring harm to Majesty or any of your other horses. Uncle Paddy trusted me; you mustn't be angry with him."

He said nothing to this, only took his time studying her as her extraordinary eyes unknowingly employed their power. As his silence and intense regard continued, she felt a small tingle of fear, mixed with another sensation, strange and foreign, that she was unable to decipher.

"Mr. Grant," she began, swallowing pride to plead. "Please, give me a chance—a fortnight, no more." She took a deep breath and moistened her lips. "If you don't want me after that, just tell me, and I'll abide by your decision. I'll tell Uncle Paddy I'm not happy with the job, that I want to be doing something else."

"Why would you do that?" His head tilted as if to gain a new perspective.

"It's what I'd have to do," she returned with a shrug and a push at her tumbled hair. "Otherwise I'd be putting him in the middle. He's devoted to you and to this place—I know that from the letters he wrote me—but he's taken me on as his responsibility now. If I told him you had fired me, his loyalties would be torn in two. I'll not be the cause of that. Will you give me a two-week trial, Mr. Grant?" *Pride goeth before destruction,* she quoted silently, trying to remember Aunt Lettie's lectures on humility.

She stood, determined not to squirm under his silent contemplation, wishing he would not look at her as if he could read the thoughts running through her brain.

"All right, Adelia," he said at length. "You'll have your two-week trial, just between us."

A brilliant smile lit her face and she extended her hand. "Thank you, Mr. Grant. I'm grateful to you."

He accepted her hand, but his returning smile faded, a frown replacing it as he turned her palm up and examined it. Her hand was exquisitely small, fingers long and tapering, but it was rough and calloused from years of the abuse of labor. The continued contact was sending odd tingles through her body, and she looked down helplessly at the hand under his critical scrutiny.

"Is something the matter?" she asked in a voice she barely recognized.

He raised his eyes and looked into hers with an expression she could not fathom. "It's a crime for such a tiny hand to be as hard and rough as any ditchdigger's."

Unaccountably stung by his softly spoken words, she jerked her hand away, holding it behind her back. "I'm sorry they're not as soft as a lily, Mr. Grant. But it's not lady's hands I'll be needing for the job I'm doing for you. If you'll excuse me now, I'll be going in."

She moved past him quickly, and he watched her run like a rabbit across the grass and out of sight.

Birdcalls broke the night's slumber, and Adelia woke with the sun. She dressed quickly, happy with the anticipation of beginning her job, a job which was to her more of a magic wish granted than labor. She was sure she could prove herself to Travis Grant. A new home, a new life, a new beginning; she stared out at the infant sun and knew it would bring nothing but wonders.

The scent of frying bacon led Paddy to the kitchen, and he stood for a moment watching her movements while she remained unaware of his presence. She was humming an old tune he remembered from childhood, and she seemed to him the essence of shining, unspoiled youth.

"Sure and it's the most beautiful sight these old eyes have awakened to in many a year."

She turned to him, her smile dimming the sunlight into insignificance. "Good morning to you, Uncle Paddy. It's a fine, beautiful day."

While they were eating, Adelia casually mentioned that she had met Travis Grant the previous night during her nocturnal wanderings.

"I was hoping to introduce you myself this morning." He took a bite of crisp bacon and raised his brows. "What did you think of him?"

She tactfully kept her opinion to herself and answered with a move of her shoulders. "I'm sure he's a fine, good man, Uncle Paddy, but I wasn't with him long enough to make judgments." *Big, arrogant bully,* her mind added. "But I did tell him about Tom's accident, and that I'd been taken on as an exercise boy."

"Did you, now?" A slow smile formed as he added jam to his bread. "And what did he say to that?"

"He's smart enough to trust Padrick Cunnane's opinion." Her fingers crossed under the table, and she wondered if she had earned another black mark in Aunt Lettie's often mentioned Record Book of the Angels.

A short time later, Adelia stood in front of Majesty,

rubbing his muzzle and holding an intimate conversation, unaware her actions were being observed by a pair of deep blue eyes.

"Morning, Paddy. I hear you've taken on a new hand."

Paddy broke off his conversation with Hank and greeted the tall, lean man. "Good morning to you, Travis. Dee told me she met you last night."

"Did she?" His lips curved as he continued to regard woman and horse.

"Wait till you see that little lady ride," Hank put in, shaking his head. "Could have knocked me over with a feather."

Travis inclined his head. "We'll soon see." He moved to where Adelia still stood speaking softly to the large Thoroughbred. "Hello again, half-pint. Does your friend ever answer you?"

She whirled, caught off guard, and regarded his amusement with indignation. "Aye, that he does, Mr. Grant, in his own way." She brushed past him to mount, and Travis stopped her with a hand on her wrist.

"Good Lord, did I do that?" He ran a finger over the dark smudge of bruises on her arm, and Adelia followed his glance before raising her eyes to his.

"That you did."

His eyes narrowed a moment, his fingers still light on her wrist. "We'll have to be more careful with you in the future, won't we, little Dee?"

"Not the first bruising I've had, nor likely to be the last, but you'll not be having any more occasion to be grabbing at me, Mr. Grant." With this, she swung herself astride Majesty and rode him onto the track. At Paddy's signal, the pair sprinted forward and galloped around the oval in a clean, steady rhythm.

"You wouldn't have been thinking I'd lost my senses hiring my niece, now, would you, lad?"

"I'll admit when she told me she'd been hired, I had a moment of doubt about your sanity," Travis answered, keeping his eyes on the small woman glued to the speeding horse. "But I've always trusted your judgment, Paddy; you've never let me down."

Later that morning Adelia worked in the stables, insisting over Paddy's objections that she assist in the grooming of some of the horses. A sound behind her caused her to turn her head, and she encountered two small boys, one the mirror image of the other. She closed her eyes in mock alarm.

"Saints preserve us, sure and it's losing my mind I am! I'm seeing double."

The boys collapsed into giggles and spoke in unison. "We're twins."

"Is that the truth?" She breathed a deep sigh of relief. "Well, I'm glad to know it. I was afraid a spell had been put on me."

"You talk just like Paddy," one boy observed, eyeing her with unrestrained curiosity.

"Do I, now?" She smiled down at their identical faces.

The boys were about eight, she hazarded, dark as gypsies, with snapping brown eyes. "The reason for that may be I'm his niece, Adelia Cunnane, just arrived from Ireland."

Two faces creased in two doubtful frowns. "He calls you little Dee, but you're not little, you're all grown up," one boy complained, the other nodding in agreement.

"That I am, as far as I ever will be, I'm afraid. But I was just a wee babe when I last saw Uncle Paddy, and I never did grow very tall, so I'm little Dee to him. And what might your names be?" she questioned, putting down the currycomb that she had been using.

"Mark and Mike," they announced, again in one voice.

"Don't be telling me who's who," she commanded, narrowing dark green eyes. "I'll guess; I'm mighty good at guessing." She circled them as they resumed giggling. "You'd be Mark, and you'd be Mike," she pronounced, placing a hand on each head. Two pairs of eyes stared at her in amazement.

"How did you know?" Mark demanded.

"I'm Irish," she stated simply, controlling a grin. "There's many of us from Ireland who's fey."

"Fey—what's that?" Mike chimed in, eyes wide and curious.

"That means I have strange, secret powers," Adelia claimed with a dramatic sweep of her hand. The two boys looked at each other and back at Adelia, suitably impressed.

"Mark, Mike." A woman entered the stables and shook

her head in despair. "I should have known the pair of you would be here."

Adelia stared at the newcomer, stunned by her beauty and elegance. She was tall and slender, clad in a simple but, to Adelia's untrained eye, overwhelmingly beautiful outfit of dark blue slacks and white silk blouse. Black, silky hair curled back from her face. Soft, rose-tinted lips and a classic straight nose led to a pair of heavily lashed deep blue eyes that Adelia identified as Travis's.

"I hope they haven't been bothering you." The woman peered down in indulgent exasperation. "They're impossible to keep track of."

"No, missus," Adelia said, wondering if there had ever been a lovelier woman. "They're fine lads. We've just been getting acquainted."

"You must be Paddy's niece, Adelia." The generous mouth curved in a smile.

"Aye, missus." Adelia managed a smile of her own and wondered what it would be like to be as graceful as a willow limb.

"I'm Trish Collins, Travis's sister." She extended her hand and Adelia gaped at it in horror. After Travis's words the previous night she was self-conscious about the state of her hands, and her mind began to work swiftly.

How could she put her hard, rough hand into such a lovely soft one! Yet there was no way out without being pointedly rude, so, wiping her palm on her jeans, she joined it with the one Trish offered. The other woman had noted Adelia's hesitation and concluded the reason for it when their hands met, but she made no comment.

At that moment, Travis entered the building, along with Paddy and a small, spare man Adelia did not recognize.

"Paddy!" The twins launched themselves at the stocky figure.

"Well, if it isn't Tweedledee and Tweedledum. And what mischief have you been up to this fine day?"

"We came to meet Dee," Mark announced. "She guessed which one of us was which."

"She's fey," Mike added soberly.

Paddy nodded, equally grave, his eyes twinkling as they met Adelia's over the two small heads. "Aye, that's a fact. There's been many a Cunnane who's had the sight."

"Adelia Cunnane"—Travis made introductions, a light smile playing over his mouth—"Dr. Robert Loman, our vet."

"Pleased to meet you, Doctor," Adelia greeted him, strategically keeping her hands behind her back.

"Rob's come to look over Solomy," Paddy explained. "She'll be foaling soon."

The pixie face lit with pleasure, and, looking down at her, Travis raised his brows. "Would you like to see her, Adelia?"

"Very much." She beamed him a smile, previous animosity forgotten.

"She's foaling quite late," Travis commented as the

group walked down the long length of stalls. "A Thoroughbred's official birthday is January the first, and normally we breed with that in mind. We just acquired Solomy six months ago, and of course she was already in foal. She's from a good line, and the stud she was bred to is by the same sire as Majesty."

"Then you must have big hopes for the foal," Adelia returned, thinking of Majesty's style and speed.

"I think," he said with a smile, "you could safely say we had hopes for this foal." Placing a hand on her shoulder, he turned her toward an enclosure. "Adelia," Travis said with amused formality, "meet Solomy."

She sighed with delight at the animal, a dark, gleaming bay mare with a mane of flowing black silk. Running her hand down the stark flash of white on the forehead, she looked into dark, intelligent eyes.

"You're a fine, beautiful lady." The caressing of the smooth hide was met with a whinny of approval.

"I suppose you'd like a closer look," Travis observed, opening the stall door and gesturing for her to enter.

She preceded him and the vet into the stall, carrying on a low conversation with Solomy as she explored the swollen belly, probing with gentle, capable fingers. After a few moments she stopped and turned concerned eyes to Travis's laughing ones.

"The foal's turned wrong."

The blue eyes lost their laughter and studied her intently.

"Quite right, Miss Cunnane," Robert Loman agreed with a professional nod. "A quick diagnosis." Entering the stall, he too ran hands over the mare's belly. "We're hoping the foal will turn before she's full term."

"But you're not thinking it's likely; her time's almost here."

"No, we're not." He turned back to her, faintly surprised and greatly curious as to her knowledge. "We have to deal with the possibility of a breech. Have you had any training?"

"More doing than training." She shrugged, uncomfortable at having the attention focused on her. "I worked with a vet back in Ireland. I've done some birthings and some stitching and splinting."

She stepped out of the stall to stand beside Paddy, watching as the vet proceeded with his work. Paddy's arm slipped around her shoulders, and she rested her head against him.

"I hate to think what a hard time she'll be having. We had a mare that carried breech once, and I had to turn the babe." She sighed with the memory. "I can still see her poor, trusting eyes on me. How I hated to hurt her."

"You turned a foal by yourself?" Travis demanded, drawing her attention from the past. "That's a difficult enough job for a full-grown man, let alone a little thing like you."

She bristled, bringing herself up to the full of her meager height. "It may be that I'm small, Mr. Grant, but I'm strong enough to do what needs to be done." She glared up at him, her pride under attack, and stuck out her chin. "I'll tell you this: for all our difference in size I can work the day through with you!"

Stifling a snort of laughter, Paddy focused on a spot on the ceiling as Travis regarded her indignation with cool, steady eyes. After a moment, she turned and began to walk toward the front of the building.

"Did you really see a horse being born, Dee?" The twins tagged after her full of excitement.

"Many a time, and cows and pigs and the like." She took a small hand in each of hers and continued over the concrete floor. "There was a time I birthed twin lambs, and that was the prettiest sight. . . ."

Travis continued to stare after her as her voice trailed off in the distance.

The next few days passed easily for Adelia as she became accustomed to a new life and new surroundings. On the occasions she spoke to Travis, she continually struggled to hold back the tongue he seemed to have a habit of provoking. He stirred strange feelings in her, feelings she could neither comprehend nor prevent, and her defense against them took shape in a quick retort and flashing eyes. Though she gave herself nightly lectures on the evils of temper, when confronted with him during the daylight hours her vow of restraint slipped through her fingers.

She found herself watching him once as he strode toward the stables, his blue denim work shirt straining over broad shoulders as he moved over the grass. He seemed to eat up the ground with a careless vitality. There was a strange pull at her heart, and she sighed, then bit her lip in annoyance. It was only that he was such a fine, strongly built man, she told herself, lean and powerful. She dismounted from the Thoroughbred she had been exercising and rubbed his neck vigorously. She had always admired strength and power, the same way she admired this strong, well-proportioned animal. Everyone she had met held Travis Grant in great respect and admiration. When he gave an order, it was carried out without question. Only Paddy, it seemed, had the right to advise or question.

But she was Adelia Cunnane, she reminded herself, and no man would get the better of her. She would not play peasant to his squire and pull her forelock when he passed by. She did her job, and did it well. He would have no cause to complain in that field. But she would speak her piece if she'd a mind to, and the devil take him if he didn't like it!

Late each afternoon, Adelia visited Solomy. She was sure the mare would deliver any day, and, knowing the birth would be a difficult one, she spent her visits comforting the mare and gaining her confidence.

"Soon you'll be having a fine, strong son or daughter," Adelia told her as she closed the stall door after her visit.

"I'd like to take you and the babe and bundle you off with me. What do you think himself would do about that?"

"He might be tempted to have you hanged for horse thieving."

She spun around, her eyes encountering Travis's powerful form resting idly against the next stall. "It's a bad habit you have of sneaking up and scaring a body to death," she snapped at him, assuming that the uneven beat of her heart was the result of surprise.

"I do happen to own this place, Adelia," he returned in low, calm tones that only increased her agitation.

"That's a fact I'm not likely to forget. There's no need to remind me." She tilted her chin in defiance of him and the continuing flutter of her stomach, knowing she should guard her words, and knowing the power to do so was beyond her. "I give you your day's work, but maybe you think I'm forgetting my place. Should I be bobbing a curtsy, Mr. Grant?"

"You impudent little wench," Travis muttered, straightening from his relaxed position. "I'm getting a bit weary of being stabbed by that sharp tongue of yours."

"Well, it's sorry I am about that. The best advice I can give is that you not be conversing with me."

"That's the best idea you've had." He grabbed her around the waist, lifting her a foot off the ground as their eyes warred with each other. "I've been wanting to do this since the first time you slashed at me with your sharp Irish tongue."

He crushed her mouth with his, cutting off a heated retort. Too surprised by his action to resist immediately, Adelia began to experience unfamiliar and disturbing sensations, a heat and weakness that she might feel on a day spent working in the field. His hands were like steel around her small waist, holding her body suspended in the air while his lips assaulted hers, entering her mouth with his tongue in a kiss that was both devastating and totally foreign to any she had ever known.

Pressed hard against him, lips joined, she felt his warmth, his essence, seeping into her, demanding and receiving her merging. She could feel the authority in the arms that held her, taste the knowledge on the lips that claimed hers, and body and mind surrendered to both. Unable to combat the turbulence of the unexplored, she felt it whirl her like a cyclone, spinning her toward the sun until the heat threatened to become fire.

And as each of her senses were assaulted and conquered, he continued to explore her mouth, feasting on it as a man who knew a woman's flavor. He took, and she knew nothing of the richness of the banquet she gave him, warm and ripe and fresh.

After a lifetime, he released her, dropping her back to the ground as she stared at him mutely, eyes huge with confusion.

"Well, half-pint, this is the first time I've seen you at a loss for words." He mocked her openly, the lips that had just conquered hers lifted in a smug, satisfied smile.

His taunt broke the strange hold over her mind and tongue, and her eyes lit with molten green fire. "You son of the devil," she began in a rich explosion, and what followed was a raging stream of Irish curses and dire predictions delivered in so strong an accent that it was nearly impossible to comprehend the words.

When her imagination had at last run dry, and she could only stand staring at him breathlessly, he threw back his head and laughed until she thought he would burst.

"Oh, Dee, you're a fabulous sight when you're breathing fire!" He took no trouble to hide his amusement, an infuriating grin glued to his face. "The madder you get, the thicker the brogue. I'm going to have to provoke you more often."

"I'm giving you warning," she returned in an ominous voice, which only widened the grin. "If you ever molest me again, it's more than my tongue you'll be feeling."

Lifting her head, she strode out of the stables, clutching the last threads of her dignity around her.

She said nothing to Paddy about her scene with Travis, and instead banged around the kitchen as she prepared dinner, uttering incoherent sentences about great arrogant beasts and strong-arm bullies. Her fury with Travis was intermingled with fury with herself. The fact that his touch had brought both excitement and unexplained pleasure angered her further, and she berated herself for the uncontrollable attraction she felt for him.

CHAPTER THREE

By the next day, Adelia's anger had faded. She was not given to prolonged periods of ill humor; rather, she exploded like a burst of flame, simmered, then slowly cooled down. There remained, however, a disturbing new awareness, an awareness both of herself and the unfamiliar longings of womanhood, and of the frustrating, attractive man who had released them.

She managed to avoid any face-to-face contact with Travis during the morning, going about her duties in the normal fashion while she kept a cautious eye alert for his approach. Duties complete, she strolled back for her daily visit with Solomy. Instead of leaning over the low barrier to greet her, as was Solomy's habit, Adelia found her lying on her side in the hay, breathing heavily.

"By all the saints and apostles!" Rushing inside, she knelt beside the raggedly breathing mare. "Your time's come, darlin'," she crooned, running her hands over the large mounded belly. "Just rest easy now. I'll be back." Springing up, she sped from the stables.

She spotted Tom in the far paddock and, cupping her hands, shouted, "Solomy's time's here. Get Travis—call the vet. Be quick!" Without waiting for an answer, she ran back inside to comfort the laboring horse.

She was murmuring and stroking the sweating hide when Travis and Paddy joined her. Soft words and gentle hands had calmed the mare, whose deep brown eyes were riveted on Adelia's dark green ones.

Travis knelt beside her, his hands joining hers on the gleaming skin, and though Adelia spoke to him, her eyes never left the mare's.

"The foal's still the wrong way; it must be turned, and quickly. Where's Dr. Loman?"

"He's had an emergency—can't be here for half an hour." His voice was clipped, his own attention on Solomy.

She turned her head and captured his gaze. "Mr. Grant, I'm telling you she doesn't have that long. The foal has to be turned now, or we'll lose them both. I can do it; I've done it before. It's God's truth, Mr. Grant, she hasn't much time."

They stared at each other for a long moment, Adelia's

eyes wide and pleading, his narrowed and intense. Solomy let out an agonizing whinny as a new contraction began.

"There, my love." Adelia switched her attention back to the mare, murmuring words of comfort.

"All right," Travis agreed, a long breath escaping through his teeth. "But I'll turn it. Paddy, call in some of the men to hold her down."

"No!" Adelia's protest caused the mare to start, and she spoke quietly again, using hands and voice to soothe. "You'll not bring a bunch of bruisers in here forcing her down and frightening her." Again she raised her eyes to Travis's and spoke with calm assurance. "She'll hold for me; I know how."

"Travis," Paddy intervened as he started to speak. "Dee knows what she's about." Nodding, Travis moved off to scrub his hands and arms.

"Have a care," she warned as he prepared to begin. "The babe's hooves will be sharp, and the womb can close on your hand quickly." Taking a deep breath, she lay her cheek against the mare's, hands circling the damp flesh in a steady rhythm as she began to croon in quiet Gaelic.

The mare shivered as Travis entered her, but remained still, listening to Adelia's comforting voice.

The air seemed to grow closer, heavy with Solomy's breathing and the mystical beauty of the ancient tongue Adelia murmured. It brought a heavy warmth to the spring afternoon, isolating them from all but the struggle for life.

"I've got him," Travis announced, sweat running unheeded down his face. His breath came quickly, and he muttered a steady stream of soft curses, but Adelia heard nothing, giving herself over to the mare. "It's done." He rested back on his heels, turning his attention to the woman at his side. She gave no sign to him, only continued her slow, rhythmic crooning, hands gently caressing, face buried in the mare's neck.

"Here it comes," Paddy cried, and she turned her head to watch the miracle of birth. When the foal finally emerged into the world, both woman and horse sighed and shuddered.

"It's a fine, strong son you have, Solomy. Ah, sure, and there's no more beautiful sight in the world than an innocent new life!"

She turned her glowing face to Travis and gave him a smile that rivaled the sun. Their eyes met, and the look deepened until it seemed to Adelia that time had stopped. She felt herself being drawn into fathoms of dark blue, unable to breathe or speak, as if some invisible shield had descended, insulating them from all but each other.

Can love come in an instant? her numbed brain demanded. Or has it been there forever? The answer was forestalled as Robert Loman arrived, shattering the magic that had held her suspended.

She stood up quickly as the vet began to question Travis on the colt's delivery. A wave of giddiness washed over her as she rose, and she sank her teeth into her lower lip to combat the weakness. Keeping the mare calm had been an enormous strain, almost as if she had experienced each pang of labor, and the unexpected rush of emotion when Travis had held her eyes had left her drained and dizzy.

"What is it, Dee?" Paddy's voice was full of concern as he took her arm.

"Nothing." She placed her palm to her spinning head. "Just a bit of a headache."

"Take her home," Travis commanded, regarding her closely. Her eyes were bright and enormous against her pallor, and she appeared suddenly small and helpless. Rising, he moved toward her, and she stepped back, terrified he would touch her.

"There's no need." She kept her voice calm and even. "I'll just go up and have a wash. I'm fine, Uncle Paddy." She smiled into his frowning face, avoiding Travis's at all costs. "Don't you worry." Stepping from the stall, she moved quickly from the building, filling her lungs with fresh, clean air.

That evening found Adelia quiet and pensive. She was unused to confusion and uncertainty, characteristically knowing what needed to be done and doing it. Her life had always been basic, the fundamental existence of meeting demands as they came. There had been no room for indecision or clouded reasoning in a world that was essentially black or white.

She lingered in the kitchen after dinner, reasoning with herself with firm common sense. The foaling had been difficult, the strain emptying her body of its strength, and the sight of the new colt had fogged her brain. These were the reasons she had reacted so strongly to Travis. She could hardly be in love with him; she barely knew him, and what she did know was not altogether to her taste. He was too big, too strong, too self-confident, and too arrogant. He reminded her of a feudal lord, and Adelia was too Irish to have any liking for landed gentry.

However, after her work was done and self-analysis complete, she remained oddly weary and disturbed. Sitting down on the floor at Paddy's feet, she laid her head in his lap with a deep sigh.

"Little Dee," he murmured, stroking the thick auburn curls. "You're working too hard."

"What nonsense," she disagreed, snuggling deeper into the still newness of comfort. "I haven't worked a full day since I arrived. The day would not nearly be over yet if I was back on the farm."

"Was it hard for you, lass?" he asked, thinking she might now be ready to talk of it.

Again Adelia sighed, moving her shoulders restlessly. "I wouldn't say hard, Uncle Paddy, but everything changed after Mother and Da died."

"Poor little Dee, such a wee thing to be losing so much."

"I thought my world had ended when they died," she

whispered, hardly aware she was speaking aloud. "I'm thinking I died myself for a time, so angry and frightened I was, then numb, feeling nothing. But I began remembering how they were together. No two people could have loved each other more. Such a fine, full loving they had, even a child could see it."

So engrossed were the man and woman in the words being spoken that neither heard the sound of feet climbing the stairs. Travis halted in his action of knocking, dropping his hand as he watched the poignant picture, and Adelia's words drifted through the screen.

"The only thing I could give them was the farm, and it was all I had left of them. Poor Aunt Lettie, she worked so hard and I was a constant cross for her to bear." She laughed as memory flickered through her mind. "She never could understand why I had to ride so fast. 'Sure and it's your neck you'll be breaking,' she used to call after me, shaking her fist. 'Who'll be helping with the plowing if you bash in your head on the road?' Then when I'd have one of my rages and go off shouting and cursing— and it's often, I'm afraid, I did just that—she'd cross herself and start praying for my doomed soul.

"Jakers, but we worked." With a long breath she shut her eyes. "But it was too much for one woman and a half-grown girl, and not enough money to hire help, and none to be made without it. Do you know how it is, Uncle Paddy, when you see the thing you need, but the closer you get the further away it is? Always moving away from you, always just out of your reach. Sometimes, when I look back, I can't tell one day from the rest. Then Aunt Lettie had that stroke, and how she hated to be lying there helpless day after day."

"Why did you never let me know how things were?" Paddy questioned, looking down at her dark head. "I could have helped you—sent you money, or come back myself."

She raised her head and smiled at him. "Aye, that's just what you would have done, and to what good? Throwing your money away, taking yourself from the life you'd chosen . . . I'd not have had that for a minute, and neither would Aunt Lettie, or Mother and Da. The farm's gone, just as they are, and so is Ireland. Now I have you, I'm not needing another thing."

Looking into his eyes, seeing the concern and regret written there, she wished suddenly she had kept her own counsel. "How is it, Padrick Cunnane, that a fine, handsome man like yourself never took a wife?" Her grin turned impish, and devils danced in her eyes. "There must have been dozens of ladies willing. Have you never found a woman to love?"

He touched her cheek, giving her a wistful smile. "Aye, lass, that I did, but she chose your father."

Deep green eyes filled with surprise that melted into sympathy. "Oh, Uncle Paddy!" She flung her arms around him, and Travis turned from the door and walked silently down the stairs.

The next morning the air seemed to sigh with spring, whispering promises of flowers and cool, leafy trees. To Adelia it brought memories of other springs. Spring was the time the earth asked to be replenished and grew pregnant with new life. Her world had always revolved around the earth, its gifts and hardships, its demands and promises.

From the balcony of Paddy's house she surveyed the land that was Travis's. It seemed to stretch on and on with the easy, gentle roll of a calm sea. Green and brown waves were dotted not with boats but with finely sculptured Thoroughbreds. It ran through her mind that she had no conception of what lay over the last hill. This land was still a stranger. From the moment of her arrival in America she had seen little else but what belonged to Travis Grant.

Over the pure, sweet air floated an occasional whinny or the quick call of a bird. But for this, there was silence. There was no strident call of rooster announcing the new day, no fields turned up waiting to receive seeds, no weeds demanding uprooting. All at once homesickness washed over her so intensely that she could only shut her eyes and weather the storm.

So much is gone, she thought, and her hands hugged her elbows as if in comfort. I'll never be able to go back, never see the farm again. Sighing, she opened her eyes and tried to shake off the melancholy. There's nothing to be done about it; the bridges are burned. This is home now, and if it's not really mine, it's the closest I'll come.

"Where are you, lass?"

Adelia started slightly as Paddy's arm slipped around her; then she sighed again and rested against his shoulder. "Back on the farm, I suppose. Thinking about spring planting."

"It's a day for it, isn't it? The air's cool, and the sun's warm." He gave her shoulder a small squeeze, then clucked his tongue as if in regret. "I've got to go into town today. It's a pity."

"A pity?"

"I was hoping to get some seeds in around the walkway. Thought I might make a flower bed in front of the house, too." He shook his head and sighed. "Just don't know when I'll find the time."

"Oh, I'll do it, Uncle Paddy. I've plenty of time." Drawing away, she looked at him with such innocent acceptance of his trumped-up excuse that he nearly broke into a grin.

"Little Dee, I couldn't ask you to do all that on your day off." He creased his face into doubtful lines and patted her cheek. "No, it's too much. I'll get to it as soon as I find a bit of time."

"Uncle Paddy, don't be silly. I'd love to do it." Her smile was blooming again, chasing the clouds from her eyes. "Just show me what you want done."

"Well . . ." He permitted her to argue a few more minutes before allowing himself to be persuaded.

Armed with a myriad of seed packs and a small spade, Adelia stood on the patch of lawn surrounding Paddy's house and mentally mapped out her landscaping. Petunias along the walks, asters and marigolds against the house, impatiens for the border. And sweet peas, she thought with a smile, for the trellis she had asked Paddy to buy. In the fall, she decided, I'll plant bulbs, as many as the ground will hold. Daffodils and tulips. Satisfied with her planning, she began to turn the earth.

The sun grew warmer, and her sleeves were soon pushed past her elbows. In the distance she could hear the sounds of men and horses going through their daily routine: a shout, laughter, the thud of hooves on dirt. But soon, lost in her planting, she drifted apart. Softly, she began to sing a song remembered from childhood, the words soothing and familiar. The scent of fresh earth eased the ache with which she had awakened.

A shadow fell across her. Twisting her head, she dropped the spade nervously as Travis looked down at her.

"I've made you stop. I'm sorry."

He seemed impossibly tall as he stood over her. She craned her neck and squinted against the sun. It glowed in an aura around his head, and for one fanciful moment she thought he looked like a knight on his way to van-quish dragons.

"No, you just startled me." Picking up the spade, Adelia told herself she was a fool and began to work again.

"I didn't mean the planting." He crouched down beside her, his shoulders brushing hers. "I mean the song. It sounded very old and very sad."

"Aye, it's both." She inched away, carefully patting soil over seeds. "A lot of Gaelic songs are old and sad."

Folding his legs under him, he sat easily on the grass and watched her. "What's it about?"

"Oh, love, of course. The saddest songs are always about love." She lifted her head to smile at him. His face was close, his mouth a breath away. The spade hung sus-pended in her hand as she only stared, wondering what she would do if the whisper of space was gone and his mouth found hers.

"Is love always sad, Adelia?" His voice was as soft as the breeze that danced around them.

"I don't know. I . . ." She felt the weakness growing stronger and tore her eyes from his. "We were talking about songs."

"So we were," Travis murmured, then brushed back the hair that curtained her face. She swallowed and began digging with renewed interest. "I never thanked you properly for your help yesterday with Solomy."

"Oh, well . . ." Moving her shoulders, she kept her eyes

on the ground. "I didn't do that much. I'm just glad Solomy and the foal are well. Do you like flowers, Mr. Grant?" she asked, needing to change the subject.

"Yes, I like flowers. What are you planting?" His voice was casual as he lifted a package of seeds.

"All different kinds," she told him, this time able to raise her head and smile. "They'll be a lovely sight by summer. Your soil's rich, Mr. Grant; it wants to give." She squeezed a handful of earth, then held it out in her palm.

"You'd know more about that than I." Taking her fingertips, he studied the soil in her hand. "You're the farmer."

"I was," she amended and tried to free her hand.

"I'm afraid I don't know much about planting— vegetables or flowers." He ignored her attempts to pull her fingers away and brought his eyes to hers. "I suppose it's a gift."

"It just takes time and effort, like anything else. Here." Concluding that if she gave him something to do, her hand would be released, she held out some seeds. "Just drop a few in and cover them up. Don't crowd them," she instructed as he obeyed. "They want room to spread. Now you cover them up and let nature take over." Smiling, she absently brushed a hand across her cheek. "No matter what you do, nature has the last word in any case. A farmer knows that here the same way a farmer knows that in Ireland."

"So, now that I've put them in," he concluded with a grin, "I just sit back and watch them grow."

"Well," she said, tilting her head and giving him a sober stare, "there might be a thing or two more, like watering or weeding. These seeds will take quick, and the flowers will pop up before you know it. I'm putting in sweet peas there." She pointed across the lawn, forgetting that she still held the soil in her other hand. "When the breeze comes up at night, the scent will drift through the windows. There's something special about sweet peas. They start off so small, but they'll just keep climbing as long as there's something to hold on to. There should be a rosebush," she murmured almost to herself. "When the scents mingle together, it's like nothing else on earth. Red roses, just starting to open up."

"Are you homesick, Dee?" The question was low and gentle, but her head whipped back around in surprise.

"I . . ." Shrugging, she bent her face to her work again, uncomfortable that he had read her emotions so clearly.

"It's quite natural." He lifted her chin with his hand until their eyes met again. "It's not easy to leave behind everything you've ever known."

"No." Moving her shoulders again, she turned away and began to spread marigold seeds. "But I made the choice, and it truly was what I wanted. It's what I want," she amended with more firmness. "I can't say I've been unhappy a moment since I got off the plane. I can't go back, and I don't really know if I'd want to if I could. I've a new life now." Tossing back her hair, she smiled at him. "I like it here. The people, the work, the horses, the land." Her hand made a wide, encompassing gesture. "You've a beautiful home, Mr. Grant; anyone could be happy here."

He brushed a trace of dirt from her cheek and returned her smile. "I'm glad you think so, but it's your home, too."

"You're a generous man, Mr. Grant." She kept her gaze level with his, but her smile was suddenly sad and sweet. "There's not many who'd say that and mean it, and I'm grateful to you. But for better or worse, the farm was mine." Sighing, she traced a finger through the soil. "It was mine. . . ."

Late the next morning when Adelia turned one of the Thoroughbreds she had been exercising over to a groom, Trish Collins approached her with a friendly smile. "Hello, Adelia. How are you settling in?"

"Fine, missus, and good morning to you." She regarded Trish's dark beauty with fresh admiration. "And where are the lads this morning?"

"In school, but they'll be here tomorrow. They're half crazy to get a look at the new foal."

"A beautiful sight he is."

"Yes, I've just had a peek at him. Travis told me how marvelous you were with the mare."

Her mouth dropped open a moment, surprised and inordinately pleased that Travis should have praised her. "I was glad to help, missus. Solomy did all the work."

"Call me Trish," she requested with a shake of her head. "Missus makes me feel old and crotchety."

"Oh, no, missus, you're not old at all," she blurted out, horrified.

"I wouldn't like to think so. Travis and I won't be thirty-one until October." Trish laughed at the stricken face.

"So you're twins as well," Adelia concluded, feeling more at ease. "I suppose that's why I saw your brother's eyes the first time I met you."

"Yes, we do bear a strong resemblance to each other, which is why I constantly tell him how handsome he is." She smiled at Adelia's light, musical laugh. "Am I holding you up? Are you busy?"

"No, missus." At the raised brow, she amended, "No, Trish. I was about to take my break and fix a cup of tea. Would you like one?"

"Yes, thank you, I would."

They paused at the top of the stairs to the garage house as Adelia bent to pick up a long, narrow white box. "Now, what might this be?"

"Flowers would be my guess," Trish concluded, indicating the printed name of a local florist.

"What would they be doing here?" She frowned down at the box as they stepped inside. "Someone must have left them at the wrong house."

"You might open them and find out," Trish suggested, amused by the frown of concentration. "As your name's on the box, they just might be for you."

Auburn curls danced as she shook her head and chuckled. "Now, who'd be sending me flowers?" Setting the box on a table, she opened the lid and gave a small cry of pleasure. "Oh, just look! Have you ever seen such a sight?" The box was filled with long-stemmed roses, deep blood red, their half-closed petals soft as velvet to her hesitant fingers. Lifting one out, she held it under her nose. "Ah," she breathed and passed the bloom to Trish. "Straight from heaven." Then, shrugging, she returned to practical matters. "Who would they be for?"

"There should be a card."

Locating the small white note, Adelia read it silently, and her green eyes widened as she read the words a second time. She brought her gaze from the slip of paper to meet an openly curious regard. "They're for me." Her voice mirrored disbelief as she handed Trish the card. "Your brother sent them to thank me for helping with Solomy."

"'Dee, to thank you for your help with the new foal. Travis,'" Trish read aloud, and added under her breath, "You certainly wax poetic on occasion, brother."

"In my whole life," Adelia murmured, touching a silky petal, "no one has ever given me flowers."

Trish looked over quickly, observing the shimmering eyes and the stunned pleasure passing over Adelia's features. Pushing tears back, Adelia spoke on a sigh. "This was a lovely thing for your brother to do. I had a rosebush at home—red roses they were, too. My mother planted it." She smiled, feeling incredibly happy. "It makes them that much more special."

Later, they walked back to the stables. As they drew near, Travis and Paddy emerged from the building, and the Irishman greeted them both with a beaming smile.

"Travis, we've died and gone to heaven. Sure and it's two angels coming to greet us."

"Uncle Paddy." Adelia tweaked his cheek. "Living in America hasn't lessened your gift for blarney." Looking up at the man who towered above the rest of them, she treated him to the pure, honest smile of a child. "I want to thank you for the flowers, Mr. Grant. They're lovely."

"I'm glad you liked them," he answered, enjoying the smile. "It was little enough after what you did."

"Here's something more for you, Dee." Paddy reached into his pocket and withdrew a piece of paper. "Your first week's wages."

"Oh," Adelia said with a grin. "It's the first time I've been paid in money for doing anything." She frowned at the check, confused, and Travis's brows rose in amusement at her expression.

"Is something wrong with it, Adelia?"

"Yes . . . no . . . I . . ." she stumbled, and brought her eyes to Paddy.

"You're wondering what it is in pounds," he concluded, grinning merrily.

"I don't think I figured it right," she answered, embarrassed under Travis's gaze.

Chuckling, he did some mental arithmetic and told her. Confusion changed to astonishment and something close to terror.

"What would I be doing with that kind of money?"

"First time anyone around here complained about being overpaid," Travis commented and received a baleful glance.

"Here." Adelia turned her attention back to her uncle and held the check out to him. "You take it."

"Now, why would I be doing that, Dee? It's your money; you earned it."

"But I've never had so much money at one time in my whole life." She sent him a pleading look. "What will I do with it?"

"Go out and buy some of those female trappings and folderol," he suggested vaguely, waving his hand, then pushing the check back at her. "Treat yourself to something. The good Lord knows it's about time."

"But, Uncle Paddy—"

"Why don't you buy yourself a dress, Dee?" Travis inserted with a grin. "I'm curious to see if you've got legs under those jeans."

Adelia's head snapped up, and she eyed Travis with a dangerous gleam. "Aye, I've legs, Mr. Grant, and I've been told a time or two it's not a trial to look at them. But you'll not have to be worrying yourself; it's not dresses I need to tend your horses."

His grin only widened as he gave a negligent shrug.

"It doesn't matter to me if you want to be taken for a boy."

Her wrath increased as he had meant it to, and her eyes fired sharp green daggers. "There's only one who ever made that mistake, he being an ill-mannered, bad-tempered brute of a man without a brain working in his empty head."

"Shopping's a marvelous idea," Trish broke in, deciding it was time to play peacemaker. "As a matter of fact, Travis"—she smiled and fluttered her lashes—"Dee's taking the rest of the day off so we can do just that."

"Oh, really?" he returned dryly, folding his arms across his chest.

"Yes, *really*. Come on, Dee."

"But I haven't finished. . . ."

Trish linked her arm through the still protesting Adelia's and propelled her to a late-model compact. Before she had time to think things through, Adelia had an account at a local bank, a checkbook, and more cash than her apprehensive brain could comprehend.

"Now"—Trish backed the compact from its parking space—"we're going shopping."

"But what will I buy?" She stared at Trish's clear profile in complete consternation.

Stopping at a red light, Trish turned to her anxious face. "When's the last time you bought something for yourself for the fun of it? Have you ever bought something because you wanted it instead of just needing it?"

The light changed, and as she joined the flow of traffic she sighed at Adelia's blank expression. "Don't misunderstand. I'm not saying people should just throw their money away, but it's high time you did something for yourself." Glancing at Adelia's furrowed brow, she smiled and shook her head. "You can afford to slow down, Dee, take a day off, buy something foolish, stretch your wings, take a breath." She grinned as Adelia merely stared at her. "The sky will not fall if Adelia Cunnane takes time off to have some fun."

No one was more surprised than Adelia when, in fact, she did have fun. The large mall fascinated her with its various small specialty shops and large department stores. There were more clothes than she had ever seen, in colors and soft materials that had her staring and touching in frank admiration.

While Adelia gazed around her, Trish examined garments critically, going from rack to rack, dismissing dozens of dresses, skirts, and blouses, occasionally removing an item and hanging it over her arm. Finding herself in a changing room, Adelia could only stare at the garments Trish had placed on a hook. Then, taking a deep breath, she stripped off her shirt and jeans and slipped on a soft jersey dress in muted shades of green.

The silky material felt strange and wonderful to her skin, clinging to gentle curves and falling gracefully below her knees. She gaped at the stranger in the mirror, her hand seeking the cross at her throat to assure herself that she was still the same person.

"Dee," Trish called from outside the curtain, "have you got one on yet?"

"Aye," she answered slowly, and Trish pulled the curtain aside, smiling in triumph at the reflection in the full-length mirror.

"I knew that dress was you the minute I saw it."

"It doesn't feel like me," Adelia mumbled, then turned to face Trish directly. "It's beautiful, but what would I do with so grand a dress? I exercise horses. I work in a stable—"

"Dee," Trish interrupted firmly. "Whatever your occupation, you're still a human being; you're still a woman, an exceptionally beautiful woman." Adelia's eyes widened, and her mouth opened to protest, but before the words could be uttered Trish took her by the shoulders and turned her to face her reflection. "Look at yourself, really look," she ordered in no-nonsense terms, then shifted to gentler tones. "There'll be times when you'll want only to be a woman; this dress is for those times. Now," she said with practical authority as she released her, "try something else on."

For the rest of the afternoon Adelia allowed Trish to take command. For the first time in more than a decade, she permitted someone else to make all the decisions, and somehow she found she was having fun. They halted in front of a cosmetics counter, and Trish began spraying scents until Adelia grumbled in protest.

"This." Trish selected one of the bottles she had sampled. "Light and delicate, with just a touch of spirit." Paying for the cologne, she handed the package to Adelia. "A present."

"Oh, but I can't!"

"Yes, you can. Friends get pleasure from giving presents. Now, that marvelous skin of yours doesn't need any help, but I think we'll accent your eyes—and some lipstick, nothing too dramatic." She stopped and laughed. "I'm bullying you, aren't I?"

"Aye," Adelia agreed, feeling caught up in a genial whirlwind and finding she liked it.

"Well, you needed it," Trish said firmly. "Is there anything else you want?"

She hesitated, then blurted out quickly, "Something for my hands. Your brother said I've hands like a ditch-digger's."

"That man!" she exclaimed in disgust. "He's the epitome of tact and diplomacy."

"Trish, hello!"

Adelia turned to see a flash of amazing silver-blond hair before Trish was enveloped in an exuberant embrace. Adelia's first startled impression was of lavish curls and musky scent.

"I'm so glad to see you, darling." A high, bubbly voice drifted with the scent. "It's been weeks."

"Hello, Laura." With an affectionate smile, Trish disentangled herself. "It's good to see you, too. Laura Bowers—Adelia Cunnane."

"How do you do, Mistress Bowers." The greeting was returned with a flash of beautiful white teeth before Laura's attention returned to Trish.

"Darling, how is that fabulous brother of yours?"

"Fabulous," Trish returned, giving Adelia a quick grin of mischief.

"Don't tell me he's not pining after Margot?" Laura sighed and gave a flutter of extensive lashes. "I was so hoping to offer him my comfort. Not even a tear or two to be dried?"

"He seems to be bearing up under the strain," Trish returned. Hearing the unexpected sarcasm, Adelia glanced at her in surprise.

"Oh, well, if he doesn't need comfort," Laura continued, obviously not affected by Trish's tone, "he's still at loose ends, so to speak. If dear Margot overplayed her hand by whisking off to Europe, I for one am not above volunteering to fill the gap. Heard from her lately?"

"Not a peep."

"Well, then, I'll take it that no news is good news." She gave Trish a wink and tossed her brilliant curls. "Such a gorgeous man. Do you know Travis, Adelaide?"

"Adelia," Trish corrected before Adelia could do so herself. "Yes, Dee knows Travis very well."

"Charming man," Laura bubbled. "Now that Margot's

out of the picture, at least temporarily, I'll just have to give him a ring. Do tell him I'll call, won't you?" With another flurry of curls, she pecked both of Trish's cheeks. "I hate to, darling, but I simply must run. Don't forget to give Travis my very best. So nice to have met you, Amanda."

Adelia opened her mouth, then closed it again as Laura scurried off in a wave of musk.

"Sorry, Amanda." Trish grinned and patted Adelia's cheek. "Laura's really very sweet and basically kind, but she's a bit short of brains."

"She has such beautiful hair." Tearing her gaze from Laura's retreating coiffure, Adelia turned back to Trish. "I've never seen hair that color before. She must be very proud of it."

Trish laughed until she was forced to wipe away tears as Adelia looked on in puzzlement. "Oh, Dee, I adore you! Come on, we'll get that hand cream; then I'll buy you a cup of tea."

Waiting patiently while her mentor weighed the pros and cons of various lotions, Adelia reflected on Laura Bowers's conversation. *Margot,* she repeated, nibbling absently on her bottom lip. Who is this Margot, and what is she to Travis? For a moment she struggled with the urge to ask Trish outright, then, remembering her manners, she kept silent. *Perhaps he's in love with her.* This thought brought such a sharp, unexpected pain that she nearly gasped aloud. *But he's not,* a part of her insisted. If Travis

Grant were ever to love a woman, he would never let her go. He would go to the ends of the earth to bring her back. Unless, of course, he had been rejected. His pride would never allow him to pursue a woman who had refused him. But who would ever refuse such a man? *It's not my concern,* she told herself fiercely, forcing herself to concentrate on Trish's detailed description of various hand lotions.

At last Trish was satisfied. Adelia was suitably outfitted and had all the cosmetics that Trish thought were necessary. Laden with parcels, the two women headed back to the car. For once, Adelia was reduced to silence. She sat bolt upright on the front seat as Trish drove swiftly over the winding country roads. She was even too excited to enjoy the rolling hills and the horses grazing in the meadows, now softly outlined by the sinking afternoon sun.

Paddy was there to open the door when Adelia burst in with her new treasures.

"Little Dee, you're looking as happy as the first time you rode Majesty round the track," he said, observing her flushed, happy face.

"This was nearly as exciting, Uncle Paddy." She laughed and stepped through the doorway. "Never have I seen so many clothes, so many people. Do you know, I think everyone in America is in a constant hurry, driving, rushing through the stores—nothing ever seems to move slowly. This place Trish took me was amazing—all these shops in one big building, and it had fountains, right inside." She sighed, then shrugged and grinned. "I know I should be ashamed for squandering money the way I did, but I'm not. I had a fine time."

"It was due time, lass, due time." He kissed her cheek as they entered the living room.

"Well, Paddy, she's lost her innocence." Travis rose from an armchair and grinned down at Adelia and her packages. "Trish corrupted her. I knew I shouldn't have let that sister of mine get hold of her."

"Your sister is a wonderful lady, Mr. Grant." Adelia tossed back her head to meet his eyes, chestnut curls falling back from her face. "She has a sweet and generous soul, and a good deal more in the way of manners than some I could name."

His brow lifted, and he glanced over her head to look at Paddy as the older man struggled not to grin. "It appears Trish has a champion, and one I don't think I care to challenge." He shifted his gaze back to Adelia's irate face. "At least," he added with a slow, enigmatic smile, "not today. . . ."

CHAPTER FOUR

Saturday dawned sunny and unseasonably warm. The trees were now in full leaf, and the air carried the sweet scent of flowers as spring approached midterm. Adelia sang happily as she groomed Fortune, a sturdy three-year-old colt who listened with approval to her high, lilting voice as she brushed him.

"Dee! Dee!" She whirled around to see Mark and Mike scurrying into the stables. "Mom said we could come down and see you, and the new foal, too."

"Good day to you, gentlemen; it's pleased I am to have you visiting me."

"Will you show us the foal?" Mike demanded, and she smiled at his enthusiasm.

"That I will, Master Michael, as soon as I've finished with my friend here. Now." She set down the brush and reached a hand into her back pocket. "Where is it that I put that hoof pick?" Her pockets were empty, and she searched the ground, frowning. "It's the little people at work again."

"We didn't take it," Mark objected.

"People are always blaming kids for everything," Mike complained righteously.

"Oh, but it's not children I'm speaking of," Adelia corrected. "It's leprechauns."

"Leprechauns?" the twins chorused. "What's a leprechaun?"

"Could it be you're telling me you've never heard of leprechauns?" she asked in amazement. The boys shook their identical heads, and she folded her arms across her chest. "Well, your education's sadly lacking, lads. It's a sorry thing to remain ignorant of the little people."

"Tell us, Dee," they demanded, pulling at her hands in excitement.

"That I will." She hauled herself up to sit on a bench as the two boys squatted on the floor at her feet. "Now, the leprechaun is a strange fellow, his father being an evil spirit and his mother a fairy fallen from grace. By nature he's a mischief-maker. He only grows to be about three feet high, no matter how old he happens to be. Some say he likes to be riding on sheep or goats, so a man knows, if his stock is tired and weary of a morning, that the little people have been up to their tricks and using them for some errand where they didn't want to travel on foot. They can be lazy when they've a mind to.

"They love to be making mischief about the house as well. Why, a leprechaun'll make a pot boil over on the stove, or keep it from boiling at all, as his whim suits him. Or he'll steal the bacon or toss the furniture about for the sheer love of the confusion. Other times he'll drink his fill of the milk or poteen and fill up the bottle with water.

"Now," she continued, her eyes bright with excitement as the two boys clung to her words, "to catch a leprechaun would bring certain fortune to the one who had the wit to hold him. The only time you can catch him is when he's sitting down, and he never sits unless his brogues want mending. He's forever running about so that he wears them out, and when he feels his feet on the ground, he sits behind a hedge or in the tall grass of a meadow and takes them off to mend them. Then"—she lowered her voice to a dramatic whisper, and the two heads inched forward—"you creep up, quiet as a cat, and grab him tight in your arms." She flung her arms around an imaginary leprechaun and shouted, "'Give me your gold,' you say. 'I've got no gold,' says he."

Releasing her invisible captive, she gave the boys a roguish smile. "Now, there's gold by the ton, and that's the truth of it, and he can tell you where it's to be found, but he won't till you make him. Now, some try choking him or threatening him, but, whatever you do, you mustn't for a moment take your eyes from him. If you do that, he's gone in a flash, and you'll not be seeing him again. The scheming devil has a pocketful of tricks for getting away, and he can charm the birds from the trees if he's a mind to. But if you hold your ground and keep your eye on him, his gold is yours, and your fortune's made."

"Did you ever see a leprechaun, Dee?" Mark asked, bouncing with excitement.

"By the saints, I thought I did, a time or two." She nodded sagely. "But I never got close enough before they had vanished, quick as you please. So"—she jumped from the bench and tousled two dark heads—"unless I'm finding me one who's traveled to America, I'll have to be working for my living." She picked up a hoof pick from the bench. "And that's what I'm doing now, or I'll be fired for laziness and be begging for pennies."

"We wouldn't let it come to that, would we, boys?"

Adelia spun around, her color rising as she met Travis's mocking smile. The thumping in her heart she attributed to surprise, and she was forced to swallow nervously before speaking.

"It's a habit you're making of creeping up on a body and frightening the wits from them, Mr. Grant."

"Maybe I mistook you for a leprechaun, Dee." His grin was annoying, but she refused to be baited and bent to lift Fortune's hoof.

He led the twins down to visit the new foal, and she set down the horse's leg and watched his broad back retreat down the passage.

Why did he always send her into a flutter? she wondered. Why did her pulses begin to race at a speed that rivaled Majesty's whenever she looked up and met those surprisingly blue eyes? She leaned her cheek against Fortune's sturdy neck and sighed. She'd lost, she conceded. She'd lost the battle, and though she fought against it, she was in love with Travis Grant. It was impossible, she admitted. Nothing could ever develop between the owner of Royal Meadows and an insignificant stablehand.

"Besides," she whispered to the understanding colt, "he's an arrogant brute of a man, and I don't believe I like him one little bit." Hearing the boys approach, she bent quickly and lifted another hoof for cleaning.

"Run along outside, boys. I want a word with Dee." At Travis's command, the twins scrambled past, chattering and exclaiming over the foal. She set down the horse's leg and straightened to face him, the color fading from her cheeks.

Blast my cursed tongue, she thought in desperate condemnation. Aunt Lettie told me a thousand times where my temper would take me.

"I—have I done something wrong, Mr. Grant?" She stammered slightly and bit her lip in frustration.

"No, Dee," he answered, slowly searching her troubled

face. "Did you think I was going to fire you?" His voice was oddly gentle, and she felt a tremor at the unfamiliar tone.

"You did say I could have a fortnight, and I've a few days left before—"

"There's no need for a trial," he interrupted. "I've already decided to keep you on."

"Oh, thank you, Mr. Grant," she began, overcome with relief. "I'm grateful to you."

"Your way with horses is quite phenomenal, a strange sort of empathy." He stroked Fortune's flank, then fixed his eyes on her again. "It would be impossible to complain about your work, except that there's too much of it. I don't want to hear about you cleaning tack at ten o'clock at night anymore."

"Oh, well . . ." Turning back to the bench, Adelia gave intense concentration to placing the hoof pick in its proper spot. "I just—"

"Don't argue, and don't do it again," he commanded, and she felt his hands descend to her shoulders. "You know, you seem to split your time between working and arguing. We'll have to see if we can find another outlet for all that energy."

"I don't argue, exactly. Well, perhaps sometimes." She shrugged and wished she had the courage to turn and face him. The decision was taken out of her hands as she found herself being turned, then lifted until she once again sat on the bench.

"Perhaps sometimes," Travis agreed, and she found it disconcerting that his smile was so close, his hands still circling her waist.

"Mr. Grant," she began, then swallowed as he reached up to pluck her cap from her hair, freeing the rich cloud of auburn. "Mr. Grant, I've work to do."

"Mmm." His comment was absent as he became involved with the winding of curls around his fingers. "I've always had a fondness for chestnuts." Grinning, he gave her hair a firm tug until her face lifted to his. "A very particular fondness."

"Would you like to check my teeth?" Seeking a defense against a swift wave of longing, Adelia stiffened and sent him what she hoped was a lethal glare. His burst of unrestrained laughter caused the glare to light with green fire, and she struggled to slide from the bench.

"Oh, no." He held her still with minimum effort. "You should realize by now that I find it impossible to restrain myself when you start spitting fire."

He took her mouth quickly, one hand still tangled in her hair, the other slipping under her shirt to claim the smooth skin of her back. She found her second trip through the storm no less devastating than the first, and while her will melted under its force, her senses sharpened. The scent of leather, horses, and masculinity rose and surrounded her, a strange, intoxicating scent she knew she would always associate with him. She could feel his strength as he plunged her deeper into the kiss, demanding every drop of sweetness from her mouth. Hard and seeking, his lips parted hers, his tongue teasing hers into mobility until she was pliant and yielding against him.

For the first time she felt the pain and demand of womanhood, the slow ache growing in the center of her being and spreading to encompass her entirely, until there was nothing but the need and the man who could assuage it. She heard a soft moan as her lips were freed, not aware it was her own weak protest at liberation, and her lids opened slowly to reveal eyes dark and slumberous with desire.

"I find," Travis commented in a low, lazy voice, "that is a more productive use of time than arguing."

Adelia watched his eyes drop to the lips still warm from his and felt his hand tighten on her hair. It relaxed slowly, and a smile moved across his face as his eyes rose to hers. "It also appears to be the only way to shut you up for any amount of time."

He dropped her cap back on her head, then traced her cheek with his finger. "I find Irish tempers have definite advantages."

He strode away, and Adelia contemplated his long, graceful stride in confusion, reaching up one hand to press the cheek his finger had touched.

Pushing away a puzzle she could not solve, she spent the rest of the day in a state of euphoria. She was staying. She had found her place on the mammoth horse farm, and an uncle who wanted as well as needed her, and a job that was a dream realized. And at least, she thought happily, she would be close to Travis, seeing him almost daily, feeding her need on the sight of his tall, powerful form, on a few snatched words of conversation. That was enough for the present, and the future was something to be faced when it arrived. . . .

Long after her uncle had retired, Adelia remained wide awake. She had tried to relax with a book, but her spirits were too high for sitting idly, and she closed it and slipped outside.

She decided to walk to the stables, promising herself she would not touch one bridle but merely look in on the horses. The night remained warm, the sky blanketed with stars, so clear and vivid that she reached up, imagining she could pluck one from the soft, black curtain. At peace with the world, she meandered toward the large white building.

Entering, she switched on a low light to dispel the unrelieved darkness. She had gone no more than twenty feet when a soft moaning sound caught her attention, and she whirled in the direction of an empty stall. A man lay in a crumpled heap, and she caught her breath in alarm.

"Merciful heavens!" She hurried in and bent over him. "What's happened? Oh!" she uttered in disgust and stood, hands on hips. "You are drunk, George Johnson, and a pitiful sight indeed. You smell like a poteen factory. What do you mean drinking yourself into such a state and lying about in the stables?"

"So, it's pretty little Dee," George mumbled thickly, hauling himself into a half-sitting position. "Did you come for a visit? Come to share my bottle?"

Adelia had found herself avoiding the groom. She had often found his eyes on her, and his leering smile had caused her to recoil instinctively. Now, however, she was angry and disgusted, and she took no pains to hide it.

"No, I'll not be sharing a bottle with the likes of you— I've no patience for drunken sods. Haul yourself up and be on your way. You've no business in here with your mind fuddled with whiskey."

"Giving orders now, little Dee?" He struggled to his feet and faced her. "Too good to drink with me?" He raked her from head to foot with bleary eyes, pausing on the swell of her breast and moistening his lips. "Maybe you don't want to drink when there's more interesting things to do." He grabbed her shoulders and closed his mouth over hers, the strong smell of whiskey assaulting her senses as she pushed against him.

"You filthy pig of a man!" she spat, infuriated that he had touched her. "You great, sniveling, drunken buzzard, don't you ever put your hands on me again. You guzzling serpent, I'll kick you into next week if you touch me again." She ranted at him until he grabbed her with such force that her breath caught in her throat.

"I'll do more than touch you." His hand clamped over

her mouth, and he pushed her down roughly in the straw-filled stall. She fought in wild fury, kicking and scratching as his hands began to bruise her body, choking back the sickness that rose as his lips violated hers. Her blouse ripped away from the shoulder, the sound exploding in her ear. Anger gave way to terror, and she struggled more violently. Her nails dug into his arms, tearing his skin, and as he cursed with pain and raised his head, her scream pierced the still night.

A hand slapped hard across her cheek, numbing her face as he closed his palm over her mouth again. She continued to thrash out as his free hand captured her breast and moved over her with cruel purpose. Her strength was ebbing, and she realized she was helpless against the violation that was to come. He was tugging at her jeans, his drunkenness causing his fingers to fumble at the snap. The hand over her mouth was depriving her of air, and a foggy dimness floated in front of her eyes.

Please, somebody, help me, she prayed desperately as nausea swamped her. Suddenly, she was released from his crushing weight. She heard a muffled curse and the soft thud of flesh on flesh. Crawling to the stall's opening, she breathed deep to force back the queasiness. *Travis,* she thought dizzily, as she made out his powerful figure in the dimly lit stable.

He was beating the smaller man with a ruthless determination, knocking him to the floor with crushing blows, only to drag him up again by the shirtfront and send him sprawling once more. George offered no resistance; indeed he could not, she realized as her mind cleared. He was already unconscious. Still, Travis's fist pounded, pulling the man up on his watery legs again and again. He's killing him, she thought suddenly, and sprang to her feet, running toward them.

"No, Travis, you're killing him!" She grabbed the hard, muscular arm. "For the love of God, Travis—you're killing him!"

He jerked back, and for a moment she feared he would brush her off like a fly and finish the man who now lay in a motionless heap on the stable floor. As he turned to face her, Adelia stepped away, frightened by his expression of rage. His face seemed to be carved from granite, his eyes steely blue and penetrating as he stared at her. She trembled at the strong, harsh mask and offered up a silent prayer that she would never have that deadly fury directed at her.

"Are you all right?" His voice was clipped, his eyes boring into hers.

"Aye." She swallowed convulsively, dropping her eyes from his stare. "Oh, Travis, your hands!" Without thought, she took them in her own. "They're bleeding; you'll have to tend to them. I have some salve that's—"

"Damn it, Dee." He yanked his hands away from hers, taking her by the shoulders and tilting her head back so her eyes once more met the icy fury in his. He surveyed the torn blouse, the bruises already in evidence on the creamy skin, the rich hair tousled around her pale face. "How badly did he hurt you?" His voice was low and uneven.

Dee struggled to keep her own voice calm and not give way to the hysteria bubbling below the surface. "Not badly—he just frightened me. He only hit me once." Travis's face suffused with color, dark and angry at her words, his hands tightening uncontrollably on her shoulders. "Is he alive?" she asked, her voice barely audible. Travis let out a long breath, released her, and turned to study the crumpled form.

"Yes, more's the pity. Heaven knows he wouldn't have been if you hadn't intervened. The police will see to him now."

"No!" Her cry of protest brought Travis's attention back to her.

"Adelia . . ." he began slowly. "The man tried to rape you, don't you understand?"

"I know very well what his intentions were." She hugged herself to control the spasmodic trembling assailing her. "But we can't call the police." She rushed on as Travis made no protest. "I don't want Uncle Paddy to know about this. I won't have him worrying and upset because of me. I'm not hurt, and I won't have Uncle Paddy upset—I tell you, I won't!" Her voice rose, and he slipped a gentle arm around her shoulders.

"All right, Dee, all right," he soothed, tightening his grip around her shuddering. "I'll call a couple of men and have him taken off the property. No police." He began to lead her from the stables. "Come on, I'll take you home."

The room began to lurch sickeningly as a roaring sound filled her brain, the dim light ebbing until she could barely see. "Travis." Her voice sounded strange and far away over the deafening roar in her head. "I'm sorry, but I'm going to faint." As she spoke, the darkness closed in and swallowed her.

Adelia opened her eyes slowly, experimentally. There was something cool and wonderful on her forehead, and someone was stroking her cheek and speaking her name. She sighed and closed her eyes again, enjoying the new sensation of pampering, before opening them once more to focus on her surroundings.

The room was lit with a warm glow, the walls a cool, soft ivory trimmed with carved dark wood. She made out a wingback chair and a dark mahogany table on which stood an antique globed lamp that softly lit the room. Her eyes traveled over to the man who knelt beside her and rested on Travis's face.

"I'm in the main house," she stated matter-of-factly, and his expression of concern was transformed into an amused smile.

"Leave it to you not to say the usual 'Where am I?'" He removed the wet cloth from her head and sat down beside her on the long sofa. "I don't know anyone else who could calmly announce she was sorry, she was going to faint, and then proceed to do so."

"I've never fainted before in my life," she told him, mystified. "I'm sure I don't like it."

"Well, your color's better now. I've never seen anyone go so white. You scared the daylights out of me."

"I'm sorry." She gave him a weak smile and sat up. "It was a foolish thing to do, and—" She stopped suddenly as her hand went to her throat, only to find the cross that always hung there missing. "My cross," she stammered, looking down to where her hand rested. "I must have lost it in the stables. I've got to find it." He pushed her back firmly as she attempted to rise.

"You're in no shape to go out there now, Dee," he began, but she cut him off, struggling against his hold.

"I've got to find it. It can't be gone." Her color had drained again, and he pushed her back on the sofa.

"Dee, for heaven's sake, you'll fall flat on your face."

"Let me go. I can't lose it."

He tried to keep his words soothing, feeling helpless against her rising hysteria. He had seen her flaming angry and deeply moved, but never incoherently desperate, and he struggled to hold both her and his own temper in check. "Dee," he said shortly, giving her a small shake. "Get a grip on yourself. It's just a cross."

"It was my mother's. I've got to have it—it's all I have left of her. It's all I have." She was trembling violently, and he drew her into the warm circle of his arms and began the ageless comfort of rocking.

"I'll find it for you, don't worry. I'll go back and find it tonight."

Resting against his strong shoulder, she felt strangely content, and both panic and the threatened tears dissolved. "Do you promise?"

"Yes, Dee, I promise." He rubbed his cheek against the silk curtain of her hair, and she wondered suddenly what it was about a man that made it so good to be held by one—or was it just one man? Sighing, she allowed herself another moment's luxury pressed against him.

"I'm all right now, Mr. Grant." She drew herself away as far as his arms would permit. "I'm sorry I acted like that."

"You don't have to be sorry, Dee." His hand lifted to brush back the full, thick waves that tumbled around her face. "And it was Travis before; let's leave it at that. I rather like the way you say it."

She felt her pulses respond to his soft words and gentle touch, her awareness of him growing until she thought her veins would burst from the pressure.

"I—Is it that you're implying I have an accent?" Her brows lifted in mock censure as a defense against the suddenly dangerous atmosphere.

"No. I'm the one with the accent."

His smile drew one of her own, but the innocent intimacy only heightened her confusion, and she felt her color rise in an unaccustomed blush, her lashes sweeping down like fragile shutters. He grinned at the uncharacteristic shyness before he rose and moved to a small bar across the room.

"I think you could use a drink before I take you home." He lifted a crystal decanter. "Some brandy?"

"Brandy's a stranger to me, but perhaps if you've some Irish . . ." She sat up straighter, grateful for the distance between them.

"I'd be hard pressed not to with Paddy as my trainer," he commented, pouring a small measure of whiskey into a glass. "Here." He walked back to her and offered the glass. "This should steady you and keep you from falling into my arms again."

She took the glass and downed its contents without a shudder as Travis watched with uplifted brows. He looked down at the empty glass she handed him before bursting into gales of laughter.

"And what would you be finding so funny?" Tilting her head, she regarded him with curious eyes.

"That a half-pint like you could down two fingers of whiskey as though it were a cup of tea."

"Aye, well, it comes with the blood, I suppose. I'm not one that drinks often but, when I do, I can handle my liquor—which is more than can be said of that slimy pig of a groom." He turned back to set the empty glass on the bar so that she was unaware of the hardening of his features. "Travis . . ." she said, hesitating over his name, and he turned, relaxing his face into calm lines. "I'm grateful to you for what you did." Standing, she moved until she stood in front of him. "I'm owing you, Travis, though God Himself knows how I'll ever repay you."

His eyes were intense for a moment, brooding over the face she turned up to his; then his features relaxed into a smile, and he ran his finger down her cheek. "Perhaps one day I'll call in the debt."

The sun streamed onto the kitchen table as Adelia removed the postbreakfast clutter. She was grateful Paddy had noticed nothing amiss, having been fast asleep when, late and disheveled, she had arrived back home. He had greeted her that morning with his usual cheery smile, and she had mirrored it, firmly blocking the memory of her night's encounter from her mind. Hearing footsteps approach the kitchen, she closed the door on the dishwasher.

"I'm just coming, Uncle Paddy. I've got the buttons all figured out now. It's amazing how— Oh!" She stopped as she turned and saw Travis leaning against the doorway. "Good morning." She pushed at her hair as her thought processes skidded to a halt.

"How are you?" He walked toward her, eyes traveling in an intense survey.

"I'm f-fine, just f-fine," she stammered, and despised herself. Will I always behave like this when he comes on me unexpectedly? she demanded of herself, and determinedly offered a slight smile. His hand cupped her chin, and Adelia held very still as he searched her face.

"Are you sure?"

She nodded; then, realizing she had been holding her breath, she let it out slowly. "I'm fine, really." Her eyes traveled past him, and he read her concern easily.

"Paddy's already gone. I told him I needed to speak with you for a minute." Releasing her chin, Travis reached into his pocket and pulled out her cross and chain.

"Oh, you found it!" Her face lifted to his, illuminating the room more brilliantly than the sun. "Thank you, Travis, for troubling. It means a great deal to me."

"There's no need to thank me, Dee, and it wasn't a question of troubling." He tucked a strand of hair behind her ear in a gentle gesture that threatened to dissolve her knees. "The clasp is broken. I'll have it repaired for you."

"You don't have to do that. I can—"

"I said I'll have it repaired." His voice was firm, and her brows drew together at the underlying anger in his tone. Letting out a long breath, he slipped the cross back into his pocket, then carefully framed her face with his hands. "Adelia, I'm responsible for what happened last night. No, don't argue," he commanded as her mouth opened to contradict. "What happens to you—to the people who work for me—" he amended, "is my responsibility. I wanted you to know I'd found your cross, so you wouldn't worry. I'll have the chain repaired and get it back to you as soon as possible."

"All right," she murmured, finding currents of pleasure brushing along her skin as his hands continued to cup her face as if it were something fragile and precious.

He smiled, and his thumb traced her lips with a teasing lightness. "At times, Dee, you can be surprisingly docile. Then, just when I think you've been halter broken, you start bucking again."

Drawing away, Adelia straightened her shoulders. "I'm not a mare to be pulled about on a lead line."

Smile became grin. Travis tousled her hair before taking her hand and pulling her from the room. "Maybe you'll find it depends who's holding the line."

The days passed slowly for Adelia as the two main men in her life were absent for a time. Paddy had accompanied Majesty to Florida in preparation for the Flamingo Stakes. She found, for one who had always taken her own self-sufficiency for granted, that the nights grew longer without Paddy's company. The house seemed large and quiet and empty. Alone in the evening, she reflected how easily a heart could be lost to another. In less time than it takes for the moon to go from full glory to a sliver of light, love had swept over her, leaving her vulnerable. Love for Paddy, a sweet, full warmth of belonging, and love for Travis, an aching, spreading need.

She built a fire, though the spring air was kind through open windows, and curled up in front of its company, her head resting on the arm of her chair. Paddy would be home the next day, and she found the knowledge comforting, for with his presence there would not be so many hours alone, so many hours to think. Travis would not leave her thoughts or her heart, and seeing him daily brought as much torment as it did delight.

As the fire grew soft and low in the grate, her mind drifted to him, her lashes fluttering down to conceal her dreams, her hair falling in a curtain against her cheek.

"Dee." She stirred in the twilight world of dreams, sighing as a hand brushed through her hair. "Dee, wake up."

Lids opened slowly, and eyes misted with sleep focused on Travis. Her hand lifted to touch his cheek before fantasy was completely dimmed. "Oh." Dropping her hand, she struggled to sit up, pushing back her hair to look up at him. "Travis." She felt fresh color warm her sleep-flushed cheeks and pulled the neck of her faded blue robe closer together. "I must have fallen asleep."

"If I could have understood how anyone could be comfortable in that position, I would have left you alone." Smiling, he moved from his crouched position to sit on the arm where her cheek had rested.

Desperately aware of his nearness, Adelia pushed far into the corner of the chair, her hands clasped in her lap. "I was just thinking that Uncle Paddy would be home tomorrow," she said with partial honesty.

"Yes. I'd like to have gone with him, but I just couldn't get away." He laid a finger under her chin and lifted it.

The dying power of the fire danced in her hair. "You've missed him."

"Aye." Her smile spread as her eyes traveled over his face. "And Majesty as well." His smile answered hers, and as the moment grew long, she felt the need to abort the contact. "I'm sorry Majesty didn't win his race." Her fingers smoothed the skirts of her robe.

"Hmm?" His hands were exploring the flickers of light in her hair, and she repeated her statement in a rush of words.

"Oh, well, he placed and made a good run. Winning takes time, Dee." With a laugh, Travis ruffled her hair. "Time, patience, and strategy. . . . Look, I have something for you." Reaching into his pocket, he drew out her cross. "I didn't have the opportunity to give it to you earlier today."

"Oh, Travis, thank you." She lifted her face again to smile. "It means a great deal."

"I know." Instead of handing it to her, Travis opened the clasp and slipped the chain around her neck. His fingers on her skin were warm and gentle, and Adelia lowered her eyes, struggling not to tremble. "Better?" he asked when the clasp was secured, and she nodded, swallowing before the words would come.

"Much better, thank you, Travis."

He studied her bent head a moment; then, taking her hand, he pulled her to her feet. "Come on, close the door behind me and go to bed. You're tired." Reaching the door, he paused, one hand on the knob. "You look like a child." Her chestnut hair hung loose and heavy over the shoulders of her robe, and he ran a hand down the length of it. "A child can't be bundled off to bed without a good-night kiss," he said softly. Before she could step away, his hand had circled her neck, his mouth lowering to linger on her cheek while her lips parted in hunger. Her hunger was to go unsatisfied, for his mouth barely brushed her other cheek. As in a dream, she watched him straighten, then turn to leave, closing the door gently behind him. . . .

With Paddy's return Royal Meadows threw itself into preparing Majesty for the Blue Grass Stakes. The race was a preliminary for the most prestigious race in the country, the Kentucky Derby. Majesty's record was impressive, and his good showing in Florida had hopes running high for his next venture on the track.

Adelia leaned on the fence surrounding the track, chin resting on crossed arms, as Steve Parker, the young jockey, raced Majesty around the large oval. There had been an immediate liking between her and the small man, an easy rapport born of a mutual love of horses. She watched their progress around the track, enjoying their fluid harmony.

Pushing the button on the stopwatch he was holding, Paddy let out a loud whoop of approval before he handed it to Travis. "If he runs like that in Kentucky, there's not another horse will come within five lengths of him at the finish. He holds the turns like a lover."

"Aye, and he runs for the sheer love of it," Adelia murmured, sighing as Steve brought the colt toward them in a slow walk.

"Let's hope he loves it as much in Kentucky," Travis put in and sauntered over to speak to his jockey.

"Are you excited about your first race, little Dee?" Paddy asked, ruffling her hair.

"You might say I'm a bit excited," she returned with a grin. "My eyes will be glued to the television; not even a ton of dynamite could blast me away."

"Television?" Paddy repeated, the skin crinkling around his eyes as he narrowed them. "What's put it in your mind about television? You'll be coming with us."

"Coming with you?" She stared back in confusion.

"Of course, Adelia." She spun around at Travis's voice, her eyes making contact with his hard chest before she tilted her head back to meet his calm, controlled gaze.

"Now, why would I be doing that?"

"Because," he answered evenly, "I say so."

"Is that the way of it?" she demanded, infuriated by the tone of command in his voice. "Well, if it's a groom you need, there's others who've been here longer. Stan or Tom deserves to go more than me."

"But, Dee," Steve protested with a wide grin as he joined them, "you're much prettier than those two. I'd rather look at you—you'll give me inspiration."

"Inspiration, is it?" she returned, amused by the compliment. "You're mad as a hatter." She turned to Travis again, shifting her eye level by several long inches. "I think you'd best take one of the men," she began, but he cut her off, narrowing his eyes and grabbing her hand.

"Excuse us," he called over his shoulder as he began to stride off, dragging Adelia in his wake. When at last he stopped some distance away, she rounded on him furiously.

"What the devil do you mean racing off like that and carting me behind you?" she panted, outraged. "Your legs are almost as long as my whole body, and I had to fair run to keep up with you."

She glared up at him, a picture of righteous indignation.

"I prefer to argue in private, Adelia," Travis said coolly, meeting her mutinous face with nonchalant command. "I run Royal Meadows and I give the orders." Even through her own anger, Adelia could see the signs of temper held in check; his eyes hard and direct, he was suddenly the essence of the master. "I will not have you countermanding my orders privately, and most certainly not publicly." His words annoyed her further simply because she knew he was right. "You're going to have to get it through that stubborn head of yours that you are no longer in solitary control of what is to be done. Now, I believe the issue here is your presence in Kentucky," he went on calmly, his face expressionless.

"I was telling you—"

"I'm telling you," he interrupted imperiously. "You're going."

Her eyes flashed at the order. Why, she thought, if it's God's pleasure for me not to be forever bursting with temper did He give me such a demanding one?

"Majesty responds better to you than anyone else," Travis went on. "I want you tending to him." Anger receded slowly at his words, and she dropped her eyes, staring at the ground while she considered his statement. "You'll come to Kentucky because it suits me to have you there, and I'm accustomed to having what suits me." His smile spread in a rapid change of mood as her head snapped up with fresh anger. His hands claimed her waist, then trailed slowly upward, resting on the sides of her firm young breasts as her anger faded into confusion. Lingering, his thumbs caressed in a slow circle, then trailed once in a lazy arch over the subtle curves, pausing at their fullness before moving to rest under their soft swell. Her lips parted, but she found no strength to protest against the unfamiliar intimacy, her body responding to his touch, eclipsing her will. She felt herself rising from the ground, and her hands went to his shoulders automatically to compensate for the loss of gravity.

"Put me down." The order emerged as a trembling whisper, and his smile grew wider before his mouth lowered.

"In a minute."

His mouth was dominant and sure, and her fingers dug into his shoulders as the force of the kiss held her in its prison. With a final flash of lucidity, she knew she could never fight Travis on these terms. Then all was lost in the dark demand of need.

"Steve's right," he murmured, his teeth nibbling at her lip and sending shooting sparks of flame through her veins. "You are prettier than Tom or Stan."

With a final hard, brief kiss, he dropped her back to the ground, to stride away with casual arrogance, whistling the first few bars of "My Wild Irish Rose." Adelia stood gaping after him, trembling with a confusing mixture of indignation and longing.

CHAPTER FIVE

Adelia found herself on a plane for the second time in her life. This plane, however, was vastly different from the crowded economy section of the passenger jet in which she had traveled over the Atlantic. Now she was passing over the relatively short distance between Maryland and Kentucky in the lush comfort of Travis's specially equipped private jet. Adelia's attitude during this flight was also a marked variation from her first. She stared, mesmerized, from the window, fascinated by the topography of far-distant West Virginia.

She looked down on patchworks of green and umber dotted by small houses, toy-train cities, and gray ribbons of roads snaking and winding to connect them. There were rivers and pine-topped mountains, their colors soft from her eagle view, and she thought with pleasure that the world was indeed a wondrous place. Engrossed in her new discoveries, she did not notice when Travis sat next to her.

"Enjoying the view, Dee?" he asked at length, smiling at the way she pressed her forehead to the glass like a child at a bakery window. She started at his voice, then turned her head to face him, pushing back the chestnut curls that spilled over her face at the movement.

"Merciful heavens, you're forever surprising me. You move like the wind through a willow."

"Sorry. I'll practice stomping." He grinned and shifted in his seat to regard her more directly. "I've often thought you move like one of those fairies Ireland's so famous for, or maybe one of your leprechauns."

"Oh, well, it can't be both. A leprechaun's not considered a fit associate for a reputable fairy."

"Only a disreputable fairy," he returned, amused at the sobriety of her statement.

"Aye, and for the most part they're on their good behavior, hoping to be readmitted to Paradise on the last day."

"Tossed out, were they?"

"When Satan was rebelling, they stood back from the fighting, not wanting to take sides till they knew how it would end. But since that was their only offense, they were banished to earth instead of tossed into the pit with the rebels."

"Seems fair," Travis concluded with a nod. "As I recall,

they have the rather awesome power to turn one into a dog or a pig or something equally undesirable, but are normally disposed to good deeds if treated with the proper respect."

"That's right," she agreed. "How did you know that?"

"Paddy saw to the holes in my education." He leaned over her, smiling, and she pressed back into the cushions, green eyes growing wide. "Relax." His voice tightened in annoyance. "I'm not going to eat you." He fastened the seat belt around her waist and leaned back. "We'll be landing in a minute."

"So soon?" She controlled her voice to casualness while the beating of her heart vibrated in her ears.

"That's right," he answered, matching her tone as he secured his own belt. "You've been staring down at Kentucky for some time now."

With amazing organization and economy of movement, the plane was landed, Majesty was unloaded and transferred to a waiting van, and the travelers were on their way to Churchill Downs.

Adelia's impression of Louisville was vague. Her mind was in the back of the van with Majesty. She worried that he might be frightened and confused by the strange sights and long transport. When she voiced her concern, she was rewarded with a deep, full laugh from Travis. The ominous gleam in her eye was ignored as, chuckling, he informed her that Majesty was a seasoned traveler and took it in his stride.

Her irritation had faded by the time the van reached the extensive stables at Churchill Downs. Travis immediately confirmed the arrangements that had been made for Majesty's stall space and feed.

Travis Grant was well known and highly respected in racing circles. Adelia noted that he was greeted with warmth by the men and women milling around the stable area. He stood head and shoulders above the group, exuding power and a virile masculinity that, she observed with a rude stab of jealousy, was obviously appreciated by the women who greeted him. Infuriated with herself for her own weakness, Adelia turned sharply back to Majesty and led the gleaming colt into his stall.

Time passed swiftly as she tended to the animal's needs, brushing and soothing as she kept up a flow of one-sided chatter. As she was completing her duties, she heard loud footsteps approaching and turned around to see who was causing the din.

"Loud enough?" Travis grinned at her with unexpected boyishness.

"Aye," she agreed and gave him a solemn nod. "You sounded like a herd of great African elephants. You're a funny man, Travis," she commented, tilting her head to the side and studying him.

"Am I, Dee? How?"

"There's times you're like the local squire tossing orders about, and the steel in your eyes could freeze a man in his tracks. Then I think you're a hard man. But then sometimes . . ." Faltering, she shrugged and turned back to Majesty.

"Don't stop now." Deliberately, he turned her back to face him, a faint smile playing on his mouth. "You've intrigued me."

She was uncomfortable now and wishing with a full heart that she would learn to think before speaking. But Travis ignored her expression of embarrassment, hands light but firm on her shoulders, eyes demanding her elaboration.

"Sometimes . . . I've seen you laughing and talking with the men, or carting one of the twins about on your shoulders. And I see the way it is between you and Uncle Paddy, and the way you treat your horses. I think then maybe there's a gentle side, and maybe you're not so hard, after all." She finished in a rush, wishing she had never started, and turned back to give Majesty unnecessary additional attention with the brush.

"That's very interesting," he commented, taking the brush from her hand and continuing the grooming himself. "She's spoiling you," he addressed Majesty, running an affectionate hand along his flank. "She'd stand in here rubbing you down for the next hour if I let her."

She tore her eyes from Travis's fingers as they stroked the rich chestnut hide. "I don't spoil him; it was just love and care I was giving. We all need that from time to time."

He turned his head and met her eyes with a long, level look. "Yes, we all need that from time to time."

That night, awake in the unfamiliar hotel room, Adelia tossed and turned, ultimately rolling over and pounding her innocent pillow. Love was decidedly uncomfortable, unpredictable, and unwelcome. Sighing, she hugged the pillow she had just beaten, determined to erase incredibly blue eyes from her dreams.

The next morning Adelia had her first real look at Churchill Downs. Leading Majesty from the stables, she stopped as she came to the track, her companion waiting with calm indulgence as she stared in open amazement.

The grounds were enormous, the wide mile-and-a-quarter track encircling a grass field bordered by fences and graced with well-shaped shrubs and flower beds of brilliant color. Moving her eyes over the vast expanse of stands, she wondered somewhat whimsically who would be left to tend to the outside world when they were filled with people. The tops of the stands were roofed, crowned with spires, she noted.

"Something wrong, Dee?" Her observations were interrupted by Travis's question, and she jumped in surprise. "Sorry," he said without bothering to conceal a grin. "Forgot to stomp."

"I should be getting used to it by now." She sighed and began to lead Majesty along once more. "What a grand place this is." Her hand swept in an expressive arch as he fell into step beside her.

"It's one of my favorites. The architecture's basically the same as it was when it was built over a hundred years ago. And, as you well know, it's the most famous track of all because it is here that the Derby is run. And the Derby, everyone remembers. On the first Saturday in May, this ribbon of track is gold, and for a few minutes the world stops, and it's only the race." He turned to her with a smile. "It all comes down to the challenge at the turn for home, when the goal is still a quarter of a mile away. Since eighteen seventy-five the best horses have run here, and the best horses have won here. It's not only the classic race, it's a breeders' race, and there isn't anyone in the States who wouldn't rather produce a winner in this than in any other contest. The winner of a Derby becomes the horse to beat for the rest of the season; the magic stays with him. And this," he continued, giving Majesty a friendly slap on the flank, "is one who likes to win."

"Aye, that he does," she agreed, giving Majesty an indulgent smile. "And he's not shy about his own capabilities. He's feeling pretty sure of himself. He wants the Blue Grass Stakes out of the way so he can move on to the Derby."

"Does he?" The corner of his mouth tilted as Majesty nuzzled Adelia's shoulder. "And how do you feel?" His finger touched her cheek, and she turned to face him. "Do you want the prep race out of the way so you can dive into the Derby?"

"I'm not ready for the first one yet." Adelia shrugged,

nearly stumbling as Majesty's head nudged at her back. "It's him that's in the hurry. But I like the looks of this place." Again, she encompassed Churchill Downs with a sweep of the hand. "I like knowing it hasn't changed much in all these years." She began to walk again, at Majesty's urging. "Never did I think to see such a place."

"There are other tracks that are perhaps more eye-catching," he commented, following her fascinated gaze. "At Hialeah in Florida, they have hundreds of pink flamingos in the center-field lake."

Stopping, she turned to him with wide eyes. "I should like to see that."

"I'm sure you will," he murmured, twining his fingers in the ends of her long, silky waves. Then, pulling the brim of her cap down over her eyes, he repeated in a lighter tone, "Yes, Dee, I'm sure you will."

The week moved swiftly, hours crammed with duties and activities. Most of Adelia's time was given to Majesty's care, talking and fondling as much as grooming and seeing to his more practical needs. She spent much of her free time with Steve Parker, teasing him about his girlfriends or watching from the rail as he accustomed Majesty to the track. Other times she spent with Paddy, discussing the Thoroughbred's qualities and the style of the other colts who would compete in the qualifying race.

"The colt that wins is automatically eligible for the Derby," he informed her, giving Majesty a thorough examination as she watched from the stall door. "Of course,

Travis nominated this fellow right after he was born, the same way he's entered Solomy's foal, and kept up with the nomination as he got older. He knows when he's got a winner. Travis is a man who keeps one eye on the future."

"He's good with the horses," Adelia commented. The obvious pride and affection in Paddy's voice warmed her. "You can see he cares for them; it's not just a matter of the money they'll bring him."

"Aye, he cares," Paddy agreed, giving Majesty an affectionate slap on the flank. "And he's fierce on the matter of using painkillers or drugs as others have been known to do. If one of Travis's horses isn't up for the race, he doesn't run and that's that. Of course, money's not a problem with Travis, but it wouldn't make any difference if it was, because that's the man he is. Now, he has a practical side as well." He moved from the stall to join Adelia and slipped an arm around her shoulders. "Investments—and he's mighty crafty about them. He knows how to take a purse or the sale of a foal and turn it into more. He's got the touch," Paddy added with a wise nod. "And a time or two, he's stretched my pennies for me, though not on as grand a scale as his. Travis takes care of his own." Squeezing her shoulder, Paddy led Adelia out into the flash of sunlight. She remained silent, thinking of this new aspect of the man she loved.

———

The sky was overcast on the day of the Blue Grass Stakes. The air was heavy. Lead-gray clouds lay thick as a blanket overhead. Tension seemed to start at Adelia's brow and spread down to her toes; the stillness of the air weighed like a stone at the nape of her neck. To take her thoughts off the coming race she kept both hands and mind busy. Glancing up she saw Travis enter the building. She smiled as he approached.

"I believe that, if you could, you'd get into the silks and ride him today."

"The truth of it is," she began, finding the ease of his smile soothing, "I think I'd be less terrified that way. But I don't think Steve would care for it."

"No." The syllable was accompanied by a slow, grave nod. "I don't think he would. Come up to the stands with me. Paddy'll take over now."

"Oh, but—" Her objection was neatly cut off as he captured her arm and propelled her to the door. "Wait!" she cried and pivoted to run swiftly back to Majesty, throwing her arms around his neck and whispering in his ear.

When she rejoined Travis, he stared down at her, both amused and frankly curious. "What did you tell him?"

She gave him a mysterious smile for an answer. As they approached the stands, she dug into her back pocket and thrust some bills into his hands. "Will you place a wager for me? I don't know how to go about it."

"A wager?" he repeated, looking down at the two

dollars in his hand. Looking up, his features were entirely too serious. "Who do you want to bet on?"

"Majesty, of course." She frowned at the question, her expression lightening as she recalled some of the terms she had heard tossed around the stables. "To win . . . on the nose."

To his credit, Travis's features remained grave. "I see. Well, let's see . . . his odds are five to two at the moment." Brows drawn, he studied the odds board. "Now, number three there is ten to one, but that's not too long for a gambler. Number six is two to one; that's rather conservative."

"I don't know about all that," she interrupted with a frustrated wave of her hand. "It's just all a bunch of numbers."

"Adelia." He said her name slowly, giving her a small pat on the shoulder. "One must never bet unless one knows the odds." Ignoring her, he glanced up at the flashing numbers. "It's three to one on number two, a nice safe choice for win, place, or show. It's eight to five on number one."

"Travis, you're making my head spin with all of this. I just want to—"

"And fifteen to one on number five." He looked down at the two crumpled bills. "You could amass a small fortune if that one came in."

"It's not for the money." Her breath came out in one impatient huff. "It's for the luck."

"Ah, I see," he returned with a solemn nod before the grin escaped and spread. "Irish luck is not to be scoffed at."

Though she scowled quite fiercely for a moment, he slipped his arm over her shoulders and led her to the two-dollar window.

Before long, she was standing next to him and gaping openly at the masses of people filling the stands. The enormous stadium would hold one hundred and twenty-five thousand, Travis had informed her, and to her astonished eyes there seemed to be no less than that. Several people greeted Travis, and she felt an occasional twinge of discomfort as eyes often passed over her in speculation. Embarrassment was soon eclipsed by excitement as post time approached. She watched the horses step onto the track, her eyes immediately focusing on Majesty and the rider in brilliant red and gold silks on his back. As Majesty's name was announced, Adelia closed her eyes, finding the combination of excitement and nerves nearly overpowering.

"He looked ready," Travis commented casually, then laughed as she jolted at his words. "Relax, Dee, it's just another race."

"I'll never be easy about it if I see a hundred," she vowed. "Oh, here comes Uncle Paddy. Is it going to start?"

For answer, he pointed, and she watched the horses being loaded into the starting gate. Her hand clutched at the cross at her neck, and she felt Travis's arm slip over her shoulders as the bell sounded and ten powerful forms lunged forward.

It seemed to her a mass of flying hooves and thunderous noise, the pack clinging together in one speeding block. Still, her eyes were glued on Majesty as though he were racing alone. Her hand reached up of its own accord to grasp the one on her shoulder, tightening as she urged the colt to greater speed. Steadily he moved forward, as if following her remote-control command, persistently passing one, then another, until he emerged alone from the field. Suddenly the long legs increased their stride, streaking across the dirt track until his competitors were left with the sight of his massive hindquarters as he lunged under the wire.

Travis's arm encircled her, and Adelia found herself crushed to his hard chest, sandwiched between his lean body and her uncle's stocky frame. It was like being caught fast between two unmoving, loving walls, and she found the sensation torturously wonderful, a heady mixture of scents and textures. Her uncle's voice was raised in excitement in her ears, and her head was snuggled, as if it belonged, against Travis's chest. Majesty's win, she decided, closing her eyes, was the best present she had ever had.

Every man, woman, and child in Louisville ate, slept, and breathed the Kentucky Derby. As the days dwindled, the very air seemed to shimmer with anticipation. Adelia saw Travis sporadically. Their conversations revolved around the colt, the only personal aspect of their relationship being the abstracted pat on the head he would give her from time to time. She began to think that quarreling with him had had its advantages, and she relieved her frustrations by spending more time with Majesty.

"You're a fine, great horse," she told him, holding his muzzle and looking into his intelligent eyes. "But you mustn't let all of this go to your head. You've a job to do come Saturday, and it's a big one. Now, I'm going out for a few minutes, and I want you to rest yourself, then perhaps we'll see about a currying."

Satisfied with Majesty's silent agreement, Adelia stepped out of the stables into the bright May sun and found herself surrounded by reporters.

"Are you the groom in charge of Royal Meadows' Majesty?" The question was fired out by one of the people who suddenly cut her off from the rest of the world with a wall of bodies. The sensation was disconcerting, and she was thinking wistfully of the dim solitude of the stables when she heard another voice.

"You don't see many grooms that look like this one."

She rounded on the man who had spoken, squinting against the sun to see more clearly. "Is that the truth, now?" she demanded, discomfort replaced by annoyance. "I thought red hair was common enough in America."

The group roared with laughter, and the man at whom

her remark had been directed responded with a good-natured grin. Questions were fired at her, and for a few moments she surrendered to the pressure and answered, valiantly attempting to keep one query separate from the next.

"By the saints!" She threw up her hands in dismay, shaking her head. "You're all speaking in a muddle." Pushing the brim of her cap back from her head, she took a deep breath. "If it's more information you're wanting, you'd best ask Mr. Grant or Majesty's trainer." She pushed through them with determination, turning when she felt a hand on her arm and finding herself facing the reporter who had made the personal observation.

"Miss Cunnane, sorry if we were a little rough on you." He smiled with considerable charm, and Adelia found herself smiling back.

"No harm was done."

"I'm Jack Gordon. Maybe you'd let me make it up to you by taking you out to dinner tonight."

She was both surprised and flattered by the invitation, gaining the pure feminine pleasure of having an attractive man pay her specific attention. He was, however, a stranger, and she was opening her mouth to decline when a voice sounded behind her.

"Sorry, my groom's off limits."

She whirled around to see Travis watching them, blue eyes cool and direct. Fury bubbled inside her, reflecting plainly in her flashing eyes.

"Don't you have some work to do, Adelia?" he asked with an imperial lift of brows. The eyes that met his told him without words what she thought of his question before she wheeled around and stalked to the stables.

Some fifteen minutes later, Travis disengaged himself from the avid reporters and joined her. She watched as he strode toward her, hands carelessly thrust in the pockets of slim-fitting jeans.

"Don't you know better than to make dates with strange men, Adelia?" His tone was deliberate, superior, and infuriating.

"My personal life is my own affair," she raged at him. "You've no right to interfere."

"As long as you're in my employ and responsible for my horses, your life is my affair."

"Aye, Master Grant," she tossed back, undaunted by the narrowing of his eyes. "I'll be certain to ask your permission before I take my next breath." Her foot stomped in temper. "I didn't arrive on this earth yesterday. I can take care of myself."

"Were you taking care of yourself in the stables a couple of weeks ago?" She paled at this and turned away. With a muttered curse, he turned her around to face him. "Dee, I'm sorry. That wasn't fair."

"No, it wasn't." She jerked away, eyes bright with angry tears. "But it doesn't surprise me you'd be saying it. You've a habit of putting me in my place, Master Grant, and I've been reminded there's work to be done. So be off with you and let me be about it." Removing her cap, she dropped a curtsy. "If it please Your Honor."

"I've had just about enough, you green-eyed witch," he muttered, taking a step toward her. "I'd like to haul you over my knee for the spanking you deserve, but I'll get more out of this sort of punishment."

He had her crushed against him with a speed that allowed her only a short gasp of protest before his mouth descended, hard, then demanding, then possessing, in rapid succession. When he lifted his mouth, she felt him drawing her soul through her eyes.

"I'm not going to make a habit of this," he muttered and took her lips again, his fingers tangling in her hair, then moving over her back until she thought she would perish from the heat.

Feather-light tremors followed the trail of his hand along her spine, touching her with an exquisite fear. She felt the pressure of his arms bending her back, his mouth hard on hers, demanding not response but submission. She became aware of her own slightness, a fragility she had never known was part of her, as his strength overpowered even the thought of struggle. Lucidity drifted from her, leaving only the feel of a hard body and a demanding mouth, which took from her until it was impossible even to breathe.

Drawing away, Travis held Dee steady as she staggered. He stood a moment looking down thoughtfully into her flushed face. "You know, Dee," he said at length, his voice as calm and unperturbed as she was ruffled and confused, "you're too little to possess such a dangerous temper."

Flicking a friendly finger down her nose, he strode out into the sunshine.

The day of the Derby was an advertisement for spring, warm with a soft, scented breeze under a clear, cloudless sky. The perfection of the weather meant nothing to Adelia, whose nerves were so tightly coiled that it could have easily been midwinter. Seeing Travis several times during the morning and early afternoon, she was both envious and annoyed by his calm, easygoing manner while she remained a massive bundle of quivering nerves. Between the lingering sensation of her last encounter with him and the prospect of the race, she found functioning at even borderline normality an effort. Waiting through the preliminary races was sheer torture.

She found herself beside Travis in the stands, thinking that if the race did not begin soon, she would have to be carted away and locked up until it was over.

"Here." Adelia glanced down at the glass he offered before raising her eyes to his.

"What is it?"

"A mint julep." Taking her hand, he placed the glass in it and curled her fingers around it. "Drink it," he commanded, then smiled at the frown she gave it. "The purpose is twofold. One, it's traditional, and you can keep the glass to remember your first Derby. And two," he continued, grinning, "you need something to calm your nerves; I'm afraid you're going to keel over."

"So am I," she admitted and sipped gingerly from the glass. "Travis, I would swear there are more people here than the last time. Where do they all come from?"

"Everywhere," he returned easily, following her fascinated gaze. "The Run for the Roses is the most important race of the season."

"Why do they call it that?" she asked, finding the combination of conversation and mint julep soothing.

"The winner's draped with a blanket of red roses in the Winner's Circle, and the jockey gets an armful. So," he concluded and lifted his own glass, "it's the Run for the Roses."

"That's nice," she approved, lifting the brim of her cap further on her head. "Majesty will like red roses."

"I'm sure he'll be crazy about them," Travis agreed with suspicious sobriety, and Adelia's dignified retort was interrupted by the first strains of "My Old Kentucky Home."

"Oh, Travis, the parade's starting!" She fastened her eyes on Majesty and the small man on his back, clad in colorful red and gold silks. The others with their brilliant contrasts of blues and greens and yellows paled before her eyes. To her there was not another animal to compare in power and beauty with Travis's Thoroughbred colt—

and, judging by the way Majesty pranced, he agreed completely.

"Saints preserve us, Uncle Paddy," she murmured as he appeared at her side. "My heart's pounding so I'm sure it'll burst. I don't think I'm made for this."

Her eyes never left Majesty's form as he was loaded into the gate. Her senses swam with the blare of the trumpets and the roar of the crowd. With a swiftness that took her breath away, the doors were released and the horses sprang forward in a turbulent herd.

Her eyes followed the colt as he galloped with steady assurance around the track. She was not even aware that as the bell had rung she had grabbed Travis's hand in a viselike grip, squeezing tighter as each heart-pounding second passed. The air shivered with the voice of the crowd, individual calls and shouts melding into one trembling roar. She rode every inch of the track on Majesty's back, feeling the rush of wind on her face and the strong rhythm of the colt's gait under her.

As they rounded the second turn, Steve brought Majesty to the inside rail, and the colt took his head and left the field with long, smooth strides. The gap between the chestnut and his nearest competitor widened with what appeared to be effortless ease as he streaked down the back stretch into the home stretch and under the wire more than four lengths in the lead.

Without hesitation, Adelia threw herself into Travis's

arms, clinging with a joy she could only express physically by babbling incoherent and self-interrupted sentences to both him and her uncle, who was improvising an enthusiastic jig beside her.

"Come on." Travis tossed an arm around Paddy's shoulders. "We've got to get down to the Winner's Circle before the crowd's too thick."

"I'll wait for you." Adelia pulled back, stooping to retrieve her dislodged cap. "I don't like all those reporters staring and snapping and jumping all over me with their questions. I'll wait on the outside and take Majesty along when it's over."

"All right," Travis agreed. "But tonight, we celebrate. What do you say, Paddy?"

"I say I've just acquired a strong yearning for champagne." The two men grinned at each other.

That evening, Adelia stared at the reflection in the full-length mirror of her room. Her hair lay full and lush on her shoulders, shining like newly minted copper against the muted greens of her dress.

"Well, Adelia Cunnane, look at you." She smiled with satisfaction into the mirror. "There's not a one back in Skibbereen who'd be knowing you in such a dress, and that's the truth of it." A knock sounded at her door, and she plucked her key from the dresser. "I'm coming, Uncle Paddy."

Opening the door with a dazzling smile, she was not greeted by her merry-faced uncle but by an incredibly attractive Travis in a dark dinner suit, the white silk of his shirt startling against his deep tan. They stood silently for a moment as his gaze roamed over her, from shining hair and deep green eyes to the soft, rounded curves outlined by the clinging jersey. His gaze rose to her face again, but still he did not smile.

"Well, Adelia, you're astonishingly beautiful."

Her eyes widened at the compliment, and she searched for something suitable to say. "Thank you," she finally managed. "I thought you'd be Uncle Paddy."

His eyes continued to hold her in the doorway, and she moistened her lips with the tip of her tongue in an innocently inviting gesture. "Paddy's meeting us downstairs with Steve."

The single-minded intensity with which she was being studied was rapidly stripping her of all composure, and her words tumbled out quickly. "We'd best be joining them—they'll be waiting."

Travis merely nodded, a slight inclination of his head, and she took a step toward him, only to stop nervously when he made no move to let her pass. Raising her eyes from his shirtfront to his face, she opened her mouth to speak, only to find her mind a vacuum. He gazed down at her for another unnerving moment, then held up a single red rose, placing it in her hand.

"Majesty sent it. He says you're fond of red roses."

"Oh." He was not smiling with the whimsy of his words, and her mind fidgeted for something to ease the sudden awareness, the physical strength of his gaze. "I didn't know you talked to horses."

"I'm learning," he answered simply, and ran a finger over her bare shoulder. "My teacher's an expert."

She dropped her eyes to the bloom in her hand, thinking that twice in her life she had been given flowers, and both times they had come from Travis, both times they had been red roses. She smiled, knowing she would never again see a red rose without thinking of him. That was a gift more precious than jewels. Open and innocent, her smile lifted for him.

"Thank you, Travis, for bringing it to me." On impulse, she rose to her toes and kissed his cheek.

He stared down at her, and for a moment Adelia thought she saw some hesitation, some indecision, flicker in his eyes before his features relaxed into a smile.

"You're welcome, Dee. Bring it along—it suits you." Taking the key from her hand, he placed it in his pocket and led her to the elevator.

The celebration dinner was a new experience for Adelia. The elegant restaurant, the unaccustomed dishes, and her first encounter with champagne combined to give her a glowing sense of unreality. The tension brought on by the few moments alone with Travis was dispelled by his casually friendly attitude during the meal. It was almost as though the awareness that had passed between them had never taken place. The evening drifted by in a haze of happiness.

The following week, however, found her back in Maryland in jeans and cap, busily fulfilling her duties and thrusting elegant meals and fancy dresses from her mind. Long hours of grooming, exercising, and training filled the days, giving her little time to dwell on the strange new emotions Travis had aroused. She avoided the reporters who were often hovering around the track and stables, not wishing to be cornered again and bombarded with questions. At night, however, she was less successful in avoiding the dreams that assaulted her awakened senses.

Days passed into weeks, and although Adelia gave all the Thoroughbreds love and attention, she continued to dote on Majesty.

"Don't forget yourself just because you've had your picture in some fancy magazines," she admonished him, failing to keep her voice stern as she completed his grooming.

Paddy strolled into the stables and laid a hand on her shoulder. "Keeping him in line, are you, little Dee? Don't want him too big for his breeches, do we?"

"That we don't." Turning, she smiled at her uncle, then studied him carefully. "You look tired, Uncle Paddy. Aren't you feeling well?"

"I'm fine, Dee, just fine." He patted her rosy cheek and winked at her. "I think I'll sleep for a week when the Belmont's come and gone."

"You've earned a rest; you've been working hard and long. You're a bit pale. Are you sure—"

"Now, don't fuss," he interrupted with a good-natured scowl. "Nothing worse than a fussing woman. Just be keeping your mind on this lad here." He patted Majesty's side. "Don't you worry about Paddy Cunnane."

She let this pass, vowing silently to keep her eye on him. "Uncle Paddy, is the Belmont important?"

"Every race is important, darlin', and this is one of the top. Now, this fellow here, with that barrel of a chest"—he inclined his head toward Majesty and winked again—"he'll do well there. It's a long race, a mile and a half, and that's what he was bred for. A distance runner, and one of the finest. Not like Fortune, mind you; he's a sprinter and can beat almost anything at a shorter distance. Travis is smart enough to breed horses with both distance and sprinting in mind. That's why he put Fortune in the Preakness at Pimlico, and he was second by half a length. And that's just fine. But this one's for the Belmont." He shook Majesty's head lightly by the muzzle. "And so are you," he added, giving Adelia a pat on the head.

"Me? Am I going as well?"

"That's right. Hasn't Travis told you?"

"Well, no. I haven't seen much of him since we got back from Kentucky."

"He's been busy."

Her answer was absent as she considered the wisdom of attempting to refuse. Recalling the result of her previous attempt, Adelia thought New York might be a fine place to visit.

Belmont Park, on Long Island, was alive with reporters. Adelia managed to stay in the background the majority of the time and, when cornered, she escaped as soon as possible. She was unaware of the speculation about her and her relationship with the owner of Royal Meadows' Majesty. The casual attire of jeans and shirt did nothing to conceal the appeal of her beauty, and her reluctance to speak with the press added a mystery that acted as a meaty bone to the hungry pack of reporters. At times she felt hounded and wished she had stood firm and refused to come. Then she would see Travis as he moved toward the stables, hands in pockets, hair ruffled by the breeze. She would admit, though it brought little comfort, that she would have gone mad had she been left behind.

Newspapers and nagging reporters were not in Adelia's thoughts as she joined Travis for the third time in the crowded stands. She noticed, with some discomfort, that Belmont and its occupants were more sophisticated than Churchill Downs. There, size had been offset by an old-world charm, the soft, lazy accent of Louisville. Somehow, Belmont seemed more vast, more intimidating, and beside the sophistication of the elegantly groomed women who occupied the stands and clubhouse, Adelia felt inadequate and naive.

Silly, she told herself and straightened her shoulders. I can't be like them, and they're certainly taking no notice of me, in any case. Most of these fine ladies can't keep their eyes off Travis. I suppose these are the kind of ladies he sees at his country club, or takes out for a quiet dinner. Depression threatened to settle over her like a black cloud, but she took a deep breath and blew it away.

Adelia had lectured herself that by this time she should be accustomed to the tension and the crush of people, but as post time drew closer she felt the familiar anxiety and undeniable excitement capture her. She could find neither words nor ability to speak, and stood gripping the rail with both hands as Majesty strutted to the starting gate. He was impatient, she observed, sidestepping and lifting his front legs in small, nervous prancing steps as Steve struggled to control him, urging him forward into his place in the starting gate.

"I'll have to bring you to the track more often, Dee." Travis gave her shoulder a small squeeze. "In a couple of months, you'll be a veteran."

"I'll never be a veteran, I'm afraid, because each time it seems like the first. I can hardly bear it."

"I'm going to keep bringing you in any case," he informed her, tangling his fingers for a moment in the ends of her hair. "You bring the excitement back. I believe I'd been taking it for granted."

She turned to him, nonplussed by the gentle tone of his voice, and had opened her mouth to speak when the bell shrilled with the roar of the crowd. Brilliant silks were now a soft blur as Thoroughbreds thundered around the track. After the first turn the field dispersed, transforming from a single mount of speeding legs to a zigzagging cluster of gleaming bodies. To Adelia, Majesty seemed to weave his way through them like a fiery comet, passing one after another until he bore down on the leader. Then, as if a switch had been flicked, came the power, the lengthening of stride, the rippling of muscles, the steady increase of his lead, until Majesty flew down the home stretch, capturing the coveted Belmont with power and style.

The crowd went wild, cheering and shouting with one deafening voice. Adelia's feet left the ground as Travis lifted her, swinging her in circles as she clung to his neck. He continued to hold her as Paddy's arms came around them both, drawing them all together in joy and excitement. The words shouted were senseless to her, and she told herself later that it was the temporary insanity of the moment that had caused her to meet Travis's lips with hers. Even on later reflection, she was unclear who had initiated the kiss, but she knew she had responded. She had flung her arms around his neck, and the thrill that had coursed through her had eclipsed even the rushing flurry of the race. When her feet touched the ground, and Travis lifted his mouth from hers, her head was still spinning with light and color, her body trembling with the backlash of emotion, the tidal wave of sensation. She could do no more than stare up at him. For a moment, it was the same as the day the foal had been born, and the crowded, noisy stands of Belmont Park faded into a solitary, private world. She was oblivious to the throng and the curious stares, aware only of his arms around her, and the feeling that she was slowly, helplessly drowning in his eyes.

"We'd best be going down, lad." Paddy made a business of clearing his throat before he laid a hand on Travis's shoulder. Her knees weakened as his eyes left hers to meet her uncle's. She felt the sudden dizziness and disorientation of one who had been awakened from a dream too quickly.

"Yes." Travis grinned, the quick-spreading grin of a boy. "Let's go congratulate the winner. Come on." Spinning Adelia around, he began to lead her away.

"I'm not going down there," she objected, making a futile attempt to hold her ground.

"Yes, you are," he disagreed, not bothering to glance back at her. "I let you have your way before, not this time. You're coming down to help Majesty accept his flowers, white carnations this time, and one's for you."

Her sputtering objections and attempts to disentangle herself went unheeded, and she found herself in the Winner's Circle with the others.

There were microphones and the flash of lights, and she faded into the background as far as possible. She was still shaken by the intensity of need that had flowed through her in Travis's embrace, a strong, wild desire to belong to him completely. It was like being assailed with an unquenchable thirst, and the sensation terrified her. Her morals were deeply rooted, a melding of religious and personal beliefs. She knew, however, that her longing for Travis, her love for him, made her weak, and any resistance would melt as quickly as springtime snow if he pressed his advantage.

She must stay away from him, she determined, avoid situations where they would be alone and she would be vulnerable to his experience and her frailty. As she glanced over at his tall, lean frame, their eyes locked, and she trembled. Her lashes swept down, and she realized helplessly what a rabbit feels when cornered by a strong, sleek fox.

CHAPTER SIX

Back at the hotel, Adelia accompanied Paddy to his room, having no wish to be alone with her thoughts. Travis walked down the carpeted hall with them, pausing at the doorway as she slipped through.

"I've made reservations for us." His teeth flashed in a grin. "Steve's doing his own celebrating with a little lady who's been dogging his footsteps since the Derby."

"Ah, Travis." Paddy sat down heavily on the bed. "You'll have to do without this tired old man. I'm weary to the bone." He gave a smile and a shake of his head. "I've had all the excitement I can stand for today. I'll play lord of the manor and have my dinner in bed like royalty."

"Uncle Paddy." Adelia moved closer, dropping a hand on his brow. "You're not feeling well. I'll stay with you."

"Go on with you." He made a dismissing gesture with his hand. "Fussing like your grandmother used to. It's tired I am, not sick. The next thing I know you'll be pouring some strange remedy down my throat or threatening me with a poultice." He glanced up at Travis with a long-suffering sigh. "She's a worrisome bundle, lad. Take her off my hands and give these old bones a rest."

With a nod of masculine understanding, Travis turned to Adelia. "Be ready in forty-five minutes," he stated simply. "I don't like to be late."

"'Do this, do that,'" she fumed, throwing up her hands. "Never a 'will you' or 'may I.' I'm not in the stables now, Travis Grant, and I don't fancy being ordered about." She tossed back her fiery curls and folded her arms across her chest.

Travis raised a quizzical eyebrow before he moved to the door. "Wear that green thing, Dee. I like it." He closed the door against any possible further outbursts.

Dee was ready at the appointed time, having been cajoled by her uncle to leave him and celebrate Majesty's victory. Telling herself she was only going out with the arrogant brute for Paddy's sake, she zipped herself into the green dress as a knock sounded at her door. Muttering disjointedly about the devil's own spawn, she swung open the door and glared.

"Good evening, Adelia," he greeted her, obviously unconcerned by her warlike stance. "You're looking lovely. Are you ready?"

She glowered at him for another moment, wishing she had something handy to throw at him. Tilting her chin, she stepped into the hall, closing the door with force behind her.

She clung to her stubborn silence as the taxi drove through surging traffic, but Travis remained unperturbed, chatting amiably and pointing out various spots of interest. He was making it very difficult for her to keep her anger on the boil.

Defiance wavered as they entered the restaurant, grander than she could ever have imagined. Wide-eyed, she gazed around her at the sophisticated patrons in their evening dress. She allowed herself to be led unresisting to a quiet corner table, greatly impressed by the elegance of the maitre d'. Softly lit and situated for privacy, the table sat high above the throbbing city, the lights blinking and speeding below a direct contrast to their quiet seclusion. She glanced up as their waiter requested her choice of cocktail, then looked across at Travis with a helpless shake of her head. Smiling, he ordered champagne.

"It's a shame we couldn't bring Majesty with us," she commented, then grinned, animosity forgotten. "He did all the work, and we're drinking the champagne."

"I very much doubt he'd appreciate it even if we took him back a bottle. For a Royal steed, he has the taste of a peasant. So"—he paused, allowing his finger to rub gently over her hand as it rested on the cloth—"it's up to us to drink to his victory. Did you know, Adelia, the candlelight scatters gold through your eyes?"

Surprised by his sudden observation, she merely stared, greatly relieved when the arrival of the champagne saved her from inventing a response.

"Shall we have a toast, Dee?"

Lifting the slender-stemmed glass, she smiled, more at ease. "To Majesty, the winner of the Belmont Stakes."

His lips curved as he copied her gesture. "To winning."

"Hungry?" he asked after an interlude of quiet conversation. "What's your pleasure?"

"Well, it won't be mutton and potatoes," she murmured absently, sighing at the strange workings of the world that had shifted her into a new life. Her attention came to a full stop as she glanced over the menu, her eyes lifting to his, wide and astonished.

"Is something wrong?"

"It's robbery, sure as faith; there's not another word for it!"

He leaned forward, taking both her hands in his and grinning at her anxious expression. "Are you sure there's no Scots blood in you?" Adelia opened her mouth to retort, highly insulted, but he raised her hands to his lips, causing the words to die before they were born. "Don't get your Irish up, Dee." He smiled over their joined hands. "And overlook the prices. I'm able to deal with them."

She shook her head. "I can't look at it again—it makes my head spin. I'll have what you have."

Chuckling, he ordered the meal and more wine as his hands held hers captive. When they were once more alone, he turned her hands over, examining her palms, ignoring the sharp jerk she made to release herself.

"You're taking better care of them," he murmured, rubbing his thumb over her skin.

"Aye," she retorted, embarrassed and resentful. "They're not quite as bad as a ditchdigger's these days."

He raised his eyes to hers, watching her a moment without speaking. "I offended you that night. I'm sorry." His gentle tone tilted her balance, and she felt the familiar weakness flowing into her.

"It doesn't matter," she stammered and shrugged and tugged at her hands again. He ignored both verbal and physical protests.

"You have fascinating hands. I've made quite a study of them. Small, exquisite, and totally capable—the three rarely go together. Capable Adelia," he murmured before his eyes fastened on hers again with an intensity that caught her off guard. "You had a bad time on that farm, didn't you?"

"I—no. No, we got along."

"Got along?" he repeated, and she felt his eyes searching her face for the words she was not saying.

"We did what needed to be done." She spoke lightly, not sure what it was he wanted from her. "Aunt Lettie was a strong, stubborn woman, and not one to be beaten easily. I often thought it strange how little she was like Da," she continued, her expression drifting into introspection. "And now I see how little she was like Uncle Paddy, for all she was their sister. Perhaps it was the demands of having to take on me and the farm that left her so little time for the gentler things. Such small things: a kiss goodnight, a word of affection . . . a child can starve with a full plate."

She brought herself back with a shake of the head, surprised by her own words and uneasy under his glance. She groped for some way to turn the subject. "I only had the farm to concern me; she had the farm and me, and I think I was more trouble than the farm." She smiled, willing him to lighten his features with one of his own. "She told me a time or two I had too loose a grip on my temper, but, of course, I've tightened the hold now."

"Have you?" At last the smile curved his mouth.

"Oh, aye." She gave him a solemn and guileless nod. "I'm a very mild sort of person."

The smile spread to a grin as their meal was set before them. As they ate, conversation drifted into generalities, an easy flow of words, as undemanding and soothing as the wine that accompanied the food.

"Come," he said suddenly and rose. "Dance with me."

Before she could voice agreement or protest, she found herself being led to the dance floor and enfolded in his all too familiar arms. Her first stiffness at the contact melted as she relaxed against him, surrendering herself to his movements and the quiet music. Surely, she decided, allowing both mind and body to float, everyone's entitled to a taste of heaven. Tonight I'm taking mine. Tomorrow will come, all too soon.

The night was magic, as if a fairy had granted her a wish, and the very briefness of it heightened her senses. She tucked all the sights and sensations into a corner of her mind to be treasured and sighed over when day broke the spell.

It was late when they stepped into the warm night, and though Adelia's eyes were heavy, she wished the evening were just beginning. Clinging to the last enchanted minutes, she made no objection when Travis drew her close to his side in the cab.

"Tired, Dee?" he murmured, his lips brushing the top of her head so lightly she was not sure she hadn't imagined it.

"No," she said in a sigh, thinking how right her head felt cushioned against his shoulder.

He laughed softly, his voice slow and warm, and his fingers stroked through the silk of her hair until her mind drifted into the world of half-dreams.

"Dee?" She heard her name but, loath to rouse herself from the heavenly comfort, she made a small murmur of protest. "We're back," Travis announced, lifting her chin with his finger.

"Back?" Her heavy lids opened, and she stared at the

face so close to hers, dreams and reality mixed into confusion.

"At the hotel," he explained, brushing tumbled hair back from her face.

"Oh." She sat up, realizing the dream was over.

He was silent on the elevator ride to their floor, and Adelia used the time to regain her grip on reality. They moved to her door, and Travis removed her key from his pocket to unlock it as she raised her head to thank him. The smile she meant to accompany her thanks faded as she met his eyes. The concentrated, steady look caused her to step backward, only to find herself trapped against the doorframe, while he closed the distance without seeming to move at all. His hand slipped beneath the curtain of her hair, while he caressed her neck in a slow, lazy motion. They gazed silently at each other; then, very slowly, he lowered his head and pressed his mouth to hers in a kiss that was as soft as a summer breeze, unlike the others he had given and ultimately more devastating. She clung to the lapels of his jacket, trying to steady her world, but soon gave up all such efforts and moved her arms to encircle his neck, rising on her toes to meet him demand for demand.

His lips moved to trail along her face, brushing easily along cheeks and closed lids as if savoring the taste. Trembling heat was replaced by a new and poignant languor, a weak giddiness induced by a far more potent potion than champagne. Her hands moved to tangle in his hair as her body melted to his, submitting to whatever he would ask, willing to give whatever he would take.

She felt his hunger when his mouth took hers again, the hardness of his body as he pressed her more urgently against him, and with a moan of pleasure at the new demand, she drew him yet closer. The longing to be possessed, insistent and clamorous, raged through her like fire. She strained against him, her heart throbbing and echoing in her ears as she felt him devour what was offered, then demand more.

Abruptly he released her mouth, his hand moving to brush against her cheek and linger a moment, and she closed her eyes again, inviting his lips to claim hers.

"Goodnight, Dee," he murmured, and giving her a nudge into the room, he closed the door between them.

Adelia stared at the smooth, empty panel, bringing her hands to burning cheeks. Stunned both by her unprecedented actions and by the sudden rejection, she found it impossible to move. She had offered, and he had refused. Even in her inexperience, she knew her willingness could not have been mistaken for anything other than full surrender. But he had not wanted her, not completely. Her own standards had dissolved in his arms, but he had walked away and left her alone. And how else could it be? she asked herself, shutting eyes tight on threatening moisture. I could never be anything to him but a groom for his horses. Someone who amuses him from time to time.

He was only being kind to me, trying to show me a pleasant evening. She trembled once. *I should be content with that and stop searching for what can never be mine.* Glancing down at the soft folds of her dress, Adelia reminded herself she was not Cinderella, and in any case it was long past midnight.

They boarded the plane the next morning in a warm, light drizzle. Again, reporters hounded them. Adelia scurried up the ramp, leaving the men to deal with them. Shaking raindrops from her hair and her cream-colored skirt, she pressed her face to a window and watched Travis disengage himself from the press.

During the flight, she skimmed through a magazine, reluctant to enter into conversation. Travis's attitude toward her that morning had been casual, friendly, and vaguely preoccupied, and the stirring need in her that lingered from their previous evening made it a strain for her to mirror his mood.

When he disappeared into the forward cabin with Steve, she let out a deep breath and began to pace the lounge. What am I to do? she asked herself desperately. How can I control the way he makes me feel? I'll be making a fool of myself over him; he's bound to see the way I love him. Then he'll be feeling sorry for me, and I couldn't stand that. I'll just have to find a way to keep more distance between us.

Her gaze wandered over to her uncle, all thoughts of her problem fleeing her mind as she observed the unhealthy cast to his normally ruddy skin.

"Uncle Paddy." She moved to him, cupping his face in her hands and studying him carefully. "You're not well. What is it?"

"Nothing, Dee." The strain in his voice drew her brows together. "I'm just tired."

"You're like ice." She knelt down in front of him so that their faces were level. "You see a doctor the minute we get home. It won't be long now. I'll fetch you a cover and a cup of tea."

"Now, Dee, I'm just feeling my age." He stopped and grimaced in pain.

"What is it?" she demanded, hands already searching to comfort. "Where are you hurting?"

"Just a twinge." The words came out in jerks before he began to gasp for air.

"Uncle Paddy! Merciful heaven, Uncle Paddy!" She clutched at him as he collapsed, falling forward out of the chair and into her arms.

She was not even aware that she shouted for Travis over and over, desperately, helplessly, as she lowered her uncle onto the floor. But suddenly he was there, brushing her hands aside, his head lowering to the stocky chest.

"Tell John to radio ahead for an ambulance," he called to Steve over his shoulder, his hands beginning to push in a steady rhythm on Paddy's chest. "He's had a heart attack."

With a moan, Adelia clutched Paddy's hand to her own heart as if to transfer her strength. "Travis, in the name of heaven—Travis, is he dying? Oh, please, he can't be dying."

"Stop it," he commanded sharply, the words as effective as a slap. "Pull yourself together. I can't deal with this and hysterics as well."

One breath came and went quickly, then she took several more, deep and steady, her hand clutching and unclutching convulsively over Paddy's. Slowly the hysteria was buried under a wall of control, and she began to stroke her uncle's head and speak in soft, reassuring tones, though she knew he probably couldn't hear her.

Seconds dragged and minutes crawled with Travis continually monitoring the unconscious man's pulse, only Adelia's murmurs breaking the silence. She felt the change in the plane's speed and the loss of altitude, heard the whine of the landing gear and felt the jerk of wheels on ground, but her flow of words continued, and she kept her uncle's hand firmly in hers.

She watched through a haze of unreality as paramedics worked on him before transferring him to the waiting ambulance. As she made to join them, Travis took her arm, telling her they would follow in the car. She went without protest, her mind and heart encased in the numbing ice of fear.

She responded only in vague monosyllables to his attempts at consolation, and after a glance at her pale, waxen features, he concentrated on weaving through the traffic toward the hospital.

The long wait began in a small, cheerless lounge scattered with ancient magazines that some read to pass the time and others stared at in desperation. Adelia did neither, but sat, still as a stone, her hands gripped together in her lap, neither moving nor speaking as Travis paced the room like a caged tiger. Her mind was screaming in protest, searching for the power to pray as fear devoured her. Her control was tight, stretching at the seams like an ill-fitting coat as the minutes passed.

When at last a white-coated figure approached, Travis whirled and advanced on him. "You're Padrick Cunnane's family?" the doctor asked, glancing from the tall, powerful man to the small, pale woman.

"Yes." His answer was curt as he too glanced at Adelia. "What's going on? How is he?"

"He suffered a coronary—not a massive attack. He is conscious now, but his condition is aggravated by anxiety over someone named Dee."

Adelia brought her head up. "I'm Dee. Is he going to die?"

The doctor studied the pale, composed features and took a step closer to her. "We're doing all we can to stabilize his condition, but his own anxiety is a factor in his recovery. His concern is focused on you. I'm going to let you see him. You must do nothing to upset him; persuade him to relax." He turned back to the dark man whose eyes were fixed on the woman. "Are you Travis?" At his nod, the doctor continued. "He wants to see you, too. Come with me."

Travis took Adelia's hand and lifted her from the chair, leading her after the retreating white coat.

"Five minutes," the doctor cautioned, and led them into the Cardiac Care Unit.

Her hand tightened in Travis's as she saw her uncle in the hospital bed, wires and tubes joining him to machines that whirled and buzzed. He was pale and drawn and suddenly old, and her mind screamed in revolt as she struggled for control.

"Dee." The voice was weak and unsteady, and she moved close to take his hand in hers.

"Uncle Paddy." Kissing the hand, she held it to her cheek. "Everything's going to be fine. They'll be taking good care of you, and soon you'll be home again."

"I want a priest, Dee."

"All right, don't worry." A cold hand gripped and squeezed her heart, and she felt the trembling start in her knees but forced it away.

"It's you I'm worried for. You can't be left all alone again, not again." His voice was rasping, and she soothed and murmured. "Travis . . . is Travis here?" He continued to fret, and she turned, fear shining from her eyes.

"Right here, Paddy." He moved to stand next to Adelia.

"You've got to take care of her for me, Travis. I'm giving her to you. She'll be all alone if anything happens to me. Such a wee thing she is and so young. It's been too hard for her . . . I should have been there for her before. I was going to make it up to her." He made a feeble gesture with his free hand. "I want your word you'll be taking care of her. I can trust you, Travis, with what's mine."

"I'll take care of her; you have my word." His answer was calm and steady, his hand closing over the two that were joined. "You don't have to worry about Dee. I'm going to marry her."

The relaxation in the taut face was visible, his breathing slowing. "You take care of my little Dee, then. I want to see the two of you married. Will you bring a priest here, and let me see it done?"

"I'll arrange it, but you'll have to relax and rest. Let the doctors do their job. Dee and I will be married right here this afternoon. All I need is a judge to sign a waiver of the two-day waiting period."

"Aye, I'll rest till you come back. Till you come back, Dee." She forced her lips into a smile and placed a kiss on his brow before she followed the doctor and Travis from the room. She whirled on him as soon as the door closed behind them.

"Not here," Travis commanded, gripping her arm. "Is there somewhere private we can talk?" he asked the doctor in calm tones. After directing them to an office, the doctor closed the door and discreetly left them alone.

CHAPTER SEVEN

Adelia jerked out of Travis's hold as the door shut, fear and despair bubbling into fury. "How could you do that? How could you tell Uncle Paddy you were going to marry me? How could you lie to him that way?"

"I didn't lie, Adelia," Travis returned evenly. "I have every intention of marrying you."

"What are you thinking of, saying such things?" she continued as if he had not spoken. "It's cruel, with him lying there sick and helpless and trusting you. You had no right to make such a promise. You'll break his heart, you—"

"Get hold of yourself," Travis commanded, taking her shoulders and administering a brisk shake. "I told him what he needed to hear, and by God you'll do what he wants if it helps save him."

"I'll not be a party to such a cruel lie."

The grip on her shoulders increased, but she was beyond physical pain. "Doesn't he mean anything to you? Are you so selfish and hardheaded that you can't make a small sacrifice to help him?" She flinched as if he had struck her and turned blindly away, her hands gripping the back of a chair. "We'll stand in that room this afternoon, and we'll be married, and you make him believe it's what you want. When we know he's strong enough, you can get a divorce and end it."

She drew her hands over her eyes, pain washing over her in turbulent waves. *Uncle Paddy lying there half dead—Travis telling me we're marrying and divorcing in the same breath. Oh, I need someone to tell me what to do,* she thought frantically.

To be his wife, to belong to him—she'd wanted it so badly that she hadn't even dared to think of it, and now he was telling her that it was going to happen, that it *had* to happen. She was hurt beyond words. It would have been easier to go through life without him than to be his wife for an hour without his love. *Divorce*—he had said it so easily. He was talking of divorce before he had even put the ring on her finger. Taking a deep breath, she tried to force herself to think clearly, but she was too overcome by the bleak realization that he was not talking of a real marriage, a marriage of love, that he didn't want her for herself, but rather for her uncle's sake. There must be another way. There had to be another way. She swallowed painfully to steady her voice, "I'm Catholic. I can't get a divorce," she said dully.

"An annulment, then."

She stared at him in horrified silence, "An annulment?"

"Yes, an annulment. It should not be any problem if the marriage isn't consummated. It will simply be a matter of a little paperwork." He spoke in calm, businesslike tones, and her hands tightened on the chair as she attempted to fight her way through to reason. "For Pete's sake, Dee," he said impatiently, "can't you go through the motions of a ceremony for Paddy's sake? It won't cost you anything. It could make the difference between his living and dying."

He took her shoulders again, spinning her around, checking his anger as he studied the transparent glow to her skin, the fear in her eyes that stared back at him. He could feel the trembling begin under his hands and watched as she shut her eyes and tried to stem it. He muttered an oath, then drew her against him and wrapped his arms around her. "I'm sorry, Dee. Shouting at you is hardly going to make it any easier, is it? Come on, sit down." Leading her to a sofa, he sat beside her, keeping her close inside his arms. "You've been hanging on to control for too long; have a good cry. Then we'll talk."

"No, I don't cry. I never cry. It doesn't help." She held herself rigid in his grasp, but he continued to hold her close. "Please, let me go." She felt her control slipping and struggled against the arms that would not give way. "I have to think. If I just knew what to do . . ." Her breath came in short gasps, the trembling no longer controllable, and her hands clutched at his shirtfront to keep from falling. "Travis, I'm so afraid."

She burst into violent sobs, and his arms tightened around her. Once the tears escaped, she could not stop them. Held in check for more than a dozen lonely years, they now flowed freely down her face pressed into Travis's chest. He kept silent, one hand stroking her hair, and let the storm run its course.

The sobs lost their force, subsiding to soft whimpering, until she lay quiet in his arms, empty and spent. She gave one long shuddering sigh. "I'll do whatever you think has to be done."

How Travis arranged the paperwork so quickly, she never questioned. She had been too numb to deal with technicalities. The only stand she had made was to refuse to leave the hospital even for a quick rest or a meal. Determinedly, she had planted herself in the waiting room and refused to budge.

She signed her name on the license where she was told, greeted the slender young priest who would make her Travis's wife, and accepted a handful of flowers from a friendly nurse who claimed a woman couldn't be a bride without a bouquet. She smiled at this, a small, frozen smile that hurt her cheeks, knowing she was not really a bride. Legally she would bear the name of the man she loved, but the vows they would exchange would mean nothing to him. The words and motions were only a charade to bring comfort to a sick man.

They stood side by side in the stark room, surrounded by machines, the air heavy with the smell of medicine, and became husband and wife. Adelia repeated the priest's words in a calm, clear voice and looked blankly at the signet ring Travis slipped on her finger before closing her fist over it. It hung loose on her finger and lay like a stone on her heart. In less than ten minutes it was all over, and she accepted his light, brief kiss without demur.

Adelia Cunnane Grant bent over and kissed her uncle's brow. He smiled up at her, his eyes lighting with a suggestion of their usual merriment. She knew in that instant that Travis had been right.

"Little Dee," he muttered, seeking her hand and clinging to it. "You'll be happy now. Travis is a good man."

She forced a smile and patted his cheek. "Aye, Uncle Paddy. You'll rest now, and we'll be able to bring you home soon."

"I'll rest," he agreed, and his eyes raised above her head to meet Travis's. "Treat her with care, lad . . . she's a Thoroughbred."

They drove home in silence. The sun broke through patches of clouds to filter on the road. Adelia watched the play of light and kept her mind a blank. Pulling up in front of the main house, Travis broke the heavy silence.

"I called ahead and informed my housekeeper of the wedding. She'll have prepared your room by now. Your things have been brought over."

She frowned. "I'm not—"

"For the time being," he cut in, his eyes narrowing, "you are my wife, and as such you will live in my house. We'll keep separate bedrooms," he added in a tone that caused her mouth to shut quickly. "We will, however, maintain the outward appearance of a married couple. There is no reason for the present that anyone other than you and I know of this arrangement. Explanations now would only complicate matters."

"I see. You're right, of course."

He sighed at the strain in her voice and went on in gentler tones. "I'll make it as easy on you as possible, Dee. I only ask that you play your part; otherwise you'll be free to do as you please. There'll be no need for you to work."

"I can't work with the horses?" Adelia broke in, eyes widening in dismay. "But, Travis—"

"Adelia, listen to me." He cupped her face in his hand. "You can do as you like. You don't even know what that means, do you?" His brows drew together at her blank, bewildered face. "If you want to work with the horses, you're free to do so, but not as my employee, as my wife. You can spend your time lounging around the country club or cleaning out stalls—it's up to you."

"All right." Slowly, she unclenched the fists that were tight in her lap. "I'll do my best to make it easy on you as well. I know you were right to do this for Uncle Paddy, and I'm grateful to you."

He stared at her for another moment, then shrugged and slipped from the car.

When they entered the house, a plump, gray-haired woman bustled into the hall to greet them, wiping her hands on a full, white apron.

"Hannah, this is Adelia, my wife."

Warm hazel eyes inspected Adelia and smiled in approval. "Welcome, Mrs. Grant. It's about time a lovely young thing lured my Travis to the altar." Adelia murmured something she hoped was appropriate. "I'm sorry to hear about Paddy; we're all fond of him." The treacherous tears started again, and Adelia closed her eyes against them. "Oh, the poor thing's dead on her feet. Travis, take her up; the room's ready for her."

She started the climb up the staircase, which seemed to take on the proportions of Mount Olympus. Without a word, Travis swept her into his arms and carried her up the remaining steps and down a long, carpeted hallway. Entering a bedroom, he crossed the floor and laid her on a huge four-poster bed.

"I'm sorry." She lifted her hand and dropped it again. There seemed to be nothing further to say.

He sat next to her and brushed the hair from her cheeks.

"Adelia, when will you learn weakness is not always a flaw? Darned Irish stubbornness," he muttered, frowning down at her. "I'd swear nothing else kept you on your feet this long. There hasn't been a whisper of color in your cheeks for the past six hours."

She stared up at him, wanting to pull him down to her and feel the comfort of his warmth. He turned abruptly and moved to a large cherrywood wardrobe.

"I don't know where Hannah put your night clothes." Pulling open the double doors, he exposed the meager contents. "Good heavens, is this all you have?"

She tried to snap at him, but found gathering the strength too great an effort. Moving over to a mirrored triple dresser, he began opening drawers, muttering and swearing, and she lay back and watched him, too weary to be embarrassed that he should handle her clothes with such familiarity.

He pulled out a plain, high-necked cotton gown and, after a brief disparaging scrutiny, brought it to her. "Tomorrow, for heaven's sake, go shopping and buy some clothes."

"Don't you order me about, Travis Grant." She sat up, unable to keep quiet any longer, and snapped at him with a ghost of her usual spirit.

He stared down at her without expression. "While we're married, Adelia, we'll be expected to socialize, and you'll have to dress properly. We'll see to it tomorrow. Now, can you manage to change by yourself, or do you need some help?"

Snatching the gown from his hands, she spoke stiffly. "I can manage very well."

"Good. Change and get some rest. You won't do Paddy any good if you make yourself ill." Without waiting for her reply, he turned and strode from the room, shutting the door behind him.

Too tired to appreciate the beauty of the light, airy room, she slipped off the skirt and blouse which had served as her wedding dress and pulled the cotton night-gown over her head. Folding down the mint-green spread, she crawled between the smooth sheets and fell instantly into the deep, dreamless sleep of exhaustion.

The birds woke her, as was their habit, chattering and chirping outside the window. Opening her eyes, she focused on the unfamiliar surroundings and remembered. She relaxed the fist that had remained tight over her wedding ring throughout the night, while her eyes made a slow survey of the room. She had thought her bedroom in the garage house large, but she estimated this would hold two rooms that size. The walls were muted green and white striped paper, trimmed with dark woodwork. The furniture was cherry, both the large wardrobe and dresser in which Travis had rummaged the evening before, and a small writing desk, two night tables, and a small pie-crust table which served a tufted-back chair. On the small table was a vase bursting with fresh flowers. Their scent drifted to her as she sat up in bed, hugging her knees close. She sighed as she gazed at the tall French windows which led to the balcony, thinking she had never seen such a lovely room. *How happy I could be here if only Uncle Paddy was well, and Travis . . .* She tried to clear her mind of such negative thoughts. Thrusting back the covers, she jumped out of bed.

After showering and dressing in her only remaining skirt, she ventured downstairs, hoping she could locate the kitchen in the strange house which was now her home.

"Good morning, Dee." Travis appeared from a room off the downstairs hall, which she later learned was his office. "Feeling better?"

"Aye," she answered, suddenly shy and uncertain in front of the man who was her husband. "I don't know when I've slept so long."

"You were exhausted." She kept herself still as he lifted her chin and examined her face like a parent seeking to find signs of ill health in a child. "Your color's back," he said at length and smiled.

"I'm fine." She managed to remain passive as his hand continued to hold her chin. "I was wondering if I could call the hospital . . . and see if Uncle Paddy—" Her hands fluttered, then clung together in front of her.

"I've already called; his condition has stabilized." His hands moved to rest on her shoulders. "He spent a peaceful night."

A tremor passed through her. She shut her eyes and buried her face against Travis's chest. After a moment, she felt his arms encircle her lightly. "Oh, Travis, I thought he was going to die. I was afraid we would lose him."

He held her away until she tilted her head to look up at him. "He's going to be all right, with a little time and care, and no worries." His features relaxed. "Of course, when he gets home, he'll have to slow down. We'll have to bully him into it."

"Aye." Her smile was like the stars through the clouds. "But there's two of us."

"So there are," he murmured, then tousled her hair. "I imagine you're starving. I couldn't wake you for dinner last night."

"I feel like I haven't eaten in a week." With a sigh, she pushed at the hair he had just ruffled. "If you'll show me the kitchen, I'll start breakfast."

"Hannah's seeing to it," he informed her, taking her arm and leading her into a large dining room. Noticing the expression on her face, he whispered confidentially in her ear as he pulled out a chair, "Don't worry, I've been eating her cooking all my life."

"Oh, I didn't mean—I meant no disrespect. It's only that I'm not used to having someone fix my meals." Her expression bordered on horror, and he leaned back in his chair and laughed.

"Don't look so stricken, Dee. Hannah will think I'm beating you already."

"Well, I wouldn't want you to think that I meant . . ." She fumbled for something to say which would release her from her awkwardness. "The room you gave me is lovely. I want to thank you."

"I'm glad you like it."

At his careless response, she was grateful for Hannah's entrance with a steaming breakfast platter.

"Good morning, Mrs. Grant. I hope you're feeling better after a good night's rest." She set the platter on the table and Adelia smiled up at her.

"Thank you, I feel fine." She was careful not to start at her new title.

"Hungry though, I'll be bound." Nodding, she studied the pixielike face. "Travis told me you ate next to nothing yesterday, so I'll expect you to do full justice to your breakfast."

"You should be warned, Dee, not to trifle with Hannah," Travis put in from across the table. "She can be ferocious. Personally, she terrifies me."

"Don't you listen to his nonsense, Mrs. Grant." She sent Travis a scowl before giving her attention back to Adelia. "You'll be busy for a while with Paddy in the hospital, but once you're settled, you let me know how you want things done. For now, if it's agreeable, I'll just plan your meals around your visits to the hospital."

"I—whatever you think best."

"We'll have plenty of time to talk about it," the housekeeper concluded. "Now, you get to your breakfast while it's hot." With this she bustled from the room.

Adelia listened to Travis's breakfast conversation,

answering only when it was required, while she slowly took in her surroundings. The dining room was large with dark wainscoting and elegantly patterned wallpaper. The furniture was heavy, gleaming oak. Everywhere was the glow of silver and glimmer of crystal.

"Travis," she said suddenly, and his brows rose in acknowledgment as he sipped his coffee. "I don't fit into all this. I haven't the way or the experience to know what's expected of me. I don't want to be an embarrassment to you, and I'm mortally afraid I'll do or say something horrible, and—"

"Adelia." The one word stopped her rambling. She saw from his expression that she had already made a mistake. From the way his face was set, she waited for him to rant at her, but when he spoke, his voice was calm and precise. "You will not embarrass me, you could not embarrass me. Relax and be what you are, that's what's expected of you."

They lapsed into silence. Adelia toyed with the remainder of her eggs. "By the way," Travis began, and she raised her eyes and saw he was smiling, "you've had your picture in the paper."

"My picture?"

"Yes." His smile widened at her frowning expression. "Two pictures, as a matter of fact. There's one of you and Steve with the two of you sitting on the paddock fence, and there's one of you and me taken after the Belmont Stakes."

Color flooded her cheeks as she realized the contents of the second picture. "I don't know why they kept following me around with their cameras and their pencils."

"I can't imagine," Travis returned, his lips curving again. "It appears that the press has had a splendid time speculating about the romances of my attractive groom. . . ."

Her eyes widened, and the color ebbed and flowed again. "Are you meaning . . . Oh, what a passel of nonsense! Steve and I are friends, and you and I . . ." She faltered, sputtered, and fell into excruciating silence.

"Married, Adelia, is what we are, friends or not." With what she thought was a very odd smile, he drained his coffee and rose. "I don't suppose it will sound like such a passel of nonsense to the press when our current relationship is leaked to them. I can keep it out of the papers for a while, but we'll have to deal with it sooner or later. . . . I take it you're done since you've been playing with your fork for the last ten minutes." Securing her arm, he brought her to her feet. "Now, if you'll take that frown off your face, I'll drive you to the hospital."

Any anxiety Adelia still harbored was dispelled by the appearance of her uncle. The color on his cheeks, which had appeared a ghastly gray the day before, was now closer to his normal, ruddy hue. His eyes twinkled as Travis brought her into the room. His voice was weak rather than booming, but steady and unforced. When he complained about being hooked up to blasted, noisy machines, her concern melted into laughter, and, kissing the hand she held in hers, she felt the last vestige of tension dissolve.

After a short visit, Travis drew her into the hall. "You won't be able to stay too long this time. The doctor says he tires easily and needs his rest. That, and seeing you, is the best medicine he can get."

"I won't tire him, Travis," she promised. "He's looking so much better, I can hardly believe my eyes. I'll only stay a little while more. As soon as I see he's tiring, I'll go."

He looked down at her smiling face, his fingers tangling absently with the ends of her hair. "I have to get back now, but Trish will be along soon to take you shopping." His hand dropped, and he stared past her as if suddenly preoccupied. "She'll know just what you need, and if you like, she can bring you back here for a while longer this afternoon."

"It's kind of you to be doing all this, Travis." She touched his arm to bring his attention back to her. "I don't know how to repay you for all that you've done already."

"It's nothing." He shrugged off her thanks and, drawing out his wallet, handed her some bills. "I've made arrangements for you to charge whatever you need. Trish will be there to see to the details, but you'll need some cash as well."

"But, Travis, it's so much, I can't . . ."

"Don't argue, just take it." He closed her hands over the bills in a final, impatient gesture. "Give it to Trish to hold for you, and for heaven's sake, Dee," he added with exasperation, "buy yourself a purse. I'll see you this evening."

He strode down the long corridor, leaving Adelia staring after him.

CHAPTER EIGHT

When Trish arrived, she greeted Paddy with an affectionate kiss and told him firmly that anyone could see he was
faking and enjoying being the center of attention. After
a brief visit, she hurried Adelia out into the corridor and
hugged her with enthusiasm.

"I'm so happy about you and Travis." Her eyes shone
with affection. Adelia began to feel the first weight of
guilt. "Now I have the little sister I always wanted." Adelia
was treated to yet another hug. "Jerry sends his best."
She referred to her husband, her face wreathed in smiles.
"The twins went wild when I told them that Dee was
now their aunt. They claim that makes them Irish and
soon they'll be fey, too."

Adelia responded with smiles and agreeable murmurs,

hating herself for the deception and wishing with all her heart that she could confide in the woman whom she felt was a true friend. But she had given Travis her word and she would keep it.

Hooking her arm through Adelia's, Trish began to stroll toward the elevator. "Travis has given me firm instructions to see that you buy a complete wardrobe." She grinned with obvious pleasure as the elevator began its slow descent to the ground floor. "Of course I told him that I would be more than happy to follow orders and spend his money with abandon."

"He said you should hold this for me." Dee handed Trish the wad of bills, which she accepted and placed absently in her tan leather bag.

"This is going to be fun."

Adelia smiled faintly.

If Adelia was under the impression that this shopping expedition would follow along the lines of her first, she was soon enlightened to the contrary. Trish ignored department stores for the more exclusive shops. Adelia began to feel as if she were caught in the backlash of a tropical storm. She was whirled through shops while Trish made selections, dismissed or accepted articles with a nod or murmur to the sales clerks. Purchases mounted into an alarming mountain, leaving Adelia dizzy and confused.

Evening dresses that shimmered and flowed, sports-

wear Adelia considered suitable for royalty, soft, cob-
webby lingerie that seemed too fragile to be real; all were
tried on, inspected thoroughly by Trish's critical eye, then
approved or rejected. Italian shoes and handbags, French
scarves and negligees were included with a nod for foreign
craftsmanship.

"Trish, surely Travis didn't mean for me to buy all this,"
Adelia objected, looking uneasily at the stacks of boxes
and bags. "One person couldn't live long enough to wear
all those clothes."

"You'd be surprised," Trish murmured absently as she
surveyed a long, sweeping evening gown in brilliant green
silk. "You'll be doing a lot of traveling, and there are par-
ties and official functions . . ." Her voice trailed off as
she held the gown in front of Adelia and narrowed her
eyes in consternation. "Travis was very specific. He told
me to see to it that you have everything necessary and to
ignore the arguments you were sure to give me. That is
precisely what I'm doing. Here." She thrust the gown into
Adelia's hands. "Go try this on. Green is your color."

"We can't buy anything else," Adelia stated flatly, attempting to hold her ground. "There'll be no room in the
car for us when the packages are put in."

"Then, little sister, we'll hire a van." Giving her a shove
into the dressing room, Trish gave her attention to a white
linen blouse.

———

Late that afternoon, Adelia stared at the packages that lay piled high on her bed. With a weary sigh, she turned and left the room. Hannah greeted her as she stood in the downstairs hall, unsure whether she should stay in the house or seek out Travis at the stables.

"Mrs. Grant, how's Paddy?"

"He's looking just wonderful. I left him only an hour ago."

"You poor thing, you look all in."

"I've been shopping. I think cleaning out the entire stable would be less of a chore."

Hannah chuckled. "A cup of tea is what you need. Just sit down and I'll bring you one."

"Hannah." She stopped the plump woman before she could bustle away. "Could I . . . would you mind if I came into the kitchen and had one with you?" She made a small, helpless gesture with her hands. "I'm not used to being waited on."

The round face brightened, and a motherly arm slipped around Adelia's waist. "Just you come with me, missy. We'll have a nice cup of tea and a little chat."

It was there Travis found them together an hour later. He stood in the doorway watching in amused amazement as Adelia and Hannah worked on dinner preparations, chattering like lifelong partners.

"Well, well, well, a miracle in this day and age." Two heads turned toward him as he gave his brief, charming grin. "I never thought I'd live to see the day when you'd let anyone work in your kitchen, Hannah." He glanced from his housekeeper to the small woman at her side. "What kind of Irish charm did you use on her, Dee?"

"Just her charming self, you young rascal," Hannah stated with great dignity. "Now, missy"—she removed the vegetable parer from Adelia's hand—"you just run along now and keep that man out from under my feet. He's always been a nuisance in the kitchen."

Travis grinned again, serenely unperturbed. "Come out on the terrace, Dee," he invited and captured her hand. "It's too nice to stay indoors."

He led her out through wide French doors and onto the smooth stone surface of the terrace. The sweet scent of plants and flowers filled the June evening. The sun still cast a warm golden light, scattering shadows on the stone.

"So, Dee," he began, seating her in a striped cushioned chair and dropping down in an identical one across from her, "did you get everything you needed?"

"Everything?" she repeated. She closed her eyes and shuddered. "Never in my life have I ever seen so many clothes, much less put them on. Trying on this, taking off that." Opening her eyes again, she met his wide smile with a look of disdain. "You won't be smiling when you have to build another room to hold them all. Your sister is a stubborn woman, Travis Grant. She just kept tossing things at me and shoving me into dressing rooms. I couldn't make her listen to reason."

"I thought Trish might be helpful."

"Helpful?" She gave a long-suffering sigh. "I felt like I was being blown about by a whirlwind. Packages growing like a great mountain, and Trish smiling and finding something else. She had a fine time," she added, mystified.

"Yes, I imagine she did. I don't see her having much trouble filling out your wardrobe." He smiled at the picture and leaned back in his chair.

"Travis," she began after a small pause, "whatever will I do with all those things?"

"You might try wearing them," he suggested. "It's the usual procedure."

"That's fine for a time. I understand I can't go about in my old clothes with things as they are now. But after, when . . ." She stumbled and searched for the right words. "When things are back as they were before, I—"

"The clothes are yours, Adelia," he interrupted with a quick gesture of his hand. "You'll keep them whatever happens. I certainly have no use for them." Rising, he paced the length of the terrace and stared out over the smooth expanse of lawn.

Adelia sat silently, concerned by his anger and bewildered over how she had caused it. She stood and approached him, laying a tentative hand on his arm. "I'm sorry, Travis. That sounded ungrateful; I didn't mean it to. Everything's happening so fast. I don't want to take advantage of what you're doing for me."

"One can hardly call it taking advantage when it's like

pulling teeth to get you to accept anything." His shoulders moved and he turned to face her. "Adelia," he said with a sigh somewhere between impatience and amusement, "you are so artless."

She did not question the ambiguity of his words, so relieved was she that his anger had faded and he was smiling at her again.

"I have something for you." Reaching into his pocket, he drew out a small box. "My signet ring was fine in an emergency, but it looks big enough to fit on your wrist."

"Oh." She found nothing else to say as she opened the box and found a small band studded with winking diamonds and glowing emeralds.

He removed the large, masculine ring from her finger and replaced it with the jeweled wedding band. "I'd say that suits a bit better."

"It fits," she murmured inadequately, overcome with the longing to throw her arms around him and cry out her love.

"I've studied those hands enough to make an educated guess as to your ring size." He spoke lightly and, dropping her hand, moved back to his chair.

Swallowing the obstruction in her throat, she followed him. "Travis." She stood in front of his chair, feeling the strangeness of looking down at him. "Travis, you're doing all the giving, and I have nothing for you. I want to . . . Is there nothing I can do for you? Is there nothing you want from me?"

He met her eyes with a long, unfathomable stare until she thought he would not speak at all. "For now, Dee," he said at length, "the best thing you can do for me is to accept what's given and not question it."

She sighed at his answer. "All right, Travis, if it pleasures you."

He stood and took her hand, a finger running over her wedding band. "Yes, it pleasures me. Come inside and we'll eat, and I'll tell you how Majesty sulked for you today."

The next two weeks passed quickly, Adelia's days full between the hospital and the stables. Paddy was moved into a regular hospital room. No longer attached to machines, he improved daily, complaining vigorously about being stuck in bed and poked with needles. The easy friendliness of the men at the stables and the soothing routine of riding and grooming brought a sense of normalcy back to Adelia's life, and at times she almost forgot she was Mrs. Travis Grant.

Travis was kind and casually affectionate, speaking of Paddy's recovery and on the general topic of horses when they took meals together. He left Adelia free to pursue whatever project she chose, making no demands, his attitude tolerant, generous, and distant. She was aware of a subtle change in their relationship, and she found it did not please her. He never raised his voice or criticized, and he never touched her in any way unless strictly necessary. She wished fervently that he would yell at her or shake her, or do something to lose his cool, composed manner. Their relationship was now far less personal than it had been when they had been employer and employee.

She was returning to the house one afternoon, wondering if Travis had returned from a business appointment, when she stopped and gaped at a large, dirty gray mound of fur exploring a bed of marigolds. After a careful study, she concluded that under the grubby fur was a dog of rather alarming size.

"I wouldn't do that if I were you," she said in a quiet voice that had the dog's head jerking up. "Now, don't be running off. I won't hurt you." The dog hesitated, eyeing her warily, and she kept the distance between them and continued to speak. "It's just that I've seen Travis's gardener—a terrifying man he is. And one that wouldn't take kindly to anyone digging at his flowers." She crouched down, and they studied each other eye to eye. "Are you lost, then, or just roaming? I can see by your eyes you're hungry, I've been hungry myself a time or two. Wait here," she ordered and stood. "I'll fetch you something."

Entering the kitchen, she commandeered a large hunk of roast beef. The whine of the vacuum cleaner was audible from the living room, and, deciding it would be foolish to disturb Hannah and vowing to apologize to her after the deed was done, Adelia slipped back outside.

"It's prime beef, my lad, and from the looks of you,

you've not seen its kind before." She placed the offering on the grass and stepped back a few paces.

He came forward slowly at first, eyes shifting from the beef to his benefactor until either his confidence or his hunger grew and he threw himself on the unexpected meal. She watched him polish off what would have fed three hungry men, finding enormous pleasure in his appetite.

"Well, now, you've made a pig of yourself, and that's the truth, and you don't look a bit ashamed." She grinned and watched the long tail thump in agreement. "Pleased with yourself, are you?" Before she could move, she found herself flat on her back, trapped under a hundred pounds of appreciation, her face being drenched by a large wet tongue. "Get off me, you great hairy brute!" Laughing, she pushed to no avail and tried to turn her face from the moisture. "Surely there's not a rib that's not cracked, and it's God's truth you've not had a bath since the day you were born."

After much pleading and wriggling, she managed to release herself, staggered to her feet, and surveyed the damage. Her shirt and jeans were covered with dirt, her arms smeared with it. She pushed at her disordered hair and stared down at the dog that sat at her feet, his tongue hanging out in adoration.

"We'll both be needing a bath now. Well—" She let out a deep breath, tilted her head, and considered. "You wait here, and I'll see what can be done about you. It might be best if you were cleaned up a bit before I introduce you."

On the way back to the house, she paused on the terrace to brush at the dirt that covered her.

"Dee, what happened? Were you thrown? Are you hurt?" Travis rushed to her, his hands claiming her shoulders, then moving to stroke her face. She shook her head, thrown off balance by the frantic tone of his voice.

"No, I'm not hurt. Travis, you mustn't touch me—you'll get your suit filthy." She tried to take a step away, only to be caught closer.

"The devil with the suit!" His voice was edged with anger as he pressed her against him, one hand cradling her head.

The small intimacy after so many days of impersonal distance swamped her with pleasure, and her arms encircled his waist before she could lecture herself on the wisdom of the action. She felt his lips tarry in her hair, and she thought, with a brief flash of joy, that if she could only have this much of him from time to time, she would be content.

Suddenly, one hand gripped her shoulder while the other tilted her face back, and she saw temper flame in his face. "What in heaven's name have you done to yourself?"

"I haven't done anything to myself," she said with a show of dignity, shaking off his hand. "We've company." She gestured to the lawn.

His eyes moved past her, narrowed, then returned. "Adelia, what in the name of heaven is *that?*"

"It's a dog, Travis, though I wasn't sure myself at first. The poor thing was half starving. That's why"—she paused and braced herself for the confession—"that's why I gave him the roast beef."

"You fed him?" Travis asked in low, even tones.

"Surely you wouldn't begrudge the poor thing a bit of food. I—"

"I don't care a whit about the food, Adelia." He shook her briefly. "Don't you have any more sense than to fool with a strange dog? You could have been bitten."

Straightening, she glared at the censure in his voice. "I know what I'm about, and I was careful. He needed food, so I gave it to him—the same as I'd give it to anyone who needed it. And as for that, he hasn't a thought in his head about biting anyone." Glancing over, she watched the dog's tail begin to thump the ground again. "There"— she pointed triumphantly—"you see."

"I see it appears you've made another conquest. Now," he said, and turned her firmly to face him directly. "Just how did you get in this condition?"

"Oh, well." She looked up at Travis, back to the dog, and back to Travis again. "You see, after he'd finished eating, he was overcome with gratitude, and he—well, he forgot himself for a minute and knocked me down and sort of thanked me in his way. He's a bit dirty—as you can see."

"He knocked you down?" Travis repeated, incredulously.

At his tone, Adelia hurried on. "He's very affectionate, and he didn't mean any harm. Really, Travis, don't be angry with him. See how pretty he is, sitting there now." She glanced over at the dog and saw he was smart enough to blink soulful eyes in Travis's direction. "I told him to wait, and that's just what he's doing. He only wants a bit of affection."

Travis turned back and gave Adelia a long look. "I'm getting the impression you intend to keep him."

"Well, I don't know about keeping him, exactly." She dropped her eyes from him, stared at a spot of dirt on Travis's jacket, and brushed it away.

"What's his name?"

"Finnegan," she responded immediately, then, seeing she had fallen into the trap, looked up frowning.

"Finnegan?" Travis repeated with a sober nod. "How did you come by that?"

"He reminds me of Father Finnegan back in Skibbereen, oversized and clumsy but with much inner dignity."

"I see." He moved over, crouched down, and inspected Finnegan. To Adelia's relief, the dog remembered his manners.

When Travis returned to her, she moistened her lips and launched into her campaign. "I'll take care of him, Travis; he won't be any trouble. I won't let him come in the house and get in Hannah's way."

"There's no need to use your eyes, Adelia." At her bewildered frown, he laughed and tugged her hair. "Lord help the world if you ever realize what you're doing. You're perfectly free to keep him if that's what you want."

"Oh, I do! Thank you, Travis—"

"There are, however, two conditions," he interrupted before she could finish being grateful. "One, that you teach him not to knock you down; he's every bit as big as you are. And two, that he has a bath." He glanced over at Finnegan and shook his head. "Or several baths."

"I think I'm due for one myself." She brushed again without success at the clinging dirt, then lifted her face with a smile. The smile wavered as she found Travis looking down at her strangely.

"You know, Dee, I'm tempted to stuff you in my pocket where I won't have to worry about you."

"I'm small," she agreed, finding it suddenly difficult to breathe, "but I think I'm rather too big for that."

"Your size is intimidating."

She frowned, wondering what he could find intimidating about a bare five feet. His hand wandered through her hair, gently for a moment; then, tousling it with a casual friendliness, he added, "I believe it would be easier if you didn't continually look fifteen instead of twenty-three. . . . I guess I had better change my clothes before I give you a hand bathing that mountain."

As her marriage approached its third week, Adelia sat in her uncle's hospital room, smiling at him as he spoke with excitement of his discharge scheduled for the following day.

"Anyone would think they'd been torturing you and starving you to death, Uncle Paddy."

"Oh, no, it's a fine place, with good and kind people," he protested. "But a hospital's for the sick and never have I felt better in my life."

"You are better, and it makes me happier than I can say. But"—she paused and gave him a stern look—"you've still got to rest for a while and do as the doctors tell you. You're coming home to stay with Travis and me for a few days, till you can get by on your own."

"Now, Dee, I can't do that," Paddy objected, patting her hand. "You two should be off on your honeymoon, not worrying about the likes of me."

With a great deal of self-control, she managed not to wince at the word *honeymoon* and went on in calm but firm tones. "You'll be coming back with us, and that's the end of it. I didn't even have to ask—Travis suggested it himself."

Lying back against the pillows, Paddy smiled. "Aye, he would. Travis is a fine man."

"That he is," Adelia agreed with a sigh. She forced a bright smile and continued. "He's fond of you, Uncle Paddy. I knew as soon as I saw the two of you together."

"Aye," he murmured. "Travis and I go back a long way.

Just a lad he was when I came to work for his father. Poor motherless child, so solemn and straight he was."

Adelia's mind wandered as she tried to picture Travis as a small boy, wondering if he was tall even then.

"Stuart Grant was a hard man," Paddy went on. "He ran the lad harder than the horses he raised. Trish he left to Hannah, barely showing the girl a passing interest, but the boy he wanted molded in his image. Always giving orders, with never a kind word or a dab of affection.

"I found myself taking the lad in, telling him stories and making games out of the work we did." He grinned, lost in memory. "'Paddy's Shadow,' the hands called him, 'cause he took to following me about whenever his father wasn't there. He worked hard, and he knew the horses even then. A fine, good lad he was, but the old man couldn't see it. Always finding fault. I wondered sometimes when he grew older why he didn't lay the old man out, goodness knows he was big enough, and the temper was there. But he took the abuse the old man handed him and only looked at him with his eyes so cold." Paddy paused and let out a long breath.

"Travis was away at college when the old man passed on . . . that would be about ten years ago. He stood there looking down at the grave, and I went over and laid my hand on his shoulder. 'I'm sorry about your father, lad,' says I, and he turned and looked down at me. 'He was never my father, Paddy,' says he, just as calm as you please. 'You've been my father since I was ten years old. If you hadn't been there, I'd have left a long time ago and never looked back.'"

The room was suddenly silent. Adelia gripped the hand that lay in hers tighter as Paddy's eyes grew moist with memory. "And now the two of you are together, I couldn't have wished it any better."

"You'll stay with him, Uncle Paddy, always, no matter what? You promise me that?"

He turned to her, surprised by the urgency in her tone. "Of course, little Dee. Where else would I be going?"

CHAPTER NINE

The following evening, after Paddy was comfortably settled into his room in the main house, Travis announced plans for a party.

"It's expected after Majesty's win, but with Paddy's heart attack it's had to be postponed." He swirled a glass of after-dinner brandy, his eyes sweeping over her, resting for a moment on her hair shimmering on the shoulders of her Nile blue dress. "Our marriage has, of course, leaked to the press, and it will seem odd we don't have some sort of gathering where you can meet some of my friends and business associates."

"Aye," Adelia agreed, unconsciously nibbling on her lip as she turned to gaze out the window. "And so they can get a look at me."

"That, too," he answered in solemn tones. "Don't worry,

Dee: as long as you don't trip over your feet and fall on your face you should get by fairly well."

She whirled around to rage at him that she wasn't exactly a clumsy fool, but his good-natured grin stopped her. "Thank you very much, Master Grant." She smiled back at him. "It's a great comfort you are to me."

She gasped out loud at the length of the list Travis gave her for the projected reception. There couldn't be less than a hundred, she estimated, staring at the paper.

"You've nothing to worry about," he assured her. "Hannah will handle the details. You're only expected to make polite conversation."

The attempt at reassurance hurt her pride. "I'll have you know I'm not a complete cabbagehead, Travis Grant. I'm well capable of helping Hannah, and I won't be making a fool of myself in front of your fancy friends."

"You're the one who said she was afraid of making a fool of herself, not me," Travis reminded her reasonably.

"It's not what I said that matters," she concluded with her own brand of logic. "It's what I'm saying." Tossing her head, she turned and stalked into the kitchen.

Despite her proud claims, Adelia found herself terrified on the evening of the party. There had been no time for nervousness in the days before; she had been too busy with plans and preparations. But now, alone in her room, with only the prospect of dressing ahead of her, she began to feel the first flutter of anxiety.

She chose the green silk gown that Trish had insisted she buy and slipped it carefully over her head. Its classic lines accentuated her softly rounded figure; its deeply scooped neckline revealed a teasing hint of her firm breasts. The silk glowed against the creamy health of her skin. She arranged her hair on top of her head, trying for a more sophisticated style, but gave up in disgust and allowed it to fall loose and full to her shoulders, a fiery auburn waterfall.

Voices were audible in the living room as she descended the stairs. She took several deep breaths before joining Travis and Paddy.

Travis broke off what he had been saying as she entered the room. He rose from his chair. She sought his eyes for approval, but found them strangely veiled and unreadable. She wished that she had chosen one of the other gowns that now hung in the large cherry wardrobe.

"Ah, now, isn't that a beautiful sight, lad?" Paddy said, surveying Adelia with uninhibited pride. "Why, there won't be another woman here tonight will hold a candle to my little Dee. It's a lucky man you are, Travis."

"Uncle Paddy." She smiled and moved to kiss his cheek. "What wonderful blarney. But don't stop—I need it. I have to be honest and say I'm scared witless."

"There's no need for that, Dee." Taking her hand, Travis turned her toward him. "You'll have them eating out of your hand. You look incredible." He smiled at her, his free hand brushing through her hair briefly before he turned away to replenish his drink.

Love me, Travis, her mind shouted suddenly. *I'd give the world and more if you'd only love me half as much as I love you.*

As he turned back, his eyes captured hers. He paused, unreadable emotion flickering over his face. "Dee?" he began, his voice questioning, but before she could speak the doorbell pealed and their guests began to arrive.

It was infinitely easier than Adelia had imagined. After the first wave of guests, she felt her tension dissolve and met the few speculative glances with characteristic boldness. The house was soon filled with people and chatter and laughter and the chink of glasses. It was apparent that Travis was well liked and respected by his associates, and his choice of bride met with acceptance and approval, if not immediately, then shortly after exposure to Adelia's natural, honest charm.

One sleekly coiffured woman who had cornered Adelia halted Travis as he passed. "Travis, your wife is refreshing and charming and more than likely too good for you." She smiled with the privilege of old friendship. "I believe it would be a treat just to listen to her read the telephone directory. Such a marvelous accent."

"Careful, Carla," Travis admonished, slipping an arm around Adelia's shoulders in the casual way she had missed in the past few weeks. "Dee claims we're the ones with the accent—and for all her sweet looks, her temper is not to be trifled with."

"Travis, darling!" The trio turned, and Adelia caught a glimpse of swirling white as the owner of the voice embraced her husband. "I just got back in town, darling, and heard about your little party. I hope you don't mind."

"Of course not, Margot. It's always a pleasure to see you." He turned, and Adelia noted that he didn't dislodge the red-tipped hand from his arm. "Margot Winters—my wife, Adelia."

Margot turned, and Adelia nearly gasped aloud. She was staring right at the most beautiful woman she had ever seen. Tall and slender, she was elegantly draped in a cool white sheath. Ash-gold hair curled softly around an oval face. Her skin was the color of rich cream. Long-lashed gray eyes, as clear and cool as a mountain lake, looked over and beyond Adelia.

"Why, Travis, she's adorable." The gray eyes focused now on Adelia, making her feel small and inadequate. "But she's little more than a child, barely out of the school-room." The sweet tone was patently patronizing.

"I'm allowed up with the grown-ups now and again," Adelia said evenly, her chin tilting to meet Margot's gaze. "I hung up my book strap some time back."

"My," Margot observed over Carla's chuckle. "You're Irish, aren't you?"

"Aye." The quicksilver temper began its swift rise. "As Paddy's pig. Tell me, Mistress Winters, what are you?"

"Dee." Trish spoke from behind, laying a hand on Adelia's arm. "Will you come out here for a minute? I need you to help me."

Adelia was pulled out on the terrace, and after she had shut the doors, Trish dissolved into a fit of laughter. "Oh, Dee," she managed between giggles. "How I would have loved to have left you there and watched you lay into her! I just didn't think it was quite the right time. Oh . . ." She wiped at her eyes. "Did you see Carla? I thought she was going to explode! She kept choking on her drink and trying to keep a straight face. I wouldn't have missed that for the world! How Travis could ever have been involved with that woman is beyond me! She's a cold-blooded snob."

"Travis and Margot Winters?" Adelia asked, attempting to keep her voice casual.

"Oh, yes, I thought you knew." Trish gave a deep sigh, wiped her eyes again, and grimaced. "I don't really think he was ever serious about her—I give him more credit than that. She would have given one of her Tiffany baubles to have him look at her the way he looks at you." Trish smiled, and Adelia made a valiant effort to respond. "They had this big blowup a few months ago. It seems she resented all the time he spent with the horses." She gave a snort of disgust and straightened her skirts. "She wanted him to sit back and let others do all the work while he spent his time entertaining her. She gave him some kind of ultimatum and took off for Europe in a cloud of expensive French perfume." Trish laughed in pure delight. "Her little ploy failed miserably, and now her nose is out of joint. Instead of pining for her, Travis is happily married to you." She linked her arm with her sister-in-law's.

"Aye," Adelia murmured. "Now he's married to me . . ." Her tone was melancholy, and Trish glanced at her sharply, but Dee refused to meet her eyes.

Paddy moved back to his own house a few days later, and Adelia missed his presence keenly. He found Finnegan to be a congenial companion, and the dog divided his time between them. He would accompany Paddy as he grumbled inside for his afternoon rest, and Adelia was never quite sure whether Finnegan's motives were duty or laziness.

Travis made no mention of Margot Winters or Adelia's comments to her, and she found their relationship drifting away again until she felt more like his ward than his wife. When they attended social functions, he treated her with the warm attentiveness expected of a newly married husband; but once they were alone again in their own home, he was distant, showing her only the casual affection he might give to a favored cousin.

The depression and frustration this caused in her Adelia hid with apparent success, responding as she believed he desired and maintaining the same casualness he directed toward her. Rarely did her temper flare, and she was aware his was under strict control. At times she imagined they were only polite puppets pulled on invisible strings. Desperately she wondered how long they could go on.

One afternoon, as July brought summer's throbbing heat to the air, Adelia answered the summons of the bell and found herself confronted with the elegantly clad form of Margot Winters. Her finely penciled brows lifted at Adelia's attire of jeans and shirt. She glided over the threshold without invitation.

"Good afternoon to you, Mistress Winters." Adelia greeted her, determined to act the part of hostess. "Please come in and sit down. Travis is down at the stables, but I'll be glad to send for him."

"That's not necessary, Adelia." Margot strolled into the living room and seated herself in a wingback chair as if she belonged there. "I came to have a little chat with you. Hannah"—she glanced over at the housekeeper, who had entered behind Adelia—"I'll have some tea."

Hannah looked pointedly at Adelia, who merely nodded and moved to join her uninvited guest.

"I shall come straight to the point," Margot began, sitting back and linking her fingers together in an imperious gesture. "I'm sure you're aware that Travis and I were about to be married before we had a slight disagreement a few months ago."

"Is that the truth of it?" Adelia asked with apparently idle interest.

"Yes, it was common knowledge," Margot stated with a regal wave of her hand. "I thought to teach Travis a lesson by going to Europe and giving him time to think things through. He's a very stubborn man." She gave Adelia a small knowing smile. "When I saw the picture of him in the paper kissing this little ragamuffin, I thought nothing of it. The press will blow these things out of proportion. But when I heard he'd actually married some little stablehand"—she shivered delicately—"I knew it was time to come back and set things straight."

"And may the stablehand ask how you mean to do that?"

"When this little interlude is finished, Travis and I can proceed as planned."

"And by interlude I suppose you're meaning my marriage?" Adelia inquired, her voice lowering to an ominous level.

"Well, of course." Slender shoulders moved at the inevitable. "Just look at you. It's obvious Travis only married you to bring me back. You can't possibly hope to hold him for very long. You haven't the breeding or style that's necessary to move in society."

Straightening her spine, Adelia hid her pain with dignity. "I'm telling you this as a fact, Mistress Winters: you had nothing to do with the reason that Travis and I were married. It's true I haven't your elegance or manner of speaking, but there's one thing I have you're lacking. I've

Travis's ring on my finger, and you'll be having a good long wait before you can add his name to yours."

Hannah entered bearing a tea tray, and Adelia rose and turned to her. "Mistress Winters won't be staying for tea after all, Hannah. She was just leaving."

"Play the lady of the house while you can," Margot advised, rising and gliding past Adelia's stiff form. "You'll be back in the stables sooner than you think." When the door closed with a sharp bang, Adelia let out a deep breath.

"She's got her nerve coming here and talking that way," an irate Hannah sputtered.

"We'll be paying her no mind." She patted the housekeeper's arm. "And we'll keep this visit between the two of us, Hannah."

"If that's the way you want it, missy," Hannah agreed with obvious reluctance.

"Aye," she replied, staring off into space. "That's the way I want it."

Adelia's nerves remained on edge for several days and showed all too plainly in increased temper. The atmosphere in the house went from a near-stagnant calm to volatile motion. Travis greeted her change in attitude with absent tolerance that changed to strained patience.

She paced the living room after dinner one evening while he sat on the sofa and brooded over his brandy.

"I'm going to take Finnegan and go for a walk," she announced suddenly, unable to bear the silence between them any longer.

"Do as you like," he answered with a shrug.

"'Do as you like.'" She whirled and snapped at him, nerves as tight as an overwound watch. "It's sick to death I am of hearing you say that. I will not do as I like. I don't want to do as I like."

"Do you hear what you just said?" he demanded, setting down his brandy and staring at her. "That is the most ridiculous statement I have ever heard."

"It's not ridiculous. It's perfectly clear if you had the sense to understand it."

"What's gotten into you? You make more sense when you mutter in Gaelic."

"Nothing," she returned shortly. "There's not a thing wrong with me."

"Then stop behaving like a shrew. I'm tired of putting up with your foul temper."

"A shrew, am I?" Her color rose.

"Precisely," he agreed with infuriating calm.

"Well, if you're tired of listening to me, I'll keep out of your way." Storming from the room, she flew past an astonished Hannah, out the back door, and into the warm summer night.

She awoke the next morning ashamed, disgusted, and contrite. She had spent an uneasy night struggling with the aftermath of temper and the realization that not only had she been unreasonable, she had made a fool of herself as well. One was as difficult to take as the other.

Travis has done nothing to deserve the way I've been treating him, she decided, pulling on her working uniform of jeans and shirt and hurrying downstairs. She determined to apologize and make a study of being as sweet and mild a wife as any man could want.

Hannah informed her that Travis had breakfasted early and gone out, so Adelia sat down in solitary misery, unable to ease her conscience.

She worked hard in the stables that morning, doing self-imposed penance for her faults. And as morning melted into early afternoon, the manual labor began to erase the depression she carried with her.

"Dee." Travis spoke from outside the tackroom, where she was busily hanging bridles. "Come out here. I want to show you something."

"Travis." She ran after him as he strode away. "Travis." Catching up to him, she tugged on his arm in an attempt to make him slow his pace. "I'm sorry, Travis. I'm sorry for the way I've been behaving, and for raging at you last night when I had no cause to. I know I've been mean and spiteful and no fun to have around, but if you'll forgive me, I'll . . . What are you smiling like that for?"

The smile spread to a grin. "You apologize just as emphatically as you rage. It's fascinating. Now, forget it, half-pint." He ruffled her hair and slipped an arm around her shoulders. "Everyone has their black moods. Look," he said simply and pointed.

She gave a cry of pleasure at the glossy chestnut mare prancing around inside the paddock fence. Moving over, she stood on the first rung of fence and scanned the strong, clean lines. "Oh, Travis, she's beautiful—the most beautiful horse I've ever seen!"

"You say that about all of them."

She smiled at him, then back at the horse with a deep sigh of pleasure. "Aye, and it's always true. Who will you breed her with?"

"That's not up to me. She's yours."

Adelia turned wide, unbelieving eyes to his. "Mine?"

"I had thought to give her to you next month for your birthday, but"—he shrugged and brushed a lock of hair from her face—"I thought your spirits needed a lift, so she's yours a bit early."

She shook her head, the still unfamiliar tears filling her eyes. "But after the way I've been acting, you should have been beating me instead of buying me a present."

"The thought entered my mind last night, but this seemed a better solution."

"Oh, Travis!" She flung herself into his arms without restraint. "No one's ever given me such a grand present, and I don't deserve it." She drew her face from his cheek and pressed her lips to his. His arms tightened around her, the kiss changing from one of gratitude to one of smoldering passion, and she offered herself, lips parting and bones melting. "Travis," she murmured as his face lifted, his cheek brushing hers.

He set her away from him abruptly. "You'd better get acquainted with your mare, Dee. I'll see you at dinner."

She watched him stride away, biting her lip to prevent herself from calling him back. Finnegan bounded over, and she swallowed the tears of rejection, burying her face in his fur. "I don't have any appeal for him," she told her sympathetic companion. "And I don't know how to go about making him see me as a woman—much less a wife."

CHAPTER TEN

Adelia woke to a blinding flash of lightning and a burst of thunder. The room glowed with brief intensity as the sky was broken with spiderwebs of light, and the wind moaned like a man mourning.

Tossing back the covers, she rose from the bed and threw open the French doors leading to her balcony to let the storm enter the room. The hands of the wind pulled at her hair and whipped the soft material of her thin nightgown, molding it against her. Rain fell in torrents like angry tears from the heavens, and she raised her arms wide, laughing in sheer delight at the raging elements.

"Dee?" She turned her head and saw Travis silhouetted in the doorway. "I thought you might be frightened. The electricity's out, and the storm's loud enough to wake the dead."

"Aye," she agreed triumphantly. "It's wonderful!"

"So much for finding you shaking with fear under the covers," he returned with a dry smile and stepped back.

"Oh, Travis, come look!" she cried as another bolt of lightning illuminated the murky sky and was followed by a deafening roar of thunder.

He watched her slimness outlined against the blackness, the fullness of her hair flying riotously around her bare shoulders. He opened his mouth to speak, but Adelia cried out again.

"Oh, come, just look at it!" Taking a deep breath, he moved to join her. "It's so wild, so strong and powerful and free!" She lifted her face to feel the full force of the wind on her cheeks. "It's angry as the devil and doesn't give a hoot what anyone thinks. Listen to the wind, screaming like a banshee! Oooh, but I love a storm that blows free!"

She turned and found his eyes on her. Lightning flooded the room, and she saw the naked desire darkening his unblinking blue stare. Her smile faded. Her heart pounded in her ears, drowning out the turbulence of the storm as he pulled her against him and crushed her lips in a violent, hungry kiss.

Her arms clutched around his waist as they fused together, and she felt the need in him she had not known existed and knew a moment's delirious pleasure that it was for her. Fire ignited fire. Her response was abandoned and uninhibited. His mouth ravished hers, hard and bruising, and she opened under the pressure like a flower to the sun. His hand slid to her shoulders, and the soft material of her nightgown sighed to the floor. Her hands fumbled with the belt of his robe until no barrier of silk came between them. With a swift, desperate gesture, he lifted her and carried her to the bed.

The passionate violence of the storm paled against the turbulence of their lovemaking. His lips moved over hers slowly, his hands roaming with gentle experience over her trembling body, releasing her desire while he kept his own in check. When he made her his, she surrendered, drawing her pleasure from the gift she gave.

Later, she slept in the warm circle of his arms, the deep, peaceful sleep of one who had been lost and searching and finally found home. . . .

Sunlight streamed warm and loving on Adelia's face, and she opened her eyes. Travis's face lay close to hers, and she studied it thoroughly and sighed, her love nearly bursting her heart. His breathing was slow and even, the deep blue of his eyes hidden by lowered lids and lashes which seemed incredibly long and thick against the strongly masculine face. Her hand lifted and stroked the dark curls away from his forehead, and she snuggled closer, murmuring his name.

His eyes opened at her movements and smiled into hers. "Hello," he said simply as his arm tightened around her waist. "Do you always look this beautiful first thing in the morning?"

"I don't know," she answered. "It's the first time I've ever woken with a man on my pillow." She rolled on top of him and peered down at his face critically. "You're not a hard sight on the eyes either." Grinning, she rubbed a hand over his chin. "Though it's a fact you're needing a shave."

He tugged the hair that fell streaming from her head to his shoulders and brought her face down, claiming her lips. After a moment she lay her head in the curve of his shoulder, sighing with absolute contentment as he caressed her back with slow, idle movements. "Travis," she said curiously, "that clock says it's after ten."

He twisted to see for himself and groaned. "That's what it says."

"But it can't be," Adelia objected, raising herself up in indignation. "Why, never in my life have I slept as late as that!"

"Well, you did this time." He grinned. "Even you can't argue the day back."

"I'll pretend I didn't see it," she decided and snuggled against his warmth.

"As much as I'd like to do the same, I have an appointment, and I'm already going to be late." He kissed her again, rolling her over, and she clung to him, moving her hands over the rippling muscles of his back. "I've got to go." His lips tarried a moment at the curve of her neck before he disentangled himself. He rose and slipped on his robe, turning back to gaze at her slim form, scantily covered by rumpled sheets. "If you stay there for a couple of hours, I'll be back."

"You could stay now and be a bit later for your appointment," she suggested with a smile as she sat up, clutching the sheet to her breast.

"Don't tempt me." Moving over, he kissed her brow. "I'll be back as soon as I can."

When the door closed behind him, she lay back with a blissful sigh and stretched. *I'm truly his wife now,* she thought, closing her eyes as memories of the previous night ran through her mind. *I'm a married woman, and Travis is my husband. But he never said he loved me.* She sighed and shook her head. *He said he needed me, and that's enough for now. I'll make him love me in time. I'll make our marriage work, and he'll not be thinking of ending it. I'll make him so happy he'll think he's found heaven.*

She jumped from the bed, full of confidence, and danced into the adjoining bathroom to shower.

Later, she paused halfway down the stairs, her face lighting with pleasure as she heard Travis's voice coming from the living room. Before she could begin the rapid descent she had intended, another voice floated to her, and she stopped, the smile fading as she recognized Margot Winters's voice raised in exasperation.

"Travis, you know very well I never meant those things

I said before I left. I only went away so that you'd miss me and come after me."

"Did you expect me to drop everything and run off to Europe chasing you, Margot?" Adelia heard the slight amusement in his tone and bit her lip.

"Oh, darling, I know it was foolish." The voice became low and seductive. "I never meant to hurt you. I'm so terribly sorry. I know you married that little groom to make me jealous."

"Is that so?" The answer was calm, and Adelia's hand tightened on the banister at his cool, dispassionate discussion of her.

"Of course, darling, and it worked beautifully. Now all you have to do is arrange for a quick divorce and give her a nice little settlement, and we'll get things back to normal."

"That may be difficult, Margot. Adelia's Catholic; she'd never divorce me." Her stomach lurched at the easy remark, and she wrapped her arms around herself to ward off the sharp, piercing stab of pain.

"Well, then, darling, you'll just have to divorce her."

"On what grounds?" Travis's voice sounded reasonable.

"For heaven's sake, Travis." The feminine voice rose in annoyance. "You can arrange something. Give her some money. She'll do what you want."

Adelia could stand no more. Covering her ears with her hands, she ran up the carpeted stairs and into her room.

Oh, 'tis a fool you are, Adelia Cunnane, she berated herself, leaning against her door. *He doesn't love you and he never will. Your marriage was just make-believe all along.* She dashed away the tears and straightened her shoulders. Now's the time to end it, she decided firmly. Uncle Paddy's strong enough, and I can't go on this way any longer.

She packed only her old clothes and those bought with her own earnings in the well-battered case she had carried from Ireland, then sat at the writing desk and penned notes to her uncle and husband.

Please understand, Uncle Paddy, she pleaded, placing the two envelopes on the smooth surface of the desk. *I can't be going on with this anymore. I can't stay here so close to Travis, not now, not after all that's happened.*

She slipped downstairs and, taking a deep breath, walked outside to await her taxi.

The airport was as busy as it had been on her arrival, throngs of people rushing around her and shaking her confidence. For a moment she felt achingly lost and alone. Sighting the ticket counter, she drew herself up and headed toward it. A hand gripped her arm and spun her around. She dropped her case to the tiled floor with a thud.

"What do you think you're doing?" she began indignantly, stopping openmouthed as she looked up into Travis's furious face.

"That's precisely what I wanted to ask you," he tossed back, his eyes boring into hers with a hard blue light. "Where do you think you're going?"

"To Ireland, back to Skibbereen."

"Are you stupid enough to think I'd let you get on that plane without a word?" he demanded, his grip on her arm increasing.

She winced at his bruising fingers but answered evenly. "I left you a note."

"I saw your note," he hissed between his teeth. "It's a good thing I got back early, or I'd be chasing you across the Atlantic."

"There's no need for you to be chasing me anywhere," Adelia insisted, pulling at her arm as the circulation began to slow down. "You're breaking my arm, Travis Grant. Take your hand off me."

"You're lucky it's not your neck," he muttered, and, lifting her case with his free hand, he began to pull her after him.

"I'm not going with you—I'm going back to Ireland."

"You are coming with me," he corrected. "And you can walk on your own two feet, or I'll cart you out like a sack of Irish potatoes."

"A sack of Irish potatoes, is it?" she spat at him, but as he towered over her, formidable and powerful, she tossed her head and went on calmly. "Aye, I'll walk, Master Grant. There'll be other planes."

Muttering an oath, he strode purposefully out to his

waiting car, towing her with him. He opened the door and gave her a none too gentle shove inside. "You've got a lot of explaining to do, Adelia," he said as he started the engine. She opened her mouth to retort, but he cut her off with a deadly look. "Save it until we get home. I have no desire to commit murder publicly."

She remained silent on the drive home, stubbornly staring out the side window. Pulling up in front of the large stone house, Travis got out of the car, slamming his door with such force Adelia was amazed that the glass remained intact. He pulled Adelia out and dragged her inside.

"We're not to be disturbed," he announced to a gaping Hannah as he hauled Adelia up the staircase. Pushing her into her room, he slammed the door and locked it. "Now, let's hear it."

"I've an earful for you, Travis Grant," she raged. "You great thundering blackguard, I'm sick to death of your shoving me and pushing me and tearing my arms from the sockets. I warn you, you black-hearted son of the devil, you'll not be battering me about any longer unless you've a mind to have a few bruises of your own!"

"If you've finished," he returned evenly, "I'd like to see you use that double-edged tongue of yours for an explanation."

"I've no need to explain a blessed thing to the likes of you." Her eyes glittered bright green in her furious face. "I told you plain in the note: I want nothing from you. I've my pride if nothing else."

"Yes, you and your Irish pride," Travis growled, stepping forward and taking her by the shoulders. "I'd like to strangle you with your pride. What was all that about divorce and annulments?"

"I thought my wording clear enough." She jerked away and backed up. "I said that, as an annulment was no longer possible, I was leaving and you'd be free to divorce me. I wanted none of your money and would pay you back for what I took with me."

"And you expect me to accept that?" he shouted at her, and she backed up another step. "Just calmly read your little note and go from marriage to divorce in one easy step?"

"Don't you shout at me," she snapped back. "It was agreed when we started that this marriage was only for Uncle Paddy, and we'd have an annulment when he was better. Now that can't be, so you'll have to divorce me. I'm not able to do it myself."

"You can talk of annulments and divorce after last night?" he threw back bitterly. "I thought it meant something to you."

"I can speak of it? I can speak of it?" she roared, out of control. "You dare say that to me? The devil take you, Travis Grant, for your hypocrisy! You'd no more than left the bed when you spoke of divorcing me with your fine lady. Give me money to buy me off, will you? You low, sneaking buzzard! I would rather die than touch one penny of your money, you low-lying snake!"

"Dee, is that why you left?" Travis demanded, shaking her as she resorted to Gaelic curses.

"Aye." Her small fists beat uselessly at his chest. "Take your hands off me, you cursed brute. I'll not wait around to be bought off like some cheap fancy lady."

He picked her up bodily, tucking her like a football under his arm, and ignoring the flailing fists, laid her gently on the bed.

"So it's back to bed again, is it? I'll not lie in this bed with the likes of you again. A curse on you, Travis Grant!"

"Be quiet, you little fool." Travis captured her mouth, shutting off the stream of Gaelic, and held it until her furious struggles lost their force. "Did you think I'd let you go after all I've been through to get you?" He cut off her reply with another breathtaking kiss. "Now, you little spitfire, keep your mouth shut and listen. Margot came here this morning without invitation. She brought up the subject of divorce, not I. In the first place— Keep still," he warned as she squirmed beside him, "or I'll have to get tough." He demonstrated by closing his mouth over hers until, for a moment, her struggles lost their force.

"In the first place," he began again, "I had never considered marrying her; any plans in that direction were her own. We had a fairly compatible relationship for a while— Adelia, *hold still*. You're going to hurt yourself." He shifted his weight, took both of her wrists in his hand, and held them over her head. "She got it into her head that I should marry her and give up my work here, with some crazy notion about traveling the world and living in high style. I told her she was out of her mind, and she took off for Europe, telling me it was her or the horses." He grinned down at Adelia's flushed face. "The horses won, hands down. She got it stuck in that small brain of hers that I married you to spite her, and when she came here this morning going on about divorce and settlements, I let her ramble, curious to see how big a fool she'd make of herself."

He took Adelia's chin in his free hand and held her head still. "Now, if you had listened to the entire conversation, you would have heard me tell her that I had no intention of divorcing a wife I loved, now or any time within the next thousand years."

"You said that?" All struggles stopped.

"Or words to that effect. The meaning was clear."

"I—well, you might have told your wife you loved her. It would have saved a great deal of trouble."

"How could I tell her I loved her five minutes after she raged at me, standing there looking like an outraged urchin?" He brushed her curls aside to kiss the creamy skin of her throat. "My first thought was to gentle you so you could stand the sight of me and go from there. Did you really think I took you to Kentucky and New York just for Majesty?" His lips explored her smooth skin. "I didn't dare let you out of my sight; someone might have come along and snatched you away. I decided to wear you down slowly." His mouth moved over her face with slow, lingering kisses. "I thought I was making some headway, but Paddy's heart attack changed everything. I felt the best way to help him was to assure him of your welfare, so I railroaded you into marriage with the promise of an annulment. Of course"—his free hand began fresh explorations—"I never intended to give you one."

"Let go of my hands," she demanded, and he raised his head and shook it.

"Not if I have to keep you here for the next twenty years."

"You thick-brained idiot, couldn't you see how I was dying for loving you? Let go of my hands, blast your eyes, and kiss me."

She pulled his head to hers with her freed hands, and buried her face in the strong column of his neck.

"It appears," he murmured in her scented hair, "we've wasted a great deal of time."

"You seemed so far away. All those weeks you never even touched me. You never even said you loved me last night."

"I didn't dare touch you. I wanted you so much it was driving me mad. If I had told you I love you last night—and how I wanted to!—you might have thought I said it just to keep you in bed."

"I won't think that now, Travis. Let me hear you say it. I've been needing to hear you say it for such a long time."

He obliged her, telling her over and over until his lips sought hers and told her silently.

"Travis," she finally whispered against his ear. "I'm wondering if you could arrange another thunderstorm?"